# SUBVERSION

ALSO BY MITCHELL HOGAN

THE NECROMANCER'S KEY
*Incursion*
*Corruption*

THE SORCERY ASCENDANT SEQUENCE
*A Crucible of Souls*
*Blood of Innocents*
*A Shattered Empire*
*At the Sign of the Crow and Moon*—novella
*The Last Arrow*—short story

THE INFERNAL GUARDIAN
*Shadow of the Exile*
*Dawn of the Exile*

THE TAINTED CABAL
*Revenant Winds*
*Tower of the Forgotten*—novella
*A Goddess Scorned*—novella

SCIENCE FICTION
*Inquisitor*

# SUBVERSION

### THE NECROMANCER'S KEY: BOOK THREE

# MITCHELL HOGAN

# SUBVERSION

Published by Mitchell Hogan

First Printing, 2021

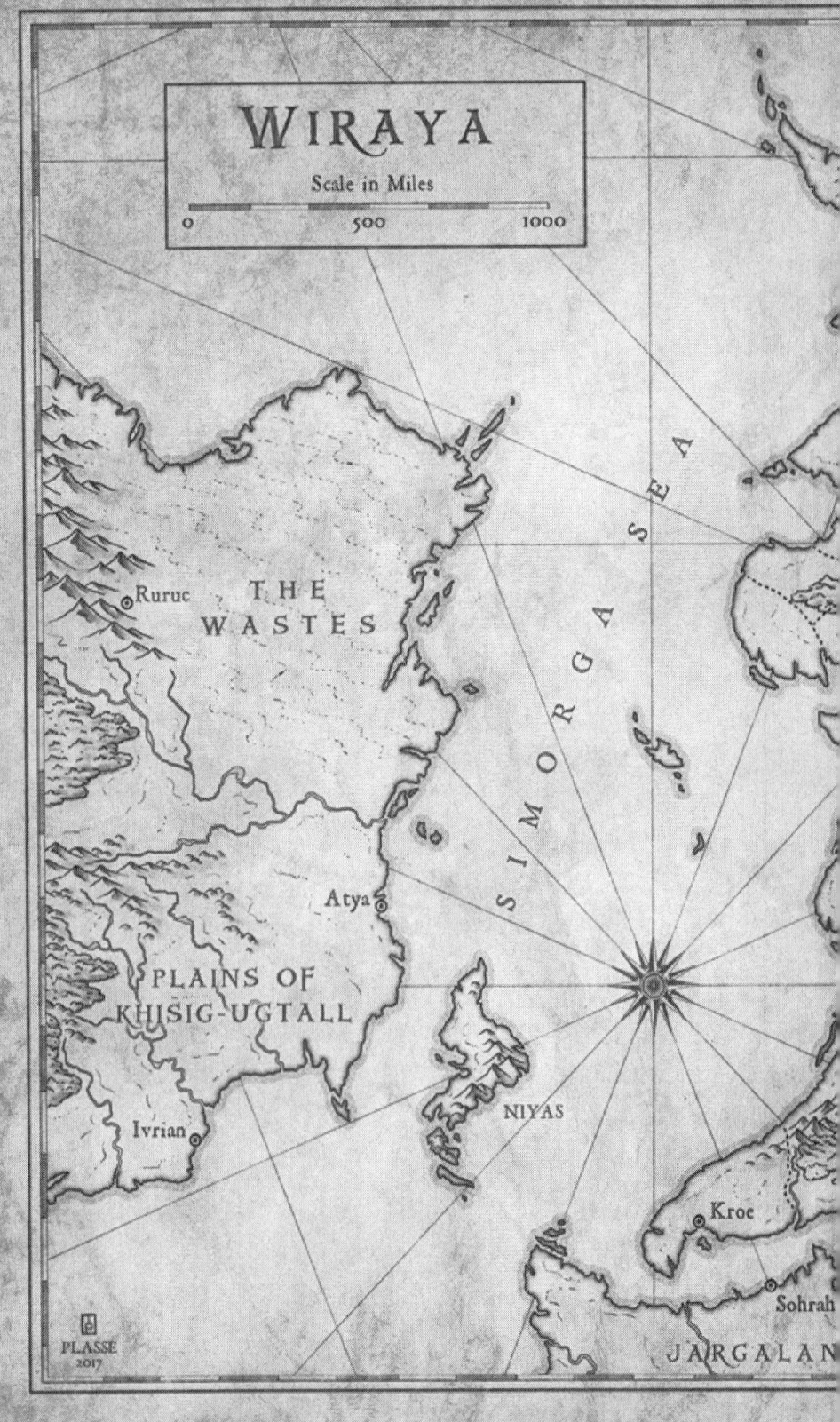

# WHAT'S GONE BEFORE

NECROMANCY BEGAN ON THE island of Niyas, when the peoples of Wiraya were little more than savages roaming the wilderness. The dawn- and dusk-tides were already known, but Niyandrian sorcerers discovered the corrupted tidal forces absorbed into the earth. They grew obsessed with the earth-tide's promise of immortality and with the secrets of the dead.

When Queen Talia of Niyas sought to raise her people to eternal life, the powerful countries of the mainland conspired to put an end to her rule. Allied armies invaded Niyas. Battles were fought with steel and sorcery. Thousands died. Cities fell. And, at last, the mainland allies, led by the Order of Eternal Vigilance, prevailed. Queen Talia died when her capital, Naphor, fell, and Niyas was placed under mainland occupation.

But there were rumors of a child: the heir to Niyas, the daughter of Talia, the Necromancer Queen. In secret, a guardian was appointed to protect the heir.

## BOOK ONE: INCURSION

**Carred Selenas**, Captain of the Last Cohort and Queen Talia's former lover, leads the resistance against the foreign invaders as they await the return of the Necromancer Queen and the reemergence of the Niyandrian people and culture. But it has been years since Talia died, and her people are losing heart. With one failure after another, Carred's resolve crumbles, but duty keeps her searching for the lost heir—the symbol all Niyandrians could rally behind and the key to Queen Talia's return from the dead.

**Anskar DeVantte** has been raised in the sacred disciplines of the Order of Eternal Vigilance, the military arm of the Church of Menselas, God of Five Aspects, his entire life. Born with the mark of sorcery and the ability to manipulate the dawn-tide, Anskar must endure the Order's brutal initiation trials if he is to become a consecrated knight. Against the Order's rules, he assists a Niyandrian postulant, Sareya, with the sword she is forging for the second trial, and they become lovers. When he is attacked by the vengeful Warrior's priest, Beof, during the final trial, an uncontrolled burst of shadow blasts from Anskar, knocking Beof unconscious.

The blind sorcerer Luzius Landav arrives with his assistant, a dwarf woman named Malady. Landav brought the trainees crystal catalysts that will enable them to draw upon the dawn-tide for their protective sorceries. Landav senses Anskar also has a dusk-tide repository, and more disturbingly, can also store the dark-tide.

Using their catalysts, the trainee knights imbue the blades they forged during the trials with strengthening cants using the dawn-tide. Anskar names his sword *Amalantril* ("Moontouched"), after Sareya's Niyandrian name.

Anskar, Orix, and Sareya are among the seven trainees to pass the trials and are raised to the interim rank of knight-liminal. The Seneschal, Vihtor Ulnar, declares he will take Anskar under his wing.

Anskar questions Vihtor about his past and his parents. The Seneschal is guarded and forbids him from asking again.

Landav and Malady implant the catalysts beneath the skin of the trainees. Anskar's body rejects the dark-threaded crystal, and he grows critically ill.

As Anskar recovers under the care of the priests of the Healer, a golden-eyed crow disturbs him in the middle of the night. Anskar enters a fugue-like state as he follows the crow through the wilderness to a Niyandrian ruin atop Hallow Hill. There, a wraithe—one of the ancient beings that haunt Wiraya—urges Anskar to enter the ruin, where he finds a statue of a woman carved from bone, upon her forearm a vambrace crafted from a peculiar silver alloy.

Carred Selenas receives word from her spies that one of the Order's newest knights, a woman named Sareya, could be the Niyandrian heir, and also that Hyle Pausus, the Grand Master of the Order of Eternal Vigilance, is on his way to Niyas from the mainland city of Sansor. She comes up with a plan to bloody the Order's nose and snatch Sareya away from them.

Carred and her rebels are attacked by Luzius Landav and Malady, who have been charged by their mainland employers with putting down the resistance. In the ensuing fight, Landav transports himself and Carred to a shadowy realm, where she meets a secret consortium who put pressure on Carred to disband her rebellion. She refuses and uses a ring Queen Talia gave her to break Landav's power and return to Wiraya. The rebels capture Landav, but Malady escapes. Carred cuts off the sorcerer's head.

Anskar approaches his namesake, the knight Eldrid DeVantte, to ask about his mother and father. Eldrid claims to know nothing except that he gave Anskar his surname at the request of Vihtor.

The trainees undertake their first mission, each mentored by a fully consecrated knight. To everyone's surprise, Vihtor announces he will join them. Ambushed by rebels, they lose almost half their number, including the trainee Petor.

As dusk approaches, they find a farm with a cottage to shelter in before dead-eyes attack in the night. Anskar hears a woman screaming inside the cottage. He and Vihtor investigate, only to find the cottage empty apart from the corpse of a woman recently killed.

After nightfall, dozens of sickly, spindle-limbed dead-eyes attack. Though the defenders fight fiercely, two more dead-eyes appear for every one slain. Vihtor is isolated and overwhelmed, but somehow Anskar steps through shadows to appear at the Seneschal's side and save him.

The knights and trainees retreat to the cottage, but dead-eyes break through the roof and windows. Anskar uses dark-tide sorcery to hold up the ceiling, which bows under the weight of dead-eyes. Sareya uses dusk-tide sorcery to incinerate the rest of the dead-eyes with violet flames, and then, exhausted, she collapses.

Carred discovers that Niyandrians are being rounded up a few at a time and sold by the Order of Eternal Vigilance as slaves. After years of failures and self-doubt, she cannot stand by. She frees Niyandrian slaves from a warehouse and burns down the building.

Carred receives word that her rebels attacked a group of knights and their trainees from Branil's Burg, but were driven back by a young knight who bristled with sorcerous energy, aided by a young Niyandrian woman, Sareya. Carred speculates that Sareya is Queen Talia's daughter and that the young knight may be the heir's guardian. Both must have been conditioned by the Order, unaware of who they really are.

After the knights' expedition returns to Branil's Burg with Petor's body, Anskar examines his vambrace using dark-tide power. He has a vision of a full suit of intricately forged plate armor and is inexplicably overcome with a burning need to possess the armor.

Grand Master Hyle Pausus gathers the Order in the chapel of the Hooded One, which has been converted into a bankers' vault. Anskar is not impressed with Hyle Pausus, who has offended the priests of the Hooded One by profaning the chapel, believing him to be a fraud who places the needs and wishes of the noble elite of the mainland above those who represent Menselas. The Grand Master announces that the

Niyandrians who built the vault have asked to be received into the family of Menselas. Anskar and Sareya watch in fascinated horror as the Niyandrians are branded with the five-pointed star of Menselas.

That same day, Luzius Landav's servant, Malady, turns up at the Burg, carrying Luzius's severed head in a sack. The decomposing head seems to speak to Anskar, who is horrified. Malady is revealed to be a demon, and tells the Grand Master that he was deceived by the new Niyandrian converts. Malady escapes, and, fearful of betrayal, Hyle Pausus orders the recently branded Niyandrians killed. Four of the Niyandrians, however, cannot be found.

The atmosphere within Branil's Burg deteriorates. Lessons become somber affairs, Forge Master Sned drinks more, Vihtor becomes aloof and unapproachable, and Sareya withdraws into herself, seldom speaking and barely eating.

The trainees are raised to the rank of knight-inferior. In another year, they will be expected to either take solemn vows or leave the Order and never return. To clear his head, Anskar rides from the Burg, intending to find some space. When he returns, he finds Naul's dead body, which speaks to him, telling him to help Sareya. Anskar finds Sareya bound and gagged, kneeling at the center of a circle formed from a golden chain. Within the circle stand four Niyandrians: the four escaped converts.

As Anskar fights two of the men, the dark-tide within him bursts its bindings. One Niyandrian's hand withers, and the second's face putrefies. The Niyandrian woman, a sorcerer, confronts Anskar, her dagger dazzling with silver fire. But she holds back and gasps with reverent awe: "*Melesh-Eloni!*"

The two remaining Niyandrians knock Sareya unconscious, drag Anskar to the center of the circle, and use a sorcerous portal to escape. They manhandle Anskar into a waiting carriage and speed away. The woman sorcerer claims Anskar is *Melesh-Eloni*, though Anskar doesn't know what the words mean. Anskar attacks his kidnappers and causes the carriage to crash. The Niyandrian sorcerer begs Anskar to come with her, but knights of the Order arrive. Vihtor kills the sorcerer and is shocked to see that Anskar's eyes are now somehow cat's eyes, like those of a Niyandrian.

Back inside the Burg, Anskar is sure Vihtor knows more than he is revealing, but Hyle Pausus decides Anskar is a gifted knight-inferior and will take him to Sansor with his retinue. Vihtor doesn't voice an objection, and agrees that it could be dangerous for Anskar to remain in Niyas.

Anskar visits Sareya in the infirmary, where she tells him that *Melesh-Eloni* means "godling."

Anskar departs Branil's Burg by ship the next morning, consumed by questions that he feels he may never get answers to.

Carred and a small group of her followers watch the passage of the lone galleon as it heads out to sea.

One of the slaves Carred rescued, a young woman called Noni, is possessed by the spirit of Queen Talia and tells Carred that there is no daughter: the heir to Niyas is Talia's son, the knight-sorcerer Anskar DeVantte. Talia reveals that Carred is Anskar's guardian, and now is the time for her to step into that role.

Carred vows to bring Anskar back to Niyas so that the entire country will rally to her cause. Under Anskar's lead, the faithful will take back Niyas for Niyandrians. Queen Talia will return. And the dead will live forever.

## BOOK TWO: CORRUPTION

Entrusted by Vihtor Ulnar to the protection of the knight Lanuc of Gessa, Anskar DeVantte sails on the *Exultant* across the waters of the Simorga Sea to Sansor. He and Orix are worked hard by Captain Hadlor, scrubbing decks till their hands are raw, while the other Order knights spend their time relaxing and drinking.

Grand Master Hyle Pausus spends his time below deck, though Anskar makes the acquaintance of his assistant, Gadius Menashin, a sorcerer with both dawn- and dusk-tide repositories.

Anskar and Orix discover Niyandrian slaves chained in the bilge. The *Exultant* detours to the coastal city of Atya, where the Grand Master plans to sell the slaves.

That night, Orix is set upon and almost raped by one of the knights. Anskar uses dark-tide sorcery, which corrupts the knight's arm, and then Orix runs the man through with his sword. Instead of disciplining Anskar, the Grand Master tells Anskar that, if he plays his cards right, he should fit in well at the Mother House in Sansor.

Carred Selenas is visited by Queen Talia, who possesses Noni and speaks through her. Talia exhorts Carred, Anskar's guardian, to find him and keep him safe—Anskar is the key to returning Talia from the realm of the dead. She commands Carred to find the old Niyandrian sorcerer Maggow, and enlist the help of Malady the demon and the abyssal realms.

Maggow summons the demon Malady and binds her to his will. He also informs Carred that the *Exultant* is heading west, away from Sansor. Carred procures a ship and gives chase.

The *Exultant* arrives at Atya, where Anskar, Orix, and Lanuc go ashore for a few days to explore the city while the slaves are sold. They are approached by a woman named Blaice Rancey, who claims her business is ransacking ancient tombs and that she's an old friend of Lanuc's.

That night, Anskar is visited by the spirit of his mother, Queen Talia. She exhorts Anskar to find her in the realm of the dead. Anskar takes no comfort from the vision, and vows to push himself to his limits to prepare for whatever is coming. He spends the rest of the night practicing sorcery.

Blaice claims to have knowledge of a recently unearthed ancient ruin, and the Grand Master Hyle Pausus puts together an expedition to explore the ruin and claim its treasures for the Order. As they journey to the ruin, they are joined by Niklaus du Plessis, who claims to be the Chosen Sword of the goddess Sylva Kalisia. Lanuc explains to Anskar that gifted knights and sorcerers, including Lanuc himself and now Anskar, are not only tolerated in secret but are called upon by the Grand Master to sacrifice their purity in the defense of the Order.

Blaice reveals that the ruin may contain a portal stone, which is thought to create a gateway from Wiraya to the abyssal realms of the demons. It was the creation of portal stones which led to the first cataclysm, the war with the demon lord Nysrog.

Orix and Lanuc are left outside the ruin to guard the group's ponies. Meanwhile, Blaice and Niklaus decipher the code that unlocks the entrance to the ruin and lead the group inside. They come to an inscribed brass circle set into the floor of a chamber—a portal. Anskar, at Hyle Pausus's urging, uses dark-tide sorcery to activate the portal, and the group are transferred to the fabled city of Yustanwyrd, buried underneath the ruins of the seven cities that succeeded it.

Carred crosses the Simorga Sea and lands near Atya, and then finds her way to a Traguh-raj tribe. The tribe's leader agrees to lead them to the unearthed ruin in pursuit of Anskar. Carred and her new companions capture Orix and Lanuc.

Blaice leads Anskar and the rest of the group to a building atop a hill of granulated quartz. As they enter, the floor blisters, and lumps form into eight statues holding black wavy blades. They resemble the ancient wraithe Anskar encountered atop Hallow Hill. There is also a massive reptile's head with jaws that open onto absolute blackness.

Anskar's vambrace grows warm and tugs him toward the lizard's maw with increasing urgency. Before anyone registers the fact, Anskar passes between the statues and continues into the reptile's gaping mouth. The statues glide across the floor and form a line in front of the lizard's mouth, their backs to him, facing his companions. The floor tilts, and Anskar is pitched into the void.

Anskar finds himself confronted with a group of wraithes, who know that he is the child of the Necromancer Queen of Niyas. The ancient beings also reveal that Anskar's vambrace is a step on the path to godhood. They deny the existence of the portal stone Blaice and the Grand Master seek, and state that the members of the expedition have seen things they shouldn't have, before using sorcery to send him back to his companions.

Anskar rejoins his companions in a chamber littered with crystal boxes. From one container, Blaice and Niklaus remove a severed hand with an ebony ring.

Fearful of the wraithes' warning, and disheartened by the claim there is no portal stone, the companions flee when there is a series of clunks and vibrations. They make it back to the entrance hall, only to find the eight statues are now living wraithes.

Anskar, Gladius, and Hyle Pausus ward themselves with sorcery, and in the ensuing fight several companions are killed, along with a wraithe. Hyle Pausus and Anskar are overwhelmed, but then Anskar's vambrace flares with brilliance, and he briefly finds himself in the realm of the dead. The shade of Queen Talia appears, with a golden-eyed crow perched on her shoulder. The Necromancer Queen says that the vambrace is not enough, and that there is much more to be done before Anskar comes here. She sends him back to Wiraya.

Anskar flees the wraithes, running for his life down the side of the hilltop in the buried city, the Grand Master panting and gasping beside him, Niklaus and Blaice up ahead. The wraithes do not give chase, instead sending birds made of smoke to attack. Anskar's sword, *Amalantril*, is ineffective against the smoke birds, as are all their weapons. Only Niklaus's sword, which bears the image of his goddess, has any effect against the birds. Niklaus saves the Grand Master and tells him and Anskar to flee. As they do, Niklaus is smothered by hundreds of the birds and is lost.

Finally free of the disastrous ruin, Anskar, Blaice, Hyle and the rest of the survivors stumble back to their camp, only to find Orix and Lanuc tied with rope. Lanuc shouts at them to run, but before they can, Traguh-raj warriors cut off their escape. With them are Carred Selenas and the demon Malady.

To Anskar's dismay, Carred reveals to all that he is the son of Queen Talia. Anskar demands to know who his father is, but Carred is unable to answer.

Anskar is exhausted, his repositories depleted, and so is unable to muster a defense. When Carred agrees not to harm his companions, Anskar agrees to go with her. Carred takes Anskar back to Atya. When they near the wharves, Anskar draws on the dark-tide and shadow-steps away to where the *Exultant* is moored. As knights come to his aid, Malady pursues him through the shadows. The demon slaughters a few knights and is about to capture Anskar when the dawn-tide arrives. Anskar uses the dawn-tide power flooding his repository against Malady, and she flees. Carred, seemingly admitting defeat, departs on her own ship.

Safe aboard the *Exultant*, Anskar is heartened when Lanuc, Orix, Blaice, and the Grand Master return unharmed with the remaining knights. On the final night in Atya, Blaice reveals to Anskar that she has the ring from the severed hand in the ruins—Niklaus had used sleight of hand to retrieve it and passed it to her that very night. Anskar is shocked to learn that Niklaus survived the attack of the smoke birds and escaped Yustanwyrd. Blaice then seduces Anskar.

One night aboard ship while they're bound for Sansor, Queen Talia visits Anskar in his sleep and begins to teach him sorcery in a twilight dreamscape. The next day, Carred's ship attacks, and the knights and rebels fight with steel and sorcery. Amid the slaughter, the knights realize they will soon be overwhelmed. At the Grand Master's behest, Anskar uses dark-tide sorcery to turn the tide of the battle, killing the old Niyandrian sorcerer, Maggow, in the process. Unable to seize Anskar, Carred and Malady abduct Orix instead.

The *Exultant* finally arrives at Sansor, and Anskar and the knights find refuge at their Mother House. Anskar makes the acquaintance of Gisela of Gessa, Lanuc's daughter, who is a priestess of the Five and a healer. Anskar asks Gisela to be his confessor, and he confesses everything to her, including lustful thoughts he has about her. After absolving him, Gisela tells Anskar he must find another confessor.

Carred is once again beaten down and depressed at another failure to secure Talia's heir. She briefly contemplates giving up, but instead goes against her better judgment and gives Malady a task: capture Anskar and the demon can go free.

After Gisela's rejection, Anskar wanders the Mother House and finds himself at a forge, where he meets Braga, a foul-mouthed blacksmith. He watches her working for a time, and despite her surliness, they strike up an unlikely friendship.

Later that night, Malady the demon uses her powers so Carred can communicate with Anskar. Carred implores Anskar to trust her and to join the rebels. Before he can decide, Queen Talia's spirit brushes aside Malady's sorcery, and chastises Anskar for consorting with demons. After she does, Anskar weaves dawn-, dusk-, and dark-tide together in order to keep his mother out of his mind.

After Carred's failed attempt, Talia once again possesses Noni and speaks through her. Talia tells Carred to seek out the necromancer Tain and to use his knowledge to create a suit of Armor of Divinity as a fallback plan, in case Anskar fails to make his own.

The Grand Master Hyle Pausus summons Anskar and, in front of senior priests, urges Anskar to make peace with his burgeoning abilities and harness them for the good of the Order. Hyle Pausus sends Anskar for further training under the ancient Abbess at the Abbey of the Hooded One, in an attempt to cure him of his disillusionment with the Order of Eternal Vigilance.

Arriving at the Abbey, Anskar is given a cold welcome by the Abbess. He is confined to a cell and left to contemplate for long lengths of time, only broken by meals, prayer, and brief talks with the Abbess. Long, lonely, oppressive days go by, and Anskar's preconceptions about the Order and its morality are broken down little by little. The Abbess's talks are his only lifeline, and Anskar clings to them as if his sanity depends on it. They speak of demons and demon lore; Malady, Carred, and Niyas; Menselas; and balance, despair and death, as the Abbess challenges everything Anskar has grown to believe.

The Abbess also reveals the lore of demon summoning and a way of inflicting sorcerous pain on demons to bend them to your will: the Wracking Nerves. Anskar practices everything she teaches him in his cell: rituals and cants and inflections that will enable him to summon beings from the abyssal realms.

When the Abbess declares Anskar ready, he summons and binds the demon Malady to his will, tormenting her with the Wracking Nerves. Anskar commands Malady to take him to Carred. Malady takes him briefly to the abyssal realms, then swiftly on to Carred before a winged demon can attack them. Malady reveals that knowing a demon's name grants a sorcerer power over that demon, and makes him a gift of the winged demon's name.

Anskar confronts Carred and Orix, who has been converted to the rebel's cause. Carred attempts to bring Anskar to her side, explaining the faults of the Order and the good Anskar could do if the Niyandrian people were liberated. Anskar rejects Carred, and Malady spirits him away, back to the abbey.

When they arrive, Malady tries to kill Anskar, and he responds by assaulting her with the Wracking Nerves. Malady proves too powerful, until the Abbess arrives and slays her with sorcery. Afterwards, the Abbess, clothed in the illusion of Carred Selenas, forces Anskar to copulate with her, again and again, until he loses consciousness.

The next day, Anskar is summoned to see the Abbess, and still reeling and confused, he is taken to a vast chamber in which are gathered all of the priests and priestesses of the Hooded One. The Abbess reveals that she is a member of the Tainted Cabal, and that with Anskar joining their ranks, she believes that they will be powerful enough to return the demon lord Nysrog to Wiraya.

Led by the Abbess, the congregation begins a ritual of summoning, and Nysrog's face begins to form in the coalescing vapors. Anskar is torn between extremes of savagery and terror. However, the demon lord's visage disperses as the summoning fails.

The Abbess is jubilant. She believes they only need to become a little stronger, and then because of Anskar's abilities, Nysrog will once again walk upon the face of Wiraya.

Anskar comes to his senses and is horrified. He has to get away from the abbey before it is too late for him, and too late for the world. Swallowing his repugnance, he forces himself to go along with the Abbess and her deranged followers until an opportunity presents itself. As the Abbess and the priests begin an orgy, Queen Talia speaks to Anskar, and tells him he must partake or all will be lost. But Anskar cannot, and he flees into the night.

Running for his life, Anskar is cornered by demons the Abbess has sent to capture or kill him. Unarmored and without a weapon, Anskar believes he is doomed, but Queen Talia speaks to him, and extorts from Anskar a vow to never shut her out again if she saves him. Talia shows Anskar how to use the earth-tide, the power behind necromancy, to raise long-dead corpses from the earth. Believing this his only chance, and the lesser evil compared to the Abbess and the Tainted Cabal, Anskar gives Talia his word. He summons a dead spirit and sends it to the Mother House in Sansor to bring help. With this done, urged by Talia, Anskar uses the dark-tide to repeatedly shadow-step ahead of his demon pursuers until his repository empties and he is too exhausted to go on as the demons close in.

Anskar fends off one demon, using his vambrace to keep its fangs from his flesh, and as he does, help arrives in the form of Lanuc, Braga, and knights of the Order. They drive the demons off, killing many, and save Anskar from certain death.

The Grand Master sends knights to the abbey, but they find the priests all dead, their veins turned black by some poison or cant. Of the Abbess there is no sign.

Once Anskar has recovered from his ordeals, he and the Grand Master walk the grounds outside the Mother House, discussing demons and the Tainted Cabal. The Grand Master's bodyguards are all slain by an assassin sent by the Abbess. The assassin incapacitates the Grand Master, and Anskar skewers the man with his sword *Amalantril*, only to find that there is no blood, and the assassin isn't slowed down by the wound.

Once again Talia tells Anskar to summon the dead using the earth-tide. Desperate, Anskar obeys and raises the Grand Master's dead guards. The assassin disposes of the animated corpses, but when Anskar scours him with dark-tide fire, the assassin is revealed as a demon.

Anskar recognizes it as the demon Malady pointed out to him in their brief sojourn in the abyssal realms. He halts the demon by uttering its name, then kills it with the Wracking Nerves.

The Grand Master declares that the Tainted Cabal have infiltrated the Order of Eternal Vigilance, and all must keep their eyes and ears open to detect the taint of corruption. He announces that Anskar must be removed from the Mother House, as the Tainted Cabal will come after him again.

Anskar is ordered to join Lanuc and a hundred knights to travel to the Thousand Lakes in the north and assist King Aelfyr, who is beset with problems from the Soreshi of the Ymaltian Mountains.

Breaking his promise to her, Anskar re-establishes the wards he had set against his mother, believing this new mission to be a manifestation of the mercy of Menselas and a way for him to atone for past sins and to give his life over to the providence of the Five. He feels free of Carred Selenas, free of the hold the Abbess had over him, and most of all he feels free of the specter of his mother.

# ONE

USPETH SUPPRESSED A SHUDDER, LEST it be taken for a sign of weakness. Probably he should have worn a second undershirt.

The air in the great hall was icy, a consequence of the tons of rock the citadel had been built beneath. If indeed it had been built, because Nax-ur-Vadim, the newly named Tainted Cabal stronghold, had the appearance of having grown out of the mountain.

It didn't matter to Uspeth how the ancient Soreshi sorcerers had constructed the stronghold in the Ymaltian Mountains. The important thing was that the Tainted Cabal now occupied it, and it was his to command.

Not that he felt much like commanding anything right now. He'd taken too large a dose of alchemicals in order to give him the energy to climb out of bed in the morning, and it had left him feeling queasy. Everybody knew about the sickly blood that trickled through his veins, rendering him pale and weak. Without his remedies, his confreres would have viewed him as prey.

He was in a bitter mood as he sat with his acolytes around the long blackwood table that dominated the hall. Uspeth had insisted on blackwood because it repelled sorcery. You could never be too careful. Any one of his acolytes might secretly acquire the power to usurp him, and the Sanctum, the five shadowy leaders who governed the Tainted Cabal, would only commend them for it. All it would take would be the successful summoning of a higher-order demon, a pact in return for dark-tide lore, and Uspeth would be an example of where weakness got you.

He winced as he took a sip of watered wine steeped with pungent herbs and sharp spices. It contained three drops of demon blood, too, carefully drawn from a captured lesser demon he kept alive in the dungeons for that purpose. There was great strength in demon blood: it was the source of the demons' innate abilities with the dark-tide, though experiments to manipulate its properties ended mostly with failure.

"Have you all broken your fast?" Uspeth asked the ten seated at table with him. It was an attempt to be convivial. He had no idea how to set others at ease nor even why he should try. He set the goblet down and ran his jaundiced eyes over his seven acolytes—men and women who each commanded fifty Cabalists, all of them sorcerers blessed with demon heritage, all of them invested in the return of the demon lord Nysrog. Alongside them sat three sun-browned Soreshi—two men and a woman—also sorcerers, albeit of the savage, wildling variety.

These three Soreshi leaders had answered Uspeth's call for a secret alliance. Ever since, King Aelfyr of the Thousand Lakes had been forced into a desperate defensive battle against the hordes of Soreshi pouring down from the mountains to sack his outlying towns and villages. Cattle had been taken, buildings burned, women and children sent to the slave pits beyond the Trackless Ocean. It was a good start to their plans, but it wasn't enough.

The seven Cabalists eyed each other slyly and said nothing, but one of the three Soreshi—Jilua, he thought she had said her name was—managed to mumble in broken Nan-Rhouric, "We have not, lord."

"Shame," Uspeth said. He had eaten nothing yet either; but then again, he seldom ate. He raised his goblet and took another sip of wine. "You can eat after."

He thought he caught an insolent flash in the woman's eyes. What did they expect—that he would order breakfast sent to the great hall so that they could munch and chew and slobber while he debriefed them? Next they'd be wanting him to endure the stench of their bodily waste. He loathed barbarians; he loathed people in general. They were nothing but eating, shitting, rutting animals, no better than the lesser demons. The higher demons were a different matter altogether. They were cultured, ordered, intelligent—superior in just about every way imaginable.

"You all know why you are here," Uspeth said. "So, brief me on our joint progress."

One of the Cabalists, a fat, indulgent piece of slime called Castellac, coughed to clear his throat. It was rumored he summoned demons in order to have them hump him like a dog. In the best Tainted Cabal tradition, Castellac had murdered his way up the pyramid to become one of the seven under Uspeth's direct command. Seven men and women whose true aim was to kill Uspeth and supplant him before Lord Nysrog's return.

"Would someone please start?" Uspeth took another sip of wine. The demon blood it contained was supposed to grant him strength, yet all it did was make him want to vomit, and the alchemicals and herbs just made him run for the privy. The way his guts had started to clench, he knew that wouldn't be long.

Finally, it was the Soreshi woman, Jilua, who spoke. She had a lithe, hard body that looked as though it had been carved from wood. Beneath her fur-trimmed cloak, she wore a strip of dyed yellow cloth that crushed her breasts and gave her a boyish look and another that girded her loins. From a string around her waist hung finger-length sticks, each carved with combinations of cuneiform letters—a fetish, to aid her sorcery, along with the eagle's claw that hung around her neck. A hatchet lay on the tabletop before her—didn't the savage know it would mark the blackwood?—and a short hunting bow rested across her lap.

"We left three villages burning," she said, "and led entire herds and flocks east into the mountains."

"Our people will eat well for months," one of the Soreshi men added. He was tall and proudly athletic, which made Uspeth instantly dislike him.

"But we were driven back by their archers," Jilua finished.

"Again?"

The Thousand Lakes archers had been a thorn in Uspeth's side ever since the Soreshi had begun their incursions into King Aelfyr's lands. Their longbows were massive weapons, and it was said it took more than ten years of training for an archer to develop the strength to fully draw the stave. The Soreshi's short bows were no match.

"We can go so far and no farther," Jilua said. "The frontiers are still vulnerable to our raids, but—"

"But Aelfyr's defenses push ever northward," Uspeth finished for her. The King had an almost mystical ability to construct palisades, earthworks, and stone fortifications wherever he perceived a threat.

He saw a flash of irritation in the woman's eyes at being interrupted, but she was clearly too frightened of him to do anything about it. That small victory helped Uspeth to relax.

"Not good enough," he added. "I thought you people were sorcerers."

"We are," the third Soreshi said, a rat-lipped man with dark rings around his eyes.

"Remind me of your name," Uspeth said.

"Traven."

"Ah, yes, Traven. From now on, speak only when spoken to. Understood?"

Traven's hands bunched into white-knuckled fists, but Jilua restrained him with a raised finger, and he slumped back in his chair.

"Our sorcery has had great effect on the enemy," Jilua said. "They have priests of the Five with them, who have shielded them from the worst of our dusk-tide attacks, but they are limited in what they can do. With a concerted effort, we will—"

She stopped, having noticed that Uspeth was distracted.

It had begun as a pressure within his head. At first he thought it was the herbs increasing his nausea, but then he realized it wasn't coming from within his skull. Rather, it was a change in the atmosphere of the hall.

He sent his sorcerous senses to the source of the disturbance: a pooling of the shadows on the floor by the unlit hearth. As he stared at the patch, the stench of mutton filled his nostrils.

"Get out," he snapped, despising the shrillness of his voice. When no one moved, he yelled, "Now!"

He barely registered the scrape of chairs, the clip of booted feet on the flagstone floor. He was watching the air above the shadow patch shimmer, dust motes swirling in a gathering maelstrom. The door clicked shut, leaving him alone in the hall. But only for a moment. The swirling air parted like a curtain, and a figure stepped through.

"Mother!" Uspeth said with a mix of feigned joy and unfeigned fear. He pushed his chair back and moved around the table so he could drop to one knee.

"Two hundred souls!" the Abbess snarled. "That is the cost of my transition here."

"You teleported here from Sansor? From the Abbey of the Hooded One?" Uspeth wasn't even sure that was possible.

"Well, I'm here, aren't I? Did you think I walked?"

"Two hundred souls, Mother?"

"The priests of the Hooded One at the abbey. I trained them myself. All those years of guidance, of suffering, of pleasure… wasted!"

"But why, Mother? What has happened?"

It must have been something grave indeed for her to emerge from the abbey within which she had hidden away for as long as anyone could remember. Longer.

"The abbey is lost," she said as she seated herself at the blackwood table. "And we were so close! The Grand Master of the Order of Eternal Vigilance sent a young man to me: Anskar DeVantte. A lad with great potential. More than potential: enormous power churning within him, and a mark of sorcery that eclipses even yours."

Uspeth felt his cheek twitch as he rose from kneeling and resumed his chair. His mother had always made him feel special as a child on account of his vast sorcerous potential, but in every other respect he had been a bitter disappointment to her. Worse, he'd been an instrument to be used. The recollection of the things she'd done with him—to him—still made him want to vomit.

"You'll never guess whose child he is," the Abbess added.

Uspeth shrugged. He hated it when she made him work for an answer that she could simply give him.

"Queen Talia of Niyas's," she said.

"The Necromancer Queen?"

"Interesting, isn't it? And he was raised at Branil's Burg, right under the noses of the Order."

"And the father?"

"That, I don't know." She gave Uspeth a long, lingering look and then shook her head.

"And he's one of us now?" Uspeth asked.

"He would have been if he hadn't escaped. We were so near, Uspeth! Nysrog came closer than ever before. With Anskar properly prepared, the demon lord could become fully manifest, free once more to walk the world."

Uspeth swallowed. "That… that is… incredible." All these centuries the Tainted Cabal had labored to bring Nysrog back, and now his mother had almost succeeded because of this son of the dead queen of Niyas. "Does anyone else know?"

He meant the four others of the Sanctum, the powerful sorcerers who governed the Tainted Cabal from the shadows within the shadows. Besides his mother, Uspeth had no idea who they were.

The Abbess shook her head. "My two hundred acolytes gave their lives to send me here, so now it is just you and me, Uspeth. Together we must determine our next course of action."

"Do you plan to stay at Nax-ur-Vadim?" The idea was not exactly thrilling.

"Where else would you have your old mother go? The abbey is in the hands of the Order of Eternal Vigilance. Even now, they will be scouring Kaile in the hope of capturing me. Do you know what they would do if they got their holy hands on a member of the Sanctum? They would torture me for weeks on end before burning me at the stake. Hypocrites, all of them! Which is why we must succeed. No matter how long the path or how hard, we must usher in a new dawn of Nysrog."

"Praise be to Nysrog," Uspeth said, and he meant it. What Wiraya needed more than anything was a return to order, to a time when the unenlightened resumed their place among the beasts, and the laws of the abyssal realms tamed the chaos of the world.

"How many trained Cabalists do you have here?" the Abbess asked.

"Sixty, plus my seven acolytes."

The acolytes were much more advanced in sorcerous lore due in no small part to their contact with the abyssal realms. For years, each had experienced progressive exposure to summonings. They had discovered how to strike bargains with lesser demons first, then with those of higher rank. And they had partaken of the blood of demons.

"Not nearly enough," the Abbess said, as if it were Uspeth's fault she had slaughtered two hundred of her own Cabalists. "Even with Anskar DeVantte's vast abilities, we lacked the power to bring Nysrog fully through the veil with more than three times that number."

"And now you don't even have this Anskar," Uspeth pointed out helpfully.

His mother responded with a cold look that promised anguish.

Uspeth snatched up his wineglass and drained the rest of the sour concoction.

"Tell me about your progress here," the Abbess said. "How close are you to taking the capital?"

"Wintotashum? Unfortunately, King Aelfyr is a formidable

opponent and quite unreachable by our usual methods," Uspeth said, referring to the spies and counselors who made up the insidious arsenal of the Tainted Cabal.

"So, not close at all."

"It is the long game we play, Mother. You were the one to teach me that."

She sighed. "And I was right. But after coming so close to reaching our goal…"

"You want to press on and force the finish?"

Uspeth winced when she opened her mouth to respond, but then she closed it again, seeming hesitant. There was a pensive quality to her expression that Uspeth had never seen before.

"We must reappraise the situation," she said. "I fear you have lost sight of the goal."

"The memory crystal of Morudjin. Believe me, Mother, it is never out of my mind."

Morudjin had been a priest of the Five who had believed it was his duty to learn all he could about the abyssal realms so the Church of Menselas could strike preemptively and end the demon wars before they started.

Morudjin had indeed learned. He had bound hundreds of demons to his service—and disposed of them one after another as soon as they had revealed everything he wanted to know. He grew in his knowledge of demon lore, and even mirrored the demons' innate dark-tide abilities within himself. He grew so adept at summoning and defeating both lesser and higher-order demons that even the demon lords themselves began to tremble. And then Morudjin made his first mistake, which also proved to be his last. He summoned Nysrog, and greatly underestimated the demon lord's cunning. The world burned, and Morudjin's death at Nysrog's hands was the stuff of nightmare.

But the priest's memories lived on in the crystal. The Tainted Cabal had long believed that if they gained the crystal, they could retrace the steps Morudjin had taken to bring Nysrog through the veil. It seemed a surer way than the Sanctum's endless experiments.

"Let me put it another way," the Abbess said. "The long game is taking too *long*."

"I still don't think we can risk showing our hand. We must continue the war by proxy. If Aelfyr suspects the Tainted Cabal are involved, his allies will come against us in force, like they did against the Necromancer Queen."

"Maybe he already suspects," the Abbess said. "I assume you know Aelfyr has sent to Sansor for aid?"

Uspeth nodded. "But against the Soreshi, not us. My spies report he has been pleading with the Grand Master of the Order of Eternal Vigilance for months. Nothing has come of it."

"I'm not convinced by your strategy, Uspeth," the Abbess said. "These piecemeal attacks by the Soreshi are getting us nowhere. All they do is stiffen Aelfyr's resolve and increase the likelihood of support from his allies."

"You think we should call off the attacks?"

"I do not. I think we should use the Soreshi aggression as a smokescreen for a much bolder plan."

"Does it involve the son of the Necromancer Queen?"

"Why, are you jealous? There's no need. I'm sure the Order are keeping Anskar DeVantte safe from the likes of me."

"So, what is your 'bolder' plan, then?"

The old crone gave a condescending smile and tapped the side of her nose. "I'll explain later."

*Only the parts you think I should know,* Uspeth thought.

The Abbess's demeanor changed. She eyed Uspeth with a look

he could easily have mistaken for a mother's concern if he didn't know her better.

"How is your sickness, dear?"

"The alchemicals and herbs are a daily torture, but I'm still here, as you see."

She leaned closer, her rank stench overpowering, and lightly stroked his cheek with a dirty-nailed finger. Uspeth had to exert all his considerable willpower not to pull away.

"So pale, so bloodless," she said. "And those yellow eyes… So like your father."

She had never told Uspeth who his father was, save for the fact that he might not have been human. Uspeth didn't waste his breath asking her now. She would have taken far too much pleasure in denying his request.

A look came into her eyes that he had seen more times than he cared to remember, and he knew with a rising sense of nausea that she was thinking of an altogether different kind of pleasure as her finger left his cheek and traced a long line down his chest, and then went lower.

Uspeth closed his eyes and suppressed a shudder, and as he tried to shut out what was happening in the hall, his thoughts turned once more to the subject of his father, who he had slowly come to suspect might even have been a demon lord.

# TWO

IT SEEMED TO ANSKAR DEVANTTE as though he were riding with a massive army rather than a mere hundred knights, given the number of pages, servants, farriers, and priests that accompanied them. Each knight had two horses: a heavy, battle-trained destrier that could carry a fully armored knight into battle and fight with its hooves and teeth, and a lighter courser to ride the rest of the time.

Unfortunately, it had started to rain again. Only an hour before, the sky had been blue and cloudless.

"That's Kaile for you," Lanuc of Gessa said, passing Anskar on his way to the front. "Frost in the morning, a heat wave in the middle of the day, showers in the afternoon, and lightning storms at night."

Anskar grimaced. It was hard to know how to dress for the day. This morning—their fifth day out from Sansor—he had been frozen to the bone, but by noon he was drenched with sweat.

As they continued around the great bay, the sea was in a foul mood. Frothing breakers crashed against the pebbled shoreline and sluiced over the groynes. The air was heavy with brine and the cabbagy stench of seaweed. North across the bay, black clouds were stacked tall as mountains. Gulls shrieked overhead, and the few fishing boats still out on the water clawed their way back to shore against the tide.

Knights muttered to one another about a big storm brewing. Some touched their fingertips and thumbs to their chests in a silent prayer for the Five's protection.

Josac, one of the priests of the Warrior, loudly disagreed. A stout-looking man with thickly muscled forearms and a long plaited mustache, he had a face ruddy from exposure and raked with old scars. When Josac removed his winged helm to scratch his bald head, Anskar saw the thick ridges of a number branded into his scalp: 24.

"The wind'll change, you'll see," Josac told them, and someone snorted in derision. "I'm not just trying to stop you boys and girls from soiling yourselves in panic," he said in a good-natured voice. Indeed, he had proven to be an amiable companion thus far on the journey, which had surprised Anskar. In his experience, priests of the Warrior were usually serious and prone to violence—especially Beof back at Branil's Burg, the man who had tried to kill him during the third trial.

"You just need to watch the scudding of the clouds," Josac said. "I tell you, the winds will change and the storm will blow back out to sea."

Anskar touched his heels to his horse's flanks and steered it in between the other riders until he came alongside Josac's bay palfrey. "How can you tell?" he asked.

"I was a sailor before I became a priest," Josac said, casting a lingering look out to sea.

"Why did you give it up?"

"Pirates." A faraway look came into Josac's eyes. He winced, remembering something, then shook his head and turned his gaze back to the trail.

At first, Anskar feared he had offended the priest, but then Josac said, "Half the crew were butchered and thrown overboard for the sharp-tooths. The rest of us, those young enough to still be useful, were sold into slavery. I ended up being forced to fight in the arenas at Ivrian in the Plains of Khisig-Ugtall. I was good at it—so good I drew the attention of a visiting bishop of the Warrior who had come to Ivrian seeking new blood for the Church. He was impressed by me, so he gave me a way out."

"No regrets?" Anskar asked.

"About becoming a priest?" Again, Josac looked out to sea. "None at all. Why would I have regrets? How about you? Do you regret signing up for the Order?"

"I was a baby when the Order at Branil's Burg took me in."

"On Niyas? You must be—what—sixteen? Seventeen?"

"Nearly eighteen." Anskar's birthday—or at least what he had been led to believe by Brother Tion was his birthday—was on the Festival of the Healer, in three weeks' time.

"So, you were a war baby?" Josac said. "I hear that was a pretty dark war, too. By the Five, the Necromancer Queen must have been an evil bitch. I only wish I'd been there to fight her myself."

Anskar didn't want to think about the fact he was Queen Talia's son. And he certainly couldn't tell just anyone in the Order—there was no point making things more difficult for himself than they needed to be. For all he knew, his mother's shade could still be inside him, but he had once more woven intricate wards of dawn-tide sorcery around his mind, preventing her from speaking or appearing to him. He was done with the Necromancer Queen.

"Were you ordained back then?" he asked Josac.

"No, I was fighting in the arenas, though I remember the Traguh-raj preparing for war. Queen Talia made overtures to the people of the Plains of Khisig-Ugtall, but the mainland nations got there first and offered an alliance. Even so, there was very little military support for the Plains from the mainland, and always the risk that a bitter Queen Talia might turn her ire on the Traguh-raj."

"But she didn't?" Anskar asked.

"She never got the chance. The Order did itself proud during the war with Niyas, and every mainland merchant, noble, and politician knows it and should be grateful."

Josac touched his heels to his horse's flanks and rode ahead.

Before dusk they came within sight of a fishing village. The boats moored at the jetties were buffeted by crashing waves, and villagers scurried around shuttering their timber homes, whose thatched roofs looked as fragile as tents against the power of the storm. Goats bleated from a lean-to within a corral, and cattle pastured in a field lay down beneath swaying trees.

Lanuc made the decision to head for the village and find whatever shelter they could in barns, homes, perhaps even the only stone building Anskar could see. It looked like a church, with its high tower, but nothing about the design spoke of the Five. He wondered then about the other faiths that still clung to the mainland, and what manner of god or goddess these fishing folk prayed to.

Lanuc called Anskar to ride ahead with him, and together they cantered down a gentle slope to the village, where a woman in an oilskin hat and cloak stood waiting.

"It's no good," she called above the wind, gesturing at the force of more than two hundred following behind Lanuc and Anskar. "We ain't got shelter enough for so many, if that's what you're thinking."

They drew rein in front of the woman. She was gray-haired, her face weather-worn and wrinkled.

"Who is the headman?" Lanuc asked.

"That'd be me," the woman said. "Molly's my name, and I say we can't accommodate so many. You got tents?"

Lanuc nodded.

"They'll do you right enough, on the lee side of yon hill you just came down. That'll keep the wind off you. But don't be fooled by all this bluster. The storm'll turn; you'll see."

"How can you be so sure?" Anskar asked.

"I have the ear of Shulni," Molly said. At Anskar's blank look, she explained: "Goddess of the bay. Like I said, the lee side of yon hill will give you shelter. When the storm passes, I'll have fish sent up to you, and a few barrels of beer. Maybe even get the bakers to make extra bread, come morning. It'll cost you, though."

"How much?" Lanuc pulled out the coin purse the Grand Master had given him.

"Couple of silvers…" Molly said.

Lanuc leaned over his saddle pommel and placed two coins on her outstretched hand.

"For the fish, that is. The beer'll be three more, and another couple for the bread. I'll add it up for you, if you like."

"No need," Lanuc said with a sigh. "Why don't I just make it a gold instead?"

Molly didn't argue with that and handed back the silvers in exchange for a gold coin.

"But that's too much," Anskar objected to Lanuc as Molly shuffled back toward the village.

"Not my money, so why would I care?"

"And Shulni?"

Lanuc turned his horse, and they started back toward the others. "Your first encounter with a rival deity to Menselas?"

"Almost," Anskar said. "Niklaus du Plessis was a follower of Sylva Kalisia."

"Her Chosen Sword," Lanuc said. "How could I forget?"

"He told me that he was tormented by her," Anskar said. "She visited him in his dreams, yet she never fully gave him what he wanted."

"That's women for you," Lanuc said. "You're better off without them."

"But you were married…"

"The exception rather than the rule."

Though the knights and their retainers made haste in putting up their tents in the shelter of the hill, the wind did indeed turn. A bank of clouds like an inverted mountain range moved ponderously back out to sea, and the lightning that had come so close flickered sporadically in the far distance.

Anskar spotted Josac tightening the guy ropes of his tent. "You were right about the storm."

The priest glanced at him. "Like I said, I was a sailor once."

Another man craned his neck to glare at Anskar over Josac's shoulder. He wore a sodden fur-trimmed cloak and leather pants, and his boots were reinforced with iron bands. His hair was long, his beard thick and full.

Anskar looked away, wondering what he had done wrong.

Was it something he'd said to Josac?

He risked another glance. The man had turned away. There was something about him that seemed familiar.

"You're wondering who he is, aren't you?" Josac said. "And why he was staring at you?"

"I thought I recognized him," Anskar said, "but I was mistaken."

"In part perhaps you were, but you were right that you recognized if not him, then some of his features. Be vigilant, Anskar, because he is a vengeful man. We all are, in a way. Vengeance is one of the excesses of too exclusive a devotion to the Warrior."

"Vengeful? Why?" Anskar asked, though he wasn't half as confused as he sounded. His mind was already starting to play catch-up, and his memories were coming together to corroborate what he had started to intuit and what Josac confirmed almost apologetically.

"His name is Gann Harril. He is also a priest of the Warrior and the brother of Beof."

Beof Harril had been the Warrior's priest at Branil's Burg charged with testing the durability of each postulant knight's newly crafted sword against his massive bejeweled mace. When it was Anskar's turn to be tested, Beof had come at him hard with strong, killing blows, but Anskar had parried with such force that his sword, *Amalantril*, had cleaved straight through the haft of Beof's mace. The Warrior's priest had been humiliated. Later, Beof had come at Anskar again, this time alone in the dark and with murderous intent. Anskar had defended himself with the dark-tide, severely injuring the priest.

"But how—?" he started.

"How does he know that it was you who wounded his brother?

News traveled with your group from Niyas, but even without that, whispers fly. Tongues wag. The Grand Master has eyes and ears in every Order house and stronghold. You know how it is. I knew before Gann did."

"And you told him?"

"Of course. We are confreres. But don't worry, I don't share his views on what happened between you and Beof, and I've already spoken to him about curbing his desire for revenge. Gann has been told many times he is out of balance with the other four aspects. He is not an easy man to confront with his failings, however. Many have tried, and all have regretted it."

"But not you?"

Josac smiled at some private recollection. "He owes me; that's all I'm prepared to say. But no, I harbor no ill will towards you for Beof. The Bishop of the Warrior, though, will punish Beof severely." Josac shuddered. "I assume it was self-defense?"

Anskar nodded.

"Beof is a fearsome warrior, but also a bully. He learned the behavior from his older brother, Gann."

"Gann bullied Beof?" It seemed hard to believe.

"Used to beat him senseless when they were kids. Then, when they grew up, they came close to killing each other on several occasions, which was what got them noticed by the Bishop of the Warrior. They learned harsh discipline during their training to be priests, and they found it was better to turn their strength and anger against their rivals instead of each other. They became allies of a sort. Cross Gann, and you have Beof to reckon with. Cross Beof…"

"I get the picture," Anskar said. "So what should I do?"

"Keep your eyes peeled, and keep limber." Josac waggled his fingers in a parody of casting sorcery.

"I've sworn to never again use sorcery, other than for shielding and making weapons and armor."

"Commendable, but not necessarily wise. One thing they teach us in the Warrior's seminary is never to forgo an advantage. All's fair in war, they say, and to my mind this is no different."

Anskar shook his head, then realized he was biting his bottom lip so hard he tasted blood.

"Should I tell Lanuc?"

"Snitching? A warrior fights his own battles, boy. This is your fight, the consequence of your actions. Use your sorcery, I tell you. Either that or grow some balls."

The promised fish came up from the village before night fell, and fires were set. There was a lot of spitting and smoke due to the wood they collected being wet, but most of the knights had brought dry kindling. Soon, orange glows were dotted about the camp, and the air was filled with the smell of roasting fish.

The beer came too, in an ox-pulled wagon driven by a sullen-looking old man. Hooded lanterns hung from poles at the front of the cart, and in between them came the reddish glow of a pipe the man was smoking as he drove. He unloaded four, not two, barrels. Presumably the headwoman felt guilty about taking Lanuc's gold coin.

Within minutes of the barrels being tapped, servants scurried around filling tin mugs for their knights, and pretty soon the storm was forgotten amid a hubbub of voices, raucous laughter, and eventually the singing of lewd songs.

After his second beer, Anskar started to relax and decided he could see himself getting used to the campaign life: riding with comrades-in-arms, setting up camp each night, sharing the warmth of a fire, drinking, eating, laughing at bad jokes. Perhaps after another beer, he might laugh as loudly as the rest of the men and women, only he'd decided not to allow himself to get drunk. Not after what Josac had told him about Gann. If he'd gotten himself embroiled in some kind of blood feud, he was going to need his wits about him.

Another chorus of laughter followed Lanuc's latest joke, which Anskar had missed. He had been thinking about what Josac had said. Should he use sorcery?

His fingers stroked the hilt of *Amalantril*. He'd already seen where the use of forbidden sorcery could lead, and he never wanted to go there again. So what should he do? Confront Gann? Challenge him?

Anskar knew he was good with a sword, but was he good enough to take on a priest of the Warrior and survive?

"Good evening, Anskar."

He looked up to see Gisela of Gessa standing beside him, white cloak hugged tightly about her. Her fair hair was braided into rounds that covered her ears, and her gray eyes sparkled with reflected firelight.

Anskar shot to his feet. "What are you doing here?"

"I thought my father and I should spend more time together," she said, nodding toward Lanuc, "so I put my name forward to join the healers on this campaign."

Lanuc saw her, and he stood and opened his arms. Gisela went to his embrace. "Sit, daughter," he said, "and entertain us." He looked around the group. "She sings very well."

Gisela stepped back from him, suddenly flustered. "I don't know if that would be appropriate. I haven't sung since I was very young, save for choir prayers to the Healer."

"Sing for us now," Lanuc said.

Gisela seemed about to refuse, but the others around the fire chanted, "Sing, sing, sing!" She cast a desperate look at Anskar, who couldn't keep himself from smiling.

And so Gisela sang, captivating her audience with a voice both melodic and haunting. It was a gentle ballad about a lord's pet hound that gave its life to save the lord's baby from deadeyes. The hound fought the creatures off until the lord and his men arrived and then collapsed, blood pouring from scores of wounds, and with its master cradling its limp body, it died.

Tears glistened in Lanuc's eyes as he watched his daughter. "Your mother used to sing that song to you at night," he said.

Gisela dipped her head in acknowledgment. Seeing her shudder beneath her robe, Anskar assumed that she was crying too.

A woman knight clapped Gisela on the shoulder and passed her a beer. To Anskar's surprise, Gisela not only accepted it but downed it in one long pull, and again the onlookers cheered. After that she resumed her singing, only this time choosing popular melodies that others could join in with. As people sang and the beer flowed and the storm fled out to sea, leaving the sky star-spangled and still, Lanuc came around the fire to sit beside Anskar.

"I tried to persuade her not to come," he said, "but she nags worse than her mother. She misses me, I think. Ordinarily, family members don't work together, in case their natural preferences interfere with the running of the Order's affairs and prove an impediment to justice. But this campaign to aid a supposed ally is not regular Order business. If it were, we would have a far larger army, and I would not be leading it."

"Supposed ally?" Anskar said.

Lanuc gave him a searching look. "If you commanded the mainland's most powerful Order and a friend appealed to you for help because his kingdom was being overrun by savage sorcerers, would you send merely a token force of a hundred trained knights?"

"Then what is this really about?"

"I suspect the Soreshi of the Ymaltian Mountains are not the sole threat to King Aelfyr's lands. They may merely be pawns in a far darker game. After what happened with you at the Abbey of the Hooded One, we can't afford to be complacent. Something has driven the Soreshi to these acts of aggression against the Kingdom of the Thousand Lakes."

"The Tainted Cabal?"

"Perhaps. The Grand Master's spies in the area have relayed rumors that the Tainted Cabal have begun to operate in the region."

"But how are we supposed to fight the Tainted Cabal, especially with such a small force?"

"The Grand Master's no fool, Anskar. Whenever there's a problem that requires more finesse than the usual blunt fist of the Order, he sends me and a team of unusual people. Remember when I told you that some within the Order have special talents?"

Anskar glanced around at those listening to Gisela's singing. "So, what is your daughter's special power?"

"Gisela is a virgin sworn to celibacy, which makes her one of the elite among the Healers."

Now Anskar understood some of her initial coldness toward him, and why, after hearing his sordid thoughts, she had told him to find another confessor.

"You must be proud of her," he told Lanuc. "I only wish that I could make some kind of grand sacrifice to the Five that would make my service feel more worthy."

"You want to be a celibate?" Lanuc said, clapping Anskar on the shoulder. "I'm told there are some men who willingly make themselves eunuchs for the sake of the Church. I have a sharp knife, if you'd like to borrow it…"

Anskar shook his head. "I was trying to be serious."

"Ah, then you have discovered one of my special traits," Lanuc said. "I am seldom serious."

Anskar let his eyes rove around the group seated at the fire. "Do they all have special powers?"

Lanuc laughed. "It's not only about power and ability. Often it's about aptitude or, more often still, attitude. Our company is made up of those who prefer to act than to sit still, who abhor routine and are always looking for the next challenge."

Anskar nodded. "I understand that. But you still haven't told me what makes *you* special."

"What's my unusual power? What makes me suited to lead missions such as this? I often wonder that myself."

# THREE

THE NEXT MORNING, WHEN ANSKAR emerged from his tent, frost coated the ground, and there wasn't a cloud in the sky. Gulls shrieked and squawked incessantly, while wedge-tailed hawks circled as they hunted for early morning prey.

The smoldering remnants of fires were relit, and soon the camp was alive with the smell of fish left over from the previous night. There were fresh-baked loaves too, sent by Molly the headwoman at first light, and another cartload of double-baked black bread for the onward journey.

After breakfast, the tents were taken down and tied into long rolls to be carried by the packhorses, and then Lanuc gave the order to move out.

No sooner had the knights, retainers, and priests moved away from the shelter of the hill than a page came cantering from the rear of the column to tell Lanuc that a laden wagon was approaching from the east. It seemed to be following the trail the army had gouged through the mud.

"Followed us from where?" Anskar asked.

Lanuc stood in his stirrups and craned his neck to look down the long line of the column. "A wagon, you say?" He frowned and shook his head, clearly unable to see much from this distance. "It must have followed us from Sansor. Probably couldn't match our pace and fell behind."

Anskar's eyes had grown keener since they had been sorcerously altered—or revealed for what they really were—by his Niyandrian kidnappers. He was even able to see things at night that he would have been blind to before. Gazing in the same direction as Lanuc, he said, "You think she drove through the night in order to catch up with us?"

Lanuc frowned at him. "She?"

But Anskar was already riding away down the column. Because while Lanuc might not have made out much more than a speck in the hazy distance, Anskar had clearly discerned the bulk of the wagon, the lumbering oxen that pulled it, and the form of the driver stooped over the reins, her graying hair held out of her face by a dark headscarf, a beige-colored smock accentuating the pendulous bulge of her breasts.

"Braga!" he called out as he cantered towards the wagon. "It's good to see you."

"You're a piss-poor liar, dung-face," Braga retorted, and Anskar had to stop himself from laughing.

"What are you doing here?" he asked, reining his horse to a halt as Braga stopped her twin oxen. The beasts looked worn out, and seemed content to dip their heads and munch on the tufts of grass poking up through the mud.

"The ghost told me to follow you," Braga said. "Any more stupid questions?"

"Ghost?"

"The lady. She didn't say much, only a few broken words. Gobbledygook. I think she's foreign."

An icy creep began at the base of Anskar's spine and worked its way toward the nape of his neck. "What did she look like?"

Braga shrugged. "Wispy. Dark. Not much I could really see. Spikes on her head—a crown, I think. But she knew your name."

Anskar might have shut Queen Talia out of his mind, but she'd found another way to get to him. He bridled with anger, and he swore under his breath.

Braga must have thought it was aimed at her. "It ain't my fault, goat-turd. It's not like I ain't got better things to do than follow your stinking ass halfway across Kaile."

"It's not you I'm angry with," he explained. "Honestly, I'm pleased to see you."

"Yes, well," Braga said, "for my part I'm pleased to see your horse. Your face, though, makes me want to take a shit."

Anskar's mouth dropped open. He had no idea how he was supposed to respond to that.

Braga's stern expression cracked, and she spluttered out a laugh. "The look on your face! I almost pissed myself!"

Anskar didn't have much time to find out what he needed to know. Lanuc was cantering toward them, watched by the tail end of the army's column.

"So, the ghost lady told you to follow me. What else did she say?"

"Not much. It was mostly gibberish. But she pointed at my smithy, and I think she meant you would need my tools. So I packed up what I could on the wagon. Even brought a portable forge and my small anvil."

"She thought I'd need a blacksmith?"

"That's all I know, dung-brain. Now, how about you find me some grub? I've eaten nothing but hard bread and cured ham for two days, and I've run out of beer."

Lanuc reined in his horse next to them. "Braga! What are you doing here?"

"What's it look like?"

"She's offering her services," Anskar said.

"We were planning to use the smithies in Wintotashum," Lanuc said. "An old friend of mine is King Aelfyr's master blacksmith. Hrothyr, his name is, and his forges are said to be the hottest in all Wiraya, built by the old gods in order to work divine alloy."

Braga hawked up phlegm and spat it out.

"Ah, of course," Lanuc said, "that was stupid of me. You already know Hrothyr."

"That goat's ass. He sucks on the udders of—"

Lanuc waved her quiet. "Whatever still festers between you and Hrothyr is of no importance. We've been tasked with riding to the Kingdom of the Thousand Lakes as quickly as possible, and a heavily laden wagon will slow us down. I'm sorry, Braga, but you should turn back."

"And who's going to tell the ghost lady why I didn't do as she asked? You, Lanuc of Gessa, you spavined pile of cow snot? Don't go worrying your pretty little head about me keeping up. I'll plod along behind like I've been doing since you left Sansor. It's not like it's hard following your trail, what with all the shit from your horses and the even bigger piles of shit that fall from your twittering gob."

"Ghost lady?" Lanuc asked Anskar. "What is she talking about?"

"What she's talking about," Braga said, "is none of your

business, you rancid discharge from a camel's ulcerated udder."

"I'll explain later," Anskar said, wincing when Braga shot him an angry glare. "And don't worry about the slowness of the wagon. I'll hang back with her."

"Then I'd better stick a peg on my nose," Braga said, "else I'll pass out from the stench."

"Fine," Lanuc said, wheeling his horse to ride back to the column. "But she's your responsibility."

Braga's wagon clattered and clanked as Anskar rode alongside, and it frequently got stuck in the mud churned up by the army they trailed behind. Braga cursed each time she climbed down from the driver's seat so she could prod the oxen to greater efforts to free the wheel. When that didn't work, she would squat down and lift the side of the wagon that was stuck—only an inch or so, but it was usually enough to get the oxen moving again. It was a prodigious feat of strength, Anskar thought, considering the combined weight of the anvil, all the tools she had brought along, and the wagon itself.

Conversation was a struggle. There really wasn't all that much that interested Braga, and Anskar became increasingly aware of just how shy she was. Her cursing and aggression were perhaps masks for her low self-esteem, he came to realize, and while she was happy enough grumbling and complaining and cursing anyone whose name Anskar happened to mention, she would immediately grow sullen and silent if ever Hrothyr's name came up. Anskar was only interested because Lanuc had mentioned the heat of Hrothyr's forges. That set him wondering about why Queen Talia's ghost had sent Braga, a blacksmith, to accompany him to Wintotashum. It could only concern the invisible vambrace he wore on his forearm.

He wondered what had happened between Braga and Hrothyr.

Had they been lovers? He doubted it. Braga was a big, brutal woman who would have terrified any man. In the end he decided it was fruitless to keep upsetting Braga, so he apologized for his questions and promised not to raise the subject of Hrothyr again.

"Good," Braga said, "because it would have saddened me to break your skull and dash your offal brains all over the ground."

While Anskar pitched his tent in the dark, Braga lay in the back of her wagon, beneath the oilskin tarp, snoring loudly. Her twin oxen grazed nearby, the air ripe with the stench of their dung.

A man limped out of the shadows, startling Anskar, who half-tripped on a guy rope as he fumbled for his sword. But then the man was lit by the flickering glow of a nearby campfire.

"Josac?"

The priest of the Warrior's face was yellow with bruises. One eye was swollen completely shut, and his bald pate was a mass of knots and welts that half-obscured the 24 branded into his scalp. His dangling mustache was slick with blood.

"You grown them balls yet, boy?" Josac growled, leaning against the wheel of Braga's wagon.

"What happened to you?" Anskar asked, dropping his voice to a whisper as Josac held up a finger for quiet.

"The Warrior's Fire is what happened. Never in all my years as a priest did I expect anyone to use it against me."

"Warrior's Fire?"

Josac waved aside the question. "I've come to apologize. I shouldn't have been so dismissive of your problem."

"Gann did this to you?"

"I believed my loyalty was to him, a fellow priest of the

Warrior. But he saw us talking and assumed I was on your side, giving you help and advice. It was a coward's attack, from behind. And he used… Menselas, I still can't believe it." Josac sighed and slumped to the ground with his back against the wagon wheel. "Gann has never exactly embodied the higher traits of the Warrior. He's not known for his honor. But as with all priests of each of the Five aspects, allowances must be made for imperfections and imbalances. Over time, our bishops believe, these flaws will be straightened out. Harmonized. And so I treated him as I would any other priest. I thought we were friends." His eyes blazed with reflected firelight. "I was wrong. I know that now, and he knows I know it. Only"—he slapped his injured leg, wincing at the pain—"there's not much I can do about it. I'm finished as a warrior."

"But the healers…" Anskar said.

"They'll not be touching me. My wounds will heal by themselves or not at all."

"But that's—"

"Stupid? That's what I'd expect you to say, because you have no pride."

"How would you know?" Anskar raised a placating hand before Josac could answer. "I don't understand. I thought as a Warrior's priest, you'd seek every advantage."

Josac's lips curled back, and his eyes almost bulged from their sockets. Then he looked away.

"You're ashamed," Anskar said. "Ashamed of what Gann did to you, and too proud to ask for help."

"The way Gann is right now," Josac muttered, "I'd say you have days at best before he makes his move. And I can no longer fight him for you."

"I don't need you to fight my battles," Anskar said.

31

Yet Josac had been a fighter in the slave pits. He'd won his freedom and gone on to endure the brutal training of a priest of the Warrior. If Gann had done this to a man as tough as Josac, then what hope did Anskar have?

*Unless you use sorcery*, said an insistent voice at the back of his mind. At first he thought it was his mother, but the wards he had set up against her were intact. So he had to assume the thought was his own.

"No," he muttered under his breath, "I won't use sorcery. I swore not to."

Nevertheless, Josac heard his words. "Then you're a fool. Because Gann will. He'll use the Warrior's Fire on you, same as he did to me. It will not be a fair fight."

"This Warrior's Fire," Anskar said, "is it a divine gift?"

Josac shook his head. "Merely an application of the dawn-tide."

Anskar crouched in front of the priest. He'd only sworn not to use the dusk and the dark. "Then show me."

"That knowledge is reserved for initiates of the Warrior's mysteries."

"Don't you want revenge against Gann?" He could see from Josac's eyes that he did.

"The Warrior's Fire is not an easy technique to learn."

"It might be for me," Anskar said. "And even if it's not, I'm a quick learner."

He helped Josac away from the camp, to a secluded spot within a copse of myrtle.

"It's not just the Warrior's Fire you're going to need if it comes to a fight with Gann," Josac said. "All of us Warrior priests are skilled fighters."

"So am I," Anskar said. "And I'm fast."

"I'm sure you are, but there are levels to these things. We don't have time for me to train you to be a match for someone as experienced and as dangerous as Gann. That would take years, and we have, at best, days. But I can tell you about any weaknesses you might exploit—not all of them physical."

"What's that supposed to mean?"

Josac's hand lashed out and struck Anskar on the side of the head, pitching him to the ground. Anskar's ears rang. White light flashed behind his eyelids.

He surged to his feet with a roar and threw himself at Josac. The bastard had tricked him, got his guard down. Josac was doing Gann's work for him!

Anskar swung a punch at Josac's face. Despite his injuries, the priest slipped aside with the merest movement of his head and shoulders. He caught Anskar's arm and twisted it, forcing him face down in the dirt, elbow locked, shoulder threatening to pop out of its socket. Anskar cursed and struggled, but he was pinned.

"Do you yield?" Josac said with a chuckle.

"Yes, I bloody yield," Anskar snarled.

Josac released the pressure, and Anskar rolled onto his back to find the Warrior's priest studying him with a serious look on his battered face.

"Let that be your first lesson. I'm smaller than Gann and severely injured, yet I was able to restrain you with ease. Why?"

"Because you know armlocks."

"Wrong. Try again."

"Because you slipped my punch."

"That's part of it. But why was I able to slip your punch so easily?"

"Because I didn't set it up with a jab or a feint."

"Not as stupid as you look, are you? But if you know such things, why didn't you set up your punch properly? Because you were angry. More than angry: you were enraged."

"You hit me without warning!"

"And stunned you, yes. And so you lost control."

Anskar shook his head and pinched the bridge of his nose. It was part of the most basic training for a knight: never allow your emotions to cloud your judgment. Always fight cold.

"And you think Gann will do the same? He'll try to make me angry?"

"I do not," Josac said.

"Then—"

"It's what you must do to him."

After that they sparred lightly with sticks. Josac worked mostly on Anskar's feints.

"You need to frustrate him. Draw the defensive parry out of him, but when it comes, your blade mustn't be there. Make him lunge, keep him off balance, irritate him. Wait till he overcommits. Then, and only then, move in for the kill."

"And if he does the same to me?"

"He might at first if he keeps calm. Which is why your first task is to rile him. Goad him with insults. He's sensitive about his gut, so call him fat. Tell him he's slow, that he hits like an old woman. Tell him how much you enjoyed beating his brother and seeing him sent to the bishop in disgrace."

"But that would be a lie," Anskar said.

"A lie that brings an advantage in a fight is permissible to the devotees of the Warrior."

"But not to the Healer, the Mother, or the Elder," Anskar objected. He was less certain about the Hooded One.

"In an evenly matched fight, the combatant who concerns

himself with such things is invariably the one who will lose."

"I'll beat Gann without needing to lie," Anskar said.

"You might," Josac conceded, "but I think it unlikely. I've faced him, remember, and felt the weight of his blows. And, of course, Gann is proficient with the Warrior's Fire. Under its influence, he feels no pain. Even if you slice off his arm, he'll not stop. I once saw a woman enraged by the Warrior's Fire eviscerated, stabbed through the heart, cleft shoulder to waist, and still she went on fighting. When he invokes the Fire, Gann will be consumed with battle lust. It will make him relentless, invulnerable. It will give him even greater strength, speed, and accuracy. Tell me, Anskar, how will you stand before such an onslaught?"

Again that inner voice nagged at Anskar to use fire of his own: black fire, the bubbling virulence of his dark-tide repository. Again he rejected it.

"You were going to teach me this Warrior's Fire," he said, setting down his stick. "So show me what it looks like."

Josac shook his head. "Once enraged, I have no self-control. I would see you as an enemy."

Instead, he talked Anskar through what he had been taught as a novice: techniques drawing on old and painful memories to evoke emotions of fear, anger, and hatred, all of which were gateways to the divine fire of the Warrior.

And so Anskar went back to the confusion and insecurity of his childhood: never knowing who his parents were or where he had come from. He remembered his disillusionment with Brother Tion, when he had discovered the priest had slept with some of the female knights-postulant he was supposed to mentor, including Sareya. And the double sense of betrayal when Tion had abandoned the priesthood for a new life with the Widow Glaena. He turned his thoughts to Sareya herself—how she had seduced him that first time in the smithing hall. He recalled his terror when the golden-eyed crow had come to his room and led him away from Branil's Burg; the dead-eye that had stalked him through the night; the wraithe atop Hallow Hill. And when the Warrior's Fire still didn't come upon him, he relived the horror of the night he and Sareya had saved their comrades from a horde of dead-eyes.

A ripple passed through his dawn-tide repository.

"You're starting to feel it," Josac said. "Go with the sensation. Let it grow within you."

Anskar directed his thoughts to the Grand Master's expedition to the lost city of Yustanwyrd; saw again wraithes wielding unimaginable powers and gigantic birds with the consistency of smoke.

The rippling of his repository became a shuddering vibration. He could feel the dawn-tide within seething and boiling as it had never done before.

There was an answering echo in his dusk-tide repository. And there was something new, something he had never detected before: a thready connection between the dusk- and the dawn-tide repositories.

He understood then that any eruption of the dawn-tide into the Warrior's Fire would involve an equal eruption from the dusk: that it was the dusk-tide's virulence that effected such a violent change in the dawn. And with that realization, he banished the burning memories, gasping as he felt the surging forces drain away into their respective repositories.

"What is it?" Josac said. "You were so close."

"You said the Warrior's Fire was a dawn-tide power."

"And so it is."

"No." Anskar shook his head. "It isn't. It also involves the dusk."

"Impossible! I have no forbidden sorcery within me."

"I'm sure you believe that," Anskar said, "but I think you are wrong."

He shut his eyes and sent tendrils of awareness inside the Warrior's priest, probing, questing, scenting. It was easy to locate Josac's dawn-tide repository. It wasn't deep like Anskar's, just about sufficient for the casting of a ward sphere. That said, the dawn-tide essence it contained held a coiled violence. It had been tainted by contact with something corrosive.

Anskar traced the impurity, following its passage through Josac's mind until he located the source: a gash so small it was almost undetectable, opening onto a sea of force that no one had yet explained to Anskar's satisfaction.

He opened his eyes. "You have a dusk-tide repository."

Josac looked as though he were going to be sick.

"Not much of one," Anskar added. "More of a gash in the fabric of your mind. A seeping scar. It makes sense. The dawn-tide was never intended for violence."

"But how?" Josac said. "I've never willingly embraced the dusk-tide. It's against the laws of our Order!"

"I don't know. Until I met you, I'd never heard of the Warrior's Fire. Are all you priests of the Warrior trained in its use?"

Josac nodded. "It is one of our closely guarded secrets."

"What about those who train you in the use of this power? Is it possible they know they are manifesting the latent dusk-tide abilities of their priests?"

"But our priests are taught to despise all sorcery other than the dawn-tide."

"What if the dusk-tide gash is a side effect of using the Warrior's Fire?"

"I don't know," Josac said, "but it changes nothing. Gann will use the Fire against you, and so you must master it."

"No," Anskar said. "I swore an oath to never again use any but the dawn-tide."

"Then you are beyond my help."

"I'll find another way to beat him," Anskar said.

"No," Josac said, looking Anskar in the eye. The priest's pupils were dilated, the sclera bloodshot. Froth spilled from his mouth as he growled, "You will not!"

Josac punched Anskar in the face, rocking his head back.

Anskar stumbled away, but Josac came with him, striking with fists, elbows, knees. All Anskar could do was shell up behind his arms and keep backing away, but then Josac grabbed his wrists, ripped his hands from his face, and head-butted him. Anskar fell on his rear. White light exploded behind his eyes. Blood seeped from his nostrils.

Josac was astride him now, raining down hammer fists as spittle sprayed from his mouth.

Anskar rolled to his side and thrust his hips, unbalancing Josac for an instant. He slid out from beneath the priest and got to his feet, staggering away to regain his stance. This wasn't a fight he was going to win by retreating.

Josac rose with a roar, but this time Anskar slipped beneath the priest's winging hook and landed an uppercut. Josac's chin snapped up, but he countered with an elbow to Anskar's face that knocked him back. Anskar slung out a kick, more to keep Josac off him than anything else, but it was wasted energy. The priest surged forward, pummeling Anskar with his fists. Anskar landed a clean jab, then a left hook, a knee, but Josac walked through them all, and then Anskar was back to circling away from the enraged priest, protecting his ribs and face.

He was tiring. His legs wouldn't obey him. His arms were

numb from blocking Josac's punches, and his face was a swollen agony. He threw a tired jab, and again Josac walked straight through it. He locked his arms around Anskar's waist, heaved him into the air, and slammed him to the ground. The back of Anskar's head hit hard, jolting his teeth. He blacked out briefly, then recovered to see Josac's blurry form astride him, beating, beating, beating…

Josac suddenly cried out in alarm as he was pulled away from Anskar—a cry that turned into a gurgle and then a whimpering moan.

Anskar propped himself up on one elbow, blinking his eyes into focus.

Braga had one arm around Josac's throat, the other forming a brace against the back of his neck. She held him a foot or so off the ground, choking him from behind. Froth spilled from Josac's mouth. His eyes bulged, his face reddened, and then he slumped in Braga's arms before she ditched him unceremoniously to the ground.

"Rancid scrotum-faced piece of horse shit," she growled, kicking Josac in the ribs.

He let out a yelp, then gasped in a snatch of air and came to with a shudder.

"I'm sorry, Anskar," the priest said. "But you see now! You see what you will have to face! Gann is bigger than me, faster, stronger. And he will not stop."

"And you would have?" Anskar asked.

"I think so. But you weren't listening to me. Better you learn now than when Gann comes for you."

"Who the fuck is Gann?" Braga said.

Anskar shook his head. Pain lanced through his skull. His ears pounded, his nose was clogged with blood and probably broken, and every limb hurt, as if the bones had been fractured in a thousand places.

"Gann is trouble," he rasped. "It's best you stay out of this, Braga."

Despite the terrifying experience, his sorcerous senses had responded to the mixture of dawn- and dusk-tide emanating from Josac, confirming that the Warrior's Fire was a hybrid power, neither fully one tide nor the other. Yet it was permitted by the Warrior's priests and presumably by the Warrior aspect of Menselas himself.

The inkling of an idea formed at the back of Anskar's mind, but before he could follow it, he slumped back and his head smacked into the ground.

"Gisela of Gessa," he muttered, as everything grew blurry and dark. "Take me…"

# FOUR

*YOU ARE ON THE RIGHT path, my son. I am pleased with you.*

The voice was a whisper on the receding tide of a dream.

A warm, pearly glow came through Anskar's eyelids, and he opened his eyes to see sunlight penetrating the gray canvas of a large tent. He shifted on the bedroll and winced in anticipation of pain, but there was none. He'd expected a pounding in his skull, agony from his broken nose, the dull ache of bruises, the stab of cracked ribs as he inhaled, but there was none of that. If anything, he felt refreshed and invigorated. It didn't seem possible.

A white-robed healer lay on a bedroll across the tent, her body curled into a ball. Although her back was to him, he could see she was racked with shudders. Fair hair, slick with sweat, trailed over her shoulders in greasy strands, freed from the tight braids she usually bound it with.

"Gisela?"

She groaned and muttered something Anskar didn't hear.

"How long have I been here?" he asked.

It had to be days, even weeks, considering his recovery, but how was that possible? Surely he couldn't have been unconscious for so long? And if he had been, where was he now? Had the army gone on without him?

"A couple of hours," Gisela replied, her voice tight and feeble.

"A couple…"

Anskar rose with surprising ease. Not a single bruise marred his skin. His pants and shirt were folded neatly beside his bedroll, alongside his boots. He quickly dressed.

"Are you all right?" he asked.

Gisela groaned and rolled over. Her face was a mass of bruises. Egg-sized knots stood out on her head, weeping blood that had stained her fair hair pink. Her nose was a crooked mess with dried blood caking the nostrils. Her lips were split, her teeth stained crimson.

She drew in a shuddering breath and winced at the pain it caused her. "I will be soon," she rasped.

"What happened? What have you done?"

"I healed you." She paused to cough up blood. "That's why you asked Braga to bring you to me, wasn't it?"

Anskar ran a hand through his hair. "Yes, I wanted your help, but this…"

Somehow she had taken his pain and injuries upon herself. Brother Tion had spoken with awe about those few healers who had the power of vicarious suffering, but Anskar had never considered that Gisela might be one of them.

"I assumed my father had told you all about me," she said, the faintest trace of a smile curling her cracked lips.

"He told me of your… your…"

"My virginity? It is a sacrifice some of us make for the Healer's blessing. We give ourselves completely to her so that she might work her wonders through us."

"I wish…" Anskar said, but found he couldn't go on. Old shame prickled his skin.

"You wish you hadn't strayed? It is not a requirement of the Order that you knights remain celibate, only that you abstain from relations with one another."

"I know. And I failed."

"A lot of people fail."

"Not me! I should be better than that."

"Is that you or your mother speaking?"

Anskar's entire body clenched.

Gisela tried to rise on one elbow and failed.

Seeing her like this, so frail—and for his sake—caused Anskar to draw in a long, deep breath.

"I'm sorry," Gisela said. "That was a stupid thing to say. What I meant was—"

"Brother Tion used to say I was scrupulous."

"A big word for a minor flaw," Gisela said. "It's easier to say you are too hard on yourself. Things are not easy for you, Anskar. They never have been."

"But they are for you?"

Gisela grimaced with pain and crossed her arms over her chest. "Why did Josac attack you?"

"I don't think he intended it to go this far. He was trying to demonstrate what I'm facing, and he wanted to persuade me to use all of my abilities in order to survive."

"Survive what?"

Gisela coughed and rolled onto her back, as if seeking to relieve her pain. Anskar noticed that already the swelling on her face was abating, and the crook of her broken nose had straightened.

"Survive what?" she repeated.

"You know Gann?"

"Ah," Gisela said. "A blood feud with a priest of the Warrior."

"He seeks revenge for what I did to his brother, Beof."

Gisela shifted on her back. "That was not your fault."

"I know that. Probably Gann knows it, too."

"But he still wants revenge. Men are like that sometimes. It's pride, an imbalance in the Five. Devotees of the Warrior seem more prone to this than others."

"I understand it," Anskar said. "I hurt his brother, so he wants to hurt me."

"I doubt Gann will be satisfied with merely hurting you. So Josac was trying to prepare you?"

"Not at first, but Gann thought he was. He took Josac by surprise and beat him half to death."

Gisela's hand trembled as she touched four fingers and thumb to her chest. She seemed to draw strength from the sign of the Five's protection, and this time managed to push herself up onto her elbows. The knots on her head were no longer visible, and she didn't wince when she said, "Your life is in danger, Anskar. Does my father know?"

"He knows, but he can't get involved. At least not until Gann makes his move."

"You're right. He can't be seen to interfere with the ways of the Warrior's priests, ridiculous as they are."

"Does this sort of thing happen often?" Anskar asked.

"Blood feuds are rife among the devotees of the Warrior, and the Order must tolerate them so long as they don't get out of hand. And Josac used the Warrior's Fire against you?"

"I thought only Warrior's priests were supposed to know about the Warrior's Fire."

"I'm a healer. We get to see the results of such excesses. It induces a berserk rage. I find it hard to believe the Warrior—an aspect of Menselas—would permit such a thing. It has the feel of madness, to my way of thinking."

"It's no simple use of the dawn-tide," Anskar said.

Gisela frowned. "What makes you say that?"

"It's tinged with the dusk-tide. Josac wanted me to learn how to evoke the Warrior's Fire so I can even the odds against Gann."

"And did you learn it?"

"I've sworn never again to use the dusk-tide."

"And the dark?"

"That too."

Gisela held his gaze for a long while. He could almost see her wounds healing, her bruises fading to nothing, her breaths growing deeper and steadier.

"Good," she said as she stood. She took a comb from her robe pocket and ran it through her tangled hair. "You're doing well, Anskar."

*You are on the right path, my son. I am pleased with you.*

It was hard not to laugh derisively. It seemed everyone thought he was doing well, but what Gisela meant was presumably a far cry from what his mother had meant in his dreams.

And what had Queen Talia meant anyway? That he had done well to get beaten up by Josac? That he'd done the right thing asking Braga to bring him to Gisela for healing? Neither, he suspected.

"What is it?" Gisela said. She was binding her hair into its usual braids. "Are you wondering about my rapid healing?"

He wasn't, but he nodded.

"The Healer grants her devotees the power to endure much pain and to swiftly recover," she explained. "Your broken bones became my broken bones, your cuts my cuts. I bled as you did. It hurt, the same as the injuries hurt you, but the pain soon passes. For some of us, the most blessed, Menselas lets the hurt flow through without touching." She read something in his expression. "But that isn't what you were thinking about, is it?"

"I'm not so sure I am doing well."

"You feel tempted to use sorcery to oppose Gann?" She stopped tying her hair so she could watch his reaction. "I can understand that."

"Not the dusk- or the dark-tide," he said. "My mind is made up. There can be no going back."

"Then what will you do?"

"Gann and I will fight. One of us will win."

She gripped his elbow. "I wish there were something I could do."

"Maybe there is," Anskar said, recalling the idea that had started to form before he lost consciousness. He was also thinking about something Gisela had said: *It has the feel of madness.*

"Teach me how to take the sufferings of another upon myself."

"Why?"

"So I can heal them." He could tell from her frown that Gisela didn't believe him. "With this power, you can take away disease, isn't that right?"

"And in so doing, sometimes the healer dies."

"I don't know if it's possible for me to learn this ability," he said, "but I feel Menselas is asking it of me. What if I'm right? What if he wants me to sacrifice my dark- and dusk-tide powers and, in their place, develop the gifts of a healer?" He hated himself for lying, but how else could he persuade her to give him what he needed?

"And this idea has just come to you?"

Anskar nodded. "An intuition, but it feels right."

Something like hope glinted in her eyes, but she quickly dowsed it with another frown. "You are no virgin, Anskar. I heard your confession, remember? It is extremely difficult for those who pursue carnal relations to receive Menselas's healing touch."

"I'm not a virgin," he agreed, "but I will swear to be chaste."

Gisela smiled. "That may not be enough."

"But this healing is a power of the dawn-tide, isn't it?"

"It is the Healer's gift," Gisela said. "The power of the Healer works through the dawn-tide, but only because that is the way the Five ordain it. If it were his will, Menselas could use any of the tides for healing, or no tide at all."

"I have the God's mark," Anskar said. "So it is possible that Menselas will bless me."

"But you lack the fortitude of one who has served the Healer for a lifetime. Any disease you take upon yourself would likely kill you."

"Perhaps. But in time, I'll grow more resistant. Isn't that how it worked with you?"

Gisela looked away, thinking. "Why, Anskar? Why would you want to take this path now?" She looked back at him. "Is it because Gann would not dare attack a healer?"

"He wouldn't? I didn't know that. No, I must fight Gann. Nothing will change that. But this… what you've done for me today… Why spend my life struggling against the dusk and the dark when Menselas is showing me another way? Remember, I was virtually raised by Brother Tion, a Healer. Don't the priests of the Elder teach us that there are no coincidences as far as Menselas is concerned? If I embrace the path of the Healer, won't I at the same time heal myself of the darkness within?"

Gisela dipped her head and closed her eyes. "Perhaps the

Healer has spoken to you through your ordeals," she said. "Maybe you're right, Anskar. Maybe this is the Five's mercy toward you, your path to redemption."

Anskar nodded. "I know it is."

"Then I'll teach you as best I can."

The army followed the coastline toward Kyuth, where Lanuc proposed to stop and resupply. The temperature grew appreciably cooler, until riding during the day was almost pleasant. There were fewer storms, too, so far north from Sansor. But as night fell, a bitter wind blew off the hills that ranged away to the northeast.

Josac had taken to pitching his tent between Anskar's tent and Braga's tarp-covered wagon. There was open hostility now between Josac and Gann, and it created an unwelcome tension among the knights. Anskar picked up from snatches of overheard conversation that most had seen such rivalry between priests of the Warrior before, and few wanted to see it again. If it came to a fight, Gann was expected to win. He had won before when he had taken Josac by surprise and wielded the Warrior's Fire against him. But despite his lingering injuries, there was a new coldness in Josac's eyes, an iron resolve in the way he practiced with his sword during the early hours and into the night.

"You are too tense," Gisela told Anskar in the healers' tent one evening. A knight's page named Rowena was seated on a folding chair between them, her foot swollen to twice its normal size from where the horse she'd been grooming had stomped on it. "Your natural aversion to sickness and pain shuts down your ability to suffer vicariously."

"Please," Rowena said, eyes glistening with tears as she grimaced. "No more training. Something for the pain."

Gisela raised an eyebrow at Anskar. "I thought you said you were a quick learner."

"It's only my second lesson," he protested.

"I'm sorry, Rowena," Gisela said. "These young knights are virtually unteachable."

Rowena forced a smile, her doe eyes resting on Anskar a little too long before she blushed and looked away.

"I'll heal you," Gisela told Rowena. "And, Anskar, this time send a tendril of the dawn-tide into my repository so you can monitor what the Healer does through me. You can do that, can't you?"

"Of course."

As Gisela rested her hand over Rowena's injured foot, Anskar separated out a single thread from his dawn-tide repository and sent it through Gisela's skull. She stiffened momentarily, then shivered as she granted him access to her repository.

Anskar gasped. It felt… He could only describe the sensation as being buried alive and then bursting above ground to suck greedily at cool, crisp air. Her repository reminded him of the Simorga Sea on a tranquil night beneath the stars.

A ripple passed through Gisela's repository, gathering force as Anskar followed its course. It became a wave surging along Gisela's arm and into her hand, then a receding tide.

Anskar winced as pain throbbed in his foot. Heat blossomed, and then the pain subsided.

Gisela smiled at him, but her eyes betrayed her own agony. She was protecting him, warding him from the worst that she felt.

The swelling of Rowena's foot diminished before Anskar's eyes, but as the page sighed with relief, Gisela let out a whimper. She withdrew her hand from Rowena's foot and held it out to Anskar.

"Help me to sit," she said. She lifted her left leg off the ground, the foot swollen and red.

"Good job you took off your sandals before you started," Anskar said.

"Good job the vicarious suffering didn't work when *you* tried it," she replied as he helped her down to the floor, where she sat nursing her injured foot. "We'd have had to cut your boot off."

"You should have warned me."

"Where's the fun in that?"

"Am I all right to go?" Rowena asked. She stood gingerly from her chair and tested out her foot. "It's better!" she said, as if she hadn't believed such a thing were possible. "I can't thank you enough."

"You might try," Gisela said, "by not standing directly behind a horse when you groom it, or don't they teach you that at page school?"

"I was distracted."

"I bet you were. What was his name?"

Rowena gave a coy smile.

"No need to answer," Gisela said. "Off you go now."

"How long until you recover?" Anskar asked, stooping to examine Gisela's foot.

"Don't get too near," she said.

"Why? Is it dangerous?"

"The smell is. It's been a long day, and I've been on my feet for most of it."

Anskar rolled his eyes, and they shared a laugh. "You're so different to what I thought," he said.

"And what was it you thought? No, let me guess: a humorless prude who is always drearily sensible?"

"Isn't that what all healers are like?" Anskar grinned to let her know he was joking.

"Even Brother Tion?"

"Well, no, not him. But Tion's—"

"A laugh a minute?"

"Married."

Gisela flashed Anskar a look, but it was so fleeting he couldn't tell whether she was amused or angry. "Fetch me some water, please," she asked. "I'll be fine in a few minutes. This was just a minor healing."

"I felt…" Anskar began as he poured water from a jug into a mug and handed it to Gisela. "I'm not sure what I felt."

"Try not to think about it," Gisela said. "Just absorb the experience. Let the Healer do the rest. If it is her will, the power will come."

"When will it come?"

"In time."

*But I don't have time,* Anskar almost blurted. Gann would make his move soon. "I'll have to learn patience."

"Now that I would like to see!" Gisela used both hands to lift her injured foot. "Go on, give it a quick try. Heal me."

"You're sure? I thought you wanted me to absorb the experience."

"I want you to stop being the one in control. Your face!" Gisela laughed. "Anyone would think I'd asked you to do something perverse. Oh, I forgot, you'd probably like… Forgive me, I'm being spiteful. Father says I get it from Mother."

"I thought you were supposed to forget the things you hear in confession," Anskar said.

"Why do you think I told you to find a different confessor? Don't answer that," Gisela said. "I've caused you enough discomfort for one day."

Anskar felt his cheeks flush. "It's I who caused you to feel uncomfortable," he said. "The things I told you in confession… they can't have been easy to hear."

"What things?" Gisela said, and when Anskar looked at her, she gave an impish grin. "In one ear, out the other."

"I wish that were true," Anskar said.

"You wish you hadn't told me? You would prefer there to be secrets between us?"

"No, I—"

"Anskar, it's all right. You made your confession. Menselas has forgiven you. Or do you want to tell him how to do *his* job as well?"

"As well as what?"

"As well as trying to effect healing by yourself. It's the Five's power alone that gives the gift of vicarious healing. I'd have thought you would have worked that out by now. All your efforts to be in control only stand in the way."

"But sorcery is all about control."

"What if the power is not sorcery? Open yourself to healing. Accept it. You are merely a conduit. Your only role is to cooperate. Trust Menselas with your whole being, Anskar. And for the Five's sake, take your boot off before you start. The left one."

Anskar did as she asked, then knelt down in front of her and extended his hand. A violent shudder ripped through his repository. Gisela raised an eyebrow and shook her head.

"Relax," she said. "Give in."

Anskar swallowed. "Menselas help me," he muttered under his breath, at the same time shutting out the mocking thoughts that arose in response. A wave of dizziness washed over him. He swayed on his knees. Warmth flowed through him, and then he shrieked in agony as his foot exploded with pain.

Gisela laughed as Anskar slumped onto his backside, clutching his swollen foot.

"See?" she said, standing and doing a little dance. "I knew you could do it." There was no longer anything wrong with her foot.

Tears stung Anskar's eyes as he bit down the urge to scream. "How long?" he asked. "How long till the pain passes?"

"You're new to this," Gisela said. "Hours, most likely." Then, with a mischievous flash of her eyes as she turned away and ducked out of the tent, "Maybe even days."

She'd been joking. The pain passed within the hour, but it was a long hour.

Over the next few days, Anskar's grasp of vicarious suffering grew stronger, but it was an arduous process, and one that left him aching and bereft of energy. Lanuc commented on the bruising that appeared on Anskar's face and arms, and on the limp he developed one day only to lose it the next.

"Is someone deliberately harming you?" Lanuc asked.

"Not yet."

"Then where are these injuries coming from?"

"Your daughter."

"Gisela?" A flash of suspicion crossed Lanuc's eyes. But then he understood. "She's teaching you healing—the vicarious kind. And you have the aptitude for it?"

"It's not so hard."

In reality, it was brutal. His senses had no difficulty entering a patient and tracing the passage of injury or disease. But then came the tricky part—when he had to empty himself of all fear, all desire for self-preservation, and effect a kind of mental flip-flop to accept the suffering of the patient as his own.

One evening, Josac joined Anskar and Braga for a campfire

supper of stale bread and salted fish. They shared the last of the beer, diluting it with the brackish water they had filled their canteens with earlier in the day. Braga still had haunches of cured ham, some dried dates, and a jar of pickled cucumbers stowed away in her wagon, but when she offered to fetch more food, Anskar advised her to save it in case there were harder times ahead.

"Use it," Josac said. "We must be only a day out from Kyuth. Lanuc says we'll stop there for supplies and maybe a day or two's rest, and I for one am sick of salted fish." He held up the piece he'd been nibbling on and then made a show of scraping off the mold with his finger.

As Braga disappeared beneath the tarp of her wagon, rummaging around for her food supplies, Josac leaned in close to Anskar and spoke in a low voice. "Gann was here after dusk," he said. "I told him you had business with the healers, but he assumed you were trying to find a way of backing out of the fight. For the most part, it's taboo for a Warrior's priest to do harm to a healer."

"Is Gann stupid?" Anskar said. "I couldn't become a priest in a matter of days, and certainly not on the trail without a bishop to ordain me."

"I know that, and he does, too, but he's doing everything he can to disparage you and make himself look just. You're aware that he's been spreading rumors about what you did to his brother?"

"Beof is a bully, and he tried to kill me," Anskar said.

"I know. But not all the knights traveling with us are so discerning in their judgments. I just want you to be aware, Anskar. Watch your back at all times."

"He won't have to," Braga said, jumping down from the bed

of her wagon, clutching a ham and a pickle jar to her massive chest. "Not if I watch it for him."

"Why would you do that?" Josac said. He still seemed bitter about Braga pulling him off Anskar and choking him unconscious.

"Because the ghost spoke to me back in Sansor. Maybe she wants me to."

"And maybe she doesn't," Josac said, accepting the ham from Braga and proceeding to slice off chunks with a knife.

"And I say maybe she does," Braga said. "So, where's this prick Gann pitch his tent? I'm thinking I'll pay the rancid cow's ass a visit… with my hammer."

"Even you, Braga, couldn't stand against a priest of the Warrior," Josac said.

"I beat you, you cockless toerag, and I could beat this Gann you're shitting your pants over. Men! I thought you were supposed to have balls."

Later that night, when Braga was snoring loudly beneath the tarp that covered her wagon, Anskar went to Josac's tent and woke him.

"Anskar?" the Warrior's priest said as he sat up on his bedroll. "What do—? Ah, clever. I'd do the same if I were you. You want me back to full strength, so I can go after Gann before he comes for you."

"I can fight my own battles," Anskar said.

"Then why are you here?"

"Because I want to feel everything Gann did to you, as if he had done it to me. And if that means healing you in the process, then so be it."

Josac frowned, then a light seemed to go on in his eyes. "You want to stare your fear in the face; experience the worst Gann can do to you before he comes for you. But it could go either way, Anskar. What if, after taking my pain upon yourself, the fear of experiencing anything like it again paralyzes you during the fight?"

"I've considered all of that," Anskar said.

"And you still want to do this?"

"If your pride will permit it."

"One thing this affair has taught me," Josac said, "is that festering anger is more powerful than pride."

"Then lie still."

Anskar touched his fingertips to Josac's temples, sending out his senses, probing for any remaining bruising, fractures, or pain. Then, with an uttered prayer, he opened himself to the Five's power.

Josac gasped, then sighed with relief.

And Anskar screamed.

# FIVE

THE NEXT MORNING BEFORE DAWN, Anskar made his way, bruised, broken, and limping, to Gisela's tent. She was awake and kneeling in prayer when he pulled aside the tent flap and entered. She opened her eyes, not betraying the slightest surprise at his battered appearance.

"Before you ask," he said, "Gann didn't do this."

"I know," she said, standing and straightening the creases in her white robe. Her fair hair was still unbound from sleep. "Vicarious suffering leaves its mark, and not just the wounds you've inherited from your patient. Judging by the limp and the bruising, I'd have to say you healed Josac completely."

"It's incredible, but I did."

"Then you're a bigger fool than I thought. The shock to your system could have killed you. Have you listened to nothing I've said? It takes time to develop the resilience necessary to heal in this manner. You're just a beginner."

"Yet I did it." Anskar winced at the pain in his ribs, his leg, his face.

"Come," she said, and he limped to stand in front of her. She placed her hands on the sides of his head and shut her eyes. It was a smooth transaction, so fleeting and expert he almost missed it. Gisela grimaced as Josac's pain left Anskar. Bruises bloomed on her face, as though daubed there by an invisible painter, and her stance shifted to compensate for Josac's injured leg. Anskar reached out to support her, but she waved him off.

"Go now," she said. "I'll be fine in a few hours. Leave the tent flap open so the cool air comes in."

Anskar smiled his thanks, then stepped outside.

The first bar of gray had appeared on the horizon. He opened his arms wide and threw his head back, waiting for the dawntide's currents to blow through him.

There was something different about Kyuth, the town that marked the coastal border between Kaile and the City States to the north. Anskar read it in the tension coming off the vanguard of the Order's knights waiting outside the town gates to receive a group of over thirty men-at-arms who marched toward them. At the group's head were three riders: an elderly man with a long white beard who was dressed in a nondescript gray robe; a woman with gray hair wearing a dress of frayed black wool; and between them, a fat man with mutton-chop whiskers he could have groomed with a horse brush. This last was dressed in a purple gown of velvet, and a heavy golden chain hung around his neck. His head was completely bald, although he'd done his best to cover it with a floppy flat hat, also velvet.

Lanuc had ordered the main force to wait a few hundred yards back from the palisade that surrounded the town, a formidable barrier of massive oak trunks sunk deep into the ground, their tops sharpened to points above which spear tips bristled. All Anskar could see above the palisade was the wooden spire of a tower—perhaps a church, but not one he recognized. Atop the spire was a figurine of some sort; at this distance all he could make out were the broad wings that extended from its back.

"Just listen and learn," Lanuc told Anskar as they sat astride their horses. "They do things differently here. Kyuth's a border town, always on the alert."

"But the City States are our allies," Anskar said.

"Officially."

"And unofficially?"

"Let's just say it's complicated. Politics always is."

Lanuc had selected one other person to ride with him and Anskar toward the three riders at the head of the town's soldiers: his daughter, Gisela, who was mounted on a piebald pony.

Anskar glanced over his shoulder. He could see Braga standing on the driving seat of her wagon, straining for a better view of what was going on. Josac was with her, mounted on his dun courser. He was unarmored, yet there was a fierceness about him as his eyes scoured the assembled knights. The whole situation with Gann was becoming ridiculous. If he did see Gann, Anskar decided, he was going to offer to settle their feud in the open, like warriors, not like thieves and assassins. Of course, Gann was unlikely to accept. Priests of the Warrior left nothing to chance. They chose the battlegrounds for their fights, they observed their enemies, they strategized, and then they struck when the odds were squarely in their favor.

"Anskar," Lanuc hissed, pulling his attention back to the three riders from Kyuth, who had drawn up in a line twenty yards away.

The men-at-arms formed a shield wall three ranks deep behind them. Each carried a curved rectangular shield that covered everything from the neck down. Their helms were open-faced, with not even a nose guard, and bands of steel protected the back of the neck. They carried long spears, held upright for the time being, and short stabbing swords were scabbarded at their hips.

"Not quite the reception I was expecting," Lanuc said to the trio of riders.

"A precaution, nothing more," the fat man with the mutton chops said. He fingered the gold chain around his neck. "It is good to see the Order of Eternal Vigilance so far from Sansor. Makes everyone feel that much safer. But I would ask, if I may, what brings you to Kyuth?"

"Just passing through," Lanuc said, "on our way north."

"Nothing to be alarmed about, then," the fat man said, glancing at the gray-haired woman in the black dress. "Just passing through. Of course," he added to Lanuc, "if we can be of any assistance… Supplies to help you on your way, that sort of thing. Just ask, and what you need will be sent out to you."

"Most kind," Lanuc said. "And you are?"

A hurt expression crossed the fat man's face. "I am Frankin Glore," he said, as if it should have been obvious. "Mayor of Kyuth."

"And your companions?"

Glore indicated the old man in the gray robe. "This is Brother Stevos, a priest of the Elder."

"An odd mode of dress for a servant of the Elder," Gisela said.

"Ubiquitous," Brother Stevos said.

"And you wear no holy symbol."

"In such an eclectic community like Kyuth, it is best to blend in, to wear nothing that could be construed as judgmental or offensive."

The old woman in the black dress rolled her eyes.

Gisela glared at her. "We all know about rival gods, Brother, but that doesn't mean we should hide what we are and whom we serve."

"Ah, a traditionalist, I see," Brother Stevos said. "Well, there is a place for everyone within the Church of the Five. But I would urge you to consider, Sister, the milieu in which you now find yourself. Harmony in Kyuth is predicated upon a delicate balance, is it not, Mayor?"

"Indeed," Glore said. "Very much so. A delicate balance, yes."

"And while it is never the intention of a priest of Menselas to give offense," Brother Stevos continued, "it is a sad reality that we frequently do, by the way we comport ourselves and even the way we choose to dress."

"I do not *choose* to wear the Healer's white," Gisela said. "It is ordained."

Brother Stevos gave her a condescending smile. "But ordained by whom? The Healer? She told you what to wear in a dream? Or is it determined by tradition? A tradition that may not be appropriate in towns where folk of different faiths intermingle. You note, I say 'may,' for I do not know for certain. We none of us know anything for certain. Isn't that so, High Priestess?"

The old woman in black snorted contemptuously.

"As I was saying," the mayor cut in, "before we were sidetracked by this little disagreement—"

"There is no disagreement," Brother Stevos said, "just an airing of theological differences." He addressed Gisela again. "It's all about acceptance, Sister. Don't you agree?"

Gisela looked as if she were about to spit poison, so Anskar interjected, "Acceptance of what?"

"The multiplicity of truth, of course," Brother Stevos said. "Whatever else? And you are, young man?"

"This is Anskar DeVantte," Lanuc said. "Knight-inferior of the Order of Eternal Vigilance."

"Inferior?" It was the first time the High Priestess had spoken. Her voice came out a grating rasp.

"Only in relation to a fully consecrated knight," Brother Stevos explained.

"How can there be a multiplicity of truth?" Anskar asked. "Surely there is only one truth. The truth is absolute."

"Ah, the definite article, yes—a somewhat outmoded concept," Brother Stevos said. "There are many roads to the truth, and many truths to follow."

"I disagree," Anskar said. "Truth must be truth, else how do we make sense of anything at all?"

"I know the theory well," the priest of the Elder said. "Many facets of the same underlying reality. Truth is truth, whatever its multifarious appearances. But is it, really?"

Lanuc interrupted with a cough. "Carry on like this and you'll have an angry army to deal with. They've ridden hard and eaten little."

"You're in a hurry, of course," Mayor Frankin Glore said. "Tell us your requirements, and I shall have supplies brought to you as soon as is practicable."

"We plan to stay in Kyuth for the night," Lanuc said. "Our people need rest and relaxation."

"Oh…" the mayor said, flicking a look at the High Priestess.

"You have coin?" she asked.

"We'll pay for any supplies you can give us," Lanuc said. "And we'll spend good money in your taverns."

The mayor beamed. "You will not be disappointed. Our beer is excellent, and the whores are—"

"They are knights of the Order of Eternal Vigilance," Brother Stevos said.

"Indeed they are. Forgive me, I wasn't thinking."

"That has never stopped your kind from using whores before," the High Priestess said. "Or are the rumors that reach my ears just malicious gossip?"

"Our knights are chaste," Lanuc said.

Anskar wondered how he kept a straight face.

"Your money is welcome," the High Priestess said, "so long as the correct tithes are paid."

"Tithes?" Lanuc asked.

"The Church of the Lady Sylva Kalisia is a cornerstone of Kyuth society," the mayor explained, "and the High Priestess and her priestesses are valued by our people. As such, a tithe is levied on all business transactions and exacted from any who enter our town's walls."

"A tithe to the Church of Sylva Kalisia?" Gisela said. "But this is Kaile!"

"Where Menselas rules supreme?" the High Priestess said. "Where his priests extort money from the populace so they can indulge their lusts in fleshpots and drinking houses?"

Anskar placed a restraining hand on Gisela's shoulder. "She's just trying to rile you."

Gisela slapped his hand away.

"Daughter!" Lanuc barked. Gisela shot him a venomous look. "How much is the tithe?"

"A silver a head," the High Priestess said. "And you must join us for our communal sacrifices."

"To the Lady?" Gisela snapped. "Never!"

Brother Stevos held up his hands. "It is no sin to worship together for the sake of friendship."

"Or the sake of peace," the mayor put in.

"Making sacrifice to a heathen goddess is immoral," Gisela said. "It is abhorrent to the Five."

"But how do you know that?" Brother Stevos said. "I mean, how do you really know?"

"The scriptures—that's how I know."

"Gisela's right," Anskar said, drawing a frown from Lanuc. "We serve Menselas because he is the one true god."

"Pah!" the High Priestess said. "A god with five faces! A god of deceptions and lies."

"Enough," Lanuc said. "Either you want our money or you don't, but either way, we will enter your town and rest, and you will bring us supplies."

"And the sacrifices?" Brother Stevos asked.

"The tithes?" the High Priestess added.

The mayor glanced behind at his men-at-arms and then back at the hundred knights plus the retainers and priests that made up Lanuc's small army.

"I suggest you take up the question of both with Grand Master Hyle Pausus," Lanuc said, "or with the Patriarch of the Church of Menselas. Kyuth is under the Church's jurisdiction, after all—unless you're going to tell me the border with the City States has shifted south?"

The mayor visibly winced. "It has not."

"Good," Lanuc said. "Then lead on, and send word to the taverns that we are coming."

"You will instruct your knights to leave their armor and weapons outside the town walls?" the mayor asked.

"Agreed," Lanuc said. "At least until the first sign of trouble."

Lanuc ordered half the force to remain outside the town with all the weapons, armor, and horses. They would have their turn in the taverns the next day. The army was to stay for two days and no longer. In truth, Anskar already couldn't wait to leave Kyuth and resume their journey north.

Braga had insisted on bringing her wagon inside the town's palisade, and no one stopped her. She parked it in the road beside the river, leaving her twin oxen in their harnesses munching the grass on the riverbank.

Kyuth might indeed have had a different feel, but there was a reassuring sameness about the Eels' Nest Tavern, where Anskar was sitting at a table in a nook with Braga. Laughter warmed the room, and over by the unlit hearth, a solitary musician was performing Kailean folk songs on a mandola. Smoke was thick in the air from the clay pipes everyone seemed to be smoking, and there was an underlying odor of beer that had soaked into the floorboards over the decades.

From above, in a loft accessed by a rickety ladder, came all manner of grunts and groans, accompanied by the overenthusiastic cries of whores. Anskar wasn't surprised to see knights of the Order, men and women, ascending the ladder.

Both he and Braga were deep in their cups, and there was a basket of bread and cheese on the table between them, along with plates of smoked ham, roasted vegetables, and… eels. The tavern, the server told them, was named after the eels that teemed in the River Sangis that snaked around Kyuth. Before the town had been founded, the site had been an elevated island of clay in the middle of marshland. The first settlers had chosen the island due to the proliferation of eels, which proved easy to catch in specially made traps. Over time, the marsh had been tamed by the cutting of drainage canals and the laying of peat, until at last the wetness had been driven back into the Sangis, whose waters still writhed with the eels the town was known for.

Conversation with Braga proved surprisingly easy. At first Anskar feared there would be an awkward silence between them, or worse still, that Braga would constantly berate and insult him. But once they settled at their table, and the beer started to flow, Braga relaxed and became good company—despite her complaints about the knights.

"They think they're better than me," she said. "They think their white cloaks and shiny armor make them holy."

Anskar was about to point out that the majority of knights were indeed holy, and it was only a few who failed to live up to the ideal, but a particularly loud thumping on the floorboards above their heads made him laugh instead.

Braga rolled her eyes in disgust. "Rancid turd-sucking rutting goats. By the flaccid ball sack of Keenos, I hate men."

"It's not just the men," Anskar said, as a female knight started down the ladder from the loft with her hair all mussed up. "And who is Keenos?"

Braga chuckled. "Just something my grandpa used to say. A god, I think."

"Never heard of him."

"That don't mean he's not real."

After that they spoke about Braga's work in the forge and how her grandfather had taught her all he knew. He had apparently been a master blacksmith until his untimely death, and the more Anskar questioned Braga, the more he realized he was in the presence of a smith of exceptional knowledge and ability. At one point he grasped the vambrace on his forearm—invisible, no more than a cool, hard weight that wouldn't let him forget it was there. He thought about asking Braga what she knew about divine alloy and whether or not she had inherited the secrets of working with it from her grandfather, but he still didn't know her well enough to reveal such a secret. And besides, there was something else he wanted to ask her about first.

"Tell me more about this ghost lady that came to you."

"There's not much to tell. She was a ghost. A woman. Maybe a queen, on account of the crown she wore. Mostly she was cloudy, like she was woven from shadows and soot."

Anskar nodded, more certain than ever that Queen Talia was refusing to leave him alone.

"I've always been sensitive to ghosts," Braga said.

"You have?" Anskar sipped his beer, watching her intently.

"Used to hear them crying when I was a child. Told my ma and pa, but they couldn't hear them. They took me to a wisewoman, who made me drink herbal tisanes, though I'd swear it was pig's piss mixed with the pus from a cow's ulcerated udder. They didn't work. I still heard the dead crying, so my folks told me to ignore them and never mention them again."

"And you saw them, too?"

"Sometimes. Not often. Just shades doing what they'd done in life: walking, sitting, stirring a pot in the kitchen."

"I…" Anskar started. Braga raised an eyebrow and he went on. "I see the dead too, only…"

"Only what?"

"Only they talk to me, and when I talk back, they respond. They're real spirits, not just the footprints of dead people like you describe."

"Like the spirit of the warrior you sent with a message to the

Mother House? Like this ghost queen?"

Anskar nodded. "Doesn't it frighten you, knowing there are spirits who still act in the world?"

"Why should it? Living people are vile and twisted." She paused to watch a knight clamber down from the loft, his pants unlaced and revealing the crack of his hairy ass. "No reason to imagine the spirits are any worse. Probably death makes them better in some way. More realistic."

Anskar chewed his bottom lip. He'd never thought about it like that. Until he'd been fitted with his catalyst and started having unusual experiences, he'd assumed the dead stayed dead, and that if there were some kind of afterlife, it was a gray limbo filled with spirits doomed to forever repeat the same choices they had made in life.

Braga downed her beer and hollered for a server. "You want another, turd-face?"

Anskar gave her a blank look, his mind awash with questions and feelings he couldn't quite put his finger on.

"Another beer?" Braga said, enunciating each syllable as if he were deaf.

And still he only half heard her. "Do you know anything about necromancy?"

"Don't even know what that is."

This ability to see and hear the dead that they shared—was it a precursor to the kind of sorcery Queen Talia was known and cursed for, in the same way the god's mark was a gateway to the priesthood?

"Beer, cloth ears?"

Anskar willed himself to focus on the world outside his head. "Yes, please."

Braga ordered, then proceeded to bang the table like a drum as she sang along with the musician in a voice like a cow breaking wind. Anskar stopped her long enough to tell her as much, and she slapped him on the arm and said, "I think I'm warming up to you, ass-wipe."

# SIX

ANSKAR WALKED BRAGA TO HER wagon. In the light of the twin moons, he rolled up his shirtsleeve and showed her the vambrace, glowing cobalt and silver upon his forearm.

Braga let out an audible gasp.

"Can you get it off me?"

"Is that divine alloy?" Braga asked. "My grandpa used to talk about divine alloy, and some bastard I knew claimed he'd worked with it, but I ain't never before seen it. I can have a go at getting it off, but don't hold your breath. My grandpa used to say the lore for working with divine alloy was long forgotten, but there are records."

"Records?" Anskar asked. "Where?"

The light of the moons and the glow of the vambrace were reflected in her eyes. "What if that's why the ghost lady told me to come with you to Wintotashum? My grandpa said the only remaining knowledge about divine alloy that he was aware of was kept in King Aelfyr's Scriptorium."

Braga turned her head aside and spat. When she met Anskar's gaze again, she looked troubled.

"What is it?" he asked.

"Only the King's master blacksmith has access to that knowledge, and that happens to be Hrothyr, the bastard I was speaking of."

Anskar remembered Lanuc mentioning the name, and the fact that Hrothyr and Braga were acquainted.

"What happened between the two of you?" he asked.

"Mind your own business, you festering pool of weasel vomit."

And with that, Braga climbed up into the back of her wagon and disappeared beneath the tarp.

The street was dark and empty as Anskar made his way to the mews behind the tavern, staggering a little due to the amount of beer he'd consumed. Too much, he knew, but he was tired from so many days on the road, and Braga had goaded him into keeping up with her prodigious drinking.

The odd bout of laughter still erupted from the Eels' Nest, and just as Anskar reached the door of the thatched-roofed block that housed his room, it started to rain—not a downpour this time, just a light, chilly drizzle.

Perhaps Anskar heard the scuff of boots, a sharp inrush of breath, a grunt of effort—he didn't know. But he sensed danger, and spun round just in time to see a glint of steel flashing toward his head. He threw himself to one side, and the axe-head bit deep into the wood of the door to the mews.

The man cursed as he tried to rip the axe free. On instinct, Anskar dipped beneath his attacker's armpit and hammered an uppercut into his liver. He expected the man to double up in agony, but instead a shock like lightning shot up Anskar's arm and flung him through the air. He hit the ground hard, and the air rushed from his lungs.

Anskar fought to clear his head of the haze of alcohol. In desperation, he reached for his dawn-tide repository and, with a prayer to Menselas, tried to heal himself of his drunkenness. His guts twisted and he had to turn his head aside to vomit onto the road. He heard wood splintering—the sound of the axe-head coming free.

"Was that a healing you just tried, idiot?"

Anskar could see the man half in silhouette, hazy and indistinct. His blurred vision was partly on account of the poor light and partly his beer-addled brain, but there was also some kind of sorcerous warping about the man's massive frame. But then the man's appearance grew clearer, as if whatever power he had employed for his stealthy attack was no longer necessary.

Anskar already knew who it was before he even registered the broad shoulders, the thick muscles that tended toward fat, the curly beard and piggy eyes that blazed with madness. Gann's upper lip was cleft, which was what caused the lisp when he spoke. He must have been a head and a half taller than Anskar, and had the bearing and manner of his younger brother, Beof.

Anskar had been a fool to go out drinking without taking precautions against the danger he had known must find him at one time or another. Because Gann Harril had at last come for vengeance, and he had come possessed by the Warrior's Fire.

"Didn't they teach you that Menselas's gift of healing is for others?" Gann said with his sibilant lisp. "The priests can't heal themselves."

As Anskar rolled to his knees then climbed to his feet, he sent out feelers of awareness—and gasped at what he found. Gann's dawn-tide repository was vast, but it was also fractured by corrosive veins of the dusk-tide, which to Anskar's *sight* gleamed crimson like rivulets of diseased blood.

Gann raised his axe, and Anskar stepped back, fumbling for his sword. But it wasn't there. He'd left his armor and weapons outside the town.

Gann laughed. "You're wondering how I got to bring a weapon into Kyuth?"

Anskar licked dry lips and managed to nod. He needed time to clear the fog from his mind.

"I didn't," Gann said. "But I brought coin, and coin will buy pretty much anything you want, if you have enough of it."

"You bought the axe in Kyuth?" Anskar said, edging away. With growing clarity, he remembered his purpose in learning the Healer's gift. It was a wild idea that might not work, and even if it did, it could kill him.

Gann took a step forward. "Not so stupid as you look, are you? So, have you worked this out by now, or did that weasel Josac tell you already?"

"Worked what out?"

Anskar grimaced against the pressure inside his head, where his dusk- and dark-tide repositories writhed against the barriers he'd erected around them. Temptation loomed large, but he wasn't going to break his oath to himself. Not for Gann. Not for anyone. Ever.

"Why I'm going to cut you up into little pieces."

Anskar felt the dawn-tide gushing from its repository and flooding his veins.

Gann glowered and advanced another step. "This is for my brother, boy. My *brother*."

"You have a brother?"

"Don't pretend you don't know!"

Anskar fought for calm as the dawn-tide surged within him. "I'm sorry, I must have forgotten. Remind me of his name. Was he fat like you?"

Gann spat his next words through clenched teeth. "Beof Harril, priest of the Warrior at Branil's Burg. You know who I'm talking about! Because of you, he has been punished by the Bishop. Have you any idea what that entails?"

"Oh, Beof!" Anskar said, feigning recognition. "Yes, he was fat. He was also weak, and extremely slow. Must run in the family."

Gann roared and lunged, swinging the axe overhead. Anskar ducked inside the arc of the swing and elbowed him in the face—and again was met with a violent shock that rocked him to his back on the road.

"Is that…" he started, then ran his tongue around his teeth until the numbness abated. "Is that some kind of ward?"

But there was no stalling now.

Gann advanced on Anskar with quick, measured steps. When he raised the axe this time, there was a keenness to his eyes, and though he was still trembling with rage, he was perfectly balanced.

Silver streaked across Anskar's vision as the axe came down, and in that same instant he flung out his right hand and sent the full force of his dawn-tide repository into Gann's chest. Gann jerked and shuddered as if struck by lightning, and his axe dropped to the mud-packed road with a thud.

Anskar's senses followed the shaft of dawn-tide essence he had lanced through Gann's chest, seeking out the root of the ailment—although it wasn't plague or disease or tumor he was looking for. He was gambling that the gift of healing applied to all that was unnatural within a patient, including a division, imbalance, or excess in any of the Five aspects of Menselas.

And then he found it: the incandescence of the Warrior's

Fire burning at Gann's core—a conflagration of the dawn-tide tainted by the virulence of the dusk.

With a silent prayer to the Healer, Anskar shredded his own dawn-tide essence into strands, as Gisela had taught him, then spoke a cant to sling each strand, one after another, into the fire.

The first shriveled away to nothing. The second merely smoldered. But the third, fourth, and fifth took hold, winding around the fiery heart of Gann's sorcery, weaving a shroud to cut it off from the twin currents that sustained it.

The Warrior's Fire vanished. Gann's legs buckled, and he flopped to his knees. Sweat streamed down his forehead into his eyes. He blinked, then looked at Anskar with bewilderment.

The stolen fire blazed along the conduits linking Anskar to Gann, then burned through Anskar's blood, scorching his bones and consuming him with fury and rage.

All he was aware of then was pounding and gouging, kicking, elbowing, hammering down blows with Gann's axe. Hot wetness spattered his face. He tasted its saltiness on his lips. And still he raged and smashed and reveled in the bloodlust. It felt righteous. It felt good. It felt…

The fire fled as quickly as it had come. Like Gann before him, Anskar dropped to his knees, shaking. Cold seeped through his veins now, in place of the burning heat. His stomach clenched and he vomited, then fell forward onto the pulpy, bloody mess that had once been the priest of the Warrior.

# SEVEN

THE FAR SIDE OF MOUNT Phyrith was so unlike the regions of Niyas that Carred Selenas was familiar with that it might just as well have been another world. A world of steaming jungle and maddening humidity.

Sweat pooled in her boots, stinging her feet where blisters had burst. Hair was plastered across her face. Her heartbeat was erratic and way too fast, and every breath burned her throat as she sucked in snatches of scalding air.

Taloc and Orix weren't faring any better, one or the other lagging behind until Carred called a halt to wait for them to catch up.

Noni was oblivious, but Noni was always oblivious. The young Niyandrian woman stumbled along, muttering to herself, occasionally blurting out her side of a conversation that no one else could hear. Her mind might have been elsewhere, but her body was suffering along with the rest of them, and not just from the walk and the humidity. Her skin was near-translucent, webbed with blue veins, her madly sparkling eyes set deep in black pits.

The necromancer Tain, on the other hand, was loving every minute of it. A head without a body, he had no lungs to fill, and for some inexplicable reason, the heat didn't appear to affect him, even encased as he was within his helm of divine alloy.

And he wouldn't shut up. By the thousand mouths of Theltek, was he ever going to stop talking?

"You are my legs propelling me back to greatness," he told Taloc, who had been tasked with carrying the head. "You are my hands, my strong right arm. Temporarily, mind, until I am reunited with my body. Serve me well and you will be rewarded beyond your wildest imaginings." Tain chuckled at some private joke. "Hah, if I could slap you on the back, I would. I'm sure you have some pretty wild imaginings, am I right? I've seen the way you look at our delectable Carred."

"I do not," Taloc said. He caught Carred's eye. "I don't!"

"Shove something in his gob to shut him up," Orix suggested.

"What's that?" Tain said. "What'd he say?"

Carred translated the Nan-Rhouric for him, though she'd hardly describe herself as fluent. "He suggested shoving something in your mouth…"

"Oh, he'd like that, wouldn't he? But he's not my type. Too much meat on his pudgy little Traguh-raj frame. Oh, and the stench!"

"I think he meant food," Carred said.

"I neither need food nor can digest it in my current state. The curse or blessing of life beyond death."

Noni giggled, and everyone looked at her—even Tain, whose head just happened to be facing the right way. A moment's anticipation, and then whatever had made Noni laugh passed, and she was back to being vacant, dumb as a child's doll.

Carred's hand flexed, as if she were clutching her childhood doll, Nally. For a second, she was four again, back in the forest, screaming for her mother.

She'd seen a helm that day—a helm that floated through the trees. Had it been Tain? Had she really glimpsed her own future? More likely, the helm had been a later interpolation in her dreams, though she had to wonder what might have caused it.

"Hold me higher so I can see the view," the necromancer's head told Taloc. "Magnificent! Just look at those trees, those creepers! By Theltek's several dicks, the sky! Oh, how I've missed it."

"Theltek has more than one dick?" Carred asked.

"I bet you'd like that, wouldn't you?"

"Shame you lost yours," Taloc said.

Carred rolled her eyes. "Don't encourage him."

"What's lost will be found," Tain said, "and then, my darling Carred, I'll give you what you've been craving."

"A head with a dick," Carred said. "Let me see, what would that make you?"

"Oh ho! A wit as well as a hard-bodied, succulent piece of—"

Taloc slammed the face plate shut. From within the helm came a torrent of muffled abuse.

"Thank the Five for that," Orix said in Nan-Rhouric. "I thought he'd never shut up."

The trees began to thin out, and the ground fell away into a deep depression. Carred went first, slipping and sliding over wet ground—it was so hot, even the vegetation sweated. Her boots squelched in mud at the bottom.

Ahead of her, reeds marked the edge of a swamp, the waters brown and thick with twigs and leaves. Lilies bunched together in islands, and it made her nervous thinking about what might lurk beneath. Something plopped into the water, but she couldn't see what it was.

"Frog," Orix said. Surreptitiously, his hand came to rest on her ass. She brushed it off.

"We say *cyllif* in Niyandrian," she said.

"Frog," he repeated, and Carred sighed.

Orix had proven both unwilling and incapable of learning. "You really should make more effort."

"I will." Orix looked hurt that she'd rejected his touch. He masked it with a grin and a raised eyebrow. "I remember the word for—"

"Grow up," Carred said.

"Sorry," he said—in Niyandrian.

"Good boy." Carred patted him on the head. "Well done."

"Sorry," he said again, then switched back to Nan-Rhouric. "That's the only word I know."

"Then please be quiet. All this Nan-Rhouric is like a spear through the center of my brain."

What had possessed her to bring Orix along? He'd been a novelty for a few nights, but… Theltek, she missed Marith.

"Now where?" Taloc asked, coming alongside.

"Ask the head," she said, rapping on the helm Taloc was carrying.

"Ouch!" came the muffled yelp from within.

Taloc pried open the face plate.

"Never do that again!" Tain said. "And don't shut me in like that! I've had an aeon in the dark, and I don't cherish the idea of going back to it."

"Directions," Carred said.

"Well, there's up, down, left, right…" Tain said. "And up

again, up your—"

"Taloc, shut the face plate."

"No, wait! Hold me aloft once more," Tain said. "Now, start a slow turn to your left—no, right. There. I think. That way. Keep clear of the water's edge. There are things in there, things with sharp teeth and slimy tentacles."

Orix must have picked up on the mock fear in Tain's voice. "What was that he said?"

Carred pressed a finger to her lips. "Speak Niyandrian or be silent. The choice is yours. And if you pout, no more fun at night. Understood?"

As far as she was concerned, there would be no more fun whatever he did, Niyandrian or no Niyandrian.

Taloc took the lead, holding Tain's head in front of him as they kept to the lip of relatively dry ground that ran around the edge of the swamp. Under Tain's direction, they veered farther from the water and tramped through ferns until they emerged at the foot of a valley. Mist curled over the valley walls, wreathing everything up top in hazy gray.

"Yes, this is the way," Tain crowed, eyes fixed on the heights. "Look! See!"

Massive shapes loomed out of the mist above, on both sides of the valley.

Orix drew his sword.

"Put it away," Carred said. "It'll rust in this humidity."

He gave her a belligerent look, but his lips remained sealed.

"You have permission to speak Nan-Rhouric," she said.

"No it won't," Orix said, running his thumb along the edge of the blade, then wincing as the skin popped. He re-sheathed the sword and sucked blood from his thumb. "We added astrumium to the blades when we made the swords, along with a sorcerous cant. Not only will it never rust, neither will it blunt."

"So, you're a genius blacksmith as well as a master in the bedroom," she said.

Orix flushed. "I had help."

Under her breath, Carred said, "You need it."

"They look like giants," Taloc said.

The figures above the valley had no arms or legs to speak of, but Carred had to admit they did appear to have heads atop long bodies.

"What are they?" she asked. "The fossils of some long-dead race?"

Noni sniggered. "We see patterns where there are none."

"Who told you that?" Carred asked. "Talia?"

"My father was a thinker."

"But not a right thinker," Tain said. "Although, to be fair, I doubt he ever ventured here. We see patterns here because that is what we are intended to see. They are statues, whittled from sandstone monoliths by the prehistoric people of Niyas."

"Statues of what?" Taloc asked.

"Those who became gods."

"It must have been common, back in the day," Carred said. "I bet they were disappointed."

"Oh?" Tain said. "And why's that, then?"

"An eternity as a pillar of sandstone. Not exactly what you'd call inspiring."

Tain sighed. "They are monuments, symbols of the individuals concerned, not the gods themselves."

"You don't say."

"So," Taloc said, "there's a real god somewhere for each of these statues?"

"That depends on what you mean by a god," Noni said.

Everyone looked at her, but she was still lost in her own world. Carred wasn't even sure that it was Noni who had spoken. The voice was hers, but not necessarily the words.

"The gods are just frustrated immortals who ascended and have grown bored of fucking each other," Tain said. "Which is why they need me among them to freshen things up."

"You've seen the gods?" Taloc asked.

"I'd be among them right now if I'd not been separated from my body. I was *this* close, I tell you! And do you know what really grates? The fact that my body is probably copulating its way through eternity right this very moment."

"That's stupid," Taloc said. "Your body can't function without a brain."

"Doesn't seem to have stopped you. Besides, my head was still attached when I first ascended. I glimpsed paradise, in all its naked glory!"

"Or you'd been smoking too much cravv," Carred said.

"Go ahead, ridicule me. Isn't that what the unremarkable always do when confronted with a superior mind? Let us be honest, Carred, you're resentful."

"I am?"

"Of how I make you feel."

"And how is that?"

"Wet."

"Oh, please! You're a disembodied head, for Theltek's sake."

"I have a tongue…"

"Not for much longer," Carred said, half-drawing her sword.

Taloc chose that moment to trip on a root—literally chose, Carred suspected. Tain wailed as his head flew from Taloc's hands to land face first in the mud.

"Oops," Taloc said as he stooped to pick Tain up, one hand

on either side of the great helm.

"Stop!" Tain yelled. "You'll make me fall out, you stupid oaf!"

Taloc had proven an expert in dumb looks. He gave Carred one now.

"Why should we care if you fall out?" Carred slid her hand under Tain, gripped his nose to hold him in place, and lifted the helm.

The necromancer spat mud. "That is none of your business."

Carred threw the head to Taloc, who deftly caught it.

"Be careful!" Tain shrieked. "For pity's sake!"

"Back to me," Carred said.

"Stop!" Tain yelled as Taloc prepared to throw.

"Then answer my question."

Silence.

"Ready when you are," Carred said, holding out her hands. "They used to call me butterfingers as a child."

"I have no existence outside of this helm!" Tain said. "Satisfied?"

"You what?" Taloc said.

"Without the divine alloy protecting you, you would simply vanish?" Carred asked.

"You'd like that, wouldn't you?"

"If it meant you'd shut up."

"I'm going off you," Tain said. "Never did like a woman with scars."

"Explain why you'd cease to exist if we removed the helm," Carred said. This might be important. Queen Talia's plan to return from the dead involved the Armor of Divinity. Was that the kind of existence her former lover could expect—an eternity encased in metal? Did Talia know?

"The armor translated me to a higher realm," Tain said.

"How do you know it was higher?" Noni again. She smirked, no longer vacant. She was fiercely attentive.

Tain scowled, but otherwise chose to ignore her. "It also transformed me. Flesh and blood as we know it cannot exist among the gods. It must be remade. Transfigured."

"And you didn't work out a way to change it back?" Carred asked.

"I didn't plan on returning."

"But there is a way?"

"There might be. But if there is, it's my secret. Rip me from the helm, and it dies with me."

"So," Noni said, her gait predatory as she approached, "what do you want in exchange for this secret?"

"Talia?" Carred asked.

"What's going on?" Orix asked.

"Niyandrian or nothing," Carred reminded him.

"If it is Queen Talia," Tain said, "get her away from me. I'll not speak again in her presence."

Noni stumbled and dropped to her knees. A sliver of drool slid from her chin, and her eyes were once more focused someplace else.

"If it was Talia," Carred said—and who else would it have been?—"she's gone."

"Or she's pretending to be. Close my face plate," Tain said.

Taloc gave Carred a bemused look.

"Do it," she said. "Until we get where we're going."

She continued along the foot of the valley, while the statues of forgotten gods looked on.

# EIGHT

ANSKAR AWOKE WITH A GROAN. The stench of blood clung to his nostrils. He was sure it wasn't his own. He was naked beneath a scratchy woolen blanket, and when he moved, he heard the creak of wood.

His eyes came into focus on the underside of an oilskin tarp. He could only see it, he realized, because of the dull glow from a hooded lantern set on the bed of the wagon—for it was Braga's wagon in which he had come to. There was barely room to move on account of the tools and supplies the blacksmith had brought with her from Sansor, but she had cleared enough space amid the clutter for a bed of straw and a blanket, which it seemed she had surrendered to Anskar.

"Clothes are by your feet," Braga said. She was seated on an anvil to Anskar's left. "I fetched them from your room. The blood-drenched ones you were wearing, I put into a sack, along with the bits of that bastard Gann."

She stared at Anskar through narrowed eyes. Her cheek twitched, and she grimaced and looked away.

"You put Gann in a sack?"

"Four sacks. Good hemp weave, too. Scraped him into them. Whatever it was you did, you did it good."

"He tried to kill me," Anskar said. "Did anyone…"

"No one saw, least not to my knowledge. I brought you here, cleaned you up, then went back and cleaned up the mess you'd left on the road. There was blood. Lot of blood. Brains too, and chunks of flesh. Dare say he deserved it, but even so…" Her eyes were dark and inscrutable in the poor light. "They were good sacks. I reckon you owe me."

Anskar levered himself up onto an elbow. "What did you do with them?"

"The sacks? Took them to the dung heaps on the edge of town. I emptied out Gann's steaming remains, then shoveled shit on top of them. If I was a poet, I'd say it was poetic justice. But I ain't a poet, I'm a blacksmith. Threw the sacks and your ruined clothes in the river. Doubt anyone'll find them anytime soon. Hopefully not before we're long gone."

"And Lanuc?" Anskar asked.

"Haven't seen him. He don't know. No reason why he should, neither."

"But he'll realize Gann is missing."

Braga hunched her shoulders and stared down at her feet. "Then I expect he'll ask you about it, sooner or later."

After that, she withdrew into herself, growing sullen and silent.

Anskar lay back on the straw, though he cast aside the blanket, which made him itch. He felt… He couldn't quite articulate how he felt. *Odd* was the best he could manage. He'd expected to at least feel a few aches and pains from being flung to the ground by Gann's sorcerous ward, but the only pain was in his knuckles, which were raw and smeared with dried blood. He felt a strange sort of tiredness too, deflated, yet with the afterglow of euphoria—the same as when he made love. The Warrior's Fire he'd snatched from Gann had consumed him. It had driven his actions and narrowed his awareness to almost nothing. He remembered snarling and pounding, gouging and biting, but it was as if he were recalling someone else's memories—or rather, the sense impressions of some savage beast.

That made a strange kind of sense. Divine gifts had to be earned. They had to be grown into over time, through trials and testing. Yet Anskar had simply wrenched the Warrior's Fire from Gann. It was no wonder he had lost control.

He could sense the Warrior's Fire within him still. A seed only, a latency, buried at his core, but a part of him now. A part he had to ignore, because although it was primarily a power of the dawn-tide, the dusk-tide could give it the destructive virulence that made it so lethal.

A niggling voice in his head told him he had already broken his oath by wresting the power from Gann and using it.

Not true, he countered, trying to convince himself. The healing that had enabled him to excise Gann's power and make it his own was a gift of the Healer that manifested through the dawn-tide. That seemed to imply that the Warrior's Fire was also a divine gift, albeit one that made use of the dawn and the dusk. But he was fudging the issue, he knew. It was a slippery slope he was on once more.

"How long since you brought me here?" he asked.

Braga shrugged, then pushed down on her thighs to stand, head bowed beneath the tarp. "Some hours. Be dawn soon, I reckon. Now you're awake, we might as well move the wagon.

Farther we are from the scene of the crime, the fewer suspicions we'll arouse."

Anskar nodded, and Braga pushed her way through the tarp at the front of the wagon to the driver's bench.

"But won't they work out it was me who killed Gann, whatever we do?" he said. "Everyone knew he had a vendetta against me. It was self-defense, but what I did to him…"

"Like I said, if anyone cares, Lanuc will want to speak with you."

And then Anskar stumbled as Braga flicked the reins and the oxen lumbered forward.

Braga parked the wagon a few streets away, and Anskar sat up front with her to greet the dawn-tide. She showed no reaction as the eldritch currents washed over him. Probably she had seen it before, living so long among the Order's knights. It felt good to fill his dawn-tide repository. The deflated feeling left him, and he grew stronger and somehow cleaner.

A swift check told him his dusk- and dark-tide repositories were safely contained by their barriers, no more than brooding presences.

Braga clambered down from the wagon, telling Anskar she was going in search of breakfast. He joined her, and they were settled at a table in a busy eatery swollen with early morning diners when Lanuc found them.

Anskar steeled himself as the older knight approached, but to his relief, Lanuc didn't mention Gann.

"Wolf your food down and meet me and Gisela outside," he told Anskar. "Just you. They only want me and two others to attend."

"Attend what?" Anskar asked, smiling his thanks to the server, who set down a steaming mug of tea in front of him and then handed Braga a beer.

"You'll see soon enough," Lanuc said. "I'm not happy about it, but if we want supplies and to get on our way without any trouble, then it's better only a few of us bear the shame."

He left without saying any more. Braga raised an eyebrow, then tipped back her head and took a long pull of her beer.

Toasted bread, smoked fish, and eggs had sounded so good when Anskar ordered them, but the tension coming off Lanuc had turned his stomach sour.

The Church of the Lady Sylva Kalisia was by far the largest building in Kyuth, but it would have been dwarfed by most of the structures in Sansor. Anskar thought it looked as if it had been thrown together in a hurry with whatever materials were to hand. Mismatched, uncut stones were heaped one on top of another in the manner of a drystone wall. The tower was a lopsided pyramid of weatherworn planks nailed about a skeletal frame. One good gust of wind, Anskar fancied, and it would fall down.

The interior was little better. The floor was hard-packed mud, the walls devoid of plaster, and the underside of the lopsided tower was draped with cobwebs. A stepped stone structure stood in the center of the floorspace, atop it a patinated bronze statue of a striking naked woman with feathered wings extending from her back: Sylva Kalisia.

A large gold-plated chalice sat at the statue's feet. It was inscribed with swirling script, some of it Skanuric, Anskar thought, but most of it indecipherable to him. Offerings were heaped around the steps of the stone structure: skulls of rodents and birds, coins, locks of hair, scraps of clothing. The air was thick with a musky incense that tickled the back of his throat, and there was a charge to the atmosphere that made his spine crawl.

The church had no seats, but the interior was packed with townsfolk standing around the central figure of the Lady. Anskar recognized the mayor, Frankin Glore, and the priest of the Elder, Brother Stevos.

"We should bring our soldiers through the gates and have them burn this abomination down," Gisela whispered in Anskar's ear.

He couldn't tell if she was joking. Lanuc ground his teeth and shook his head.

As they waited, Anskar ran his eyes over the locals, some of them coughing due to the incense, others watching the flickering shadows on the walls cast by the hundreds of rushlights set on ledges. Brother Stevos bobbed his head and flashed smiles at the worshipers, as if doing so could make everything all right. But there was nothing right about the worship of heathen gods.

At the far end of the church—he took it to be north—Anskar glimpsed a rippling of the shadows, and then a slender, dark figure emerged. Anskar's first impression was of some demonic entity shadow-stepping into the church. Then, as the figure resolved into a woman, he thought it might be Sylva Kalisia herself.

The locals made claws of their hands and placed them over their breasts. Brother Stevos did the same, at the same time dipping his head in a deferential bow. Lanuc's jaw clenched. Gisela narrowed her eyes and muttered under her breath.

For it was no demon that had emerged from the shadows at the end of the church, and it was no goddess either. Anskar hadn't noticed it before, in the gloomy interior, but it was a heavy black veil that had rippled, not the shadows, and the figure, while indeed a woman, was gray-haired and more emaciated than slender. In the reflected glow of the hundreds of rushlights, her eyes blazed like embers. Involuntarily, Anskar touched four fingers and thumb to his chest. Gisela noticed and nodded in approval.

Wreathed in a black gown that fell to her feet, and aided by an effect of the flickering rushlights, the High Priestess glided across the floor, the locals parting for her, until she came to rest upon the lowest step of the central stone structure, where the gifts to the Lady had been left. She stood there a long while, running her eyes over those gathered before her, turning slowly to take in those behind. Anticipation hung heavy in the air, and there was a hungry look in the eyes of many of the worshipers.

The High Priestess lifted the gold-plated chalice from the feet of the statue and raised it above her head.

"The realm of the dead is as nothing to those who serve the goddess," she said.

Anskar held his breath, feeling as if the High Priestess's words were intended for him.

"That realm is a limbo for the unbelievers," she went on. "The abode of necromancers and the source of their unnatural power. But we who serve, we who are carried above that gloomy half-existence in the arms of the Lady, we who are borne aloft by her outstretched wings, we will pass over the realm of the dead in the blink of an eye. For us, it will be merely a bridge into the plentiful pastures and mountainous glory the Lady has prepared for us, her servants. But only if we are united to her."

She held the chalice out before her. In its depths Anskar saw a bubbling red liquid. Mist or steam poured over the lip of the chalice, pooled at the High Priestess's feet, and crept out across the floor of the church.

Gisela met Anskar's eye and gave a barely perceptible shake of her head. He interpreted it as a warning not to participate in whatever was about to happen.

The High Priestess raised the chalice to her mouth and sipped from it; then her tongue snaked out to lick a red smear from her lips. She closed her eyes and turned her face toward the ceiling, smiling rapturously, then shuddered and gave a low moan.

Opening her eyes, she poured a measure of the liquid over the feet of the representation of her goddess atop the stone structure. Crimson cascaded down the steps, an impossible volume of glistening blood-like sludge that coated the entire structure and the gifts at its base. And still the chalice was not empty.

Turning back toward the north of the church, the High Priestess returned to the heavy black veil she had emerged from, turned back to the congregation, and held out the chalice.

The worshipers formed a long line and went before the High Priestess one at a time to drink from the chalice. No matter how many devotees came, how many drank, the chalice remained full to the brim, mist billowing from the surface of whatever liquid it contained.

Anskar saw Mayor Frankin Glore take a long drink, then wipe his mouth with the back of his hand, which seemed to irritate the High Priestess.

Lanuc, Anskar, and Gisela lingered at the back of the line, as if they might somehow be spared. Brother Stevos hung back with them, giving nods of reassurance and smiling like an imbecile. For a priest of the Elder, he struck Anskar as a fool, a man who had blurred right and wrong to justify all manner of atrocities in the name of some misguided sense of tolerance.

Anskar's attention was drawn away from the priest as Lanuc leaned in to whisper, "I went to see Gann early this morning to persuade him to end this nonsensical blood feud, and was told he hadn't been seen since late last night."

Anskar swallowed. He didn't know what to say.

Lanuc shook his head in irritation. "The last thing our mission to the Kingdom of the Thousand Lakes needs is a blood feud, and while it is traditional for Order knights not to interfere with the ways of the Warrior's priests, I thought it was at least worth a try. A pity I couldn't find him."

"A pity," Anskar agreed.

Brother Stevos hissed at them to be quiet. "Respect is due to the worshipers and their beliefs," he whispered.

Lanuc clamped his jaw shut, but Gisela said, "No respect is due to heathens, Brother. As a priest of the Elder, you of all people should know that."

Slowly, the line went down as those who had drunk from the chalice made their way outside.

And then it was Brother Stevos's turn to drink, which he did with a little flourish, giving Anskar, Gisela, and Lanuc a nod and a wink before barely wetting his lips with the red liquid. He sighed as if he had just enjoyed a fine wine, and handed the chalice back to the High Priestess.

As he made his way toward the exit, he mouthed to Lanuc, "It's perfectly all right. Menselas understands."

The High Priestess held the chalice out toward Lanuc, who visibly stiffened.

"Father," Gisela warned, but Lanuc took a step forward and accepted the chalice, raising it to his lips.

"Oh, by the Five!" Gisela cursed, and stormed out of the church.

The High Priestess raised an amused eyebrow.

Lanuc grimaced at his daughter's retreating back and switched his gaze to Anskar, eyes wide in an unspoken question as he wiped the red stain from his lips. "And you?" he seemed to say. "Will you embarrass me too?"

The High Priestess held out the chalice.

"I've already made too many compromises," Anskar said.

He turned his back on the High Priestess and her chalice and strode after Gisela.

# NINE

THE VALLEY FLOOR ROSE ALMOST imperceptibly, mile after mile. The hills on either side leveled out as they left the valley of the gods, until there was only an endless expanse of white flatland tufted with spiny grasses.

At first Carred thought the whiteness was due to chalk, but then Orix, who'd said nothing for hours, bent down to touch the ground and brought his finger to his lips.

"Salt," he said in Nan-Rhouric.

"*Ulluar*," Carred translated for him.

"*Ulluar*," he said, then continued to repeat the word under his breath.

"This was once a sea?" Taloc asked, the helm that contained the necromancer Tain's head tucked under his arm.

"It was not," Noni said.

Carred glanced at her, but already the young woman was staring vacantly ahead. She looked incapable of speaking.

"We go on?" Taloc asked. He seemed hopeful they would not.

"Missing Vilintia?" Carred asked.

"Who?" Then Taloc laughed. "I guess I am. A little."

"Just a little?"

"A lot, then."

"Just think about how pleased she'll be to see you when we get back to the hideout."

"I've been thinking about nothing else!"

Carred smiled as she swigged the last of the water from her canteen.

"I have some left," Orix said. "I've been saving it for you."

"Then keep saving it." She was about to chastise him for once again speaking Nan-Rhouric, then told herself to stop being so harsh. Answering in kind, she said, "It may not be enough. But thank you. How about you?" she asked Taloc. "You still got water?"

"A little."

"Noni? No, forget I asked. We go on."

She led them toward a smudge on the horizon. The farther they trekked across the salt plain, the more the plant life thinned out, until all that remained was white as far as the eye could see, save for the steadily growing smudge.

Little by little, a gigantic structure came into focus: interconnected cairns made from massive stones that glimmered blue where the sunlight touched them.

"Be wary, my love," Noni said, and this time the inflection of her voice was definitely Talia's.

"Wary of what?"

"Something. I feel it, but I've not been here before. Just… be wary."

"Open the helm," Carred said.

Taloc grumbled about it but did as she asked.

"Is she still here?" Tain said, blinking against the sunlight outside his helm.

Carred glanced at Noni. "She's still here, but I'm sure you're quite safe."

"I long ago told Queen Talia I wanted nothing to do with her schemes," Tain said.

"What did she do to upset you? Reject your advances?"

"Hah! I'd like to see the woman who could resist me."

"You're looking at her."

"Tain is jealous of what I might achieve," Noni—Talia—said.

"Jealous? Me? I rose among the gods!"

"A headless god. You failed, Tain, and you wish me to fail too."

"I couldn't care less whether you succeed or fail," Tain said, "so long as I get back to my body. Where are we?"

Taloc turned so that the necromancer's head faced the cairns.

"There you go," Tain said. "We've arrived."

"You've been here before?" Taloc asked.

"In search of relics of Armor of Divinity. I found a complete suit to learn from."

"And what did you learn?" Carred asked.

"That there were flaws in their design—presumably why the owner remained in the world. Dead."

"So what's the point of coming here?" Taloc asked.

"Because he knows how to modify the armor," Noni said. "He wrote a book about it, didn't you, Tain?"

"Private notes," Tain said. "Not for the prying eyes of power-mad sorcerers."

"He melted the armor down," Noni said, "and added a key component that the original maker had been ignorant of."

"Astrumium," Tain said.

"Did he say astrumium?" Orix asked Carred in his own tongue. "Like I said, we used that at Branil's Burg during the trial of sword crafting."

"What did the savage say?" Tain asked.

"Perhaps you should learn Nan-Rhouric," Carred said. "Maybe you two could teach each other."

"Why would I want to speak Nan-Rhouric?"

"So," Carred said, "all we need do is find a full suit of ancient armor, melt down the pieces, and add astrumium before reshaping them?"

"There's more to it than that," Noni said.

"There is not," Tain said. "I thought you'd read my notebook."

"I've also seen the result of your experiments," Noni said. "A head without a body. Believe me, there is an additional component, which even you didn't think of."

"There is no missing ingredient," Tain insisted.

"You're sure about that?" Carred asked. "I mean, only your head came back."

"I was not supposed to come back at all. If I had wanted to, I'd have designed the armor differently."

"With the missing ingredient," Noni said.

Carred flashed her a glare and then wished she hadn't. Talia hadn't been the most forgiving woman in life, and there was nothing to suggest that death had mellowed her. "I assume you want me to find the missing ingredient, then. Do you mind telling me what it is?"

"At the appropriate time," Noni said, then she shuddered and grew vacant again.

"If you weren't supposed to come back," Taloc asked Tain, "then why did your head?"

"Good question," Carred said. "What did happen, Tain? You

said you glimpsed the realm of the gods, so I assume your head made it through with your body."

"It did. I opened my face plate to see—and what a sight I saw!—but it slammed shut of its own accord, or something I didn't see closed it for me, and I was alone in the dark. The gods are capricious and full of unabashed lust; I dare say they wanted my body and not my brain. I could feel nothing—couldn't even wiggle my fingers and toes. It was only when that bitch Talia found me that I realized I had returned to Wiraya, and that I was a head without a body."

With a glance at Noni, Carred said, "And Talia came to learn from you?"

"What she learned, she stole. Her sorcery is depraved. You have no idea how depraved."

"Yet you've agreed to help her?"

"I've agreed to help you find a suit of armor so that you can use it to carry me back to the realm of the gods and reunite me with my body."

"Yes," Carred said. "But how will I return?"

"Ask her," Tain said, eyes flicking toward Noni. "Because that was not part of our arrangement. Besides, what if you don't want to return? I tell you, the gods live for pleasure, and you have the look of a ripe and lusty woman."

"I must return. It's my duty."

"Oh, yes, to give the armor to this Anskar DeVantte so he can bring his mother back from the dead. Then let's hope her so-called secret ingredient is all she claims it is."

"Right," Carred said. "How do we get in?"

"Around the far side," Tain said. "It took us weeks of digging, but we excavated an entrance tunnel when I first came here."

"We?" Taloc asked.

"They, technically," Tain said. "I directed, they dug. Hirelings from the villages. Not that I paid them. None of them returned."

"The danger you spoke of?" Carred asked, but Noni was back to vacantly staring ahead, an empty vessel. What had Talia done to her? Was there anything of Noni left?

"What danger?" Tain asked.

"Before we opened your face plate, Queen Talia sensed something and said to be wary."

"Wary of what? It was quite safe when I came before."

"How long ago was that?"

"I see your point."

"So, what happened to your hirelings?" Taloc asked.

"You killed them, didn't you?" Carred said.

"King Lowanu's orders, and who am I to disobey a king? They didn't go quietly, let me tell you, but what good are picks and shovels against necromancy? I'm no Queen Talia, but I know a thing or two."

Taloc held the necromancer's head out in front of him as he led the group around the gigantic structure. Beneath the shade thrown by the cairns, the heaped stones lost their bluish tinge and grew cold and gray.

The scale of the construction was staggering: eight burial halls, as Tain called them, that extended like the spokes of a wheel from a central hub, also made from stacked stones. Each of the halls was over thirty feet high and ten times as long.

"If there was no sea here," Orix said, "why all the salt?"

"Sorcery?" Carred said with a shrug. "Have you seen anything living here? Save for us, of course."

"No, nothing."

He gave her a look so intense it made her feel there was something wrong with her. It was the kind of look her mother used to give her. "What?" she said.

"You didn't yell at me for not speaking Niyandrian."

"I don't yell."

"Sometimes you do."

Carred sighed. "What is this about, Orix? It was fun for a while. It's no longer fun."

"I know that. I'm not completely stupid. I'm just hoping we're doing the right thing… now… being here… The right thing for Anskar."

"You miss him?"

Orix made a scoffing noise and looked away.

"Yes, you miss him."

"I don't understand why he wouldn't join us," Orix said. "He and I both saw what the Order's really like, yet when he had the chance—"

"That is not how I left it!" Tain cried out in a shrill voice. "I concealed it with the earth-tide, and warded it with the dusk."

Taloc had stopped in front of a square-shaped pit. The jagged remains of a wooden cover were still attached to the edges. The wood must have been ancient, but it showed no signs of rot or wear. Something had smashed through the cover at some point in time. Steps of the same stone as the cairns, dusted with grains of salt, led down into the dark.

"The earth-tide?" Carred said.

"It's not just for necromancy, you know," Tain said. "If you have the aptitude, you can use it for shaping things. All kinds of stuff: animals, people, wood, stone. I made the cover resemble the salt of the plains. Even if it was located, anything that tried to enter would have been incinerated."

"But they weren't," Taloc pointed out. "There aren't even any scorch marks."

"I don't understand how that's possible," Tain said.

"Perhaps your sorcery wasn't as good as you thought it was," Carred said. "I mean, just look at what happened to your body."

"An oversight, nothing more. You'll see, and then you'll eat your—"

Noni walked between them as if she were asleep, and descended the steps into the pit.

# TEN

ANSKAR SAT UP FRONT NEXT to Braga as she drove her wagon out through the gates of Kyuth. Anskar's horse was tethered to the rear of the wagon, and the priest of the Warrior, Josac, who had made a complete recovery following Anskar's vicarious healing, rode alongside. They were among the last of the army to leave the town, and already falling behind the rest of the column.

Lanuc was out of sight, riding in the vanguard. He didn't meet Anskar's eyes when he came out of the Church of Sylva Kalisia, and Anskar hadn't dared to approach him. Lanuc was as furious with him as he was with his daughter.

Gisela hadn't said anything to Anskar either, and was now just a white robe among the dozen or so healers who rode with the army.

"Do you think I did the right thing?" Anskar asked.

"Depends on what's most important to you," Braga said.

"Doing what your god expects, or obeying your superior, even when he's being a fool." She sniffed and spat a wad of phlegm over the side of the wagon.

No longer following the curve of the bay, the army made a beeline for the north. The terrain rose gradually toward the great mountainous region of the Thousand Lakes—a land of crags and cliffs, extinct volcanoes, wending rivers, and inland seas. The famous lakes, Josac told Anskar, were a combination of rain-filled calderas of extinct volcanoes, water pooling in natural depressions, and man-made reservoirs left over from the rule of a long-forgotten race, back when the Thousand Lakes had been an arid wasteland with a different name.

The column slowly ground to a halt, and Braga's wagon caught up with the rest of the army. They had come to a fast-flowing river that no one seemed to know the name of.

A knight—a surly man with a neatly trimmed mustache— came to summon Anskar up front to see Lanuc. Josac remained behind with Braga. The two of them seemed to be getting along now, judging by the generous measure of insults Braga was constantly dishing out to the Warrior's priest, who responded in kind, though with a twinkle in his eye.

Following the knight's horse, Anskar made his way to the front of the column on foot. He needed to stretch his legs.

He found Lanuc standing on the riverbank, hands on hips, scanning the white water in both directions. Two women stood behind him. They were dressed in padded jackets, thick-weave pants, and scuffed leather boots, and each carried an unstrung longbow stave.

Lanuc turned around, a grim expression on his face. An uncharacteristic growth of stubble covered his chin, and his eyes were sunken and red-rimmed. He manufactured a meager smile and gestured for Anskar to follow him upriver.

When the knight with the mustache and the two women made to follow, Lanuc said, "Just Anskar. You three wait here."

The women shrugged and settled themselves down on the riverbank. The one with dark hair even tugged her boots off and dangled her feet in the water. The knight, though, narrowed his eyes in what looked like resentment at being left out. Anskar gave him a friendly smile and a shrug, as if to say this wasn't his idea, but that only seemed to make matters worse, and now the man positively glowered.

Anskar walked with Lanuc for perhaps five minutes until they came to a ruined bridge that had once spanned the river. All that remained were the thick wooden pilings driven into the riverbed.

"You plan to repair the bridge?" Anskar asked. It would be a mammoth task, given the river was, at its widest, three hundred or more yards across, and at its narrowest a good two hundred. Whoever had built the bridge must have possessed great patience and skill.

Lanuc seemed to be thinking along the same lines, and when he saw Anskar studying the pilings, he said, "It's a tidal river, so they would have waited until the water was at its lowest before boring the holes and driving the pilings home. Probably would have taken months."

Anskar nodded, not sure what else to say. There was an atmosphere between the two of them, and Lanuc clearly had other matters on his mind. Anskar opened his mouth to broach the subject, but Lanuc spoke at the same time.

"Is Gisela still angry with me?"

Anskar grimaced. He should have expected this. "I've not spoken to her since…"

"Since I apostatized?" Lanuc sighed and shook his head. "Gisela is right. I taught her, growing up, never to compromise her values. I told her stories of heroic priests and knights who endured torture and death rather than betray the will of Menselas. I don't know when I stopped heeding my own advice."

Anskar knew what it was like to rigorously follow the laws of the Order, the statutes of their god, only to find that intention whittled away little by little.

"I used to be so strict—" he started, but clammed up when Lanuc turned back to face him.

"We all start out that way," Lanuc said. "Well, most of us do. But then we see the things our superiors are willing to do in the name of diplomacy or expedience or even some desperate bid to survive. It's like a slow corrosion that passes unnoticed until…" He sighed. "Until a fully fledged knight of the Order of Eternal Vigilance, a follower of the Five, the father of a virginal priest of the Healer, drinks from the cup of Sylva Kalisia."

"Brother Stevos…" Anskar said.

"Is an idiot," Lanuc said. "Too clever for his own good. Too clever to see the truth when it's staring him right in the face. But Stevos isn't to blame. The mayor implied trouble if we didn't show respect to the Church of Sylva Kalisia, and it was my decision to play the High Priestess's game. For the sake of supplies and a peaceful journey, I put my soul in peril. Worse, I ordered you and Gisela to do the same. Thank the Five you both had the courage to disobey me."

"I…"

"No need to say it, Anskar. Your loyalty, your obedience, is not in question. And neither is my daughter's. I'm the one at fault." And now there was a pleading look in his eyes. "Will you forgive me?"

Anskar's cheek twitched and his throat tightened. "Of course I forgive you. You're my commander, and I'm entrusted to your charge."

"By Vihtor, yes. How do you think he'd have reacted to what I did back in Kyuth?"

"He would have understood."

"I sincerely doubt that, and I don't expect you to understand either. There's no need. I was wrong. I see that clearly now. Pray for me to Menselas."

"I will," Anskar said.

"And talk to my daughter for me."

"I'm sorry?"

"Gisela is so like her mother: stubborn, willful, and unforgiving. You didn't betray the Five. Maybe she'll listen to you."

"But she's a healer," Anskar objected. It was part of a healer's duty to forgive and to convey the forgiveness of Menselas to others.

"Even so…"

"What do you want me to say?"

Lanuc hesitated, thinking things over. "Just tell her that I was wrong. Ask her to pray for me. Tell her… tell her I crave her forgiveness."

"I will," Anskar said, though it wasn't a task he relished.

Lanuc puffed out his cheeks and exhaled sharply, then put a hand on Anskar's shoulder. "Thank you. And now to the other reason I wanted to see you."

"Oh?"

Lanuc gestured toward the river. "This is an obstacle I hadn't expected. Last time I came this way, several years ago, this bridge was intact."

"Someone destroyed it? Why?"

Lanuc shrugged. "Relations between Kaile and the City States have soured over the past few years, as have most of our major alliances. Pretty much the entire mainland came together in order to defeat Queen Talia."

Anskar dipped his eyes, heat rising to his face.

"I'm sorry, Anskar. But that's the reality of how it was. Your mother's ambitions united a continent, and the Order of Eternal Vigilance was the glue that bound those alliances together. But now that the threat has been lifted, old rivalries have been reborn. Oh, there's still the veneer of peace, but cooperation has been sorely lacking of late. It's part of the reason our mission is so important. Ignore the requests for aid from King Aelfyr, and he will seek the aid of others. But if we honor our alliance with the Kingdom of the Thousand Lakes, even with so paltry an army as I've been tasked with leading, then the City States will be isolated, at least geographically, caught between Kaile to the south and the Thousand Lakes to the north. I suspect the rulers in Sansor, not to mention the Patriarch and the Grand Master, hope this will force the City States to renew their commitments to the greater good."

Politics was an entirely new concern for Anskar. In Branil's Burg, life had been simple, but since he'd left Niyas, it seemed that every day heaped complexity upon complexity.

"What is it you want me to do?" he asked.

"Go with the three we left back at the bank, follow the river east, and find a place for the army to cross, whether it be another bridge, a ferry crossing, or a ford. The two women are scouts, the best I know, and the man who fetched you, Flavin Reider, is…" Lanuc struggled to find the right words. He settled upon: "He's a capable enough knight."

"Capable enough?"

"Reider is a difficult individual," Lanuc said, "but as you progress in the Order, you'll be expected to deal with such people, both above and below you.

"We're still in Kaile, but we're close to the border, and while the City States are still officially our allies, I was warned by the Grand Master to tread warily once we reach their lands. If we can cross the river near here, we should be able to cut across the corner of their territory and head into the Kingdom of the Thousand Lakes within a day or two. And that's when our problems truly begin."

# ELEVEN

HANDS ON THE WALLS EITHER side, in case she should slip, Carred descended the steps into the gloom. Footfalls behind told her the others were coming. She could see Noni below her, silhouetted in a hazy, violet glow.

At the foot of the steps, Carred came to a tunnel. The walls were scabbed with violet scaleskin fungus, the source of the glow.

Noni turned to face her and smiled. A flash of eagerness shone in her eyes, but it was quickly gone.

Carred slipped past her and continued along the tunnel, testing each flagstone before she put her weight on it.

"Hurry it up!" Tain called from behind. "There are no traps. Least there weren't when I came here before."

Noni followed Carred like a dog. Orix was next, with Taloc bringing up the rear, Tain's head under his arm. The necromancer's eyes blazed with an inner, greenish light. The sight of it made Carred nauseous, and she quickly looked away.

If she'd not neglected her repositories all her life, she might have recognized the sorcery that made his eyes glow, rather than being alerted to it by feelings of queasiness.

After a couple of hundred feet, the tunnel branched into three passageways with walls of stacked stones and no mortar.

"There are levels above us," Tain said, "though I never found a way to access them."

"What's that smell?" Orix asked in Nan-Rhouric.

"What did the peasant say?" Tain again.

"Was that stench here when you came before?" Carred asked.

"I don't remember," Tain said. "I don't think so. It's probably a combination of rot from the burial chambers and the degradation of the armor."

"Armor of Divinity degrades?"

"Some of the components are organic. While the sorcery that binds them together preserves the materials, over time it fades. These cairns are old, my luscious beauty. Prehistoric."

Carred rolled her eyes. "Which way?"

"It matters not. All passageways lead to a burial hall. Like your delectable orifices, one's as good as another for our purposes."

Gritting her teeth lest she say something she might live to regret, Carred chose the central passage, thankful for the growth of phosphorescent fungus on every surface.

She entered a cavernous hall divided into sections by walls of unmortared stone. Rocks were piled on the floor from where some of the walls had partially collapsed.

"Each wall defines a separate burial chamber," Tain said. "My team were responsible for breaking into one, but not the others. What happened here?"

Virtually every chamber had been entered, Carred saw as she turned a slow circle. Within the nearest, she could see a central stone slab, atop which was a skeleton.

"No armor," she said as she peered inside. The bones had a metallic tint that shimmered in the light of the scaleskins.

The next tomb was the same, and the next.

"What happened to the armor?" she asked. "Did they remove it before burial?"

"Remove it?" Tain said. "Of course they didn't remove it. That would have spoiled the illusion—or should I say 'deception.' The people were hoodwinked, as soon as it was apparent to the priesthood that the experiments were failures. The rulers who put on the Armor of Divinity weren't translated to the realm of the gods as they had expected. They died inside their suits. As you can see, their bones were somehow fused with divine alloy, an odd and unforeseen side effect. Of course, I solved the problem with my own armor, but…"

"You had problems of your own," Carred said.

"Or I was sabotaged by jealous gods," Tain said. "We shall know soon enough, if we're successful here."

"So let me get this straight," Carred said. "The corpses of these rulers were interred here as gods? And people believed that?"

"No one was allowed to remove the armor," Tain said. "The priests gave the impression the wearers had ascended and only the armor remained behind—a relic, or even a sacrament, you might say. Then they made the sandstone statues we passed in the valley on the way here: a locus of worship for each new god."

"And people were so stupid they would believe without evidence?" Carred said.

"While these suits of armor might not have worked as intended, there are legends of even earlier suits that did. Or are you saying you don't believe in the gods?"

"I've yet to see one," Carred said.

"Believe me, when you do, you won't be able to keep your hands to yourself."

"But if the suits of armor were buried here," Taloc said, "what happened to them?"

"Stolen," Tain said, as if he couldn't believe it. "I only took one suit for my experiments, and several others were missing when I found this place, but…"

"There are tomb robbers all over Niyas," Taloc said.

"But my wards should have stopped them. And besides, I concealed the entrance."

Orix was breathing down Carred's neck. She found his proximity annoying. "Spread out," she said. "See if anything's left."

At the far end of the hall, one of the dividing walls was still intact, though there were fragments of rock on the floor, where someone had discarded a pick.

"Before I found these cairns, I discovered the locations of several other suits of Divine Armor in various places around Niyas," Tain said, as Carred began to chip away at the wall with the pick, "but they were not easily accessible. If my suspicions are correct, all of them started out here."

"Who would have known about this place?" Carred asked. "Relic hunters?" *Like that Blaice Rancey woman back in Atya.*

"Or knowledge seekers," Tain said. "Anyone with ideas of becoming a god. Each chamber would have been dug out, one at a time. If it was relic hunters, their finds would most likely have passed through the Ethereal Sorceress's depots. They could be anywhere in the world."

Setting down the pick, Carred worked a stone loose, amid a shower of dust. She winced in case the entire wall should come crashing down, but it had been made too well for that, each stone perfectly shaped and slotted into place.

"Lend me a hand," she said to Orix.

Together they removed stone after stone until there was a hole in the wall large enough for Carred to squeeze through.

No violet light from scaleskin fungus here, just a faint aura coming from the body atop a stone slab—or rather, from what it was wearing.

"There's a full suit of armor in here," she said.

"There is?" Tain said. "Carry me there, oaf. Let me see!"

Something moved in the corner of Carred's eye. As she turned her head, shadows uncoiled from the base of a wall. She gasped and tried to back away, but her legs were rooted to the spot. More shadows detached from the ceiling. Others wafted up from the floor. They drifted toward the armor on the slab, as if drawn to its light, swirled around it, through it, over it, and then launched themselves at Carred.

Her scream caught in her throat as hands grabbed her and pulled her back through the hole. Arms wrapped around her, pressed her face into a chest not quite hard, not quite soft. Orix. Theltek, he stank!

"Don't Traguh-raj ever wash?"

She was trembling all over. The shadows would have killed her—every instinct she possessed told her so. When Orix stroked her hair, she didn't pull away. His smell no longer repulsed her; it made her feel like a child. Not that anyone had comforted her when she'd been one.

"Thank you," she said.

"I love you," he whispered.

"No, you don't." With a deep breath to steady her nerves, she pushed Orix away and looked behind at the hole in the wall.

Noni stood in front of it, blocking her view.

"We can't leave without the armor," Noni said, though the

inflection was all Talia.

"I'm not going back in there."

"Carred, you must."

"Because I'm expendable?"

"Because I command it."

Carred faltered. She'd never before disobeyed an order from the Queen, and she prided herself on her loyalty, even so many years after the fall of Naphor. "Talia, please, those things in there…"

"Fine, then I'll do it myself."

"But it's not your body! You've no right to use Noni like that."

Noni stepped through the hole in the wall. She made it halfway to the armor, when once more the shadows swarmed.

Carred started toward the opening, but Orix restrained her. She put up a token struggle, but she was relieved he'd stopped her. "Sorry," she mouthed at Noni's back. "I wish I were braver."

With Tain's head still tucked under his arm, Taloc ducked through the hole and reached Noni before the shadows did. Noni clawed at the back of his hand, drawing blood, as Taloc spun her round and shoved her toward the opening. Orix and Carred pulled her to safety.

"Get me out of here!" Tain screamed. "They know who I am!"

Shadows streaked towards Taloc. He took a stumbling step, then faltered as the shadows swept in front of him. Panic flashed in his eyes. He turned, but the shadows swirled around him. He turned back again, and threw the necromancer's head. Tain wailed as he spun through the air.

"Got it!" Orix said as he caught the helm and clutched it to his chest.

As one, the shadows veered away from Taloc and streaked in pursuit of the necromancer's head.

Only as far as the opening.

As Orix stepped back, the shadows remained where they were, a seething of the dark. Wisps of blackness reared up like serpents. They bent close together, conferring.

Taloc started to edge around behind them, wide-eyed with fear. Sweat beaded on his forehead as he tiptoed. He met Carred's gaze. She swallowed. He nodded: *I can do this.*

Carred's shirt rippled from the patter of her heart. She shook her head: *Please don't.*

Taloc seemed to bounce with anticipation, then he bellowed at the top of his voice. The shadows scattered like startled fish, and at the same time, Taloc flung himself headfirst toward the opening.

Almost, he made it, but then strands of blackness whiplashed and snagged his ankle, yanking him back. He hit the floor with a thud and immediately pushed himself up on one elbow. Shadows wound around both legs, working their way up his body. Taloc shook all over. Blood trickled from his lips from where he must have bitten his tongue, but his mouth remained clamped shut, as if he refused to scream. The shadows wound about his waist. Where his legs should have been there was only ash. As the shadows reached his neck, Taloc found Carred's eyes again, his own bloodshot and frenzied. His mouth opened, and Carred steeled herself for the cry of pain and terror that was bound to follow; only it didn't.

"Carred…" he uttered.

If he'd had a hand left, he would have reached for her. Tears spilled from his eyes.

And then he was gone.

Carred just stood there, glaring at the dark. Hating.

Noni pulled her away and looked at her, not with her usual blankness, but with sympathy.

"I'm sorry, my love," the Queen said. "Truly, I'm—"

118

Carred shoved Noni so hard she slammed into the wall.

And then she was striding for the tunnel they'd entered by.

"Idiot Queen," she heard Tain say behind her. "Going in there like that! Didn't I say I knew the location of other suits? We fail here, we go after one of them. I'm not saying it will be easy, but here we have no chance."

Carred drew up sharply, fists bunched at her sides. Without looking round, she asked, "What were those things?"

Orix approached with the head.

"They feed off the dead," Tain said. He was moderating his tone for once, as if he knew how close to violence she was. "But they prefer the living when they can get it. These ones were starving: the skeletons on the slabs were fused with divine alloy and couldn't be consumed."

Orix held the head at arm's length as if he feared contagion. He raised his eyes to Carred's, but she kept her focus on Tain. "Where did they come from? You said they knew you."

"No, I didn't."

Carred took a step toward him. "Yes, you did."

Noni pushed herself away from the wall. She frowned as she put a hand to her chest, where Carred had shoved her, then she felt the back of her head.

"We call them residuals." It was Queen Talia who spoke.

"We?"

"Those of us who have mastered the earth-tide. We necromancers. Their bodies were slain by the stagnant tidal forces that pool at the world's core. Their souls, too. Sometimes, there are unforeseen side effects. There is an exchange, rather than the annihilation of life. Out of the void, a terrible hunger is born."

Carred came to loom over the head in Orix's hands.

"You did it, didn't you, Tain? When you slew your helpers

with necromancy, this is what they became."

"I had no idea."

"Your grasp of the earth-tide was incomplete," Talia said.

"If you're so powerful," Tain said, "why don't you go back in there and banish the shadows? Or better still, destroy them?"

"Because I can't. No one can."

"Then there's no point in us spending another minute here," Carred said.

"You don't blame me, do you?" Tain said. "I didn't know."

"Tell that to Vilintia."

"Who?"

Carred turned away and headed for the steps to the outside.

"Let's hope you never get to meet her."

# TWELVE

"HAVE YOU DONE THIS SORT of thing before?" Ravenni asked Anskar as their group headed east through the woods that skirted the river.

She was the dark-haired scout, lean and flat-chested, with a vicious scar that cut a jagged line across her chin. Anskar was hard-pressed to keep up with her as she strode through the trees.

"Never," he said. "The closest I came was when I once left Branil's Burg and walked across country for some days."

"A holiday?" Ravenni asked.

Korine, the older woman with gray-streaked auburn hair, rolled her eyes.

"No," Anskar said, wishing he hadn't brought up the nightmare trek to Hallow Hill. Just thinking about it seemed to make the vambrace on his forearm grow heavier, and he rubbed it through his sleeve.

"You were bored, then?" Ravenni pressed.

"I thought you were supposed to be scouts," Flavin Reider said, lumbering along behind them, the metal plates he wore over his mail hauberk grating. "The way you keep nattering, every blasted City Statesman across the river will hear you and come running."

"You telling me to shut up?" Ravenni said.

Again Korine rolled her eyes.

"What I'm saying," the knight replied, "is that we should all at least attempt to keep it down."

"Tell that to your armor," Ravenni said. "Only an idiot would—"

"Ravenni…" Korine warned.

"I'm just saying—"

"Well, don't."

"What do you want me to do?" Reider said. "Go naked into the fray?"

"Sounds good to me," Ravenni said. "Unless you ain't got nothing worth seeing."

"Show some respect!" Reider said.

"How about you just go back to the others and let us do our job?" Korine suggested.

"Are we expecting trouble?" Anskar asked.

"First rule of scouting," Korine said. "Expect the worst."

She wasn't even breathing heavily, despite the pace Ravenni was setting. Anskar was beginning to sweat.

"And hope for easy pickings along the way," Ravenni added.

"Always looking for plunder, our Ravenni," Korine said with a grin. "When she's not looking for cock."

"I don't need to look for that," Ravenni said, smirking for Anskar's benefit. "Cock comes looking for me."

They pressed on at the same relentless pace, Ravenni

occasionally exiting the woods to gauge the river's depth.

"Tide's retreating," she told them. "So, if there is a ford, it should show itself."

Anskar's knees ached and his limbs felt heavy. Flavin Reider was struggling to keep up too, and Anskar found himself walking beside the knight.

"You're from Branil's Burg, you say?" Reider sounded affable, but there was an edge to his question that brought Anskar's guard up.

"That's right."

"Born in Niyas, were you? During the war?"

"I was."

Reider said nothing for a minute or two as they continued through the forest. Korine and Ravenni had moved so far ahead Anskar could no longer see them, though he heard them talking from time to time.

"My father fought in that bloody war," Reider said. "Died there, too. At Naphor. That evil bitch of a queen and her bloody sorcery did for him."

Anskar said nothing.

"So, being born there and all, does that make you Niyandrian?" Reider said. "That would explain the eyes."

"What about my eyes?"

"Settle down, boy. I'm just making conversation."

"I thought you wanted us to keep quiet."

"The way those old girls are wittering on, what would be the point? You got a surname?"

"DeVantte."

Reider stuck out his bottom lip. "You related to Eldrid?"

"No."

"It's not a common name. Surely there must be—"

"We're not related," Anskar said, and picked up his pace, knowing Reider wouldn't be able to keep up in his armor.

He emerged from the tree line to find Korine sitting on her haunches by the river and Ravenni bending her yew stave so she could string the bow. He noticed the knotted muscles of her arms, the broadness of her back and chest. It took prodigious strength to draw a longbow to its full extent, he had heard, years of practice with ever stiffer and stronger bows. Most men couldn't effectively fire a longbow, let alone a woman, yet Ravenni strung her stave with ease.

"What is it?" he asked.

"Water's shallow here," Korine said, standing and proceeding to string her own bow. "And Ravenni spotted movement on the far bank."

Anskar squinted across the white water, but all he could see was dense undergrowth—bushes and briars and stands of bracken as tall as a man. He could smell woodsmoke on the breeze.

A clash and clatter from behind made Anskar turn. Reider was on his back, flailing around like a flipped turtle. With a great effort, the knight rolled first one way then the other and managed to reach his knees. He paused to catch his breath, then pushed his gauntleted hands against his plate-armored thighs to stand.

"Bloody shitting damn," he said, kicking an exposed tree root. "Never saw the bloody thing poking up out of the ground."

"Quiet," Korine said.

"No need to be so rude," Reider said, smoothing down his mustache.

"Shut up, idiot," Ravenni said.

Reider began to protest, but was cut short by the whistling rush of an arrow from across the lake. It struck his breastplate and bounced off. Reider made a pathetic mewing noise and backed away into the trees, fumbling for his sword.

Anskar spoke a cant, and instantly his ward sphere sprang into existence around him, pure and silver, drawn solely from the dawn-tide. He extended it to encompass Korine and Ravenni, both of whom nodded in acknowledgment.

Reider cast his own ward sphere, but it was watery and weak and flickered as if fear had made him forget how to hold it steady.

Another arrow zipped across the lake to ricochet harmlessly from Anskar's ward. Two more followed in swift succession, one burying its head in the mud with a wet *phwat*, the other vibrating as it embedded itself in the trunk of a tree.

Before Anskar could even register where the bow fire came from, Korine and Ravenni had drawn back their strings and released. There were two muted thuds, twin spurts of blood misting the air across the lake, and a strangled cry.

Half a dozen men poked their heads above the bracken on the far bank, drawing back the strings of short hunting bows, but before they could release, Korine and Ravenni fired their second arrows, and two more men dropped. There was a quick rat-tat-tat as three arrows pinged off Anskar's ward, sending up sparks, and the fourth sailed overhead. Then Ravenni and Korine released again.

This time, Korine's arrow pierced a man's throat, causing him to jerk backwards and collapse into the undergrowth. Ravenni's arrow missed, but she already had another nocked, and as the attackers turned to flee, she took one in the back.

Korine felled another. It looked as though the last man was in the clear, but Ravenni tracked him with her bow, drew the string back to her ear, and sent a shaft looping across the river to rip through his back.

Reider edged out of the tree cover, sword in hand, ward

sphere stuttering. His face was pale, and his sword wavered in his trembling hand.

Ravenni dropped her bow, drew a long hunting knife, and sprinted for the river. The water was shallower there, as Korine had said, and there was a land bridge of steeped mud maybe an inch or so beneath the surface. Ravenni splashed her way across, Korine close on her heels. When they reached the bracken on the far side, Anskar saw their blades go up and down with savage efficiency.

He lowered his ward sphere as Reider approached, the knight's own ward flickering out.

"Had to be done, I suppose," Reider said, wrinkling his nose in distaste as the two women finished off the men they had dropped with arrows.

A pleading cry drifted across the water, terminating in a wailing scream that was abruptly cut off.

"We should join them," Anskar said, drawing *Amalantril*. "In case there are more of them."

"Of course," Reider said. "After you."

Anskar led the way across the partly submerged land bridge, ready to summon his ward sphere at the slightest sign of danger. There was no sign of the two scouts save for the bloody mess they had left behind.

Anskar looked away from the corpse of a man with an arrow protruding from his chest and a grisly red line across his throat spilling blood over the greenery. There were more bodies to the left and right. Reider touched four fingers and thumb to his chest.

"Have you seen battle before?" Anskar asked.

"You call this a battle? I call it a skirmish. Of course I've seen battle. Been fighting since before you were born."

That hardly seemed likely. Reider couldn't have been more than a handful of years older than Anskar.

"So you know how to handle that sword," Anskar said as he scanned the lush pasture beyond the undergrowth. Ravenni and Korine came jogging back toward them.

Reider slammed his sword home in its scabbard. "It would be prideful of me to comment, but let's just say these poor bastards were lucky they didn't come in range of my blade." He made a couple of feints and raised an eyebrow at Anskar, as if he expected applause.

"Maybe next time I'll get to see you in action," Anskar said.

"Well, if you do, stand back, watch, and learn."

"There was a force of about twenty of the bastards hidden out of sight," Ravenni said, tucking her knife back in her belt.

"City States standing army, judging by their livery," Korine said. "They didn't want to be seen, neither, not by the way they fled so fast."

"Why would they attack us?" Reider asked.

"Maybe someone should have sent word ahead that our army needs to cross their lands?" Anskar suggested.

"Why would we do that?" Reider said. "They're supposed to be our allies."

Korine sniffed and shook her head. "Did you bring our bows across the river?"

"Bring?" Reider said. "Bows? Do I look like a pack mule?"

"What you look like," Korine said, "is a useless bleeding fool."

"Or a cock with no balls," Ravenni added.

By the time Ravenni had retrieved the bows and fetched the rest of the army, the tide was high once more and the ford impassable.

There was some discussion between Lanuc and his closest advisors—the trio of knights, Borik, Nul, and Rindon—as to whether they should swim the horses across, but Anskar objected that Braga and her heavily laden wagon would be left behind until the tide was low again. Lanuc's shrug in response annoyed Anskar, so he left the discussion, determined to wait behind with Braga if it came to that.

In the end, though, Lanuc decided it was best to wait for low tide. They hadn't brought enough oilskin to wrap their armor and weapons so they wouldn't rust from exposure to the water; nor did they have enough vinegar and sand to scour the rust away once it set in. Further, the healers complained that some of their herbs and powders wouldn't survive being immersed in water. And so the army set up camp for the night and waited.

Anskar took the time to once again examine his vambrace under the light of the twin moons. Now that he'd resolved never again to use the dusk- and the dark-tide, he was feeling the vambrace's weight, and he had an irrational need to rip it off and cast it into the river. He knew it was futile, but he tried, abrading his fingertips in his efforts to unfasten the clasps that closed the vambrace about his forearm. In frustration, he hammered the divine alloy with a stone, which he then discarded by skimming it across the water.

Braga came from her wagon and offered to take a look at the vambrace for him. She had brought heavy pincers with which she attacked the clasps, and when that didn't work, she returned to her wagon and came back with a hammer, a chisel, and a fine-toothed hacksaw. After an hour of not even scratching the surface, she gave up.

"It's a tough bastard metal," she said. "Keenos's man-tits, how they worked it is a bloody mystery."

"Heat, I imagine," Anskar said. "A lot of it."

Braga made a scoffing noise. "Drakkon's breath, I'd wager. Or a drakkon's fart."

"The forges in Wintotashum…" Anskar started, then remembered that Braga hadn't reacted well the last time they had spoken of the master smith in King Aelfyr's capital city.

"Hrothyr," Braga said, sounding more sullen than enraged this time. "But it makes no difference. We can't use that kind of heat when the vambrace is on your scrawny forearm. Well, we could, but crowds would come, thinking we were cooking bacon, and then everyone would know your dirty secret."

Anskar laughed. *Dirty secret.* He supposed that was what it was, this invisible vambrace: something that bound him to his mother's designs.

He looked up. "Scrawny?"

Braga bellowed a laugh and clapped him on the shoulder, then gathered her tools and returned to the wagon.

Examining the vambrace once more, and thinking about his mother, unsettled Anskar to the point that he knew he wouldn't sleep. Rather than return to his tent, he sought out Josac and asked if he were up to an evening practice.

Josac had been teaching Anskar elements of the combat skills reserved for the Warrior's priests, much of it mental warfare designed to intimidate an opponent, to elicit a particular action from them, which could then be countered; or to goad them into overcommitting to their strikes, thus leaving them off-balance. There was little Josac could teach Anskar about the physical craft of fighting, but the mental edge… Anskar was determined to gain every advantage he could.

Tonight, though, Josac was weary and wanted to rest. However, he offered to speak about the Warrior's Fire ability

Anskar had stolen from Gann.

"You may be able to temper it," Josac said. "Eke out its power a little at a time, so that you don't leave yourself drained—though I never mastered the technique."

"What would be the point?" Anskar said. "It's tainted by the dusk-tide, so I'll never use it again."

Leaving Josac to bed down for the night, Anskar walked along the river's edge, wrapped in his cloak. The night was cold, but there was little wind and no rain. He filled his lungs with cleansing air and wandered toward one of the patrols Lanuc had set up along the bank in case of more trouble from the City States' side.

As he drew nearer, he recognized the three knights bundled up beneath cloaks as Lanuc's men: Rindon, Nul, and Borik. Anskar had never seen any of the trio alone, and he had the odd impression that they were bound together in some way, three persons in one. There was something in the way the three men shadowed each other as they moved, the way they finished each other's sentences, laughed at each other's jokes, ate together, drank together.

Of course, Anskar realized, he could be reading too much into it. The most likely explanation was that they had trained together and fought side by side for many years—they weren't exactly young men. Anskar put Rindon and Borik in their late thirties, and Nul looked even older, but that might have been because he was rake thin with scarcely an ounce of fat on him, and his thickly curled beard and close-cropped hair had more gray than black.

"Anskar DeVantte," Rindon said, good humor in his rumbling voice. Rindon was the shortest of the three and also the fattest. He was moonfaced and ruddy-cheeked, with a shock of hair starting to gray, and a thick, unruly mustache that dangled down to his chin. "Something to warm your cockles?" he asked, proffering a wineskin.

"Thank you, but no," Anskar said, immediately cursing himself for his stiff, awkward manner. Drinking on duty wasn't permitted, and he knew his manner conveyed criticism to the older man.

"If it's Lanuc you're worried about, lad, you've no need," Rindon said, taking a swig of wine and wiping his lips with the back of his hand. "He's a stickler for the rules, but even he makes an exception for heroes."

"More a case of pitying the drunkard who was once a half-capable knight," Nul said, his eyes on the far shore of the lake, which was wreathed in heavy shadows.

"Hah!" Rindon said. "A palpable hit. You have wounded me mortally, old friend. Borik, defend me against this cadaverous old fiend."

Borik, by far the largest of the three, said nothing. He was a head and a half taller than Anskar, who was by no means short, and he had the neck and shoulders of an ox. Like the others, Borik wore no armor, only a cloak, though his was of bearskin, fastened at the neck by a heavy steel chain. Both his hands were clasped around a staff that came up to his chin, and which was for some reason wrapped in oilskin. And then Anskar saw: beneath Borik's hands was what looked like a cross-guard angled down toward the ground, bound about with strips of oilskin.

"Is that a sword?" Anskar asked.

"Uh-oh," Rindon said, glancing at Nul, who rolled his eyes.

"*The* sword," Borik said.

"The?"

"It's not just any old sword," Rindon put in helpfully.

"Not one sword among others," Nul said, feigning a yawn.

"This," Borik said, raising the oilskin-wrapped weapon above his head and gazing up at it, "is the Sword of Supremacy, a perfect facsimile of the Sword of Menselas, which smote so many of the pretender gods."

"You've seen the Sword of Menselas?" Anskar asked. The way Brother Tion always spoke about the god's sword, Anskar had assumed it was a metaphor for righteousness and truth.

"The Five inspired me," Borik said, lowering the blade. The hilt was a good foot and a half long, more than enough to accommodate two gauntleted hands. The blade was close to six feet in length. The Sword of Supremacy must have been a fearsome weapon: a two-handed greatsword that only a giant like Borik could wield.

"What he means," Rindon said, taking a slug of wine, "is he was drunk."

"Was not," Borik said.

"More likely it was a case of the nightmares that come when a man stops drinking too suddenly," Nul said.

"It was a vision, I tell you," Borik insisted.

"Like the harlot back in Kyuth with the pendulous breasts?" Rindon said. "For there was a vision to widen the eyes of Menselas—all five aspects of him!"

"You may mock," Borik said, no trace of anger in his voice, only a weary good humor, "but you have seen what this old blade can do. You have seen her sated on the blood of our enemies."

"And rusted by it," Nul said. "You really should oil the blade and scour it with sand and vinegar."

"Don't let a little rust fool you," Borik said. "Many have made that mistake, only to find their own blades shattered by the Sword of Supremacy, their bones crushed, their flesh ripped asunder."

"Last time I looked, it wasn't just a little rust," Rindon said. "And the blade is so chipped, I thought you'd made it that way to saw through the spines of your foes."

"Let not the outward appearance of a thing blind you to the reality of what it is inside."

"I am not in the least bit blinded," Rindon said. "The reality is, the Sword of Supremacy is as riddled with rust inside as she is outside. The only wonder is—and here I am willing to grant the possibility of a miraculous intervention by the Five—that the blade has not shattered into a thousand brown and crumbling pieces yet. But it will, I'll wager."

Borik shook his head and gave Anskar a look that said he despaired of his companions. "You see where lack of faith leads a man? There is no wonder in the world these days, no belief in a higher power."

"Now you go too far," Nul said. "To express doubt about your claim that the sword is rusty on the outside but somehow divinely blessed and beyond compare in contradistinction to its appearance is hardly the same thing as a denial of the truth of Menselas."

"One and the other are intrinsically bound," Borik said. "If the sword's crafting was divinely inspired, then it is a sacrament of the god's hidden nature, an instrument of his will."

"Of course it is," Rindon said in a kindly tone. Then to Anskar, "That which is corroded by rust isn't necessarily a poorly crafted piece of shit. Isn't that right, Nul?"

"Indubitably."

Borik shook his head and gave a wry smile, followed up with a good-natured chuckle.

"May I see it?" Anskar asked, feeling a certain reverence despite the mockery of Nul and Rindon.

"No," Borik said, suddenly grim. "And you must never ask again."

"I'm sorry," Anskar said, wondering what he had done wrong.

"It's not you, lad," Rindon said. "Borik is superstitious about the sword. He only unwraps it just before a battle. Reveal the blade under any other circumstances, he believes, and the god's power will leave it."

"That is true," Borik said.

"The reality, of course," Nul said, "is that he doesn't want any more damp to get at the metal and speed the spread of the rust."

"And you made the sword?" Anskar asked Borik.

"For my trials before rising to the rank of knight-inferior."

"That was a way back," Nul said. "For all of us."

"We were postulants together," Rindon said, taking another swig of wine. "With Lanuc. Good times."

"But what I don't understand," Anskar said, unconsciously fingering the hilt of his own sword, "is why the blade would rust if you imbued it with the dawn-tide and blended astrumium into the steel."

He had done as much with *Amalantril*, before the blade was tested against the mace of Beof Harril—thus starting the feud that had only now ended with the death of Gann. At least, Anskar hoped it had ended. Beof, of course, was still alive.

"Ah, now you come to the crux of the matter," Nul said.

"I did blend in astrumium," Borik said, adding, with a narrow-eyed glare at his two companions, "in just the right quantity. And I did imbue the blade with dawn-tide sorcery so it would never lose its edge."

"Then what happened?" Anskar asked.

"A witch cursed him," Rindon said.

"Technically, she was a whore," Nul put in.

Rindon made a show of clutching his crotch. "Gave him the pox, she did. A foul-faced, big-bottomed pig of a woman. Poor Borik was scratching and moaning for weeks. He had weeping sores all over his… It was horrible. The only way we could help him was to pray for Menselas to remove the pox, which he graciously did, under the ministrations of the healers."

"But Menselas does not simply remove things from existence," Nul explained. "The pox he took from Borik had to go somewhere."

"And so it went into his sword," Rindon finished, as if everything was now crystal clear.

"They jest," Borik told Anskar. "And not in good taste."

"Do I look like I'm laughing?" Rindon said. "The sword has a sexually communicated disease."

Nul nodded solemnly, then gave Anskar a discreet wink. Anskar laughed, feeling as if he were back on the *Exultant*, listening to Captain Hadlor's tall stories and bad jokes.

"So, enough about Borik and his pox-ridden weapon," Rindon said. "Tell us about yourself, Anskar DeVantte, and how you came to be under Lanuc's protection."

"Lanuc told you that?" Anskar asked.

Nul grinned. "With enough booze inside him, Lanuc blabs like an old woman. Vihtor Ulnar was your mentor in Branil's Burg, I hear. A good man. One of the few remaining."

"I like Vihtor well enough," Borik said. "Broke my arm once in a fight."

"You fought Vihtor?"

"Over that fat pig of a woman," Rindon said. "Despite his broken arm, Borik won, though I imagine in hindsight he would rather have not."

"You're joking again," Anskar said. "Vihtor isn't like that."

"Not like what?" Rindon said.

"He doesn't go with whores."

The trio exchanged looks, then Nul changed the subject.

But they had sown further doubt in Anskar—not just about Vihtor, a man he looked up to and respected, but about the Order of Eternal Vigilance and what it stood for. After all Anskar had observed of the knights' behavior, not only in Kyuth but also at sea, and in Atya where they had stopped to sell the Niyandrian slaves, the Order struck him as little different to Borik's sword. Indeed, the Sword of Supremacy struck him not so much as a sacrament or a symbol of Menselas as it did a symbol of the Order itself: rusted through and through, corroded, brittle, and ready to shatter into a thousand pieces at the slightest application of force.

Of the three companions, Anskar judged Nul to be not only the oldest but the wisest, the most prudent; and while he shared the good humor of Borik and Rindon, there was a serious edge to Nul that kept the others in check.

"So, what do you know about the foul mood that's overtaken our Lanuc? I've never seen such a scowl on his comely face."

"Gisela," Anskar said.

"Thought as much," Rindon said. "Didn't I say as much?"

Borik grunted in affirmation.

"They've had a falling-out," Anskar explained.

And then he remembered that he hadn't yet spoken with Gisela. But he couldn't face doing that tonight, and so after he had filled in the three knights about the conflict that had arisen between Gisela and Lanuc, Anskar bade Rindon, Nul, and Borik goodnight and retired to his tent, where he triggered his ward sphere on and off until its strobing light eventually lulled him to sleep.

# THIRTEEN

THE ARMY FORDED THE RIVER at midmorning the next day. The tide had receded so that the land bridge became visible just beneath the surface of the water. Even so, it was a slow crossing, the knights and the retainers walking their horses to lighten the load.

The riverbed grew treacherous from the passage of so many horses, and when Braga attempted the crossing in her wagon, the wheels gouged deep ruts in the wet earth and became bogged down.

Josac and Anskar unloaded Braga's heavy equipment and carried it across, aided by Nul, Rindon, and Borik. It was hard work, and by the end of it Anskar's knees were burning and his pants sodden from the steadily rising water. But with the wagon emptied of its load, the twin oxen were able to pull its wheels free and cross to the far side.

As Anskar rested a few short minutes before reloading the

wagon, he caught sight of Gisela watching him, but the moment he glanced at her, she looked away.

Once the army got underway again, they made quick progress, following an old cattle track across sparse and brown grassland, heading north toward the border with the City States. By nightfall, they were a mere few miles away, but the scouts spotted the orange glow of campfires half a mile to the east.

"City States patrols, no doubt," Josac said as he, Anskar, and Braga shared a supper of jerked beef and double-baked bread around a fire of their own. "Bastards are supposed to be on our side, but they've been nothing but trouble."

"You're not wrong there," Anskar said, thinking back to the skirmish by the river. "But what can we do?"

"I know what I'd bloody well do," Braga said around a mouthful of bread and jerky. She patted the hilt of her sword, which lay beside her on the ground.

To Anskar's mind, the weapon had more the look of a giant cleaver, but he knew how devastating it was in Braga's hands. It wasn't as long as Borik's greatsword, perhaps, but it was just as impressive. He shuddered as he imagined the two blades clashing in the hands of their gigantic owners. And then he chuckled. The Sword of Supremacy would disintegrate into a million rust-browned fragments, and Borik would lose.

In the morning, Nul woke Anskar and told him Lanuc wanted him to go with them to confront the City States patrol that had clearly been trailing them the previous day. For good measure, Lanuc sent out parties of scouts east, west, and back south the way they had come. Korine and Ravenni were among them.

Lanuc's group, which seemed dangerously small to Anskar, rode the half mile east through a straggle of trees until they could smell roasting pork on the embers of the previous night's fires.

"An early breakfast, methinks," Rindon said. "Do you suppose they'll let us join them?"

Before anyone could answer, Anskar felt a tug inside his skull, and his ward sphere flashed into existence. He whirled his horse to face the threat, but already it was neutralized. A cloaked and hooded man rose from his crouched position and raised his arms overhead, letting his loaded crossbow drop to the ground, where it discharged harmlessly.

From the trees behind the man emerged Ravenni, arrow nocked to the string of her longbow. On the other side of the City States scout stood Korine, her bow bent so far back that the goose-feathered flight of her arrow almost touched her ear.

"I thought I sent you two south," Lanuc said, riding his horse up to the captured man.

"We saw this cretin circling behind you," Ravenni said. "Did we do wrong to follow him?"

"No," Lanuc said, though he spoke through clenched teeth. "You did well."

"I meant no harm," the City States scout said.

"Then why was your crossbow loaded?" Korine asked, taking the tension off her bowstring but leaving the arrow nocked.

"I was going to hail you," the man insisted. "The crossbow was just in case. You can't be too careful these days."

Rindon let out a guffaw and twirled one end of his dangling mustache. "I like you, lad," he said. "Can't be too careful! And I thought we were among friends."

"You are," a woman's voice said.

Anskar turned his horse, as did the others, to see a line of City States soldiers step from the trees to the east. They were armed with short stabbing swords and carried round wooden shields with iron bosses and rims. The woman who had spoken wore a crimson cloak, and her long gray hair was bound with silver twine. Like the dozen or so men and women she stood at the center of, she was armored in a chain hauberk, above which she wore a dark blue surcoat with the crenellated tower emblem of the City States embroidered on its front in white.

"And you are?" Lanuc said.

"Commander Lyrian Albec. I know what this must look like to you."

"Not good," Lanuc agreed. "I assume you know what happened at the crossing?"

"The ford over the River Untwep? Yes, I know. Those responsible have been disciplined."

"Court-martialed, I would hope," Lanuc said.

"Disciplined. The captain made an error of judgment. He hadn't expected a friendly force so close to our lands. No one told us the Order of Eternal Vigilance was sending a small army into the City States. Or why."

"Your people would have recognized our livery. They knew who we were," Lanuc said.

"An experienced officer would have," Commander Albec agreed, "and in less tense times."

"Times are tense?"

The commander hesitated before she answered. "To the north, there is trouble between the Soreshi and the Thousand Lakes."

"I'm aware of that," Lanuc said. "King Aelfyr no doubt sent to the City States for aid, before, in desperation, he came to us."

"That's why you're here? You ride to the aid of the Thousand Lakes?"

"And you did not?" Borik said, steering his horse alongside Lanuc's, the bundled-up Sword of Supremacy slung across his back.

Lanuc waved the big man to silence.

"It's a delicate balance," the commander said. "The Soreshi are not our enemy, and neither is King Aelfyr."

"But the Soreshi are the aggressors," Lanuc said. "And the terms of our alliance state—"

"I know what our obligations are, as do our rulers in Selemis."

Selemis: the City at the Juncture. Anskar had been taught that it had been built to appease the leaders of the chief cities that comprised the City States, who couldn't decide which of them should be preeminent. The solution had been to build a new city some two hundred years ago at a point roughly equidistant between the rivals. Of course, the distance wasn't entirely accurate, but the sentiment was genuine, and the rivals had been appeased. And so the City States came to have a new hub, a capital purpose-built for government. It was a bland place, according to Brother Tion, who had once been sent there in penance for a minor transgression. "Everything looks the same," he had complained to Anskar. "The houses, the walls, the churches—all built from the same nondescript white stone. And it's clean! Too clean for human habitation."

"The Soreshi are not united in their attacks upon the Thousand Lakes," Commander Albec went on. "A faction has emerged among them: a large and powerful group from the Ymaltian Mountains, which acts independently."

"A Soreshi civil war?" Lanuc asked.

"Not yet, but it probably soon will be. The Soreshi were ever a tribal people, given to warring among themselves; but as you know, that came to an end with the appointment of a High Sorcerer to lord it over them. The current High Sorcerer has been invited to Selemis to give an account of what is happening. She has yet to respond."

"And meanwhile," Lanuc said, "these other Soreshi—what do we call them? Rebel Soreshi? Insurgents?—are free to make incursions into King Aelfyr's land."

Commander Albec shrugged. "That's as much as I know. I'm not privy to all the dealings of the League of Cities that govern in Selemis. All I can say is, the political situation is complex, and my betters are trying to work out the best way forward."

"While Thousand Lakes burns!" Borik said, and this time Lanuc flashed him an angry glare.

"The important thing," Commander Albec said, "is that there is no ill will between the City States and Kaile."

"You should have thought about that before opening fire on my people," Lanuc said.

"It was a mistake," the commander repeated, though she was convincing no one.

Anskar couldn't see what the City States had to gain from angering neighboring Kaile, but then he was new to the politics of the mainland. Perhaps there was opportunity in the chaos currently enfolding the Thousand Lakes kingdom to the north. Perhaps the League of Cities that met in Selemis sensed a shift in the balance of power and were starting to flex their muscles. Or perhaps it had indeed been a mistake made by an inexperienced and jumpy captain. Anskar was glad that he wasn't the one having to make decisions.

"As I stated earlier," Commander Albec said, "the captain responsible has been disciplined, and I can personally guarantee there will be no further mistakes on our part."

"Oh?" Lanuc said. "And how do you propose to do that?"

"Because we will escort you to the northern border."

"But that's a good three days' ride."

"Two, if we take the old road the ancients built. Much of it is grown over and hidden, but it's familiar to me."

Lanuc clenched his jaw, considering for a long moment. Finally he nodded his agreement. "Then I accept, Commander. You have my thanks."

Lanuc's force followed the City States patrol north along the disused roadway. Its flagstones were cracked and furred with moss and mold, and some of the stones were missing, scavenged no doubt by locals for use in the drystone walls that enclosed the few farmsteads they passed. Nevertheless, the road was a wonder to behold, crossing hundreds of miles of otherwise untamed wilderness. In places, the ancients had cleft a path through the center of hills, forming their own artificial valley for the road to pass through, and Anskar wondered how they had achieved such a feat.

"Giants with mattocks," Braga suggested. Anskar was once more riding up front with her in the ox-drawn wagon.

"Which begs the question," Josac said, riding alongside, "of what happened to the giants?"

"My great-grandpa was one," Braga said. Anskar glanced at her, but she was straight-faced. "Borik's was too."

Braga had been impressed by the knight's size when Anskar had introduced them. Borik, for his part, had been wide-eyed and incapable of speech, though it was hard to tell if that was from attraction or fear.

"Seriously?" Josac asked.

Braga shook her head and snorted.

Commander Albec advised that they stop and make camp beside the road before dusk. There were creatures that stalked the night this far from the population centers, she said—dead-eyes and worse—and the sooner they got their campfires blazing the better.

As had been their way since leaving Sansor, Lanuc's force split into groups, each with their own fire, around which their tents were clustered. Commander Albec's patrol kept to themselves, setting up their own camp on the brow of a low hill a few hundred yards away. She claimed it was a good vantage from which to watch for danger, and she was probably being truthful, Anskar decided, but there was no denying the tense atmosphere that remained between the City States soldiers and the knights from Kaile.

As usual, Braga prepared the bed of her wagon for her to sleep in. Anskar helped her move the anvil and other heavy equipment to make space for her bedroll.

Dusk arrived as they finished, and Anskar winced as the tide blew over and through him. He tensed every muscle in his body as he refused it entry. His dusk-tide repository clenched and twisted in what he could only describe as anger. The barriers he had erected around it buckled and stretched, but as the dusk-tide passed, his repository settled back down.

After he had pitched his tent, Anskar left Braga to feed grain to her oxen and exchange insults with Josac while he went to find Gisela.

The night was clear and still, the air cool but with no breeze to speak of. The twin moons were both razor-sharp crescents, one white, the other crimson, and the stars spangling the velvet blackness of the sky shone with a steely intensity.

Gisela was at prayer with half a dozen other priests of the Healer when Anskar found her. The healers' tents were arranged in a circle around the healthy blaze of a heaped fire. The priests were all cowled and kneeling, but it wasn't hard to recognize

Gisela from her slender frame and the way she managed to keep her impeccable posture: shoulders back and chest proud, despite her head being dipped in prayer.

Anskar waited until they had finished, then approached Gisela as the priests began to share out their rations.

"You've come to speak for my father?" she said as they moved to the edge of the camp so they could talk privately.

"Can you read me so easily?"

"I know him."

"He's sorry, Gisela. I see it in his face. He looks terrible."

Gisela sniffed. Her shoulders hunched up around her ears, and she tucked her hands into the sleeves of her robe.

"He was trying to assuage any trouble we might have had at Kyuth," Anskar said.

"By consorting with heathens?"

"It wasn't consorting."

Though in actual fact it was. Lanuc had drunk from the Lady's chalice, after all.

"This is difficult for me," he told Gisela, "because—"

"Because you agree with me," she said. "Don't deny it. I know you do. I was your confessor, remember?"

Anskar felt the hot flush of embarrassment on his cheeks.

"You take your faith seriously," she went on. "You meet the demands head on."

"Not always," Anskar said.

"But you admit your faults, you crave forgiveness, and you strive to do better."

"Isn't that what your father's trying to do? He's sorry, I tell you. He knows he made a mistake."

"This is not just about *his* soul," Gisela snapped. "He tried to coerce us into committing the same abomination."

"I wouldn't use the word coerce," Anskar said.

"To endanger another's soul is the worst of offenses. It's right there in the scriptures!"

"So," Anskar said, suddenly growing cold toward her, "this is about you, about *your* soul?"

"It is not about me!"

"Your father didn't make you stay and drink from the chalice. He never even protested when you stormed out of the church like that."

"He had no right to!"

"Do you think he's drawn down a curse on himself?" Anskar asked. "Or worse, cursed our mission?"

Gisela shrugged, then shook her head. "That is not the nature of Menselas."

"No," Anskar said, and added pointedly, "It's his nature to forgive."

"I'll think about it," she said.

"Gisela…"

"I said I'll think about it. And pray. And tell my father…"

"Tell him what?"

"Tell him to pray too."

Commander Albec hadn't been lying: following the ancient road shaved a whole day off their journey north. When they arrived at the border, Anskar was surprised there was no line of demarcation, no checkpoint like the ones the Order had established in Niyas after the conquest. One minute the road cut through City States lands, the next, Commander Albec informed them they had arrived in the Kingdom of the Thousand Lakes.

Anskar knew he was being foolish, but he had expected some change in the scenery—a lake perhaps. Lots of lakes. Smoke-topped mountains. Forests of pine. But it was just the same endless scrubland, the same straight road, the same distant low hills and thin forests.

As Lanuc bade Commander Albec and her troops farewell and watched them ride away back down the road, Braga, seated beside Anskar at the front of the wagon, sniffed the air, and eyed the black clouds stacked high on the northern horizon.

"My tits are tingling," she said. "That means it's going to snow."

She was right. Within the hour, the snow came, hard and fast and freezing. Anskar hunkered down beneath a bearskin cloak Braga dug out from the back of the wagon for him, which he wore over his white woolen one. Still, he felt frozen to the bones.

The oxen that pulled the wagon wore a fine dusting of snow, though they showed no indication of being bothered by it. Onwards they plodded, pulling their heavy load, and for once the wagon didn't fall far behind the rest of the army, for the horses could only make slow progress through the white and frigid blanket covering the ground.

Braga seemed unperturbed by the drop in temperature. If anything, it improved her usually irascible mood, and Anskar wondered if that was because she enjoyed watching the knights riding ahead of them shivering in their saddles and grumbling about the cold.

The ancient road petered out a few miles beyond the border, as if these were untamed lands that even the might of that ancient civilization had been unable to conquer. One plodding step after the next, Lanuc's small force made its way north, always heading toward a distant range of mountains that never seemed to get any closer.

Whenever they stopped, it was all but impossible to get a decent fire burning, so everyone ate mostly dried rations, which only added to the ill temper of the knights and those traveling with them.

It was when they reached the foothills of the mountain range that Josac spotted the watchers and rode his horse up the column to report what he had seen to Lanuc.

The four riders stood high up on a steady incline of shale and scree that skirted the first stepped ascent to the snowcapped peaks in the distance. It wasn't horses they were mounted upon but some kind of large, long-horned mountain goats fitted with bridles and saddles. The riders were cloaked against the cold in what looked like wolfskins, and each held a long-shafted spear. All had long, wild hair, but other than an impression of pale skin, Anskar could make out no more of their features at such a distance. As he watched, they turned their mounts and rode away up the incline and out of sight behind an outcrop of rock.

"Goat-shagging, piss-stinking, turd-eating Soreshi," Braga said.

"You've seen them before?" Anskar asked.

"Nope. Just heard stories about them, and don't like what I heard."

"Don't you think you're being unreasonable?"

"I'm always unreasonable. That way idiots like you leave me well alone."

Anskar was so taken aback that he swallowed the lump that had formed around any retort he might make.

Braga rumbled out a laugh and slapped him on the back, and then he felt foolish.

"You snot-sucking piece of cow dung," he said, and she

nodded approvingly.

"Finally. I was starting to think you as slow-witted as something that drizzled from a dead-eye's…" She trailed off as Josac came riding back down the column.

"Lanuc wants you," the Warrior's priest told Anskar as he reined in beside the wagon.

"Is this about the Soreshi?"

Josac scowled. "It should be, but it isn't. He reckons there are too few of them to threaten us, even if they wanted to. Ignore them, he says, and they'll go away."

Braga grunted with derision. "So what's he want to speak with ass-wipe about, then?"

"I can guess," Anskar said, jumping down from the wagon and going to untether his horse.

As he'd expected, Lanuc was angry that Gisela hadn't accepted his apology, or if she had, she was making him wait in order to prolong his agony.

"You told her I'm humiliated by what I did?" Lanuc said as he rode ahead of the army with Anskar.

"I told her you regretted drinking from the Lady's chalice. I told her you seek her forgiveness, and that it is the nature of Menselas to forgive."

"And?" Lanuc prompted.

"She said she would think about it."

"She said what?"

"That she would—"

"I know what she said! But who in the name of the Five does she think she is? She's my daughter, for the Five's sake! I thought priests of the Healer were sworn to humility and obedience."

"I think maybe she's struggling—"

"She's struggling with family duty!" Lanuc said. "Too damned rigid, she is. I tell you, those bloody healers… it's like a cult."

"You want me to speak with her again?" Anskar asked. "I'm not exactly comfortable as the go-between."

Lanuc looked up at the white-capped peaks that grew taller and more oppressive with every mile. The army was threading its way along a broad gorge that gouged a path through the foothills, and Anskar repeatedly scanned the heights for any sign of goat-riding Soreshi.

"No," Lanuc said. "I've done my part. The next move is hers."

Anskar fell back behind, eventually rejoining Josac to ride alongside Braga's wagon.

"How did that go?" the Warrior's priest asked.

"Like shit, I'd say," Braga said, "judging by your face, asswipe."

Anskar didn't even bother to laugh. He wasn't in the mood.

# FOURTEEN

SOMETHING ABOUT THE SORESHI THEY had spotted earlier had unnerved Anskar, and there was a growing pressure in his skull. In response, his ward sphere almost burst unbidden to life around him, but he quickly shut off the flow from his dawn-tide repository. His ward was growing too sensitive, taking it upon itself to manifest at the slightest intimation of danger. In some ways that was a good thing, but he didn't want the silvery sphere appearing at an inopportune moment, or if he needed to retain the element of surprise.

A steady snowfall started around midmorning and showed no sign of relenting, so Lanuc called a halt for the night in the shelter of a craggy escarpment.

After avoiding the worst of the dusk-tide by hunkering down in the back of Braga's wagon, Anskar ate a few scraps of jerked meat and hard bread, then worked with Josac on swordplay—feints, stance-switching, and the use of posture and eye-contact to intimidate and convey confidence.

Some of these ploys of the Warrior's priests struck him as mere trickery, but Josac tried to impress upon him the need for every advantage when fighting at the highest level.

Again, the priest tried to encourage Anskar in the use of the Warrior's Fire, and again Anskar refused. Mitigate his vow in one thing, he knew, and he would make exceptions in others.

During the night, when he lay shivering inside his tent, he became aware of the relentless scratch of the dark-tide against his repository. His barriers were strong, but it felt as though he were in a bubble of air surrounded by an endless expanse of angry, corrosive sea.

At some point in the night, the Soreshi must have made their way into the camp, evading the sentries Lanuc had positioned about the site. In the morning, there were boot prints in the snow. Salted meat and double-baked bread had been taken, along with grain sacks for the animals. Several knights complained of weapons or pieces of armor stolen from their tents as they slept.

"Harassment," Josac explained around the breakfast fire, after he and Anskar had greeted the dawn-tide together, to the accompaniment of Braga's loud snoring from the back of her wagon. "It's a tactic to wear a force down."

"You think they'll attack us?" Anskar asked.

"Not if numbers are anything to go by. We saw four, and now they're saying there's a dozen or more, but still not enough to threaten us in the open. Probably they've been told to make our lives miserable, in the hope that we'll run out of food and decide we're better off turning round and going back home."

"And will we, do you think?"

"I'm not the man to ask," Josac said. "Your friend Lanuc's in command, remember. But if it were me, I'd make the bastards pay for what they did last night. It's the only way to discourage them from doing the same thing in the future."

"Bastards never pay," Braga said as she poked her head out from beneath the tarp that covered her wagon. "That's why they're bastards."

The next night, after a long hard day of picking their way through snowdrifts and ascending an ice-slicked incline that took them higher into the mountains, the army sheltered in a network of blowholes in the surrounding rock faces. Josac said he'd seen such things before, and that long ago the caves were probably made by surges of boiling mud that had erupted from the roots of the mountains.

"Not lava?" Anskar asked.

"Mud, I tell you," Josac said. "Steaming hot mud."

"Sounds a whole lot like dung to me," Braga said. "Makes you wonder about the size of the ass it came from. A demon lord, probably. Or a drakkon."

Josac rolled his eyes. "A priest of the Elder told me about the mud and the blowholes. Said it was a phenomenon peculiar to the Thousand Lakes. Probably that's why they have so many lakes, on account of the mud leaving craters all over the place."

"I still ain't seen a lake," Braga complained. "Not since we crossed the border."

"You will, don't you worry," Josac said. "Soon you'll be complaining of seeing nothing else."

Braga snorted, then her eyes widened as she caught a glimpse of something outside the shallow cave they were sheltering in. When she stepped out into the bracing night air where she had left her wagon and oxen, Anskar went with her.

Smoke plumed like misted breath from the caverns that pocked the rock face. Some of the knights had chanced lighting fires, trusting that the smoke wouldn't fill the interior. Anskar, Braga, and Josac had thought about it but eventually decided to rely on the warmth of their cloaks and the cave walls to shield them from the night breeze.

The sky was starless, but not uniformly black. Braga pointed across the gorge to where wispy green lights were capering and dancing high up on a mountain ledge. Higher still, the sky surrounding the summit was awash with green and blue and purple: a shimmering sea of light that bathed the mountainside in an undulating glow.

"Bloody sorcery," she said.

Faint upon the gathering breeze, Anskar could hear an echoing, repetitive chant. He strained to listen but didn't recognize the language.

"They're cursing us," Josac said. Anskar hadn't heard the priest step outside to join them. "By the Five, I hate Soreshi. They have an affinity for sorcery that, to my mind, makes them no better than demons. Like the bloody Niyandrians. No offense, Anskar. And in any case, you're not Niyandrian, are you? Well, maybe half, but the stronger half is winning out, isn't it?"

Anskar didn't take offense, which surprised him.

"Yes," he said. "Yes, I think it is."

Braga had run out of the hard bread she claimed sustained her and had drunk her last skin of beer, and she had done nothing but grumble about it as the wagon clanked and clattered along behind the rest of the army.

The mountain road they were following wound its way deeper and higher into the range. The wagon made slow progress, and once or twice Anskar had to jump down and clear rocks from the road.

"All we need now's a bloody broken wheel," Braga grumbled.

Josac, riding ahead, shot back over his shoulder, "Maybe then you'll leave that hunk of junk behind and take one of the spare horses. Least then we might look like we were part of the army and not just easy prey for the Soreshi."

"I don't ride, camel face," Braga said. "And I ain't leaving my wagon behind. It was my ma's wagon, and her ma's before her. And who's going to pay for all the equipment I'd have to leave behind? You?"

"Certainly not," Josac said. "Not that it's worth anything."

"Not to you maybe, you festering piece of toad shit," Braga said. "But it is to me."

Braga's bad mood showed no signs of relenting, and Anskar untethered his horse so he could ride up front with Josac.

"What do you know about the Soreshi?" Anskar asked the Warrior's priest as he came alongside.

"I know that I don't like them. I once faced off against one back when I was a slave fighting in the pits. Shifty bastard, he was. Pale-skinned and long-haired. The other slaves mocked him, called him a woman, but he killed most of them in the pits, one after another. As his reputation grew, the insults stopped. Me, I was never one for insults back then, and us Warrior's priests are taught that careless use of insults make you appear weak to your foe, so we employ them strategically."

Anskar edged his horse closer and whispered, "You think Braga's weak, then?"

"I do not. That there is a strong woman, and a big one to boot. And those jugs!"

"You like Braga? You fancy her?"

"I fancy those breasts. What man wouldn't? But, by Menselas, I pity the man who tries anything on with her. She could crush your spine with those massive hands, not to mention what she could do to your nether regions. No, far safer to observe from a distance and admire."

"So, what happened?" Anskar asked.

"With Braga? Nothing, more's the pity."

"Not with Braga. With the Soreshi in the fight pits."

"I killed him."

"With sorcery?"

Josac shook his head. "Didn't have none back then. It was before I became a priest of the Warrior, remember?"

"Then how?"

Josac grimaced, remembering. "The Soreshi bastard used subtle sorcery that the fight crowd couldn't see. Whenever he touched his opponents with his hands—when he punched or poked or grabbed hold of them—they would shriek and writhe and sometimes spasm. Most of the people who watch pit fights are morons, ignorant as… I'm sure Braga would have the words. My point is, the crowd didn't notice. They would've put down the screams and the twitching to some high-level skill the Soreshi possessed. But by then I'd been fighting for years, and I knew a cheater when I saw one. I watched his fights carefully and examined the corpses he left in his wake."

"They were fights to the death?"

"A pit fighter is only as good as his last victory. You lose in some of these so-called civilized fight squares and you live to fight another day. But that doesn't happen in the pits. Lose there and you lose for good. Which is why it's important to take steps to ensure that you don't lose."

"You learned to cheat too?"

Josac glared at him. "I did not, and don't you ever imply that I did."

"I'm sorry," Anskar said. "Then what…?"

"Like I said, I observed the cheating bastard. When it came time to fight him, I feinted, he raised his hands to protect his face, and I grabbed him by both wrists. He struggled like a demon, but I was stronger than him and I forced his hands into his own face. Menselas, how he screamed. Foam came from his mouth, and a lot of blood—I think he bit his tongue. All I felt was intense heat radiating out from his hands, and ripples of… not quite pain… that shot along my arms and made me twitch. Then the skin of his face started to slough away and drip into his neck. His eyes swelled and bubbled until finally they burst. And the smell—it was like you get at a pig roast, when the fat sizzles on the flames below. There were those in the crowd who jeered—they thought I was the one cheating. But the owners knew—the men who organized the fights and put vast amounts of coin on their slaves to win. Many of them had long suspected there was Soreshi sorcery involved, and they'd lost a lot of money to the bastard's cheating. That was why they supported my victory—vengeance against the slaver who had owned the Soreshi, and a chance to promote a new champion: me."

"You have burn scars?" Anskar asked.

Josac shook his head. "Never once let the bastard touch me with his hands. When it came time to select weapons, I asked only for thick leather gloves, the sort blacksmiths use." He nodded over his shoulder toward Braga, who was glowering from the driver's seat of her wagon. "First law of fighting, Anskar: know your enemy, then turn his strengths against him."

As Lanuc's force navigated a series of high passes, the Soreshi began to follow them openly, riding along the ridges on their massive goats. There were now more than a dozen visible at any one time.

Lanuc ordered the knights to wear full armor and to ride their destriers instead of the faster-moving palfreys. Of course, that slowed their progress considerably, but it also meant Braga's wagon wasn't left lagging so far behind.

At night, sentries were doubled, yet things still went missing. Not just small items, either. On their third night in the mountain range, Anskar awoke to hear Braga swearing and Josac trying in vain to calm her.

"What is it?" Anskar asked as he emerged from his tent.

There were tears streaking down Braga's cheeks as she pointed at her wagon. "My oxen! The goat-shagging scrotum-faces have stolen my oxen."

Lanuc was sent for, and shook his head in bewilderment. "How in the Five's name could they sneak into our camp unnoticed and spirit away two oxen?"

Josac hawked and spat. "Sorcery," he said, then to Anskar, "Know your enemy."

It was agreed that Braga had to abandon her wagon and proceed on foot, because nothing anyone said would entice her to ride a horse. Anskar suspected it was because she was conscious of her weight and wanted to avoid the embarrassment of crushing the horse beneath her.

Braga insisted on bringing a selection of tools, and even tried to carry her anvil. She managed to struggle on with it for half a mile, then dropped it into a snowdrift and left it behind.

"The ghost lady will curse me," she said miserably.

"Because she wanted you to work on my vambrace?" Anskar asked.

Braga shrugged. She didn't really know.

"Did she say anything about trying to forge similar pieces of armor for me?" He was remembering his vision of the armor crafted from divine alloy: the Armor of Divinity.

Braga shook her head. "If that's what she wants, my portable forge wouldn't be up to the task anyway. Nor would my forge back home. We'd need something hotter to work the divine alloy. Much hotter."

"Hrothyr's forge in Wintotashum?" Anskar asked.

Braga's only reply was a grim set to her bristly jaw.

The Soreshi raided again the next night, this time stealing more rations—and it wasn't as though the army had a good deal left. They needed to find a town and resupply, but first they needed to get through the mountain passes alive.

Lanuc was furious at the failure of his sentries to thwart the Soreshi during the night, and finally he decided to do something about it. He assembled a team to double back and get behind the raiders: Rindon, Nul, and Borik; the scouts Korine and Ravenni; and the knight Flavin Reider.

Josac objected. "The Soreshi are sorcerers, so we need to send sorcerers against them."

"Then you will go," Lanuc said.

Josac nodded. "And Anskar. If anyone can counter their sorcery, it's him."

Lanuc frowned, but before Anskar could object that he had vowed not to use any but the dawn-tide, nodded his agreement.

"I'm going too," Braga said. "The goat-shaggers stole my oxen, and to say I'm pissed is putting it mildly."

"There were more than twenty of them this morning," Reider said, cheek twitching as he stroked his mustache.

"Fine, then take them with you." Lanuc indicated the three

knights who shared Reider's campfire at night.

When the knights glared, Reider looked as though he wished he'd kept his mouth shut.

Despite his cloak, Anskar was freezing. With the rest of the team Lanuc had selected, he was hunkered down in a gorge. His fingers burned with the cold, and he constantly had to flex them in order to keep the blood flowing.

Josac was crouched at Anskar's shoulder, and behind them were Reider with his three comrades, Devuin, Klimp, and Storig.

Devuin was a shaggy-haired, bearded ex-vagabond from the eastern cities—probably Caronath, Josac said—and no one seemed to know how he'd made it to the rank of full knight. He carried a spiked morning star and a round wooden shield with an iron rim and boss. There was nothing left of the shield's emblem other than flakes of red and blue paint.

Klimp, so Reider said, was from some forsaken wasteland across the Trackless Ocean, though Josac didn't believe it. "Scum from Mazin, most likely," he told Anskar. "It's a wonder some of these bastards managed to get accepted into the Order."

Klimp was tall, lean, and rangy, but there was nothing obviously holy about him, nothing overtly religious. He might have dressed like a knight, but his armor was tarnished and scabbed with rust, his cloak patched and stinking of mildew. That he was a hard man and a killer, Anskar had no doubt. Perhaps the Order of Eternal Vigilance had need of such people, the same as they had a need for those gifted with both dawn- and dusk-tide sorcery, and Menselas knew what else.

Storig was even more of an oddity. He was a short man, on

the plump side. With his rosy cheeks, big gray mustache, and whiskers, he looked more like a kindly old farmer than a knight, but he was said to be quick with a blade and above average with the casting of a ward sphere.

Nul, Rindon, and Borik were seated on the frozen ground farther down the gorge, acting as a rear guard. They looked as though they were there to enjoy the scenery as they passed around scraps of rations and wine in a skin, which Rindon claimed was watered down. Borik's greatsword was still wrapped in oilskin, but from time to time he unbound the massive hilt only to swiftly bind it up again.

"There!" Korine hissed, waving her hand to make sure the others kept still.

It was Ravenni she had spotted, making her way down the ice-rimed scarp face.

Anskar marveled at the skill of both the scouts, who had led their group away from the main force when they were convinced they couldn't be seen by the Soreshi, and then laid several false trails, all the while seeking an alternative passage through the heights. Both knew how to keep downwind of an enemy and how best to use the terrain for cover. Twice they had evaded Soreshi outriders and gotten the group into a position where they could observe the enemy scouts watching Lanuc and the army. If they'd chosen to, Ravenni and Korine could have easily killed those scouts, but they didn't want to risk alerting the rest of the Soreshi and allowing them to get away.

"You found them?" Korine asked as Ravenni slid down into the gorge.

"Amateurs," Ravenni said.

"They're Soreshi," Josac said. "What do you expect? Nothing more than witches and warlocks."

"They know the mountain paths well enough," Ravenni said.

"Enough to harass the army," Josac conceded.

"But not," Ravenni continued, irritated by the interruption, "the more difficult paths. I was able to get behind them and observe their camp."

"You think they were sent to follow us?" Anskar asked.

"No idea if they were sent, but they are following and not making much of an attempt to disguise the fact."

"How many in the camp?" Korine asked.

"Fifteen that I saw."

"Can we take them?" Reider asked. He'd approached as they were speaking and now stood with his hand resting on the pommel of his sword.

"They're sorcerers, remember," Ravenni said.

"And we are knights," Reider replied. "Some of us, at least."

"The Soreshi aren't just any old sorcerers," Nul said. "Like the Niyandrians, they have an innate talent for the tides. More so in some respects, and they are trained from childhood."

"A hero does not worry about such trifles," Reider said.

"Oh, I'm no hero," Nul said.

"Me neither," Rindon said. "Save for when I've had too much to drink."

Reider shook his head, as if drinking was for cowards.

"I'm a hero, though," Borik said, leaning on his monstrous sword, which he'd still not unwrapped.

"So, what do we do?" Reider asked.

"We do," Nul said, indicating Ravenni and Korine, "whatever these ladies tell us to do."

# FIFTEEN

THE WAGON RATTLED ALONG THE Iron Road, the ancient highway between the Ymaltian Mountains and the Thousand Lakes capital of Wintotashum.

The Tainted Cabalist Castellac sat cross-legged in the back, eyes closed, his heart beating at a snail's pace. For the thousandth time, he checked the wards he'd established about himself, designed to alert him to the presence of hostile sorcery. A surprise attack could come at any moment—from the Thousand Lakes priests of the Five or from the Soreshi who hadn't allied themselves to the Tainted Cabal—and even those who had. Castellac trusted no one, least of all his fellow Cabalists.

This madcap scheme had been proposed by the Abbess, curse her withered tits for coming to Nax-Ur-Vadim and upsetting the apple cart. But it had been her pallid shitbag of a son who'd chosen Castellac for the mission. What that meant in reality was that Uspeth considered him a threat and wanted him out of the way.

Castellac took no comfort from the thought that he was so near the top of the heap. All he felt was an impending sense of doom. Of course, that was how he always felt. The only thing that had changed was the magnitude of the feeling, the closeness of the doom. He was always on tenterhooks, expecting the figurative knife in the back. That was why he ate so much—to quell the ever-rising tide of panic. It was why, over the long months since the Tainted Cabal had come to the Ymaltian Mountains, he had grown so fat.

"Wintotashum ahead," called the driver from up front—a newly ordained Cabalist named Haleki, a petty sorceress who had stumbled upon the more destructive elements of the dusk-tide and had run afoul of the Order of Eternal Vigilance in the Pristart Combine. That had brought her to the Cabal's attention, and she had been rescued from the knights' dungeons right under their pious noses. Haleki hadn't realized it yet, but her plight hadn't improved. It had considerably worsened.

When the Cabal's agents had recruited Castellac all those years ago, they had forced him to give up his comfortable life as an alchemist, where he was making good money selling fool's gold to the rich and stupid, and instead introduced him to their own harsh disciplines and perversions. Those perversions disgusted him, yet he craved them more and more. Waking or sleeping, unsavory needs boiled within him, and he threw himself headlong into the orgies and the unnatural couplings with lesser demons. He'd even enjoyed them for a while, until the revulsion returned, along with an unhealthy dose of shame. Not that either stopped him. The compulsion was too great.

If Wintotashum was near, he had to stop moping and start preparing. It was no easy task, he had been reliably informed, to break into King Aelfyr's Scriptorium.

Of course, even if Castellac were to succeed, he'd be the last person to benefit from retrieving the memory crystal. Morudjin's firsthand experience of the summoning of Nysrog was the most sought after secret in the Tainted Cabal. It followed that, once the memory crystal was safely in the hands of the Abbess or her cretinous son, Castellac would be disappeared.

In an effort to contain his fear, he went over his mission once more in his mind.

Although the Necromancer Queen of Niyas had been dead for years, rumor had it that her agent, an old Niyandrian sorcerer named Lengar, still lived in the city. More fool he, if that were the case. Lengar, it seemed, had achieved with stealth what the Tainted Cabal hadn't managed with force.

Uspeth had been trying for months now to rouse the Soreshi into a hammer to wield against King Aelfyr, and all he had achieved was a few burning villages—until his mother, the Abbess, had arrived with her own ideas of how things should be done. Of course, she gave Uspeth the credit, but everyone knew who was really in charge.

And so Castellac and Haleki had been sent to find the old Niyandrian sorcerer and persuade him that helping them was in his best interests. It wouldn't be, of course. Once he had served his purpose, he would be given two choices: join the Tainted Cabal or join his beloved queen in the realm of the dead. The difficult part, though, was finding him. Wintotashum was a big city, and neither Castellac nor Haleki had contacts there.

The wagon slowed, then came to a faltering stop. Outside, Castellac could hear Lakelander accents—gate guards, presumably—and Haleki answering with her own passable impression of a Thousand Lakes citizen. They had arrived.

He briefly entertained the idea of leaping from the back of

the wagon and begging the King's protection, then revealing the presence of the Tainted Cabal in Aelfyr's lands. But fear gripped him in its paralyzing clutch. No one, not even a king, could help him. He was in for life, a fact that had been made painfully clear to him at his initiation.

And so he didn't leave the wagon and beg for help. Instead, he prayed to Nysrog, and as ever, he couldn't tell if the response he received was the demon lord's voice in his head or his own twisted thoughts, clutching at straws.

*Every petition you make to me, every heartfelt prayer, is one step closer to liberation from fear, one rung of the ladder higher than your mediocre brothers and sisters.*

He shuddered, but at the same time he wondered: Was he ready to challenge Uspeth, or even the Abbess herself? Did he even want to, when the reality was, the higher you rose in the Tainted Cabal, the bigger the target on your back?

"Are you ready?" Haleki called from outside as the wagon got underway again, bumping along an uneven street.

"Of course I'm ready!" Castellac replied.

He cursed himself for not masking his irritability.

What if she construed it as a weakness?

# SIXTEEN

ANSKAR COULD SEE TWELVE SORESHI from his vantage point on top of an overhang. Ravenni was crouched beside him, her unstrung bow clutched in one hand. An icy drizzle was falling, and Anskar's cloak was heavy with damp that made him shiver. His hands were chapped and frozen stiff, so much so that he worried he might not be able to wield his sword should it come to a fight.

The Soreshi had made their camp—if that was what it could be called—in a gully between two sheer faces of rock. They had no fire to speak of, just a soft orange glow that effused from the snow-covered ground beneath each of them. Where they sat, no rain seemed to touch.

It had been a long climb to get above the camp. Ravenni had led Anskar in a wide loop along treacherous mountain paths so the Soreshi would have no chance of seeing them coming. How the scouts knew which way to go was beyond Anskar.

Korine had led Josac around the opposing rock face, aiming to come out above the far side of the Soreshi camp from Ravenni and Anskar.

Reider had been instructed to lead Klimp, Storig, and Devuin up the most obvious mountain path directly toward the Soreshi, but Korine had told him to wait an hour before setting off. Of course, Reider had objected: waiting was for cowards, he said, and besides, he was keen to come at these bloody savages head on and teach them a lesson. Nevertheless, he waited.

Braga remained below the camp with Borik, in case the Soreshi numbered more than the fifteen Ravenni had seen and tried to get behind Reider and his men.

Nul and Rindon had set off on the longest trek of all, working their way to the rear of the Soreshi position, where they could block any attempt to escape.

To Anskar's mind, the Soreshi were cornered rats, and he and his companions were a pack of wildcats that had stalked them to their lair. But he could still see only twelve of them, and there was no sign of the mountain goats they had been riding earlier.

Ravenni raised her hand and waved. Across the gully, lying flat atop a ledge a good hundred feet above the Soreshi camp, Korine responded with a wave of her own. Anskar could just make out the prone form of Josac next to her. Now those two were in position, it was a matter of waiting for Reider and his men. Of course, no one had spelled out to Reider that his group were bait to draw a response from the Soreshi, thus exposing them to the surprise of attacks from above and from Nul and Rindon in the rear. If the Soreshi somehow made it past Reider and his team, Braga and Borik would be waiting for them. Anskar pitied anyone who went toe-to-toe with either of those giants.

Despite the cold, his palms began to sweat, and there was a

niggling sensation at the base of his skull. It had to do with sorcery, he was sure, but what sorcery? So far, all the Soreshi had done was heat the ground where they sat and keep off the rain, and there was no indication they knew they were in any danger. But there were three Soreshi unaccounted for.

Anskar reached out with his sorcerous senses, sending them high into the mountains above, then scouring the gully below. There was nothing save for the footprint of Soreshi repositories—he could feel vast reserves of corrosive essence, but it wasn't purely dusk-tide. He could also feel the dawn-tide, its presence blurry and somehow meshed with the dusk—not two repositories but one.

Someone must have noticed him probing, for all trace of Soreshi sorcery suddenly vanished. It was as if a black cloth had been slung over a dozen candles, snuffing them out at once. The Soreshi grabbed their weapons—short spears, long knives, hunting bows.

Without thinking about it, Anskar whispered a cant and wove an obscuring cloak around all three of his repositories. The tickling probe of sorcerous feelers crept over him, then passed him by. Nothing to see here.

He let out a sigh of relief, then realized what he'd done. He'd broken his oath and drawn upon the dark-tide, and it had been as easy as breathing.

Too late to worry about that now. The Soreshi were all on their feet, and three of them were nocking arrows to strings and aiming upwards—not towards Anskar and Ravenni, but the other side.

Of course! The Soreshi's sorcery had failed to locate Anskar, but Josac's dawn-tide repository was wide open.

Arrows thrummed through the air. One clattered from the

ledge, another bounced from the rock face behind Korine. The third arced down toward Josac. Anskar blinked against the blinding flash of Josac's ward as it sprang to life. The arrow struck the sphere of light and ricocheted away.

Effortlessly, Ravenni strung her bow, bending the yew stave with one hand while gripping the lower half between her knees and feet.

Korine stood and unleashed an arrow into the gully below, ripping it through the throat of a Soreshi woman. Already she had a second arrow nocked, the string pulled back to her ear. This time her target tried to swerve aside, and the arrow grazed the man's shoulder, causing him to cry out and drop his bow.

Ravenni drew her own bow and, with unerring accuracy, dropped the last Soreshi archer.

Josac was on his feet, bellowing at the remaining Soreshi, drawing their attention to him and away from Korine and Ravenni.

Lines of coruscating fire, lurid and green, streamed from Soreshi fingers to converge on Josac's ward. There was an eruption of sparks, a succession of sizzling pops, and then plumes of dirty smoke writhed and twisted around Josac on the ledge. But his ward remained intact, and he taunted the Soreshi with their failure.

While the Soreshi were gathering their inner reserves for a second assault on Josac, Korine's and Ravenni's arrows ripped into them. Anskar marveled at how quickly and devastatingly accurately the two women could fire. Before one arrow had hit the target, a second was already in the air. Beside him, Ravenni dipped her right hand over and over into the hemp bag that held her goose-fletched shafts, nocked, drew, and released with scarcely a thought.

Three more Soreshi went down under the arrow storm, and then Reider and his men charged.

Flashes erupted beneath the knights' feet. Klimp disappeared inside a crimson fire that billowed black smoke. Storig changed his course at the last instant, but was thrown into the air by a second burst of red flame. He shrieked, and then there was a sickening thud when he hit the ground. He writhed on his back, clutching at the stump where his leg had been. Anskar could see that the wound had been cauterized by the crimson fire, the lower part of the leg incinerated.

Devuin crouched behind his shield of wood and rust, but Reider turned and ran.

Anskar cursed himself for not detecting the Soreshi wards. But as with their repositories, the Soreshi had found some means of hiding any trace of their sorcerous defenses. The wards had been activated when the knights' feet passed over them.

On the ledge opposite Anskar's position, Josac still drew the Soreshi's sorcerous attack, but then one of the sorcerers realized that continuing in that vein would get them all killed. Instead, he pointed his index finger at Korine, who immediately dove for cover. Lightning streaked from the Soreshi's fingertip and struck the rock wall behind where Korine had been standing. Stone exploded in a shower of dust and shrapnel.

Josac extended his ward sphere to encompass Korine, and she stood once more, shooting arrows through the silver barrier.

Three of the Soreshi broke away and ran at Devuin, who growled and stepped to meet them, wooden shield raised to protect his body, sword glinting dangerously in his other hand.

And then a many-colored spray of motes and light shot toward Anskar from the ground. He recoiled on instinct, shouted a cant, and his ward sphere burst into life just in time.

He felt the concussive impact of the prismatic force, and for a moment saw it swirling and flickering around his ward before dissipating into the air.

Ravenni wasn't so lucky. She teetered on the edge of the overhang, smoke snaking from her skin in a thousand writhing plumes. She turned her eyes on Anskar, and he saw they were gold and silver and burning red. Her mouth parted as if she tried to speak, and then she tumbled into the gully, her bow clattering against rock as it fell with her.

Anskar heard Korine's scream, saw her fire arrow after arrow into the Soreshi below.

Josac shaped his ward sphere into a hammer and flung it down with such force it pulped a Soreshi woman and left a crater where she had been standing. The priest staggered with the loss of so much energy, but he was grinning like a drunkard.

Regaining his senses, Anskar thought to do the same—to attack the three Soreshi attacking Devuin—but two of them were already down, one with blood gushing from his neck and the other missing half her face. The third had managed to slip past Devuin and was running in terror the same way Reider had fled.

"Don't worry," Josac yelled, "Borik will get the bastard. Him or Braga."

That was when Anskar realized that the Soreshi were dead, all barring the one who had fled.

"Reider?" he called down to Devuin, who was wiping his cleaver clean on a dead Soreshi's hair.

"He won't catch nothing but a cold," Devuin said. "Probably halfway back to Sansor by now."

Anskar gritted his teeth and clenched his fists. Reider was a coward. How could there be such a thing—a knight and a coward?

He saw that Korine was watching him from the ledge opposite, her eyes blazing with rage and grief. Anskar had to turn away. Did she blame him for Ravenni's death? Maybe she was right to. Why hadn't he thought to extend his ward and protect Ravenni? He shouldn't have waited for the Soreshi's sorcery to strike. He should have been prepared.

"Uh-oh," Devuin said from the gully, his eyes on the ledge where Korine and Josac were standing.

Anskar saw that some fifty feet above Korine and Josac's position, more Soreshi had come into view. There were six of them, mounted on goats, atop a rocky plateau that wound its way out of sight around the mountain. The Soreshi were armored in boiled leather and wore black cloaks. Each held a white-painted staff raised overhead.

Pressure built in Anskar's skull as the air around the six staffs shimmered. Their tips touched, and an inky dark vortex appeared, springing up high above the Soreshi, swirling, growing.

The vortex coursed away from the staffs and dropped lazily into the gully, still expanding so that it touched the walls on both sides and swelled to fill every inch of space.

"Anskar!" Josac yelled.

"Oh, shit!" Devuin said, turning to run—just in time, for where he had been standing, a sheer wall of flame burst from the ground.

Korine and Josac also turned to flee, but they were too late. Sheets of fire thirty feet tall hemmed them in on every side, and the black vortex simply passed right through the flames as it continued to fall.

Anskar thought frantically, then sent out waves of dawn-tide from his repository. In response to Josac's urgent cries and the rapidly expanding vortex that was mere feet now from the top of his own head as well as from his comrades, Anskar gave in to pure sorcerous instinct, and the dawn-tide left him in a flood. He fashioned it into a bulwark against the descending vortex; then, with an effort of will, forced it upward and spoke a hastily prepared cant.

The vortex started to rise, and Anskar heard Josac's cheer of encouragement. But within seconds the vortex seemed to grow heavier and pushed back against his dawn-tide flow.

Anskar narrowed his eyes and redoubled his efforts. As dawn-tide ruptured from his well in a flood, his stomach clenched, and a cold sweat beaded on his brow. But the sorcerers controlling the vortex were too strong for him. His body began to shake, his legs buckled, and he dropped to his knees.

The vortex dropped lower, and both Korine and Josac screamed at him. Anskar pushed back again, but felt something intangible rip deep inside him, and his dawn-tide repository ran dry.

Unthinking, he unleashed blind, desperate rage, and before he'd realized what he was doing, a roaring blast of dusk-tide smashed into the vortex, which erupted into fiery motes that dispersed on the wind.

Every muscle in Anskar's body clenched, and he leaned forward to vomit. Heat washed over him, and he shut his eyes against a sudden brightness. He opened them a crack and saw fire, then turned his head to see that he was surrounded by a cylinder of flames that rose twenty feet above him. Worse, it was contracting around him, its heat scalding. His cloak began to smolder. Acrid smoke filled his nostrils. The cylinder contracted again, and his cloak burst into flames.

Anskar screamed, and thrashed about in panic. The self-imposed bindings around his last repository fell away, and he raced inward to his core, to the black stain that clung there and seemed to define him. Abandoning himself once more to instinct, he threw back his head, opened his palms, and let the dark-tide burst the dam of his flesh and collide with the Soreshi fire. There was a brief flicker and sizzle, and then the cylinder of flames went out.

Anskar stood, no longer himself. Darkness swamped his mind and body, swathing him in its shadow. Only dim recollections of the dawn and the dusk lingered, along with the sense of who he had been moments ago—a young man, a knight, the child of a queen.

A malign laugh echoed about him as he drew his sword, and he realized that he was the one laughing. No longer weak or sickened by the overuse of sorcerous power, he was invigorated by the dark, intoxicated with it.

He looked up to see the goat-riding Soreshi aiming their white staffs at him. Lines of emerald sorcery streaked toward him, but before they struck home, Anskar poured himself into the shadows and emerged behind the goat-riders.

Dimly, he was aware of the rise and fall of his sword. Black fire coursed through the blade, rendering it a thing of shadow and flame, a thing possessed, a thing alive.

Dimmer still was the sound of his laughter, the splash of hot blood on his face and arms. He swam in a sea of screams and crimson. He felt tendrils of the dark-tide snagging the seed of the Warrior's Fire within him, prying it open and joining themselves to its lust for battle.

He killed mindlessly, brutishly, a beast slaughtering its prey, relishing in the song of his sword as it screamed for blood and souls.

# SEVENTEEN

"ANSKAR?"

He recognized the far-off voice but couldn't put a face to it.

Anskar lay on his back. Cold air caressed his skin. He frowned, but his face was like a mask, coated in something sticky.

"Anskar, it's Josac. By the Five, you killed them, lad. You killed them all!"

Anskar tried to prop himself up on one elbow and failed. He groaned as his head smacked against stone.

"Killed? Where…?"

"You're on the ridge above the ledge Korine and I were on," Josac said. "How in the Five's name did you get up here? Your abilities, wasn't it? Your forbidden sorcery."

"You approve?"

"In war, all things are permissible. Use every advantage, is what the Warrior tells us, and you did just that."

"It was sinful," Anskar said, despair rising from his guts.

"Prudent is what it was. Good judgment that saved all our lives."

Anskar shut his eyes as hot tears pressed for release. "Korine?" he asked.

"She's alive," Josac said, "though heartbroken. She and Ravenni were closer than sisters."

Anskar grimaced, remembering Ravenni's fall into the gully. There was no way she could have survived. Probably the sorcery had killed her even before she fell.

"Hey!" It was Braga's voice, coming from far below.

"Ho!" Josac exclaimed. "She has that Soreshi bastard who escaped, dragging him by his hair. And here comes Borik. Still hasn't unwrapped that bloody great sword of his. Wait here. Of course you'll wait—you don't exactly look fit to be going anywhere. I'll fetch Korine, and together we'll help you back below."

"You should have saved her," Korine said, as she and Josac lowered Anskar to the ground in the gully, resting his back against a boulder.

"I couldn't," he muttered. His tongue felt as though it belonged to someone else. "There was no warning."

"They're Soreshi," Korine snapped. "Sorcerers, like you. You should have known they would use sorcery. You should have warded Ravenni against them."

"But—"

"You should have warded against them," Korine said again, stalking off as if she couldn't bear to associate with him any longer.

"You're right," Anskar said, but his words came out as a barely audible whisper. "I should have protected Ravenni."

"Leave her to stew for a bit," Josac said. "She'll come round."

"But I could have saved Ravenni," Anskar protested.

"Maybe. Maybe not. But you saved the rest of us; that's the main thing."

"Is it?" Anskar suspected he had only unleashed the force of his dusk- and dawn-tide repositories in order to save himself.

It hadn't been as cold and self-centered as that, he knew. He'd acted out of panic. But therein lay the problem. It was all very well to deny his forbidden abilities in what he was increasingly seeing as a misguided attempt at piety, but whenever his life was in peril, he behaved no better than a wild beast: no control, no holding back. And yes, it was effective. He had saved himself and the rest of their group. But it had been too late for Ravenni.

Was that some kind of sin he had not previously considered—to have the power to do something yet refuse to use it out of concern for his own soul?

Anskar looked up and saw Braga watching him. She'd seen what he had done—the blood, the slaughter—and Anskar felt ashamed. He opened his mouth to say something that might reassure her, but could think of nothing.

The Soreshi was watching him too, from where he lay trussed up on the ground.

It was the first time Anskar had seen a Soreshi up close. When he'd killed the sorcerers above the gully, he had been possessed by fire and darkness. He'd seen nothing but shadows; heard nothing but distant screams and the song of his sword howling for blood.

The Soreshi prisoner had a broad, flat face, and a nose that looked as though it had been squashed. There was a haughty nobility to his high cheekbones and slanted blue eyes. His long black hair was bound into dozens of braids with leather cords that glistened with crystal dust.

Anskar sent out his sorcerous senses, and found the Soreshi had two sizable repositories—dawn and dusk—but they seemed to be fused together.

Reider chose that moment to return, huffing and puffing.

"Thank Menselas!" the knight said, bending double to catch his breath. "I thought I could get behind the bleeders. By the Five, I wanted to punish them for what they did to Klimp and Storig."

Devuin stood from examining the charred corpses of his comrades and pocketed whatever he had just pilfered from them. "You ran away," he said. "Like a startled turkey."

Reider straightened. "I did no such thing."

"You did," Braga said. "I watched you go, and it weren't nowhere near the Soreshi."

"Always said you was nothing but a shit-squirting coward," Devuin spat.

"How dare you!" Reider half-drew his sword but then seemed to think better of it. "I was trying to find a way to outflank those blasted Soreshi."

"You shit yourself?" Braga asked, pinching her nose.

"What?" Reider's face turned beet-red, and he looked about to explode.

"This one, on the other hand," Devuin said, turning to face Anskar, "did us all proud."

"You'll get no argument from me on that," Josac said.

"What I did," Anskar said, trying and failing to stand, "I'm not proud of."

"Trust me, lad," Josac said, "you did well. You can't be a warrior and forgo all your advantages."

"Yes, you can," Anskar replied. "Or are you saying that if I had sorcery that could destroy an entire city and all its peoples, I should use it if they refused to surrender during a siege?"

"I would," Josac said. "It's the way of the Warrior."

Anskar shook his head. "No. It's the way of imbalance."

"It's not so different to what that bitch Queen Talia did during the siege of Naphor," Korine put in. It sounded as though she blamed Anskar for that too. "Rather than surrender the city, she destroyed it with her sorcery."

"You were there?" Anskar asked.

"I'm not as young as I look," Korine said as she turned away.

"I'll do penance for this," Anskar told Josac. "For breaking my oath and for using… sorcery." Dark-tide sorcery.

"What penance?"

"I've no idea." But no sooner had the words left his lips than he knew exactly what he must do. He unbuckled his sword belt and handed *Amalantril* to Josac. "Look after this for me."

The sword seemed lighter somehow, different. It made his skin crawl just touching the scabbard. Superstition, he supposed. A manifestation of his guilt. The sword was no longer the symbol of virtue and truth he had intended it to be when he made it. It had become a thing of the shadows that he'd tried so hard to keep buried inside.

Before they left the gully, Reider insisted on questioning the Soreshi prisoner. Devuin trussed the man's wrists behind his back with his own belt and then pulled down his pants around his ankles in case he decided to run.

Borik turned away and walked toward the northern end of

the gully, where Nul and Rindon were returning, chatting as if they were out for an afternoon stroll. The three "heroes," as Anskar had started to think of the trio, stood apart, casting the occasional glance toward Reider and Devuin as they went to work on the prisoner. Clearly, the heroes didn't want any part of the interrogation, and neither did Anskar.

"How are you feeling?" Josac asked, crouching beside him.

"Cold." Anskar had been sitting on the frozen ground by the boulder for far too long, yet he still lacked the strength to stand unaided.

"Come on," Josac said, "let me help you up."

Anskar was unsteady on his feet, but the sight of Devuin punching the Soreshi in the stomach and winding him brought on a surge of anger, and with anger came strength, if only a little.

"Fucking knights," Braga muttered.

"Has to be done," Josac said. "Know your enemy and know what he's up to. It's the Warrior's way."

"You think there could be more Soreshi out there?" Anskar asked.

"This is how we find out," Josac said.

Devuin hit the Soreshi in the stomach again, and this time the man crumpled into a ball, gasping for breath.

"Bloody him up a little," Reider said, "and then we'll start the questioning."

"You bloody him," Devuin said. "I've done my bit. All you've done is run away."

"All you did was punch him twice," Reider objected.

"I punched him twice, I trussed him up, and you ran away."

"I have already told you—"

"And you pissed your pants," Devuin added.

"That was melted snow!" Reider leaned in close to Devuin and kept his voice low. "Not in front of the prisoner. Division gives them hope. We must stand united."

"Bullshit," Devuin said, walking away to the far side of the gully, where he perched on a rock. He took out a pipe and stuffed tobacco into its bowl, then cursed because he had no way of lighting it.

"Here," Josac said, a sorcerous blaze blossoming on his palm. "Let me."

The Soreshi, curled up on the ground, craned his neck to look at Anskar, pain and torment in his eyes. Reider kicked him, then winced and bent down to rub his booted foot.

Once Josac had gotten Devuin's pipe alight, he made for the prisoner, palm still ablaze with sorcerous fire, and Anskar recalled the story the Warrior's priest had told him about the Soreshi with the burning hands he had fought in the fight pits. Anskar's fists clenched. He tried to say something, but fatigue or shock or just the horror of what was about to happen choked the words in his throat.

"I'll handle this," Josac told Reider, who seemed happy to let him.

"Right, you savage piece of shit," Josac said, crouching down in front of the prisoner. "How about we start with why you and your offal-eating friends attacked us?"

"We did not," the man said in thickly accented Nan-Rhouric.

"You hear that?" Josac said to Reider. "He says they didn't attack us." The flames in his palm flared brighter.

"We stole your supplies," the Soreshi said, "but we did not attack."

"And why'd you do that?" Josac snarled. "Don't they teach you goat-shaggers that stealing is wrong?"

"We…" The man faltered, looking around as if he sought the

answer in the rocks of the gully.

"We what?" Josac prompted.

Anskar didn't like what Josac was doing, but as a knight-inferior he was the priest's subordinate. Besides which, he lacked the strength to argue with Josac or Reider, let alone fight.

He felt the prick and crawl of sorcerous senses and knew the Soreshi was probing him.

"We needed them," the Soreshi said, switching his gaze back to Josac.

"You attacked the Order of Eternal Vigilance, savage," Reider said, "and there will be a reckoning."

"My people have been driven from their homes in the Ymaltian Mountains," the Soreshi said. He rolled to his side, then managed to rock himself to his knees.

"By whom?" Josac asked.

"Others of our kind. A faction has arisen among the Soreshi—"

"What kind of faction?"

The Soreshi shook his head, then glanced at the fire welling on Josac's upraised palm. It wasn't fear Anskar saw in the man's eyes; he thought it might be the sparkle of amusement.

"Rebels, under the command of three Soreshi traitors. They're led by a woman named Jilua."

"What are they rebelling against?" Josac asked.

"Those they believe stole our ancestral lands an aeon ago."

"King Aelfyr and the Kingdom of the Thousand Lakes?"

The Soreshi nodded.

"And now the Soreshi war among themselves?" Josac pressed.

"It isn't war. Not yet. The rebels came, they burned our homes, they committed abominations against our people."

Josac snorted. "The loser in any conflict always says such things."

"They have laid claim to the fortress of Molas Drythe in the Ymaltian Mountains, which lay abandoned for five hundred years."

"Never heard of it," Josac said. "And why would they do this now?"

"I do not know," the Soreshi said.

"I think you do. Or you could make a good guess."

Josac's hand flared again, and he brought the flames toward the Soreshi's face. Before it could burn flesh, the fire went out.

"What?" Josac stared at his hand. He shook it, then rubbed it vigorously with his other hand as if to get the circulation going.

"Has Menselas abandoned you?" Reider asked.

Menselas, Anskar thought, had nothing to do with it. He'd felt the gushing flow of sorcery from the Soreshi's braided repositories.

Josac ignited a new and more virulent fire upon his palm. Again he reached for the Soreshi's face, and again the fire went out.

"It's you, isn't it?" the Warrior's priest said. "You sneaky Soreshi shit-sucker."

"Perhaps there is another explanation," the Soreshi said. He nodded at Reider. "Maybe your god has not abandoned you but is sending you a sign."

"A sign?"

"We are not your enemy, priest of Menselas. We stole from you, true, but only so that we might survive. We are victims of this Soreshi uprising—refugees, survivors. But I will admit that we were curious, too. Why would the Order of Eternal Vigilance ride north into Thousand Lakes? Could it be that you are in league with these rebels? That you come against King Aelfyr?"

"Quite the opposite!" Reider said, then clamped his mouth shut at a warning glare from Josac.

"So you come to Aelfyr's aid?" the Soreshi said. "That is good."

"It is?" Anskar said, finally finding his voice. "Why?"

"Because your enemy is our enemy. The majority of my people do not want war with the Thousand Lakes kingdom, but we are scattered far and wide, easy pickings for those who would take our towns and villages. If we were to unite…"

"But you won't," Josac said. "That was always the Soreshi weakness, thank Menselas, else your kind would have infected the whole mainland by now."

"Conquest has never been our way," the Soreshi said.

"Until now," Anskar said. "Something must have happened."

"Oh, something happened," Josac said, "and this scumbag knows what."

"Then maybe I should take over," Devuin said, drawing a slender dagger as he returned to the group. "You won't be getting fancy sorcerous tricks from me," he told the Soreshi. "You'll be getting pain and blood. A shitload of both of them."

"No!" Anskar said. "That's not what we do."

"Who appointed you leader?" Reider said.

Devuin advanced on the Soreshi, sunlight glinting from his dagger.

Anskar felt the swell of essence in the Soreshi's strange repository.

"Don't make me do something I might regret," Anskar told Devuin.

Devuin turned on him. "You what?"

"You heard him."

Anskar turned to see Nul striding towards them, Rindon and Borik in his wake. "You're supposed to be a knight, Devuin, so act like one."

Rindon and Borik came to stand beside Nul. For once, there

was no good humor in Rindon's eyes; they were glittery and hard, the cold eyes of a killer.

Devuin muttered a curse under his breath, but he sheathed his knife and moved away from the Soreshi.

"I say we take the prisoner back to Commander Lanuc," Reider said.

"I'd say that's a very astute choice you just made," Rindon said.

# EIGHTEEN

ANSKAR FELT LIKE A CHILD as Braga carried him down the mountain. He would have preferred to walk, but now that his anger at the treatment of the Soreshi had abated, so had his strength.

The three heroes walked with Braga, while Josac and the others led the Soreshi prisoner on a leash.

When Borik offered to take over and carry Anskar, he was met with a barrage of foul language and curses so strong that he actually blushed.

"I think she likes you," Rindon mouthed to Borik.

Anskar winced. If he'd seen, then so had Braga.

"About as much as a goat's dripping ass," the blacksmith said.

Rindon chuckled and clapped Borik on the back.

"What you laughing at, maggot groin?"

"Maggot?" Rindon said, feigning outrage. "My good woman, if you'd only care to take a look…"

Braga snorted and quickened her pace, and Anskar started to feel queasy from the motion.

He let his heavy eyelids close and tried to relax into the rhythm of her strides. The playful banter of the three heroes brought a smile to his lips, and he wondered how it must feel to have friends like that, to really belong.

He thought briefly of Orix, but the memory was still painful. His friend had switched sides to join Carred Selenas, and for what? The warmth of her bed?

Without realizing he'd fallen asleep, he was startled awake when Braga set him down. His toes and fingers were numb from the cold, but he found himself beside the heat of a crackling fire. They were back at the camp.

"Where's the prisoner?" he asked blearily.

"They've taken him to Lanuc," Nul said.

By 'they,' he must have meant Reider, Devuin, and Josac.

"You should have gone with them."

"No need," Nul said, and Rindon nodded his agreement. "Lanuc won't dishonor himself with torture. It's not always easy to see, but there's still goodness in the Order."

Borik stood warming his hands over the flames, glancing at Braga as she resumed her grumbling about the loss of her oxen and having to leave her wagon behind. There had been no sign of the beasts at the Soreshi camp. Either they had been eaten or driven off to some nearby settlement.

"Where the fuck am I going to sleep?" Braga grumbled. She glared at Anskar, and he feared she was about to insist on sharing his tent.

"You could have my tent," Borik stuttered.

"Huh," Braga snorted. "Then where are you going to sleep?"

Rindon and Nul eyed Borik expectantly.

"I'll be fine," he said.

"The wielder of the Sword of Supremacy does not need sleep," Rindon put in, producing a metal flask from his boot and unscrewing the cap.

"Don't worry," Nul said with a sigh. "You can come in with me, Borik. But no farting."

"We take him with us," Lanuc said the next morning as the army smothered their breakfast fires with fresh snow and prepared to get underway. "He's your charge now." He shoved the Soreshi prisoner toward Anskar.

"Why me?"

"You're the company sorcerer," Lanuc explained.

"I am?"

"There's no point denying what you are any longer. Not after yesterday."

The Soreshi offered Anskar a thin smile. It was not at all convincing.

"He's unbound," Anskar said.

"I accept his story," Lanuc said. "We're all on the same side."

Lanuc turned on his heel and left the prisoner standing there by the smothered remains of the fire.

"Make yourself useful," Braga said, shoving a bag of smithing tools into the man's arms. "Carry this."

The Soreshi accepted the burden without reaction, his eyes locked to Anskar's. "I am Zekil Silvertongue," he said, "though I am more often known as Zek."

"Silvertongue?" Braga said. "Is that another name for lying, stinking toerag?"

Zek almost laughed at that. "My people give each other second names on account of their behavior. I am told that I talk too much and too glibly."

"Then you'll like Rindon," Anskar said.

Zek frowned. "Rindon?"

"One of the group that came out against your… You'll see."

"Enough natter, ass-wipe," Braga said. "Don't encourage the loquacious bastard."

"Ass-wipe?" Zek said.

"It's what she calls me. A term of affection. So, you're no longer our prisoner?"

Zek shrugged. "What would you do if I chose to wander off?"

"I'd tell Lanuc."

"And he would have me brought back. You decide: am I a prisoner?"

The Soreshi was provided with a horse that had belonged to either Klimp or Storig. Braga still insisted on walking, and while their pace was faster without her wagon, she, Anskar, and Zek lagged behind the rest of the army.

The ground continued to rise as they trekked northward, deeper into the Kingdom of the Thousand Lakes. Far to the east lay a sprawling mountain range, and to the north, snowcapped peaks poked above the clouds. For the most part, they crossed frozen tundra, here and there pocked with tufts of hardy grasses and spiny leaves flanged like spear tips, which Zek said could survive all the extremes of hot and cold.

They saw their first lake the second day after the fight with the Soreshi: a vast inland sea rimmed with ice at the edges, but teeming with brightly colored fish. Gulls swooped and squawked overhead, along with the occasional big-beaked pelicans trawling the waters for prey.

The army camped beside the sea overnight, and in the morning some of the archers tried their hand at bow-fishing.

"The water is good to drink," Zek told Anskar, and after a brief taste test, waterskins were refilled for the onward journey.

Forage parties were sent out into the wastes. One knight failed to return, but the others came back with a stag, a few white-furred rats, and some tubers and herbs. The rats made surprisingly good eating when baked over a campfire. The stag, though, according to Zek, was an ill omen.

"They should not have killed it," he told Anskar as the army got underway again, "for now the mulag will be angry."

"Mulag?" Braga said, huffing and puffing as she tried to keep pace with the horses. "What's that?"

"Bad is what they are," Zek said. "Now they will stalk us, and many will die."

"What if we tell Lanuc to order the stag buried?" Anskar asked. "If we give it back to the tundra, perhaps the mulag will leave us alone."

"Perhaps," Zek said, sounding unconvinced. "So long as its flesh is not defiled. So long as no one eats of it."

Anskar said as much to Lanuc, who, to Anskar's surprise, did indeed order the stag returned to the ground. Some of the knights and retainers grumbled, but the three heroes stood alongside Lanuc, and no one seemed to want to disagree with them.

The stag was buried and petitions for forgiveness were made, most of all to Menselas, but Zek also pleaded with the mulag, whatever they were.

"We have done all that can be done," the Soreshi said to Anskar as the army moved out. "Let us hope it is enough."

At dusk, Lanuc ordered the army to make camp in the lee of a frosted escarpment. Within an hour, tents were pitched, horses tethered together and fitted with feedbags, and a dozen or so fires were lit.

The sky was black and cloudless, the stars pinpricks of silver that seemed to seep light from some other realm. The moon Jagonath was full and bloody and for once alone. Despite the clear, calm skies, away from the shelter of the scarp face the wind howled, picking up particles of ice and snow and churning them into an undulating sheen of white.

"Our apology has not been accepted," Zek said. He touched both shoulders and then his forehead with the tips of two fingers.

"These mulag are coming?" Anskar asked.

"Good." Braga tapped the hilt of her monstrous sword. "I need something to kill."

Josac, who had rejoined them, caused his hands to flare with the sorcerous fire he had attempted to harm Zek with.

"That will not help you," the Soreshi said. "I was able to nullify such borrowed sorcery with ease. The mulag will do it without thinking."

"Borrowed?" Josac said, clapping his hands together and snuffing the flames out.

"It's a Soreshi technique. Where did you learn it?"

"I stole the idea from a cheater in the fight pits."

Zek frowned, then shrugged.

"Tell us about the mulag," Anskar said.

"There are many. And they hunt like wolves."

"I eat wolves for breakfast," Braga said.

"They hunt like wolves, but they themselves are nothing like wolves," Zek explained. "What I mean is, they are cunning, and they will pursue us over many miles. They will weaken us, and when we can no longer defend ourselves, they will move in for the slaughter."

"Then we turn the tables," Josac said. "We hunt them instead."

"You might," Zek said, sounding unconvinced. "My advice would be to run and keep on running till we reach the lands King Aelfyr has garrisoned. The mulag will not pursue us there. They are not stupid. They know we would find shelter behind the walls of the burgs, and that archers would cut them to shreds."

"So they can be killed," Josac said. "Then we've nothing to worry about."

The night passed uneventfully, but Anskar slept only fitfully. It was so cold that the blood felt frozen in his veins. When he woke in the morning, he had to rub warmth into his limbs before he could stand.

The entire camp was subdued. Knights and retainers ate a poor breakfast of dried rations around feeble fires that seemed to shrink from the cold. Most were bleary-eyed from lack of sleep.

The mulag had already weakened their prey, Anskar thought, without having to even show themselves.

# NINETEEN

THE ARMY MOVED ON ACROSS snow-dusted plains and through steep valleys slick with ice. Lakes glimmered on high, where melted snow and frigid rain had collected in the calderas of extinct volcanoes. There were great bodies of water lower down, too: lakes and reservoirs connected by snaking waterways and ruler-straight canals, which had presumably once carried the grain and trade goods of whatever ancient race had lived in the far north. In the early morning, mist rose from the water and covered the sky with its haze. Visibility was poor then, and at times fog pressed in tight around the army, bringing with it the sense of something stalking them beyond its obscuring blanket.

By afternoon, the mist had lifted, and the view of snow-topped mountains and shimmering lakes was something to behold. Despite the relentless grip of the cold, Anskar's heart was warmed by the sheer beauty of the land and the burgeoning hope that soon they would reach the end of their journey.

Hopefully before the mulag came.

As they traveled, Anskar found himself speaking more and more with Zek, asking him questions about the nature of the blended dawn- and dusk-tide sorcery he had witnessed the other Soreshi use back at the gully.

Zek was at first reluctant to divulge much in the way of knowledge. The Soreshi, he said, guarded their lore jealously, because in the past they had been generous with their teaching and their sorcery had later been used against them.

In exchange, Anskar spoke about the conflicts that had forced him to bury his dusk-tide powers. He didn't mention the dark.

"What I fail to understand," Zek said as they rode alongside each other, "is why you assume the dawn-tide is benevolent but the dusk is malign. Are not dawn and dusk but two ends of the same day? Does their light not come from the same sun?"

Anskar had never thought of it like that. Little by little, Zek was able to challenge some of his preconceptions about sorcery and the tides that fueled it. Did the knights, did Frae Ganwen, his sorcery tutor at Branil's Burg, really believe there was a qualitative difference between the dawn and the dusk? A moral one? The more Anskar thought about it, the more it made no sense.

"Light is light," Zek explained, "no matter the angle or the degree of shade. Even when it refracts through a prism into a myriad of rainbow colors, it is still the same light."

"But the effects of the dawn-tide and dusk-tide are fundamentally different," Anskar objected.

"True. It is a conundrum, is it not?"

As they pressed on, the cold entered Anskar's bones, seeped into the marrow, and turned his thoughts to somber things: to disease and hopelessness and death. And with thoughts of death, he was never far from thinking of his mother.

The horses grew skittish and difficult to ride. That night, some of them screamed, but the retainers guarding them could find no reason why. Not a single horse was harmed.

"We're almost there," Lanuc told the assembled army as they prepared to leave in the predawn twilight.

He was met with grumbles of relief.

There was something in the mist.

Anskar could sense it, but he could see nothing.

Zek suddenly sat alert in the saddle.

Josac went on talking, oblivious, taking great pleasure in telling Zek how he had fought his way free of the fight pits by defeating the cheater. "The look on the bastard's face when I…" Josac trailed off. "What is it?"

"I'm not sure," Anskar said.

Braga loosened her sword in its scuffed and battered scabbard.

Zek's eyes panned along the mist behind them until he was squinting at the retainers toward the rear of the column. One of the horses whinnied and reared, and its handler spoke calming words in its ear.

Anskar followed Zek's gaze, but still he could see nothing, only the encroaching mist caressing the cloaks of the knights and their retainers.

He sent out feelers of awareness, but they recoiled as soon as they made contact with the mist, whiplashing back into his dawn-tide repository.

Zek snapped his head round. "That won't work, not against the mulag."

"They're here?" Josac drew his sword and offered to return

Anskar's.

"No," Anskar said. "Not this time."

"A warrior needs every advantage."

"I said no."

Josac slid from his saddle and handed the reins to Anskar. "Then I'll use it."

The Warrior's priest stood beside Braga, glaring into the mist, his own sword in one hand, *Amalantril* in the other.

It made no sense, but Anskar felt sure *Amalantril* was mocking Josac, as if she resented being touched by anyone but her maker. And now Josac was going to pay for the offense.

"They have passed around us," Zek said. "They know my people. Their anger is not directed toward me."

The mist hazed red, and a knight screamed, thrashing about wildly before something dragged him into the cloaking fog, and all went quiet.

All along the column, knights and their retainers stood frozen to the spot. Horses nickered and stamped. Anskar could hear the thud of his own heartbeat. Within him, the dark-tide writhed and strained against its barriers.

"Wards!" Lanuc yelled.

In quick succession, silvery spheres of light burst into existence around the hundred or so knights. Anskar did the same, expanding his ward sphere to encompass Braga. Josac's ward was threaded through with gold.

"Zek?" Anskar asked, intending to extend his ward further, despite the huge cost in energy.

"I have my own defenses," the Soreshi said. Three emerald spheres appeared in the air above him and began to orbit his head. "No one will listen to me, a Soreshi," he added, "so you must tell them all to flee."

"What?" Anskar said, but as he looked at the fear and resignation on Zek's face, he knew that if they tried to hold their ground and fight, they would all die.

"Flee!" he yelled at the top of his voice, trusting that Lanuc would hear him. "Flee!"

The knights' wards expanded to encompass the retainers, and the army set off again at a much faster pace.

Josac, though, stood his ground, and Braga remained with him.

"Come on!" Anskar told them.

Somewhere within the fleeing column, a woman screamed, and then a man. Blood sprayed.

A ward sphere morphed into a hammer that slammed through the mist. Swords were drawn, glinting in the silver light of the wards.

"Keep running!" Zek yelled.

While most of the army heeded him, three silver ward spheres wove their way back through the ranks: Nul, Rindon, and Borik.

"We are to be the rearguard," Nul said from within the central sphere.

Borik's greatsword was finally unwrapped—rust-scabbed and dull, the blade nicked in a hundred places. Rindon, bright-eyed and grinning beneath his mustache, held a vicious-looking hatchet in either hand.

"Just you three, or the rest of us?" Josac asked.

"Stay if you must," Borik said, running a thumb along the dull edge of his rusty blade, "but give me space to swing."

"I will stay too," Zek said. "And do what I can."

Anskar had already decided that he would stay, not to fight, but to ward the others as best he could. After all, it was sorcery that made him "special" to the Order, not swordplay.

"Braga?" he asked.

She didn't answer, merely gripped her sword in her massive fist and waited.

"What if the mulag follow the army and leave us behind?" Josac said.

"They won't," Zek said. "I have made certain of that."

"How?" Anskar asked.

Zek glanced up at the three emerald spheres circling his head. "They will recognize these, and take them as a sign of aggression. They remember what my ancestors did with such sorcery."

"Why would you do this?" Josac asked.

"To show that we are on the same side."

"Thought you said these bastards wouldn't attack until we were weak," Braga put in.

"We are weak," Zek said. "Even if you are too stubborn to realize it."

The Soreshi was right. Anskar's mind was clouded by the same cold that numbed his limbs, and he was exhausted from sleepless nights and long hours in the saddle.

"There are too many of us," Borik growled.

"Aye," Rindon said. "It's supposed to be the three heroes, not the seven."

Even as Rindon spoke, Zek flung out his hand, and his emerald spheres streaked ahead of him, illuminating the mist as they passed through it. Within the spreading radiance they shed, shadows moved. Hundreds of shadows.

"Aim for their heads," Zek said as a dagger of light materialized in his hand.

Borik didn't need telling twice: he swung the Sword of Supremacy in a murderous arc. Rust and iron struck shadow, and the shadow howled. More shadows converged on Borik, who stood his ground, scything about with his greatsword.

Nul moved to Borik's left, thrusting with his slender blade, and Rindon went to the right, twin hatchets a blur of motion. The three heroes' silver wards overlapped and grew denser—and then a deluge of shadows smashed into them. For a long tense moment, their ward spheres were eclipsed, then their weapons pierced the dark shroud—Rindon's hatchets, Nul's blade, Borik's mighty sword. Shafts of silver light burst through the smothering pall, widening as the trio killed and killed and killed again.

Shadows screamed and snarled and roared, and then Josac was in among them, hacking left and right with his own sword and *Amalantril*.

"Look out!" Zek cried as a shape rushed from the mist straight at Anskar, shaggy and tall and broad as a bear. Anskar had an impression of horns and fangs, of glistening sickle claws, a whiplashing tail—and then Braga stepped in front of him, outside the protection of his ward.

Her sword swept down, cleaving the mulag from shoulder to belly, but the beast just roared and swiped at her with a taloned hand. Braga caught it by the wrist, but she lacked the space to swing her sword. The beast's other hand came toward her, but Zek was there, stabbing the mulag in the face with his dagger of light. The mulag screeched and fell back, and Braga's sword took its head off.

Anskar stepped in close to Braga, the better to shield her with his sorcery. And then the three of them were in the thick of the mist and the mulag were all around them. He saw flashes of silver from where the three heroes still fought; glimpsed the blaze of Josac's ward, the whir of his blades; and then his own ward was hit by a succession of impacts.

Zek also stood within Anskar's ward sphere now, and another

emerald sphere manifested above the Soreshi's head, swelling until it burst, its green light merging with the silver of Anskar's ward. As the trio advanced, the mulag recoiled from the ward's glare, and Braga cut them down.

For a moment, it looked as though it was going to work, as though the heroes were holding their own, as if Josac, possessed with the fury of the Warrior's Fire, could slaughter an army of the mulag on his own, as if Braga's sword and Anskar's ward and Zek's emerald sorcery would be too much for the beasts.

But more and more dark forms emerged from the mist to throw themselves snarling onto sword, axe, and dagger. An increase in the gloom told Anskar someone's ward had been snuffed out, and the subsequent scream told him it was Josac's. The overlapping ward spheres of the three heroes flickered, close to breaking.

Pain spiked in Anskar's head as he sought to preserve his own ward. Zek, beside him, cast another emerald sphere, but it fizzled out uselessly.

A colossal mulag hammered its fists against Anskar's dwindling ward. Braga hacked at it with her sword, but even her prodigious strength was waning, and the blade failed to penetrate the beast's hairy hide. Another mulag added its weight to the attack, and another. Anskar staggered under the ferocity of the assault. Sweat poured into his eyes. His knees buckled, and his ward collapsed.

The mass of mulag stood still, as if in disbelief; then the massive one that had first damaged the ward sprang.

And died, the goose-feather fletching of an arrow protruding from its forehead.

That first arrow was quickly followed by another, and another, and then Korine cried out, "Run, you stupid bastards! Wintotashum's just beyond the next rise!"

"We stay and fight!" Borik roared above the clamor of battle.

"Not this time, Borik," Nul cried. "Retreat!"

Anskar backed away, pulling Braga with him. Each time the mulag took a step forward, Korine unleashed another arrow. As Anskar and Braga drew level with her, she said, "Go! I'll cover you."

Legs trembling, Anskar stumbled. Braga looped her arm under his, and together they hurried toward the rise. Zek, running with them, tried conjuring all manner of minor sorceries, but each attempt made him weaker, and none had much of an effect.

Behind them, Anskar could hear the thrum of Korine's arrows, then the quick tramp of the archer's boots as she followed them.

He caught glimpses of the three heroes and their fighting retreat. Rindon was facing the encroaching mulag, driving them back with flurries of blows from his hatchets; and then he broke off, circling away to the left as Nul circled back from the right to take the rearguard. The trio exchanged positions over and over: run, circle back, fight. It kept the mulag off-balance and ensured that no man was left behind. Anskar felt his heart swell with pride. These were the kind of knights he had imagined all his young life. They were what he wished he could be.

"Last one," Korine said, cursing. She was out of arrows.

"You goat turds go on ahead," Braga snarled. "I'll keep them off you."

"No," Anskar said. "Just keep running."

But the big woman wasn't listening. She stood her ground, taking a two-handed grip on her sword as the mulag swarmed toward her. Anskar stopped and tried to ward her, but his dawn-tide repository was empty.

Zek gripped his shoulder. "Use what's left of mine," he urged, his dagger of light fizzing away to nothing.

Anskar felt the trickle of blended dawn- and dusk-tide energy leaving Zek. His dawn-tide repository shuddered under the touch of the tainted essence, but then something peculiar happened. The barriers he had erected around his dusk-tide repository melted away as the repository itself yawned and engulfed the dawn-tide.

Anskar doubled over to vomit, but the nausea quickly passed. When he stood straight again, he felt an absence within his skull where his repositories seemed to reside. The dawn-tide was missing. So was the dusk. The two had somehow merged into one.

There wasn't any time to think about what it meant. Anskar reached into his conjoined repository and cast a ward around Braga as the mulag swarmed over her. It wasn't the simple silver of his old ward sphere: this one was blue and purple and flashing with streaks of green.

Flesh sizzled. Mulag screeched. The ward fizzed, popped, and died as Anskar's dusk and dawn-tide mixture ran out.

Braga was surrounded by dozens of smoldering mulag corpses. And this time, before the rest of the mulag could recover, she turned and ran.

"Keep going!" Korine called back to them. "Just over this rise."

The trio of heroes continued their revolving rearguard, using what was left of their dawn-tide to ward them during the moments each fought at the back, then dowsing the ward as soon as they recommenced running.

Still the mulag came after them, no longer obscured or invisible. The mist was evaporating with the ascending sun, and the sunlight seemed to give the beasts more solidity, as if without it they were not fully real but monsters from nightmare, only half formed.

Braga stumbled, and Anskar caught her arm. She was

wounded—a flap of skin and muscle hung from her thigh, and blood spattered her boot. Both arms were raked and gouged, and a bloody score mark seeped beneath her eye. Zek took Braga's sword arm and lent his support, but even with his help, they were too slow, and the mulag started to close on them.

Korine sprinted ahead, up and over the rise. Anskar couldn't blame her. She was out of arrows and had nothing more than a dagger with which to defend herself.

The mulag were a great tide of shaggy hair and glistening claws, and there seemed no end to them. Anskar forced himself to take one step after another, but Braga's weight bore him down. Zek was sweating profusely and struggling for every breath. Braga stumbled again, and this time Zek and Anskar lacked the strength to stop her from pitching to her knees. Her sword slipped from her grasp.

The mulag roared as one.

Anskar stooped and reached for the hilt of Braga's sword, but before he made contact, before the first of the mulag fell upon him, a great cry went up from the beasts. Blood sprayed, flames roared into the sky, and the mulag parted, howling in rage and pain, as Josac flopped forward out of the mass of hairy bodies.

The priest's entire body was slick with blood. Even his hair and beard were sodden with gore. His eyes were wide, and his mouth hung open as he lay on the ground, gasping for breath. Somehow, he had fought his way back, seemingly from the dead, for Anskar had seen the Warrior priest's ward snuffed out and assumed he had fallen.

Flames surged again, this time wreathing Josac's body as well as scorching the closest mulag, and drove them back. Josac grimaced but didn't cry out, and then his grimace turned into a grin. "That... bloody showed them."

He extended his arm and the bloodied sword in his grip. *Amalantril.*

Anskar crouched and pried the hilt from Josac's twitching fingers. Fire singed his skin, but he pulled the blade away, then fell back as the flames surged once more, consuming Josac.

While the priest's body burned with some manifestation of the Warrior's Fire that Anskar had never guessed at, a great roar went up from the top of the rise.

He turned at the thunder of hooves. Silver spheres flashed into being one after another as a disciplined line of armored knights came charging down the incline, opening their ranks to accept the heroes and Anskar, Braga, and Zek. With swords extended like lances, the knights smashed into the mulag.

More people came over the crest of the rise—the retainers and healers. They swarmed down the hill to help drag Braga away from the fray. Anskar felt the warm glow of healing, and turned to see Gisela frowning in concentration as she poured dawn-tide essence and the god's power into his weary body.

And then the mounted knights were backing up, creating a wall. The mulag pressed and snarled halfway up the rise, where they stopped and would go no further.

When Anskar reached the top, Korine was waiting with Lanuc and the rest of the army.

And the high walls of Wintotashum were before them.

# TWENTY

ANSKAR GAZED AT THE CURTAIN walls that surrounded the city. They weren't as high as those at Branil's Burg nor as well built. To his eye, it seemed as though the base of the walls had been constructed at some time immemorial, then added to over the centuries. There was layer upon layer of gray stone, roughly mortared and overgrown with moss. Sandwiched between the layers were seams of reddish bricks, then more stone, then more bricks. There was no discernible pattern save that of necessity. Probably the walls had been damaged in long-ago wars, then patched and repaired.

The worst repair was to a section far to Anskar's left, where the breached stone had been replaced with a wooden palisade— dozens of stripped pine trunks sharpened to points. Some kind of fighting platform must have stood inside the wall, as the helmeted heads of crossbowmen could be seen peeking above the palisade. There were more crossbowmen along the length of the stone sections—grim-looking warriors who aimed their weapons across the valley between the city walls and the rise Lanuc's army now occupied. Before the walls was a steep embankment and in front of that a ditch, one side of which was spiked with rotting wooden stakes. There was a squat barbican flanked by two crumbling towers, and the barbican's brown-rusted portcullis was closed.

"No wonder those mangy shit-sacks won't come any closer," Braga grumbled, and she was right. Any attacking mulag would be cut down before they reached the ditch, never mind the walls.

"My people call it the fortress city," Zek said. "King Aelfyr is famed for the manner in which he defends his kingdom. There are fortifications all over the Thousand Lakes. Some among my people have long cautioned against Aelfyr's expansionism. Me, I'm not so sure. A king has the right to defend his own territory, and Aelfyr has always respected the natural border of the Ymaltian Mountains."

Something was troubling Anskar, and after wrestling with the question for a moment, he gave it voice. "Why didn't they ride out to our aid?"

Zek shrugged. "They fear the mulag as much as we do. Perhaps now the pursuit has ceased, they will raise the portcullis and come to greet us."

Lanuc rode out in front of the army, organizing the knights into ranks five abreast, mounted on their destriers, fully armored and in their white cloaks. Anskar set about wiping the gore from *Amalantril* by drawing the blade repeatedly across the snow-covered ground.

The newly ordered column descended into the valley, Lanuc and the knights at the front, the retainers and healers following. Anskar, Braga, and Zek came last, along with Nul, Rindon, and

Borik, who seemed no worse for wear after their battle with the mulag. The three heroes were passing around a wineskin and talking boisterously.

As the knights in the vanguard rode up the incline on the far side of the ditch, approaching the barbican, the portcullis still hadn't opened, and no one hailed them from the battlements.

Lanuc drew rein and held up a hand to halt the column. "Ho, Wintotashum!" he called. "We come from Sansor in answer to the King's request for aid."

The crossbowmen atop the walls remained motionless.

Lanuc tried again. "I am Lanuc of Gessa, sent by Grand Master Hyle Pausus. We're here to help."

A man in a black fur cloak and wearing a simple circlet of bronze pushed between a pair of crossbowmen and leaned out over the parapet. He was long-haired, though his beard was trimmed short, and both hair and beard were shot through with gray. He held a bejeweled finger aloft for a long moment, then jabbed it toward Lanuc.

A hundred crossbows clattered as they were brought to bear. In response, dozens of silver wards sprang into being around Lanuc and his knights.

"Do they mean to fight us?" Anskar asked no one in particular.

But then the King—for it had to be King Aelfyr atop the wall—laughed and called down, "Well met, Lanuc of Gessa. Forgive me for testing you, but the ward spheres are more than enough proof you are who you say you are. Come; I will have the portcullis raised. Only yourself, mind, and five others of your choosing. A routine precaution. Tell your people to set up camp in the valley for now, until we straighten a few things out. And tell them not to worry: the mulag won't pass the rise, not if they know what's good for them."

With that, the King ducked out of sight, and within a few minutes the portcullis began to grind upwards.

It was no surprise that Lanuc chose Rindon, Nul, and Borik to accompany him into the city. What was surprising was that he asked Anskar and Zek to go, too. In some ways, the Soreshi was an understandable choice, Anskar thought: he claimed his people wanted peace with King Aelfyr, with only a small faction desiring war. That faction had driven Zek's people from their homes, burned their villages, and committed atrocities on those left behind.

The only reason Anskar could come up with for being invited along was his sorcerous ability. Lanuc clearly hadn't expected such a cold reception.

But the biggest surprise was that Lanuc left Flavin Reider in charge of the army. Lanuc looked awkward as he informed the other knights of the decision, then endured their shaken heads and dark murmurings.

"Reider's from a rich family in Sansor," he explained to Anskar as they made their way on foot toward the barbican. "They're close to the Grand Master."

A dark-robed priest of the Elder appeared in the mouth of the barbican, glancing up uneasily at the iron teeth of the portcullis suspended above his bald head. Anskar could tell he was a devotee of the Elder because of his wispy white beard, his rounded shoulders from too much time studying at a desk, and the fact that he wore a thick-lensed monocle.

Lanuc led the way toward the barbican, Zek on one side, Anskar the other. The three heroes brought up the rear, uncharacteristically stern and serious. From what Anskar overheard of their muttered conversation, none of the three approved of poor hospitality, especially when the army had come such a long way in response to the King's plea for aid.

As they drew nearer, Anskar could see that the priest of the Elder had an unsightly hump high up on his back, and the eye covered by the monocle was in constant squinty motion. He was an ugly man, too: his nose a hooked beak with flaring nostrils and his skin pocked with the scars of some childhood disease.

"Welcome, Lanuc of Gessa," the old man said. "I am Brother Bonavir. Bonavir by birth, brother by vocation. I'm not much to look at, I'm afraid, though one shouldn't complain. A touch of goiter, that's all. Lazy eye. A bit of the palsy. The skin… that's just plague, when I was a child. Survived it, though, thank the Five. Not many do, I tell you. But do you know the really interesting thing?"

"Forgive me," Lanuc interrupted. "But the King…"

"Waiting, yes. The King will be waiting, and he's not a patient man. A decent man, mind, and holy. Certainly more pious than many a priest, and a good friend to the Church of Menselas."

Lanuc gave a polite cough.

"Ah, yes. Can't keep the King waiting. Silly old fool, Bonavir. Follow me. Try to keep up."

Brother Bonavir walked with his feet turned out like a duck. Keeping up was hardly the problem; it was trying not to overtake him that was the difficult thing.

"Quite spry for a man of… what am I? Seventy-five, or is it eighty? I lose count. Too much study will do that to a man. Addles the brain, trying to sift through all those contrary opinions and integrate them into something one can call one's own. If I could live my life over again, I'd raise sheep, I think.

Or cattle. Anything but pore over dusty tomes by the light of a guttering candle."

Bonavir led them at a snail's pace through the barbican and along cobbled streets lined with a mix of thatch-roofed wattle-and-daub houses and older stone buildings. Many were badly patched with wood, some with reddish tiles clinging like scales to their roofs. The air was thick with woodsmoke, which plumed from holes in the thatch or from brickwork chimneys atop the stone buildings.

Townsfolk stared at the passing strangers, none of them looking exactly pleased to see them. Probably they resented the fact that their king had sent to Sansor for aid months ago and it had only just arrived.

Brother Bonavir led them across a market square, then over a narrow bridge that spanned a canal. They came at last to a great hall of cut stone patched with wattle and daub and roofed with mildewed thatch. Set back from the hall was a newer building made almost entirely from thick tree trunks that lay one atop another, the gaps between them sealed with pitch. A framework tower jutted above the crude structure, atop which hung a large bell. On the gable facing them was a five-petaled rose: one of the emblems preferred by the Church of Menselas.

Bonavir took them into the great hall. Two guards in scale armor with round wooden shields and spears stood at the entrance, but didn't ask them to leave their weapons outside.

There were six more armored guards just inside the double doors that opened onto the hall, and many more faintly discernible in the hall's gloomy interior. Rushlights had been set in iron holders around the walls, many of them flickering and ready to be replaced. It was noticeably warmer here, and already Anskar was starting to sweat beneath his cloak and mail. The soles of his boots grew hot if he stood still long enough, and he wondered why that should be. It was as if the hall had been built above a fire pit that released its warmth through the stone of the floor.

Anskar guessed there were in the region of fifty armed men pressed back against the walls, forming a corridor that led to a dais atop which stood a throne. The throne was surrounded by at least fifteen priests—of the Healer, the Elder, the Warrior, the Mother, and even the Hooded One.

Upon the throne sat King Aelfyr, eyes sparkling with fierce intelligence, and while he looked more like a priest than a king, there was a hardness to his long face and a sense that he had seen his fair share of battle.

"Such a small army Hyle Pausus has sent me," he said. "I suppose it gives the impression of the Grand Master answering my request for aid without overcommitting the Order of Eternal Vigilance."

"We are indeed a small army," Lanuc conceded, "but we are an army of knights."

"I can see that," King Aelfyr said. "And a knight of the Order of Eternal Vigilance is worth ten ordinary men-at-arms—is that not what they say in Sansor?"

"An exaggeration, sire," Lanuc said.

"Statistically, the evidence would support such a contention," Brother Bonavir interjected.

King Aelfyr flicked the Elder's priest a look of irritation, then manufactured a thin smile for Lanuc's benefit. "You know, Lanuc of Gessa, our situation?"

"The Soreshi come down out of the Ymaltian Mountains to harass your subjects, sire."

"Harass… That must be Sansor-speak for burn our town and villages, defile and plunder. The skies are clear today, Lanuc, but most days there are plumes of black smoke from the east: our towns burning. Of course, we counter. We push them back into the mountains, we rebuild, we fortify as best we can, but always they return."

The King's eyes alighted on Zek. "Yet you see fit to bring a Soreshi into our presence. I'm sure there is a good explanation."

"This, sire," Lanuc said, "is Zekil Silvertongue. We… encountered Zek and some of his people on the journey here. Their own villages have been burned, sire, by the same Soreshi who attack your lands."

"The same? Are not all Soreshi the same?"

"No, Majesty, we are—" Zek started, but stopped when the King snapped his fingers.

"Lanuc of Gessa," Aelfyr demanded, "are not all Soreshi the same?"

Lanuc licked his lips and shifted his weight from foot to foot. "It would seem not, sire. A faction has arisen among the Soreshi…"

"The Soreshi are at war with themselves?" the King asked.

Zek opened his mouth to reply but promptly closed it again.

"My understanding, sire," Lanuc said, "is that the aggressors struck hard and fast, and there was no time for Zek's people to organize an effective defense."

"Not a minority uprising, then?"

"It would appear not, sire," Lanuc conceded.

The King shifted on his throne. "What concerns me most is what has brought about this change in the savages of the mountains. For centuries the Soreshi have left us alone, and our two peoples have co-existed peacefully."

"Perhaps we will be able to help you find out what has changed, and set things right," Lanuc said.

"Magnanimous of you. Hyle Pausus is so good to us folk of the provinces." The King's eyes seemed to lose focus for an instant, but then he shook his head. "Come closer," he said, speaking to the three heroes who stood just behind Lanuc.

Nul, Rindon, and Borik advanced then dipped their heads in unison. The King's eyes alighted on the massive oilskin-wrapped sword Borik was leaning on as if it were a staff.

"Is that… the Sword of Supremacy?"

"It is, sire," Borik replied.

"I would very much like to see it."

Borik grew suddenly awkward and glanced at Nul.

"And you shall, Majesty," interjected Rindon, "when we engage the enemy for you. Until such time, the Sword of Supremacy must remain hidden."

"Yes, yes," King Aelfyr said, "else bad luck will befall the wielder, and we can't have that, can we? So, it's true: the legendary blade will never break in battle?"

"So long as she sups on blood," Borik said.

"And if you reveal the blade, you must kill with it?"

"That is the nature of the sword," Nul said. "It takes a special kind of man to wield her."

"A hero," King Aelfyr observed, appraising first Borik and then the other two. "Your fame precedes you, gentlemen, and I am truly grateful to have you with us. If the stories of your exploits are true, I would sooner have the three of you fighting alongside me than an entire army of lesser men. And this is?" the King asked, directing his gaze at Anskar.

"Anskar DeVantte, sire," Lanuc said. "He is under my charge at request of the Seneschal of Branil's Burg on Niyas."

"A Niyandrian? I thought there was something about the eyes."

"No," Anskar said, then added, "Sire."

King Aelfyr raised an eyebrow, which Brother Bonavir took as his cue to step forward and examine Anskar.

As the Elder's priest inclined his head, ostensibly appraising Anskar's eyes, Anskar felt the probe of sorcery. On instinct, he erected wards to thwart it, but Bonavir's was a subtle kind of sorcery that somehow slipped through the gaps in Anskar's barriers, leaving him feeling inadequate and exposed.

"You're a knight, you say?" Bonavir asked in a congenial voice.

"Inferior," Anskar confirmed.

Bonavir seemed amused by that. "But more than a knight in other respects, I'll warrant. Interesting, Majesty. Very interesting indeed."

"You serve the Five?" one of the priests huddled around the throne asked Anskar—a healer.

"Of course."

"You're sure?" asked a priestess of the Hooded One. "I smell a taint."

"He is sure," Lanuc said.

"Enough," King Aelfyr told the priests. "Let us not be impolite to our guests."

The gaggle of priests all nodded enthusiastically at that, vying with each other for the King's favor.

"The important thing is that Lanuc of Gessa and his army of knights are here. It has been a long wait—but a worthwhile one, I'm sure. And how blessed we are to welcome the three greatest living heroes of our day: Rindon, Nul, and Borik. You have my thanks for making the long journey from Sansor, Lanuc of Gessa. When we are done here, you will be accommodated in the royal barracks behind this hall. And please accept our humble apology that there is insufficient room for the rest of your brave force within the city walls at this juncture. Rest assured, we will bring them inside once suitable arrangements can be made."

A likely story, Anskar thought. King Aelfyr was clearly a cautious ruler, and probably reluctant to permit almost a hundred armed knights inside the city walls. Fighting men and women were known for their drinking and carousing—and Anskar had seen that knights were no exception. Things could soon turn ugly if swords were drawn.

"But first," King Aelfyr said, "Brother Kenaith will outline where we are in this war with the Soreshi, and, now that help has arrived, what we intend to do next."

Brother Kenaith stepped away from the group of priests gathered around the throne. He was a short man and stocky, with shoulders so huge he appeared to have no neck. Judging by his steel breastplate embossed with a fist clutching a sword, he was a priest of the Warrior, and there was an air of self-assurance about him that bordered on arrogance. He wore a round, steel-rimmed shield strapped to his back, and held the long haft of a single-bladed axe.

In a clipped and oddly high-pitched voice, Brother Kenaith explained how the Soreshi had suddenly streamed down from the Ymaltian Mountains earlier in the year and devastated the settlements in the foothills on the Thousand Lakes side of the border.

"By the time word reached us here in Wintotashum, it was already too late," the priest said. "His Majesty dispatched a force to counter the invaders, but when our army reached the settlements, the Soreshi had already disappeared back into the mountains. We rebuilt, and constructed stout palisades to guard against future incursions. We garrisoned the towns and relayed messages between the border and Wintotashum to make sure we would be forewarned of any future attacks. The Soreshi simply ignored our defenses and attacked settlements deeper into our lands. By the time we sent a response, they had looped back behind us to ravage the first settlements again. They use sorcery to cloak their movements, and rained down sorcerous fire on our villages and towns. There are too few priests of the Warrior among us," he finished, "else we could have repulsed their attacks."

"Be that as it may," King Aelfyr said, and his tone conveyed the impression that it would have made very little difference to have more priests of the Warrior among his army, "we have repulsed the enemy several times with our longbows. Virtually every peasant in Thousand Lakes is trained as an archer from the age of seven, and I suspect that's the only reason we've not yet been overrun. Even so, the Soreshi are persistently sacking the towns between the mountains and Wintotashum, and we have been scurrying from one site of devastation to the next like fools. Kenaith here believes I have been overly cautious and we should take the fight to the enemy—into the mountains."

"Where the Soreshi would possess all the advantages," Lanuc said.

"Exactly."

Brother Kenaith smarted at that. "Soreshi aggression must be met with an iron fist. It's the only thing the bloody savages understand."

King Aelfyr stifled a yawn.

Beside Anskar, Zek folded his arms over his chest.

"Your Majesty, if I may?" Lanuc said, and King Aelfyr nodded for him to go on. "Do you plan to fight a defensive war from behind Wintotashum's walls?"

"And leave the rest of my kingdom to burn? I do not. Three months ago—well after I first sent to Sansor for aid—the royal decree was given that every able-bodied man and woman was to practice with sword and arm themselves with a bow. My forges here in Wintotashum have been perpetually ablaze, and the city's armorers and fletchers have worked tirelessly day and night to ensure our people have adequate weapons and armor. Each town has been garrisoned by several hundred seasoned veterans. There will be no more easy pickings for the Soreshi.

"As to Wintotashum, the city is nestled within a complex network of lakes and canals, which form a natural defense—although scholars like Brother Bonavir here might tell you that there is nothing haphazard about the placement of the lakes. Already fords have been flooded, bridges destroyed, and the larger lakes are patrolled by heavily armed longships with crews of sixty fighting men. That all leaves an invading army few good options if they plan to come against Wintotashum head on."

"Why would the Soreshi attack Wintotashum?" Anskar asked, and Lanuc flashed him a warning glare.

"Why attack Thousand Lakes at all?" King Aelfyr said. "Perhaps Zekil Silvertongue can enlighten us?"

"Something has happened, sire," Zek said. "Some kind of influence."

"Indeed," King Aelfyr said. "Some among my priests have gotten a whiff of it. An evil stain, they say. A madness that has afflicted the Soreshi—or at least some of them, as you would have it. What do you call it, Brother Bonavir?"

"The tides, Majesty. There is a discoloration of the tides, if such it can be called. The tides, of course, have no pigmentation, so when we speak of color, we mean something quite different. The same when we speak of scent or smell. But there is an anomaly in the tides that blow through the Ymaltian Mountains. Of course, it could be entirely natural, something cyclical that only happens once every few thousand years."

"But you don't think so," Anskar interjected.

"No," Brother Bonavir said. "I do not."

"Well," King Aelfyr said, wincing as he stood from his throne and clutching his stomach. "I think that's enough talk for now. Let's get you people settled into the barracks, fed, and watered. Tomorrow we'll meet again and lay our plans."

# TWENTY-ONE

AS LANUC'S GROUP OF SIX stood outside the great hall, Brother Bonavir approached Anskar.

"I sense great conflict in you, young Anskar. If you need to talk while you're here, I am at your service. Conflict is something I know all too much about. No, of course you don't want to talk with an old fool like me. Whatever was I thinking?"

"I'd like that," Anskar said.

It was clear that Bonavir knew things about sorcery he did not, including how to penetrate another's sorcerous defenses. There were bound to be other things he could learn from this old man, and there were questions he wanted badly to ask—about balance, about morality, about what was and was not permissible to a fully integrated follower of Menselas. He felt as though he had been kept in the dark about a wealth of knowledge the priests and consecrated knights had access to.

Bonavir's smile lit up his face. "Excellent. I shall look forward to it. Once you've had a chance to bathe and eat, I shall call upon you at the barracks. And don't worry, Anskar. I have seen what lies within you. As with everything else along the paths the Five sets before us, it is all a matter of perspective. It will turn out well for you, have no doubt, but wellness, as any good healer will tell you, seldom comes without suffering, and often a good dose of purgative remedies."

The three heroes took a barracks room together. Borik accepted the floor, while Rindon and Nul laid claim to the bunks. Lanuc, as commander, was given a single room of his own.

Anskar agreed to bunk down with Zek. He felt a growing connection with the Soreshi; both possessed sorcerous abilities that made the knights if not fearful of them, then at least mistrustful.

After being allocated their room, Anskar and Zek were directed to a communal bathhouse. The water was blessedly warm, and afterwards they sat in a room thick with steam from a cauldron filled with smoldering coals.

The King's men they spoke with were cordial enough, though they eyed Zek with suspicion. They recommended a tavern they called the Piss-Pot, which in reality was named the King's Throne, and Anskar and Zek went there for their evening meal and a mug or two of beer.

It was surprisingly pleasant inside, warm and homey, but then Anskar supposed it had to be, given the frigid weather that plagued the Thousand Lakes. What else would there be to do in such a place, other than eat and drink and warm yourself in front of a blazing fire?

The tavern was packed, and they had to wait until a table in a nook became free. The locals—laborers and soldiers intermingled—stood around the bar or sat on tall stools. A few of the Thousand Lakes soldiers glanced over at Zek, muttering to one another. Anskar touched *Amalantril*'s hilt beneath the table, glad that he'd taken her back from Josac's dying grip.

With that small gesture, he was reminded of the reason he had so readily agreed to speak with Brother Bonavir. It had to stop, this locking away pieces of himself and trying to pretend he was something less than he really was.

"Perhaps we should leave," Zek said.

"We're under the King's protection," Anskar said.

"We are?"

"I think so. Let's at least wait until our food comes."

As he spoke, the door opened and in walked Nul, Rindon, and Borik. The atmosphere changed in an instant.

Rindon strolled up to the bar, greeting soldiers with a handshake and a pat on the back, and loudly offered to buy everyone a drink. Nul joined him, engaging the locals in friendly banter, but Borik merely stood by awkwardly, leaning on the wrapped Sword of Supremacy, and sipping his beer once Rindon handed him a mug.

Pretty soon, Rindon was regaling the entire tavern with highblown tales of Borik's exploits with his mighty sword, and the local soldiers lost interest in Zek and Anskar.

Nul caught Anskar's gaze and raised his mug, shaking his head at Rindon's overembellishment of what was now a ballad of Borik, which Rindon sang in a tenor voice a bard would have been proud of.

When Anskar turned back to Zek, the Soreshi was watching him.

"I was wondering, Anskar, why you did not use your sword against my people."

Before Anskar could answer, the serving girl set two bowls of steaming broth on the table before them, along with a wooden platter holding a loaf of freshly baked bread.

Anskar leaned over his bowl to sniff at the broth. "Beef," he said, and something else—a hint of mushrooms and spices that made his mouth water.

"Your sword…" Zek prompted.

Anskar ripped off a hunk of bread and trailed it through his broth. "I lent it to Josac."

"Because he was a better swordsman than you?"

"No." Anskar popped the broth-soaked bread in his mouth and chewed ravenously, at the same time picking up his spoon.

"I cannot believe you were afraid to fight," Zek said. "So why?"

Anskar set down his spoon. "It wasn't about the sword."

Zek steepled his hands in front of his face, his food forgotten. He said nothing, just waited patiently for Anskar to speak.

And so Anskar told him about the battles he'd fought within himself since the eve of the trials at Branil's Burg. How he had tried to contain his arrogance, his anger. How he had succumbed to lust with Sareya—a Niyandrian.

Zek laughed at that.

"What's so funny?" Anskar said.

"You worshipers of Menselas, always fretting about where you stick your…" He coughed and tried again. "Coupling comes naturally to us Soreshi. It is one of the greatest blessings of life—something to be embraced, enjoyed."

Anskar frowned. Brother Tion would have condemned such ideas as heretical, but then Brother Tion was hardly one to talk. And Anskar had to admit, he wanted to hear about this Soreshi view of sex. It was hard to imagine a world in which such pleasures could be enjoyed without the crushing weight of guilt that invariably followed. Of course, the knights he had observed at Kyuth, rutting in the loft with the town's whores, had shown no signs of contrition. Rather, they'd reveled in the fact that they were doing something wrong and getting away with it.

"We do not marry as your people do," Zek went on. "We are like ships passing in the night. Sometimes we pause awhile and get to know each other intimately. Often we embrace the tides together, the dusk and the dawn. Have you ever..." He stopped.

"Have I ever what?"

"Have you ever welcomed the dusk-tide naked, with a woman in your arms?"

"Can't say that I have," replied Anskar, heat flooding his cheeks.

"Then you must! A hot-blooded Soreshi woman, mind, with a brimming repository, not one of these desiccated-on-the-inside Thousand Lakes peasants, or those painted Sansor harlots."

"You've been to Sansor?"

"I hear things."

They both laughed, then both took sips of beer at the same time.

"So you thought that by not fighting with your sword, you would please your god?" Zek said.

"I'm not saying I was right."

"Which god, though? You worship five."

"Ah, now that's where you're wrong," Anskar said, downing the rest of his beer and raising the empty mug till the serving girl saw. "Menselas is one god, but he has five aspects."

"He is divided among himself?"

"Not divided. The five aspects are in perfect harmony. And that's what we, his followers, are supposed to imitate. We must come to know all the aspects that make us what we are, and hold them together in balance."

"This is why you gave up your sword? That makes no sense at all."

"I was wrong," Anskar said. "I think. I'm confused."

Zek leaned across the table, keeping his voice low. "About sorcery too?"

"About sorcery above all else."

Zek thought for a moment before he spoke again. "Menselas is a god of balance, yes?"

"Five aspects held in equilibrium."

"And if out of balance, what happens then?"

"Too much of any one aspect leads to excess, corruption, perversion."

"And if you take one aspect and examine it by itself? Say, for example, the Hooded One."

Anskar recalled his time at the Abbey of the Hooded One, when the Abbess had convinced him that what he'd once thought was bad was good. The thought of what he had done with that vile woman still made his innards clench.

"Taken in isolation," he said, "devotion to the Hooded One leads to death, disease, and corruption. On its own, it is depraved, demonic."

"It is the same with the tides of sorcery," Zek said. "They are in essence one, though, like light striking a prism, they are in some mysterious way refracted. Our role as sorcerers—at least in the Soreshi tradition—is to gather all that the tides bring to us and bind them back together as one."

"And that's possible?" Anskar said. "I mean, I know that your dawn- and dusk-tide repositories are melded in some way, but—"

"You do? Not so unknowing as you make yourself out to be, Anskar DeVantte, are you? Yes, my repositories are braided, but it is a crude braid. The more adept sorcerers among my people weave their repositories together seamlessly."

"The dawn and the dusk?"

"Of course. There are no others, at least not this side of the abyssal realms."

"But the other one…" Anskar started.

"The dark-tide?"

"Does it also come from the same source?"

"I would have to assume so, but you would know more about that than me. I saw what you did back at the gully. Saw, but did not fully understand. But I'm guessing it had to be the dark-tide."

Anskar swallowed and just about managed to nod.

"Don't worry," Zek said, "I'm not judging, just intrigued. How did you, a holy knight, gain access to the dark-tide?"

"I'm not holy," Anskar said. "And I'm only a knight-inferior."

"Only?" Zek said, and when he laughed this time, it sounded false. "Perhaps…" He hesitated. "Perhaps you could teach me?"

They paused to allow the serving girl to pour them both more beer from a pitcher.

"Me, teach you?" Anskar said when the girl had gone. "But you're Soreshi. I was going to ask you to teach me."

"And I will… about balance. I can show you how to make your repositories work with each other. The dusk and the dawn, I mean. But if, in return, you were to introduce me to the rudiments of the dark-tide…"

"I don't know," Anskar said. "You say that the tides have one and the same source, that it's possible to hold them in balance, but my experience of the dark-tide has been…"

"Dark?" Zek said with a wry grin. "Demonic?"

"Unpredictable. It doesn't feel right, Zek."

The Soreshi steepled his hands in front of his face. "Maybe it will once we figure out how to bring it into balance with the dawn and the dusk."

"I'm not so sure. And why would you want this knowledge anyway?"

"Because I'm Soreshi. For us, all knowledge is good knowledge. A sorcerer is measured by how much they know, and there are few among my kind who know the ways of the dark-tide. One or two, maybe, and a handful of great sorcerers from the past—all of whom died horribly and mysteriously."

"Yet you still want to learn this ability?" Anskar said.

"Let us start with me teaching you to balance the dawn and the dusk. I see your repositories have already melded together, albeit in a clump of knotted strands that no doubt impedes the full flow of your casting. If you're satisfied with what I teach, maybe you will repay me with an iota of your dark-tide lore."

"Maybe," Anskar said, still not convinced. He hadn't yet laid to rest the idea that Menselas cursed those who used the dusk-tide, let alone the dark. And if it were indeed a sin to use the lore of the abyssal realms, he would only be compounding that sin by teaching the knowledge to someone else.

The tavern door swung open, admitting an icy gust of wind. "Anskar DeVantte?" a Thousand Lakes soldier bellowed.

Shrugs and blank looks passed around the tavern until the three heroes turned to face Anskar and pointed. Rindon, of course, raised his mug and beamed.

The soldier, a gray-haired man who looked too old to fight, hobbled over to their table. "Brother Bonavir asked me to fetch you, sir, and bring you to the barbican gate."

"Bonavir? Why? Is something the matter?"

"Says there's a large woman outside who's demanding to see you. Something about a ghost telling her she's not to stray from your side."

Braga's shouted curses and insults had offended even the Thousand Lakes guards. When Anskar and Zek arrived, Bonavir was concerned that the big woman might be deranged. Dangerous, even.

"The ghost lady was angry this time," Braga said once all four of them were gathered in the barracks room Anskar and Zek shared.

The Soreshi sat on the top bunk, legs dangling over the edge. Bonavir stood in the doorway, watching Braga intently.

"Why would she be angry?" Anskar asked.

"Because I failed. She's going to curse me, isn't she? The rancid bitch is going to curse me."

"You're not making sense, my dear," Brother Bonavir said. "Just who is this ghost lady? And why would she curse you?"

"Who's talking to you, turd-face?"

"Is it the vambrace?" Anskar asked. "She wants you to remove it?"

"No," Braga said. "She wants me to examine it so I can make more."

"More vambraces?"

"She showed me, in my head. A whole suit of armor—you were wearing it. She wants me to make it for you."

"She told you this?" Anskar said, recalling the vision he had seen.

"Not with words, but I think that's what she wants. I could be wrong."

"Never heed ghosts and spirits, my people say," Zek put in. "Those who return from the realm of the dead serve only their own selfish ends."

"What kind of armor?" Brother Bonavir asked.

"Who is this maggot?" Braga said. "Why's he here?"

"He let you into the city, remember?" Anskar said. "His name is Brother Bonavir. He's a priest of the Elder."

Braga spat. "Bloody squinty, shortsighted book-lovers. Bet you've never done a hard day's work in your life, have you, shag-face?"

Bonavir raised an eyebrow. "I thought I was turd-face."

"That too, dung-breath. You need to show me the vambrace again, ass-wipe."

"We'll have to go outside in order to see it," Anskar said.

Brother Bonavir stepped forward. "In the moonlight?"

Anskar stared at him. How could he know?

"This vambrace," the priest continued, "you have it on your person?"

Despite his misgivings, Anskar rolled up his sleeve.

"May I?" Bonavir said, then proceeded to feel about Anskar's forearm with his fingers, murmuring when he encountered the cold metal of the vambrace. "Where did you get this?"

Anskar withdrew his arm without answering and tugged down his sleeve.

"Of course," Bonavir said. "You barely know me. You must be wondering how I knew about the vambrace. In truth, I didn't, but I listened to what was said between you and this good woman here, and I pieced things together. As Braga has so astutely observed, I read a good many things. We all do, we priests of the Elder. We learn all the myths and legends of Wiraya, so I have heard the Niyandrian folk tales of the Armor of Divinity."

"That's what this is?" Anskar asked.

Bonavir removed his monocle and cleaned it on the sleeve of his robe. "Who can say? In one tale—the most famous—a suit of Armor of Divinity was forged by the necromancer Tain for the Niyandrian King Lowanu, but when it was completed, Tain took it for himself."

"Why?" Anskar asked.

"Because the armor is supposed to bestow immortality on the wearer, and immortality is what Niyandrians most desire. Their whole culture is based upon the acquisition of eternal life, and Tain had long claimed he knew how to attain it. All he had previously lacked was the funding and the materials necessary for his work."

"And the King provided both," Anskar said. "Wouldn't Tain taking the armor for himself be considered an act of treason?"

"It was, and the King condemned Tain to torture and execution, but no one could find the necromancer or the armor he had crafted."

"So what happened?" Zek asked.

"That," Bonavir said, "is where the legend grows hazy. Some say Tain put on the full suit of armor and vanished from the world. Maybe he became a god—one among many. Perhaps the other gods accepted him, perhaps they did not. I suppose we shall never know. But what is important is that the last ruler of Niyas, the Necromancer Queen Talia"—he touched the tips of four fingers and his thumb to his breast in the sign of the Five—"sought to emulate Tain. She searched far and wide for the knowledge to replicate the Armor of Divinity, sending her agents even as far as Sansor in Kaile, and subsequently here, to Wintotashum's Royal Scriptorium, where we have an ancient notebook written in Skanuric that scholars have long contested contains Tain's instructions for making the Armor of Divinity."

Zek sniffed derisively. "And where did Tain get his knowledge?"

"Wouldn't we all like to know?" Brother Bonavir said. "But the important question to ask is, how far did Queen Talia get in her attempt to replicate the armor? Wouldn't it be exciting if this ghost lady proved to be none other than Queen Talia herself, and the vambrace Anskar wears is part of her Armor of Divinity?"

"Concerning is what it would be," Zek said. "Like I said before, we Soreshi pay no attention to the wishes and plans of the dead."

"My vambrace might be something else altogether," Anskar said. "I mean, was the Armor of Divinity invisible like this?"

"There is no mention of it, so I would have to assume not. And besides, invisibility is a power of the dark-tide working through void-steel."

"Void-steel?"

"Interesting metal. It reacts to moonlight, if I understand correctly. I read about it in a confrere's thesis."

"What thesis?" Anskar asked.

"Oh, some abstract nonsense—you know how scholars tend to overspecialize, until no one else can make head nor tail of—"

"Tell me," Anskar said, face pressed up close to Bonavir's. As soon as he realized he was angry, he stepped back and took a breath to calm himself. He didn't know how or why, but Bonavir had struck a nerve.

"It was a study of the legends of Shimrax. Apparently, void-steel is only found in the abyssal realms."

"So whoever made Anskar's vambrace had the aid of demons?" Zek said.

"Or was a demon," Anskar said.

"So what's your interest in this Armor of Divinity?" Braga asked. "You want to find it for yourself?"

Bonavir shook his head. "I doubt it exists. Tain's Armor of Divinity, the legend tells us, vanished along with him, and Queen Talia's… I suspect it was never finished. Probably it was barely even started, given the difficulties of producing and working with divine alloy. You need a very hot forge."

Anskar shared a look with Braga, and she scowled.

"You think my vambrace was made here in Wintotashum?" Anskar said.

"If it was, I know a man who could tell us for sure."

"Hrothyr," Braga said.

"You know the King's blacksmith?"

"I know him."

# TWENTY-TWO

"ALL RIGHT, ALL RIGHT, I'M coming!" a man hollered from the other side of the door.

Braga stopped her knocking. "That'll be an improvement on last time," she said. "So you got that course of leeches from the physiker to fix your flaccid little maggot, did you?"

"Braga?"

The door swung open and a huge man stepped out. Hrothyr had a ruddy, round face and a thick, curly beard. His eyebrows were bushy and singed black, and his ginger hair was so far receded it was basically a tonsure with a fringe of greasy ringlets that fell to his shoulders. When he gave Braga an uncertain smile, the gap in his teeth was revealed—or rather the teeth in his gap, for he only had two front teeth, both of them yellow.

He glanced at Anskar and Zek, then widened his eyes when he saw Brother Bonavir. "What are you doing here?" But before the priest of the Elder could answer, Hrothyr focused on Braga once more. "You came. After all these years, you—"

"Don't waste your breath, slug-crotch," Braga said. "I ain't forgiven you." She stepped aside and nodded toward Anskar.

"What do you want, waking me up at this hour?" Hrothyr said. He wrinkled his nose. "Are you a Niyandrian?"

"Waking you?" Zek said. "But you're fully dressed."

Hrothyr had on a stained once-white shirt, thick-weave pants, and long socks riddled with holes. Over his clothes he wore a leather apron that, like his eyebrows, had been burned at one time or another.

"He's always dressed," Braga said. "Save when he's doing it, and that ain't a pretty sight, I can tell you. Other than that, the filthy bastard sleeps in his work clothes, which is why he stinks like something that slopped out of a mule's ass."

"I'm waiting, boy," Hrothyr said, pointedly ignoring Braga's insults. "Why did you wake me up?"

Anskar held up his arm and pulled back the sleeve of his shirt. Hrothyr shielded his eyes against the glare. Beneath the silvery light of Chandra and the red of Jagonath, the vambrace rippled with an oil-sheened brilliance.

Hrothyr reached out a hand but stopped shy of touching the metal. "It can't be. How did you get hold of this? I made it. Twenty years ago, give or take." A pained look passed across his face, and he glanced at Anskar. "You'd better all come inside. Some things it ain't safe to talk about in the open, and certainly not in the moonlight."

He led them into the house, where they were met by the feeble glow of grime-smeared crafted globes set into the ceiling.

The place was cramped, almost claustrophobic, and there was far more furniture than seemed necessary. Every wall had a sideboard against it or a chest of drawers. Stacked on top of every piece of furniture were wooden crates and boxes that contained everything from rivets and nails to earthenware casks and clear-glass bottles of solvents, oils, and acids. There were wooden handles for tools, iron heads, whetstones, blocks of river stone of various grades, ingots of iron, copper, and bronze. The whole house stank of grease and oil, reminding Anskar of the smithing hall at Branil's Burg.

The blacksmith guided them through the organized clutter to a kitchen-cum-dining room, the walls of which were also lined with boxes all the way up to the low ceiling. There was an island of space in the center, where a butcher's-top table stood, along with a single chair.

Hrothyr didn't have guests often, he explained, and Braga muttered something under her breath. He slid four crates across the floor as seats for the others, then plonked himself in the chair.

"I would have offered you a hot drink, only…" He cast a look toward the stove, which was buried beneath yet more boxes.

Anskar, Zek, and Brother Bonavir seated themselves on the crates, but Braga remained standing, her head almost brushing the ceiling beams.

"You really made ass-wipe's vambrace?" she said.

Hrothyr glanced at her. "I never told you all my secrets, Braga."

"No. Some I had to find out for myself."

"And I'm sorry for that."

"That just makes you a sorry turd," Braga said.

"Show it to me again," Hrothyr said, and Anskar rolled up his sleeve once more, this time revealing only the bare skin of his arm. Hrothyr reached out, and his fingers touched the invisible metal of the vambrace. "Just wanted to be sure," he said. "But you've still not answered my question. How did you come by it?"

"Can you remove the vambrace?" Anskar asked.

"I could. And I probably should. I'll fetch my tools."

"No, wait," Anskar said. "This is all happening too quickly."

He frowned, not sure exactly what he should and shouldn't tell them. That he was Queen Talia's son? Probably not a good idea. The fewer people who knew that, the better. How he had found the vambrace? Maybe. He looked at Zek, who was watching him through slitted eyes.

"How about I start?" Hrothyr said. "I told you I made the vambrace. Well, I put together the alloy too, though I scarce remember how. Twenty years flies by in the blink of an eye, but it's still a long time."

"If I may," Brother Bonavir interjected. "You were granted access to the Scriptorium's restricted shelves?"

"I was."

"That's a relief," the priest said. "As far as I know, the instructions for smelting—is that the right word?—divine alloy exist nowhere else, not even on Niyas. The necromancer Tain left nothing behind save the notes we have here in Wintotashum, which no one can access without the express permission of the King."

"What I did back then," Hrothyr said in a faltering voice, "ain't something I'm proud of."

"Here we go," Braga said, folding her arms beneath her massive breasts.

"But I had my reasons."

"Course you did."

Hrothyr shifted uneasily on his chair, a grimace that could have been pain or annoyance crossing his face. "They accosted me in the street one night after I'd had a bit too much to drink. Niyandrians they were, which was strange in these parts. I later learned they were agents of Queen Talia."

Anskar held his breath and leaned forward.

"They said they could hurt my family," Hrothyr said. "Told me the names and addresses of my ma and pa, my two sisters."

"Those fat slappers," Braga said.

"They gave me instructions, from the Queen of Niyas herself, they said. One word to anyone and they would kill my family and then kill me. So I cooperated. An agent of Queen Talia's broke into the Scriptorium and found what we needed."

"The necromancer Tain's notebook," Bonavir said.

"The agent didn't steal it," Hrothyr said, "just memorized the parts we needed: the instructions for making divine alloy. It took me a while to get the ratios right, and I've forgotten half the ingredients—copper there was, and iron, astrumium, and half a dozen other ores. Some of the ingredients came by way of the Ethereal Sorceress. And the forges... Bloody darkness, them forges had to be hot. Singed more than my eyebrows back then, I can tell you."

"But you managed to make the vambrace," Anskar prompted.

"Aye, I made the damned thing right enough, and the bloody Niyandrians paid me well in gold for it."

"And to think you was always grumbling about having no money," Braga said. "Turd."

"It was before I met you, Braga. Nine, maybe ten years."

"Eight," Braga said emphatically. "A man with his head screwed on would've invested all that coin, maybe bought a decent home."

"Nothing wrong with this place."

Braga looked away in disgust.

"And it was you who made the vambrace invisible?" Anskar said, sharing a look with Zek.

"There was another ingredient I was told to add to the alloy—something not mentioned in Tain's notebook. One of the Niyandrians spoke words in a foreign language, and the vambrace faded away before my eyes."

"Void-steel," Anskar said.

"Maybe. If I knew what that was."

"So did they take the vambrace back to Niyas?" Brother Bonavir asked.

Hrothyr nodded. "Took it to their queen. They was supposed to come back for more—said she wanted the entire suit of armor, exactly as Tain had made it—but no one ever returned."

"Probably because of the war," Bonavir said. "There would have been a few years yet till the liberation of Niyas by the mainland allies."

"I'm certain Queen Talia is your ghost lady, Braga," Anskar said.

"I figured that out for myself, ass-wipe," she said. "And now I think I've figured out why she came to me."

Hrothyr met her gaze. "Because of the skills I taught you when we—"

"You taught me nothing I didn't already learn from my grandpa," Braga cut in.

Hrothyr looked about to object but thought better of it. "And perhaps because she knew I was the one who made the vambrace in the first place, and she somehow knew that we were related."

"You and Braga are related?" Zek said. "Like brother and sister?"

"We're married," Hrothyr said.

"Were," Braga corrected.

"Hrothyr's your husband?" Anskar said incredulously. "You didn't tell me you were married, Braga."

"Because I'm not. Not any longer."

"Nothing that the Five joins together can be sundered,"

Brother Bonavir said.

Braga turned on the priest. "He joined your teeth to your gums. But that's about to change if you don't shut your trap."

"I'm sorry, Braga," Hrothyr said. "I was a fool. I made a mistake. How many times do I have to say it?"

"So did I, marrying a slime-covered piece of dripping shit like you."

"You could make the full armor?" Bonavir asked.

"I could not," Hrothyr said. "A vambrace is one thing, but a full suit of plate…"

"Then give me your notes," Braga said, "and I'll bloody well do it. But I'll need your forges."

Hrothyr stared at her for a long while before he replied. "Even if I let you, how will you smelt enough divine alloy? The components aren't easy to come by. And as for this other stuff, this void-steel…"

"If its only purpose is to render the armor invisible," Zek said, "would we even need it?"

"If," Brother Bonavir said. "From what I read in my colleague's thesis, void-steel has many properties, so long as you know the cants to coax them out of the metal. Of course, finding void-steel may be beyond us, but the other ingredients…"

Anskar flashed him a look. Why was the priest of the Elder so invested in all this?

"This is an unparalleled opportunity," Bonavir said, as if he had intuited Anskar's question. "The lore of the ancient civilizations that preceded our own is the most sought after, the most prized, among those of us dedicated to the pursuit of knowledge. That this vambrace, made according to ancient sorcery retrieved by Queen Talia, should present itself in this manner tells me that Menselas has willed that such forgotten knowledge be brought back into the light."

"And you think that's a good thing?" Anskar asked. "My…" He almost said "My mother" but caught himself. "Queen Talia wants this Armor of Divinity for herself. I've seen it in a dream."

"My people view the Niyandrians as demons," Zek added. "Obsessed with immortality, and with bringing the dead back to life."

"Then we shall proceed with caution," Bonavir said. "Let me make some enquiries with Sheelahn, the Ethereal Sorceress. She'll know where we can obtain the necessary ores—at a cost, of course. On second thought," he said, "you should go to her, Anskar. She'll want to see the vambrace and make a note of it, and I'm sure there's good advice she can give you… about any number of things. And you are probably better suited to pay her price."

"And if I don't want to?" Anskar said. "What if I just want Hrothyr to remove the vambrace and destroy it? Maybe I want to forget all about the Armor of Divinity."

"You can't," Braga said. "She'll be angry."

"So what if she is?" Hrothyr said. "It ain't like you to be frightened of anyone, Braga."

"Aren't you forgetting something?" Zek said. When everyone turned to him, he added, "The instructions?"

"The necromancer Tain's notes?" Brother Bonavir said. "I'll speak with the King and see if he'll grant me access to the Scriptorium."

"You think that's likely?" Hrothyr asked.

"I do not."

"Well, if you're looking for someone with the skills to break in…" Zek said.

"I'm not sure about this." Anskar realized he had gone from being totally against the idea to being on the fence about it.

He had to admit that the mystery of the vambrace and the myth of the Armor of Divinity were oddly compelling. A series of thoughts rose unbidden to mind, all of them persuading him that there could be no harm in finding out more before destroying the vambrace. After all, the vambrace had saved his life several times already. And did it matter that Queen Talia desired the Armor of Divinity for her own ends? Maybe history had been unfair to her. Maybe Wiraya needed her again, to restore some sort of balance, to oppose the corruption Anskar had witnessed within his very own Order, not to mention elsewhere on the mainland.

"I don't suppose it will do any harm to find out more," he said. "But not now. I have to sleep. I have a meeting with the king in the morning."

"I'll be at the meeting too," Bonavir said. "But perhaps…" He cast a sly look at Zek.

The Soreshi waggled his fingers in a parody of a sorcerer casting an enchantment. "I'll get the notes, don't you worry. And no one will have a clue they're gone."

"And I'll copy them by hand so you can return them as soon as possible," Bonavir said.

The priest was a little too invested for Anskar's liking. Was there more to him than met the eye? Or did his enthusiasm, like Zek's, really stem from a desire for ever greater knowledge?

"A moment, please," Hrothyr said as his visitors stood up to leave. "Braga, could we—?"

"No," she said, already heading for the front door.

"I am concerned about you, my friend," Zek said.

He was once more seated on the top bunk in their shared

barracks room, and all Anskar could see of the Soreshi from the bottom bunk were his bare feet, the soles hardened with calluses.

"What's to be concerned about?"

"You have—for a non-Soreshi, at any rate—a significant sorcerous mark."

"The priests say the same about my god's mark. Others say they are one and the same thing."

"Though viewed from different angles," Zek said. "I have heard this too." He slid from the bunk and landed gracefully on the floor, where he seated himself cross-legged so he could look at Anskar. "Sometimes, I think, they overcomplicate things that are straightforward and natural."

"Priests?"

"Not just priests. The lowlanders, as my people call those whose ancestors conquered the mainland all those centuries ago."

"Conquered? I thought they were native."

"Those with gray skin, or dark—even the green-tinged Ilapa—you think they all came from one and the same place?"

"I hadn't thought of it like that."

"My people believe there were seven invasions of the continent, some from the east: Niyas, the Plains of Khisig-Ugtall, even the Orgols of the Jargalan Desert—though they did not settle here, as they prefer hotter climes. Others came from the north, from across the Trackless Ocean: a fierce people who relished warfare and slaughter."

"And they all settled on the continent?" Anskar said.

"Over time. They came in waves in their longships, and little by little drove the indigenous people west into the Ymaltian Mountains."

"The Soreshi?"

Zek nodded.

"But where are these savages now?" Anskar asked. "These warriors who love to slaughter."

"They stayed and bred with those who had invaded before and those who came after. They learned to farm the land. They built homes and villages and towns and cities. They are you, Anskar, and the people of Kaile, the City States, the Pristart Combine. They are King Aelfyr and his subjects."

"But we're not all the same."

"Indeed you are not. But the blood of the conquerors is in a good many of those who call the mainland their home. The only thing that differs is the degree. It is those who rule, I think, who have the greatest portion of that savage blood. Some, I have heard—the elite among the nobles of Kaile—claim they are pure blood. It matters not. What matters is that you are all lowlanders to my people. You stole our lands, brought your strange religions, and imposed your ways on us."

"Strange?" Anskar echoed.

"A god with five aspects? Don't you find that strange? I do."

"Menselas is all about balance," Anskar reminded Zek.

"When it's convenient. But then why do his followers revile the dusk-tide and not the dawn? Why is one deemed good and the other forbidden?"

It was a good question. The answer Anskar had been taught was that the dusk-tide was destructive. It made use of the dying light, and therefore brought dissolution and death. The dawn, on the other hand, was a growing light, the rebirth of the day after the darkness of night.

He said as much to Zek, who shook his head.

"Does not the entire world of Wiraya act in the same way? Do not plants grow, then wither and die? Do not their seeds spawn new life? There is an ebb and flow to all life in this world. People are born, they grow, they die. If they are fortunate, they leave offspring behind to continue the cycle of death and rebirth. Do your priests condemn a wilting flower, or an old man inching toward the grave? Do they believe it an act of evil for a person to age and die?"

"It's not the same thing," Anskar said.

"It *is* the same thing. You cannot embrace one tide and deny the other. That would be like breathing with only one lung or fighting with just one arm."

"Something happened when we fought the mulag," Anskar said. "Something changed within my repositories."

"I know. May I take a closer look?"

Anskar nodded, then stiffened as he felt invisible threads of awareness penetrate his mind.

"As I perceived earlier," Zek said, "your dawn- and dusk-tide repositories are braided, though crudely, as if they have been crushed together."

"And that's not good?"

"It is better than it was. How your so-called sorcerers function with two distinct repositories is a wonder to me. We Soreshi are born with ours separate, but the more we embrace the tides, the more they weave together and work in harmony. Wait—what's this?"

Zek closed his eyes and fished deeper with his tendrils of awareness. He jerked and his eyes snapped open, and his senses recoiled from Anskar as if scalded.

"That," Anskar said, "is the dark-tide."

Zek eyed him warily. "I knew you had—" He broke off then started again. "I have never before come so close, felt it for myself."

"And now you have, you don't approve? Is not the dark-tide

from the same source as the dusk and the dawn?" Anskar said sarcastically. "Is it not the same sunlight dimmed?"

"No," Zek said. "I don't think it is. It is the absence of light. The dusk and the dawn are both positive forces drawn from the same source, but the dark… the dark is pure negation."

"Is it? And you know this how?"

"As I told you before, there have been sorcerers among the Soreshi who went further than they should have."

"Who's to say how far they should have gone? Isn't this the same thing you were criticizing us lowlanders for—denying one of the tides?"

"That is not my intention," Zek said. "But to my people, the dark is unwholesome. It is emptiness, a bottomless pit. The stuff of the abyssal realms."

"Then why do we have a dark-tide repository?" Anskar asked.

"Most of us don't."

"But these Soreshi sorcerers you spoke about…?"

"It's there, sometimes: a latency. A very few have the potential for the dark-tide, but most are never aware of it, and the rest are usually too sensible to cultivate it."

"But not you?"

"It fascinates me. Draws me. But now that I have felt it…"

"You're not so sure," Anskar finished for him. "I never asked for it, and sometimes I think the dark-tide influences what I do—a temptation. But I have used the dark-tide. I used it in the fight with you and your people."

"Perhaps we should save this talk for another time," Zek said, standing and climbing the wooden ladder back to the top bunk. "You have a meeting to attend in the morning, remember? And I need to think about what we have discussed."

"Good night," Anskar said, his voice coming out colder than

he intended.

And then he just lay there, pondering, feeling the throb of the darkness welling within him.

# TWENTY-THREE

IT WAS A BRIGHT MORNING, though bitterly cold. Outside the barracks, a glistening frost dusted the tufts of hardy grasses poking through the cracks in the road, and frost-rimed puddles filled the depressions. The cloudless sky glimmered a brilliant blue, and the hills visible above the north city walls wore caps of snow.

Anskar walked with Lanuc, Rindon, Nul, and Borik to the great hall, where the council of war was to be held. Zek hadn't been invited, so Anskar had left him in their shared room shortly after they greeted the dawn-tide together.

The sensation of the eldritch current weaving its way between the rills of dusk-tide in his meshed repository was still fresh in his mind. As an experiment, he had briefly cast his ward sphere before meeting with the others. Rather than its usual silver, it had shimmered with red, purple, and jade, silver webbing the sphere like veins. When Zek threw a stick at it, the ward held as well as normal. Better: the stick had sent up sparks of flashing colors before falling to the ground, reduced to ash.

A trestle table had been set up outside the great hall, upon which were stacked all manner of weapons the guards insisted the attendees leave in their care. Anskar reluctantly handed over *Amalantril*, Rindon laid down his hatchets, and Nul and Lanuc their swords, but Borik refused to be parted from the Sword of Supremacy. Instead, he elected to remain outside and make sure no one interfered with his friends' weapons, though Lanuc pointed out he risked the displeasure of the King by not attending.

Inside the great hall it took a few moments for Anskar's eyes to adjust to the gloom. A stifling heat rose through the floorboards, and newly set rushlights gave off a warm and flickering glow—for the hall's windows were all shuttered.

High-backed chairs were arranged in a broad circle, with the King's throne at the far end, elevated on a dais. Most of the thirty or so chairs were occupied by grim-looking men in thick winter cloaks, their upper arms adorned with the rings of silver and gold that denoted valor on the battlefield in the Kingdom of the Thousand Lakes. The practice, according to Lanuc, was a throwback to the ways of the savage invaders who had plagued mainland shores in ages past. Of all the mainland peoples these days, Lanuc added, those of the Thousand Lakes were the most like those barbarians. It seemed to Anskar, as he scanned the men seated on the chairs, that they were proud of it.

King Aelfyr, upon his throne, was deep in conversation with Brother Bonavir and Brother Kenaith. The stocky priest of the Warrior was wearing his steel breastplate with its insignia of a fist clutching a sword, and his shield was strapped to his back. Notably, he had been permitted to retain his axe. He glanced at Lanuc's group as they entered, curled his lip slightly, and then resumed his conversation with the King.

A man in a long black robe with a silver chain of office around his neck guided the newcomers to six empty chairs that had been reserved for them. When only five were taken, the man frowned. "Perhaps I miscalculated?"

"Our colleague chose to remain outside with his sword," Rindon said. "I think it's love."

The King stood to speak.

"Lords of the Thousand Lakes," King Aelfyr said, "it will be another ten days before our brothers, the earls and barons of the northlands, can join us for a full council."

"Then why are we here?" an ancient-looking lord asked the man seated next to him. Clearly he was partially deaf, for he had spoken loud enough for the King to hear him.

"We are here, Lord Silan," Aelfyr said, "to formally greet our new arrivals, the long-awaited help sent from Sansor."

Grumbles passed around the hall.

"Long-awaited," the King said, and the muttering stopped at once, "but warmly welcomed." He gestured toward Lanuc, and the lords dutifully clapped.

The King resumed his throne, and Brother Bonavir invited each of the lords present to name himself, the region he governed, and how many he could bring to the King's service. Then each lord kneeled before the throne to reaffirm his allegiance.

Finally, Brother Bonavir invited Lanuc's small group to say who they were and what they were offering to the Kingdom of the Thousand Lakes. Lanuc went first, and there were grunts and nods of respect from the lords. They obviously knew who he was, and, despite the small force he led, considered him a worthy contribution to the war effort from their allies in Sansor.

The presence of Nul and Rindon evoked even stronger shows of appreciation from the lords. Both knights bowed before the

King, but there was no pledge of allegiance. The lords were awed to learn that the mighty Borik was also in Wintotashum but had remained outside with his legendary sword, and they were immediately won over by Rindon, who bowed ostentatiously as he said, "I, sire, lords, am Rindon. I am a hero, and my contribution to your war effort will be my heroism."

"I hear," the King said, "that you enjoy a drink or two, Sir Rindon."

"A malicious rumor, sire. It is never less than six or seven."

The lords laughed aloud at that, and the King smiled.

Brother Bonavir invited Anskar to introduce himself in a tone that suggested he had saved the best for last. It was nonsense, of course, but Anskar's mouth felt suddenly dry when the King leaned forward on his throne.

"Your Majesty," Anskar started uncertainly, "my lords of the Thousand Lakes. I am Anskar DeVantte, knight-inferior of the Order of Eternal Vigilance—"

"Inferior?" Lord Silan said loudly, as if he had been short-changed.

"Newly consecrated," Lanuc explained. "A transitional title."

"Not a veteran, then?"

"Not in the usual sense, my lord, but Anskar has several times proven himself above and beyond what we would expect from a new knight."

Anskar glanced up and found the King scrutinizing him.

"You have an above average ability with sorcery, young man," Aelfyr said. "Isn't that what you detected, Brother Bonavir?"

"More than above average, sire. Exceptional. Maybe even unique."

"So," the King said, "what else can you do with the dawn-tide?"

The implication hung heavy in the air: that only the dawn-tide was acceptable to Menselas.

"As Your Majesty is aware," Brother Bonavir put in tactfully, "balance within the Five aspects occasionally requires that, in Menselas's service and in adherence to his will, it is sometimes necessary to harness the... shall I say, less salubrious aspects of his blessed creation. Is that not so, Brother Kenaith?"

"That is so. In war, we are told to use every advantage."

King Aelfyr shifted his weight on his throne, and a pained look crossed his face. Anskar wondered if he were suffering some physical ailment or perhaps struggling to accept what he was hearing.

"So," the King said at last, "you have gifts from Menselas that might bring us an advantage?"

"An advantage against Soreshi sorcery," Bonavir answered for Anskar.

"Then it is good you have come to us, Anskar DeVantte. Now tell me," the King said to Lanuc, "about this Soreshi you brought to Wintotashum."

Lanuc explained once more—presumably for the benefit of the lords—how he had come to believe that most of the Soreshi tribes had peaceful intentions toward the Thousand Lakers, but a faction had arisen from among them that had other ideas, leading to civil war between the Soreshi.

"And how is it you know all this?" Lord Silan asked.

"From the Soreshi we captured."

Lord Silan exchanged a look with the King. "And we accept the word of our enemy uncritically? Majesty, this sounds to me like folly."

"Perhaps, Lord Silan. But Lanuc of Gessa is no fool, and I am inclined to trust his judgment."

"But, Majesty—" Lord Silan began.

"Bring this Soreshi into our presence," Aelfyr ordered.

"Majesty, we cannot protect you from every aspect of his sorcery!" Brother Kenaith said.

"You won't need to," Aelfyr said.

He smiled at Anskar, who had the impression that the King knew a lot more than he was letting on.

Zek was brought into the great hall far more quickly than Anskar would have thought possible, and shoved before the throne on his knees. His hands had been shackled behind his back, and the two men who had fetched him and now loomed over him were priests of the Elder. Anskar's senses flared, and he sensed that both men had deep marks of sorcery.

"I do trust you, Lanuc of Gessa," King Aelfyr said, "and I have no doubt that young Anskar here is more than capable of protecting everyone present from a sorcerous attack—though I have not personally seen him in action. I even think there is credence to what you have told us about the Soreshi and this—if not a civil war, then at least some kind of insurgency, a faction that has split from the main population. What I still fail to understand is what drives the Soreshi to such acts of aggression against my kingdom. Explain, for the benefit of the lords here, what you told Lanuc of Gessa about the disagreeable behavior among your own people, Zekil Silvertongue."

"It is no small matter, sire," Zek said. "Other Soreshi burned our villages, stole our children, defiled—"

"I have never before heard of the Soreshi acting so"—the king circled his hand, trying to come up with the right word—"bestially."

"I tell you, something has happened to turn them," Zek said. "Does no one believe me?"

The king locked eyes with Lanuc, who gave an almost imperceptible nod. Zek's words were only confirming something they already knew, Anskar realized.

"These villages of yours that were burned," Brother Kenaith said. "Where were they located?"

"Along the line of the central Ymaltian Mountains."

"Why?" Lanuc asked. "Is there a pass there that would afford them faster entry into the Thousand Lakes kingdom?"

"A narrow and treacherous one, but there are numerous better crossings all along the mountain range." Zek shook his head. "It makes no sense. If I were plotting an invasion of the Thousand Lakes—"

"The Soreshi is right," Brother Kenaith said, cutting him off. "I have given much thought to how an invasion from the Soreshi side might best be planned. This pass he speaks of might be one point of incursion, but there are others that would reap easier rewards and give the invaders a more secure foothold in our territory."

"Then what is in this region that these rogue Soreshi have focused their efforts on?" the King asked.

Zek didn't reply. Perhaps he didn't know.

The King held the Soreshi's gaze for a moment, then addressed the assembled lords. "Which towns and villages have been hit to date?"

There was a murmuring among the lords as Brother Kenaith recited the names of towns and villages in the north that had been attacked. The Warrior's priest concluded with, "All within fifty miles either side of the Iron Road, sire."

"Brother Bonavir," the King said, "enlighten our guests."

"The Iron Road," Bonavir said, his monocle reflecting the glow of the rushlights as he stepped forward, "is so called because of the legions that once marched its length, not because of the material it was constructed from. As if," he said with a shrill peal of laughter, "a road could be cast from iron."

No one else laughed, so he pressed on.

"Our remote ancestors built the road, and we have always maintained it, as it provides swift and secure travel between the principal towns, cities and villages along the spine of the kingdom. One must assume the ancestors built the road in order to invade the lands of the Soreshi, who had fled there from all over the mainland.

"The road terminates at this pass we have been talking about, and the Soreshi built a stronghold there—presumably with outside help. It is fashioned from the very rock of the mountains, and was considered unassailable. The only time our ancestors made a determined assault, it ended in disaster, with a sea of the dead left outside the citadel's walls, they say, though you all know how the chroniclers love to exaggerate."

"And this citadel is still there today?" Anskar asked, then clamped a hand over his mouth because he hadn't been invited to speak.

To his surprise, the King answered his question. "The citadel was abandoned centuries ago. Probably the Soreshi felt there was no further need of it. It is likely the structure has fallen into disrepair, if it hasn't been collapsed by an earthquake or rockfall. Unless..." The King shut his eyes, thinking. "Unless the citadel is what the insurgents were after when they attacked the Soreshi villages in the area."

"But why?" Zek said. "My people need no such defense. Your kingdom, Majesty, has left us alone for centuries."

"But it would make an excellent base for a Soreshi invasion of our lands," Brother Kenaith said.

"How many do the enemy number?" the King asked Zek.

"It is hard to say, Majesty. Hundreds came against my village, but I have heard estimates of thousands."

"Our scouts say as many as twenty thousand," Brother Kenaith said.

"Twenty thousand Soreshi, rampaging across our north lands," the King said.

"And coming slowly south, Majesty," Brother Kenaith pointed out. "We have pushed them back a little with our bolstered defenses, but several towns were utterly destroyed; burned to the ground."

"So, Lanuc of Gessa," the King said, "you see our predicament. You really think one hundred knights is going to be enough?"

"How many men does Your Majesty have?" Lanuc asked.

"Our professional army is ten thousand strong, but we can raise another twenty thousand from among the laborers on the lords' lands who are sworn to the defense of the realm."

"Unskilled compared with professional soldiers," Brother Kenaith added, "but good enough to man a city wall. Not, however, good enough to face Soreshi sorcery. And that disadvantage is shared by the majority of our professional soldiers."

"Then it is not so much the number of your enemy as the powers they can wield against you," Lanuc observed.

"Quite right," the King said. "There is little we can do to counter Soreshi sorcery in a pitched battle."

"Then, Majesty," Lanuc said, "my one hundred knights will help to even the odds."

"Excellent," the King said. "In that case, we should waste no more time. I grow tired of reacting to what the enemy does. Far better, don't you think, Brother Kenaith, to go on a little offensive of our own?"

"Indeed, Majesty," Brother Kenaith said, and Anskar had the impression the decision had been made before the meeting.

Voices were raised in protest, but the King quelled them by raising both hands.

"Don't worry, my lords, we will take no decisive action until the full war council. But in the meantime, we will bloody the nose of the Soreshi and get an idea of just what these Knights of the Order of Eternal Vigilance can do for us. As for him"—the King indicated Zek—"while I am inclined to believe what he's told us, in times of war a king must be certain, and I am far from that. We will take him with us, but until we leave…"

He nodded to one of the priests of the Elder looming over Zek, and both men grabbed the Soreshi by the arms and led him away.

"Where are they taking him?" Anskar asked. Lanuc squeezed his arm for silence.

The King didn't deign to answer. Instead he said, "Ready your warriors, lords, Lanuc of Gessa. We leave in five days."

# TWENTY-FOUR

"WELL, THAT RATHER SCUPPERS OUR plans," Brother Bonavir said as he followed Anskar from the great hall. Lanuc had stayed behind at the request of the King. "Zek was supposed to steal the notes from the Scriptorium. Without them, we'll have no idea how to smelt divine alloy."

"Perhaps we should abandon the idea," Anskar said.

"Join us for a drink and a bite of lunch?" Rindon said, when Anskar went to reclaim his sword from the table outside the great hall.

Rindon had already retrieved his hatchets, and Nul was strapping on his sword belt. Borik leaned on his oilskin-wrapped greatsword with a bored expression on his face.

"I'd like that," Anskar told Rindon, and didn't miss the flash of irritation in Bonavir's eyes. "Where will you be?"

"Tavern called the Tall Man," Rindon said. "We're hoping the ceiling beams are high enough for Borik here not to bang his head."

"I know the place," Bonavir said. "I trust you don't mind me joining you?"

There wasn't much Anskar could say other than to agree. He started toward Braga, who was leaning against a post surmounted by an alchemical globe—dull and inert now the sun had fully risen. Bonavir followed him like a stray dog to which he should never have fed scraps of food.

Braga glowered as she pushed away from the post. She hadn't been invited to the meeting, and no one had seen her since last night. For all Anskar knew, she could have gone back outside the city to camp with the army, or found herself a tavern room. Or maybe she'd gone back to Hrothyr's…

"What happened to you last night?" he asked.

"Nothing, more's the pity. So, what did they talk about in there?"

"War. Are you thirsty?"

"For beer, I am."

Rindon, Nul, and Borik were already seated at a long table in the tavern, and had kept chairs for the others. Borik's greatsword was leaning precariously against the side of his chair, and the big man kept steadying it with his hand.

Nul waved as Anskar, Braga, and Bonavir entered. Rindon was in deep conversation with a redheaded server, who showed an unseemly amount of cleavage as she leaned over their table, mopping up spilled beer with a cloth.

Despite the tavern's name, the ceiling low enough that Anskar could have reached up and touched its black-stained beams. Borik no doubt had had to stoop when he entered. The walls were roughly textured wattle and daub, painted a pale color that had probably once been white. The wooden floor was scuffed and bore the dark stains of spilled beer, and the bar was unusual in that it was made from mortared stones and topped with oak. A fire was burning in the big hearth, a young boy tending it with an iron poker. Smoke collected beneath the ceiling and curled away through the gloomy interior.

Brother Bonavir tried to make conversation with Braga as they headed for the heroes' table.

"So, you lived in Wintotashum when you were married?"

"I did not."

"Not even when your husband was here?"

"You've got a big nose, dung-breath."

Bonavir breathed into his hand and sniffed.

Braga saw and laughed. "Silly fool," she said, shaking her head. But when she'd seated herself at the table next to Bonavir, she added, "When I was married to Hrothyr, we lived in Sansor. With the skills he brought from Wintotashum, he made a good living. Taught me most everything he knew, and I already knew a fair bit myself. Best blacksmiths in Kaile we were. Until he went and fucked everything up."

"I'm sorry," Bonavir said.

"Course you are."

Anskar took the seat on the other side of the priest and let his eyes roam around the tavern. The Tall Man was packed with laborers in thick coats or woolen cloaks. Several pairs of shifty eyes met his and then quickly turned away. He patted the coin purse at his belt to make sure it was still there. As he did, he accidentally bumped the Sword of Serenity, and it started to fall. Borik gasped and was half out of his chair before Anskar's hand lashed out and caught the bundled-up blade. Awkwardly, he guided it into the big man's grasp.

Borik emitted a low growl, but nodded his thanks.

Anskar had thought about asking Borik about the Sword of Supremacy—how he had made it, what techniques he had employed—but now thought better of it.

As if sensing the tension that had arisen at the table, Rindon launched into a lewd song. The serving girl, now perched on his lap, let out a cry of delight and joined in, apparently familiar with the song's vulgar lyrics.

Anskar caught sight of the landlord, a fat bald man behind the bar, glaring at the girl and trying to get her attention, but when Nul raised an inquisitive eyebrow, the man shook his head and went back to wiping glasses with a dirty rag.

Bonavir leaned close to Anskar. "So what are we going to do about making this divine alloy now that Zek's out of the picture?"

The three heroes looked at each other, then at the priest. Rindon's song petered out, and the serving girl made a face at him, slid off his lap, and resumed her duties.

Braga sniffed. "Hrothyr should know how to do it."

"He said he doesn't remember the exact ingredients," Anskar reminded her.

"Divine alloy?" Nul said. "Am I missing something?" When no one answered, he added, "Borik claims there's a strain of divine alloy running through the Sword of Supremacy."

"Really?" Brother Bonavir said. "May we see the sword?"

Borik took a long pull of his beer.

"It's bad luck to reveal the blade unless it is to be wetted with blood," Rindon explained.

Nul nodded. "If he were to unwrap the sword, someone would have to die. And seeing as you made the request…"

Bonavir paled.

Anskar saw Rindon and Nul exchange looks, and Rindon's

chin began to quiver.

"They're pulling your cock," Braga told Bonavir.

"Ah, good lady," Rindon said, "you judge us too harshly. We would never pull a priest's cock, no matter how much he begged us to." He snapped his fingers to get the serving girl's attention. "Beer for our companions, my lovely."

"Not for me," Bonavir said. "I rarely touch strong drink. Water, please, my dear."

"You sure that's safe?" Nul asked. "The water back in Sansor's undrinkable. People have gone blind from drinking it, or worse."

"For all its wealth, Sansor is not a sanitary city," Rindon added.

"The same could be said of Wintotashum's water," Bonavir said, "but I have picked up one or two tricks over the years. If I may return to what we were talking about? Anskar, it seems you will have to retrieve the notes from the Scriptorium yourself."

When Anskar frowned, the priest added, "It is just a minor sin and in a good cause."

"What's good about it?" Anskar asked.

"All knowledge is good, and this is exceptional knowledge."

There was a brief silence as the serving girl brought beer for Anskar and Braga, and water for Bonavir. Anskar sensed a trickle of dawn-tide from the priest as he waggled his fingers above his drink before sipping it.

"You have to go to the Scriptorium, ass-wipe," Braga said. "I think that's what the ghost lady expects, same as I think she wants me to make the armor."

"Now that I'd like to see," Nul said. "Armor made from divine alloy. Can it even be done?"

His question was aimed at Borik, but the big man merely went on sipping his beer.

"You can't get Zek out of the dungeons?" Anskar asked Bonavir.

The priest shook his head. "I might be able to arrange for you to visit him, but that won't be much help to us."

"It might," Anskar said. "Zek had a plan for getting hold of the necromancer's writings. I need to know what it was."

"Necromancer?" Borik said, without looking up from his beer.

"What is it you're up to?" Nul asked. "Is it something that might bring harm or dishonor to the Order?"

"Of course not," Bonavir said.

"No," Anskar said. "It concerns my past on Niyas."

"Oh?" Rindon said.

Nul patted Rindon on the arm. "None of our concern. Anskar has assured us this doesn't impact upon the Order, so we'll speak no more on the subject."

Rindon worried his lip for a moment, then grinned. "Does that mean it's time to sing again?"

Nul sighed. "If you must."

Anskar's head was pounding by the time he left the Tall Man with Bonavir and headed for the dungeons. Nul and Borik left at the same time to return to their barracks room, but Rindon remained in the tavern, drinking with Braga and laughing uproariously every time she swore.

The guards at the dungeons knew Bonavir, so the priest left Anskar with them, claiming he had important duties to attend to for the King. One of the guards let Anskar into Zek's cell. It was dark, and the air was thick with the peppery smell of mold.

When the door closed behind Anskar, a soft pearly glow sprang up—a glow on the palm of a hand.

"I wondered if you would come," Zek said.

The glow intensified until it formed an island of light in the darkness. Anskar saw that the Soreshi was seated cross-legged on a pile of mildewed straw. There were rings around his eyes, and on the floor in front of him were a wooden bowl and a cup, both empty.

"They feed you, then," he said.

"Bread and water. But at least the bread comes with blue mold."

"But no light?"

"They left me a box of rushlights, but they give off too much smoke, and the air's thin enough in here already. And there are no windows, of course."

"Of course?"

"No windows, no tides. Another day down here and my repositories will be dry. That makes me less of a threat."

"But you aren't a threat to them," Anskar said. "They must know that."

"The King knows, I think. He is no one's fool. But he is probably right to be cautious. My people—at least some of them—are attacking his lands. It would be imprudent to trust me. However, I assume Brother Bonavir is concerned now that there is no one to go after the necromancer's notes?"

"Just a little," Anskar said, seating himself on the cold floor.

"Is that why you came?"

"In part. I was worried about you."

Zek studied him for a long moment. "I am surprised you agreed to Bonavir's mad scheme."

"It's not just him. Braga's even more insistent."

"You trust her?"

Anskar thought about it, then nodded.

"And you trust this ghost lady she talks about?"

"I believe it's my mother," Anskar said.

"A woman you never met in life, but you seem all too willing to obey in death."

"Hardly willing. I shut her out of my mind."

"Impressive," Zek said. "Even untutored, you have sorcerous skill a Soreshi would be envious of."

"You couldn't do such a thing?"

"I did not say that. For a dead woman, Queen Talia is persistent. Failing to manipulate you, she has gone instead to Braga."

"It would seem so."

"What do you plan to do about it?"

"What choice do I have?"

Silence grew thick between them, until eventually Zek said, "The Armor of Divinity—an odd name."

"The necromancer Tain believed it would raise him up among the gods," Anskar said.

"Is that what your mother wants—to be a god?"

"There are fanatics who still follow her. They claim she'll return from the realm of the dead and liberate Niyas."

Zek gave a rueful smile. "And does Niyas need liberating? From its mainland rulers? From the Order of Eternal Vigilance?"

"Maybe," Anskar said. "I don't know."

"So, your mother plans to use the Armor of Divinity to return from the realm of the dead? That seems a different purpose to that of the necromancer Tain when he crafted the original."

"I've wondered about that," Anskar said. "I don't even know if the armor is *for* Queen Talia."

"You think it is for you?"

Anskar shrugged.

"How would you feel about becoming a god?" Zek asked.

"That's blasphemy."

"But you have considered it?"

The idea frightened Anskar. And yet…

"The people of Niyas have a belief in a future immortality for their race," he said. "Maybe that's what this is about—a small step in that direction."

"With Anskar DeVantte as the first immortal?"

Anskar shook his head, and again silence descended. He really didn't know where this business with the Armor of Divinity was going, and while his instincts screamed that it was a manipulation, a trap, another part of him wanted to see where it led.

"Perhaps you are clutching at straws, holding on to the barest sliver of a connection with the mother you never knew."

"Just tell me how I can retrieve Tain's notes from the Scriptorium," Anskar said.

"You are resolved to try, then?"

Anskar nodded.

Zek drew in a long breath, then let it out. "Here is what I had planned to do. But remember: if you are successful, if you manage to forge this Armor of Divinity, there will be a cost. In sorcery, there always is."

As Anskar had suspected, it was dusk-tide sorcery that Zek had planned to use to break into the Scriptorium, and the Soreshi patiently instructed him in some of its basic uses.

It was difficult at first to separate out the enmeshed strands of the dusk-tide from entanglement with his dawn-tide repository, but Anskar was a quick learner. And Zek was going nowhere soon, so they had hours alone in which to practice.

By itself, Zek told him, Anskar's dusk-tide repository would have been a roiling vat of chaos, its surges unpredictable and ungovernable. Perhaps that was one of the reasons the Order eschewed its use: one mistimed burst could cause untold destruction. But when the two repositories blended together—albeit crudely in Anskar's case—the dawn-tide tamed the dusk and provided a degree of stability. With practice, Anskar learned to discharge measured pulses of dusk-tide power, and Zek showed him several ways in which to apply it.

By the time Anskar left Zek at sunset, he was surprised that the Order of Eternal Vigilance hadn't found some way to justify the dusk-tide's use, for such sorcery had the offensive potential to turn a battle.

The problem was, he thought, as he hailed a two-wheeler trap outside the great hall, there was nothing subtle about the dusk-tide. Corroding door locks with dusk-tide sorcery, or using stronger bursts to blow them apart, not only ran the risk of someone hearing or even smelling the burned metal, but there would be a trail of evidence leading to the manuscript room where Bonavir claimed Tain's notes would be found. Someone would follow that trail, conclude the notes had been taken, and suspects would be rounded up and questioned. Suspicion would rest most strongly on the newcomers to Wintotashum, and it would only be a matter of time before Anskar was discovered. So he considered alternatives as he rode in the trap, but could come up with no better options.

He was about to give up the whole enterprise, when a nagging thought tugged at the back of his mind. He ignored it at first, focusing instead on the clop of the horses' hooves and the clatter of the wheels on cobbled streets. But the nagging became a persistent pull. At first he thought it was coming from his dark-tide repository, but then, with a growing sense of trepidation, he realized it came from the wards he had set up around his mind. Wards intended to keep his mother out.

"Anskar," whispered her voice inside his head.

He must have unpicked the wards without realizing it—just a little—during his lessons with Zek. Enough to grant Queen Talia the slightest entry.

"Anskar?" she said again, as if uncertain whether he could hear her.

Anskar widened the gap in his wards, and heard an answering sigh from his mother.

"Am I forgiven?" she said.

"Tell me about the Armor of Divinity," Anskar demanded.

There was a long moment of silence, and then a shadow coalesced on the bench beside him, formless at first, but swiftly resolving into a woman woven from soot. There was a reciprocal tug in Anskar's guts, as if she were drawing substance from him. No crown this time, just wisps of smoky hair that blew in some intangible wind. She turned her head to face him, and eyes emerged from the blackness, the only thing about the queen that bore any semblance of solidity. They held an unnatural tinge of emerald, and the pupils were slitted like a cat's.

Anskar shifted away from her, and she raised an insubstantial arm to touch his face. He flinched, expecting her fingers to be icy, but there was no sensation at all, as if she weren't really there.

"Did I desire your presence?" he wondered aloud. "Or did you make me will it?"

"A bit of both. You are my child. We share the same essence."

Anskar grimaced and looked away from her, at the dusk-grayed buildings racing by, the loiterers on the street—urchins, whores, men who had once presumably had better luck.

"The Armor of Divinity is necessary," Talia said.

"For you to return from the dead?"

"For you, my child, to fetch me."

Anskar turned to face her, and saw that her emerald eyes had dissolved back into the black haze that defined her.

Again something tugged at his guts, and again he had the feeling his mother was taking something from him to sustain herself in the world.

"You want me to come to the realm of the dead?" he asked.

"I need you to."

"Why would I do that?"

"Oh, Anskar," she said, stroking his face, though he didn't feel a thing. "The greatest crime the Order of Eternal Vigilance committed was to fill your young mind with hatred of your own mother."

"I don't hate you," he said before he could stop himself. His heart began to pound, and tears welled at the corners of his eyes.

"That is good. All will be revealed in time, Anskar, but time is something we lack at this moment. I can remain here with you but a minute or two longer, and then I must return to the realm of the dead. I know what you plan to do. Let me help you."

# TWENTY-FIVE

ONLY CHANDRA, THE SILVER MOON, remained in the sky amid a scatter of stars. Red Jagonath had already dipped below the city walls.

There was a lull in the raucous singing coming from the tavern across the road, and Anskar felt suddenly cold and exposed as the carriage pulled up.

"This ain't the most well-to-do district," the driver called over his shoulder. "But it's the oldest, built before the invaders came from across the Trackless Ocean. You're braver than me, lad. People round here don't go out at night. They say the ghosts of the old folk who built the original city still walk the streets."

Anskar settled his fare and climbed down from the carriage. There were no ghosts here. If there were, he would have seen and heard them. He'd done so before.

At the end of the road stood the Scriptorium, a vast white tower with windows in the top few stories only. Teams of guards in fur-trimmed cloaks patrolled around the base, and the blackwood doors—the only way in from the street—were guarded by six heavily armored men with swords and halberds, at least one of whom was a sorcerer with a potent dusk-tide repository.

Zek's plan now seemed reckless. Anskar was glad he'd accidentally relaxed the wards he'd set against his mother— if indeed that was what had happened. Her advice had been sound, and he saw no better alternatives.

He made his way along the street to a second tower, on the opposite side of the road. It was built of unpainted brick, crumbling and ancient, though its structure and height were identical to the Scriptorium.

As he climbed the iron staircase that wound around the outside of the tower, he cast glances over at the Scriptorium, nervous of the patrols catching sight of him. He didn't know why that should be, considering the residents of this second tower must come and go at all times, but still the guilty feeling that he was doing something wrong nagged at him.

By the time he reached the top floor, where Queen Talia's former agent, Lengar, still resided, his heart was pounding, and sweat poured from his brow, stinging his eyes.

Lengar, his mother had told him, was a sorcerer of rare talent, even among the Niyandrians. It was he who had agreed to the task of finding the necromancer Tain's notes so that Queen Talia could have Hrothyr commence work on the Armor of Divinity. Lengar had devised a way to enter the Scriptorium unseen, and once inside, he had memorized the relevant portion of the notes rather than removing them, which he'd believed too risky. It had been enough for Hrothyr to craft the vambrace that Anskar now wore.

"He was going to break in again," Talia told Anskar, "to

memorize more of the process once Hrothyr reached that stage, only…"

"Only Naphor fell," Anskar finished for her. "But why didn't you contact Lengar from the realm of the dead?"

"It takes a special type to hear the shades of that grim place," she said. "The talent is not in Lengar's blood."

But it was in Anskar's, and it was obviously in Braga's.

He knocked on the weathered wooden door and waited. It almost didn't matter if there was no response. It wasn't the sorcerer's abilities he needed, it was access to the Scriptorium.

Queen Talia had explained that Lengar's room was situated directly opposite the restricted chamber where Tain's notes were kept. Using techniques Talia had shown him during the carriage ride—techniques Anskar had immediately understood, as if he were remembering them—he planned to leap from Lengar's window to the opposite window in the Scriptorium. It was the most direct route and the least likely to be noticed.

Commands from the patrols drifted up to where Anskar was standing, and he held his breath, listening. More voices, this time farther off, and peals of laughter followed whatever had been said. Anskar allowed himself to relax.

He knocked again. Maybe Lengar was out, although that didn't seem likely. He must be an old man by now, with little reason to be out and about at such an hour.

The faint sounds of the music from the tavern once more reached his ears, and then he heard something through the door—the scuff of feet? The creak of a floorboard. Probably Lengar was worried about someone knocking on his door in the middle of the night. Perhaps he thought he was about to be burgled, or worse.

Figuring he had come too far to back out, Anskar tried the

doorknob. It turned, but the door remained stubbornly shut, which only told him Lengar had locked it.

Queen Talia hadn't prepared him for what to do in a situation like this, but thankfully Zek had. During their practice session in the dungeon, the Soreshi had shown him a few applications of the dusk-tide. He needed metal, something small enough to fit into the lock. He had no key of his own—the barracks room where he was staying didn't have a lock—but he did have his coin pouch. He rummaged through it till he found a twisted half-shekel—literally half, cut up by traders to facilitate low-cost transactions. He inserted the half-shekel into the lock and directed a pulse of dusk-tide essence into it. He smelled heated metal, then came a thin plume of smoke, followed by a muffled thud and a crack.

Anskar eased the door open and slipped inside. The first thing that hit him was the stench—sulfur and excrement. Despite the darkness, he could make out the shapes of a table and chairs. A dripping sound came from beyond the curtained opening opposite.

"Murder!" a voice hissed.

Anskar's heart lurched. He stood still and strained to hear. Had he really heard the voice?

And then he realized: the single word had been spoken in Niyandrian, and he had understood it at once. Lengar?

Edging around the furniture, Anskar parted the curtain and entered a wood-paneled hallway. Lamplight flickered from the open doorway at the far end. As he crept closer, he could see scorch marks on the walls—they were still warm to the touch.

*Evidence of Lengar's dusk-tide wards,* Queen Talia said, her inner voice clearly distinguishable from the man's voice Anskar thought he had heard. *He always said a sorcerer could never be too careful.* She chuckled, but there was no mirth in it. If anything, she sounded worried.

The windows inside the room—Lengar's bedroom, judging by the cot with the rumpled blankets—were shuttered.

*Lengar never did like the daylight,* Talia said. *His eyes are sensitive. Too much poring over old scrolls in his youth.*

Against one wall there was a writing desk with a high-backed chair, beside which stood shelves crammed with books and scrolls. The dripping was louder here. Anskar looked up at the vaulted ceiling to locate the source. At the same instant he found it, Queen Talia cried out, *No!*

An old Niyandrian—it had to be Lengar—stared down from the ceiling, as if he had been pinned there with invisible nails. Blood dripped from his open mouth to pool on the floor.

"Judging by the size of your dark-tide repository, you must be Anskar DeVantte," a man said.

The high-backed chair scraped as its occupant turned it around. A man sat upon the chair, obese, wearing a long black coat, a broad-brimmed hat shadowing his face.

"The Abbess told me all about your distinctive talents. She is, I fear, quite taken with you. If she'd known you would be here, she'd have come herself."

Anskar spoke a cant, and his ward sphere erupted around him with its oily sheen. He drew his sword, then froze at the scuff of a boot behind him.

"Such an unexpected bonus." A woman, her breath hot on his ear. Somehow, she had slipped inside his ward!

Something cold and hard pressed against his temple. "Are you and Lengar old friends, or did you come here for some other reason? You know how some sorcerers like young boys."

Anskar extinguished his ward, but when he tried to face the

woman, a jolt of pain shot through his skull and he jerked violently.

"Put the sword away," the man said. "Unless you want Haleki to demonstrate the full force of her unique powers."

Anskar's hand shook as he returned *Amalantril* to her scabbard. "Dusk-tide sorcery," he said.

"Aren't you the clever one?" the woman said.

"What else can you discern about the two of us, and what is going on here?" the fat man said, rising and approaching Anskar.

"You murdered an old man."

"A tedious man. He was given plenty of chances. He chose to use them all up."

"Why did you come here?" Anskar asked.

"Why did you?" the woman countered.

Anskar felt a surge of dark-tide power from the fat man, then something invisible wrapped around his legs and arms, holding him tight. He struggled with body and mind, reaching for his own repositories.

"Settle down," the woman said, prodding him with the cold object she had rammed against his head.

*Be still, my son,* Queen Talia said within his mind.

"What was that?" the fat man said. "Did you hear that?"

The woman removed the pressure from Anskar's head and stepped away, presumably to look for the cause of the noise.

Had they heard? Had the fat man, at least, heard Queen Talia's voice?

Anskar could feel his mother's presence within the very marrow of his bones now. Perhaps he had made a mistake slackening his wards. But that was a question for another time—if he got out of this alive. Right now, he sensed Queen Talia teasing out threads from his dark-tide repository, weaving them together in complex patterns. He wanted to ask her what she was doing, but dared not speak. One word from either of them might prompt the fat man or the woman to act.

"Are you ready to tell me why you're here?" the fat man said, walking a tight circle around Anskar. "Did you know Lengar?"

Anskar's skin itched at the proximity of the man, yet he was unable to move a muscle to track his course. An odor he didn't recognize filled his nostrils—it evoked so many feelings blended into one and gave him the overwhelming impression of madness.

"Who's Lengar?" he said.

He squirmed as he felt the fat man lay a finger on his spine through his shirt. "I think you know."

The man's finger tracked down his spine and lingered above his buttocks.

"Nothing," Haleki said, returning to the room.

She came to stand in front of Anskar and stared at him with eyes so dark they looked black. She was pale skinned and rake thin, with dark hair twisted into ropes that hung to her shoulders. Like the fat man, she wore a black coat, though hers was adorned with silver buttons. In one hand she held a slender rod of iron.

She caught Anskar noticing and held the rod up. "You know what this is?"

"Inert metal," he replied. "Save when it's in the hands of one proficient in the use of the dusk-tide."

"He is very good, you know," the fat man said, continuing his orbit of Anskar back to the front, his finger trailing around to rest on Anskar's belly. "I must say, I'm quite taken with him." Something about the way the man's eyes glistened made Anskar want to be sick. "I can see why the Abbess likes him."

"You're with the Tainted Cabal?" Anskar asked.

The fat man smiled a crooked smile. "I am Castellac, and this is—"

"Haleki," Anskar finished for him. "I heard. And this is a coincidence, you say? You weren't sent after me?"

"Alas, no," Castellac said. "We came seeking the services of Lengar. Am I right to assume that you are here for the same reason?"

Anskar remained silent, conscious of the way Haleki was rubbing her thumb along her iron rod, glancing at Castellac as if she needed his permission to use it.

"What use would an old Niyandrian sorcerer be to the Tainted Cabal?" Anskar asked.

"What use would he be to a knight of the Order of Eternal Vigilance?" Castellac countered. "Albeit one with the most exquisite cat's eyes." The tip of his tongue poked out and slid along his lips.

The man disgusted Anskar. There was something unwholesome about him.

When Anskar didn't reply, Castellac said, "We had hoped Lengar would help us get into the Scriptorium."

Anskar's eyes widened.

"Ah, so you had a similar aim. Why? What are you after?"

*Say nothing,* Queen Talia hissed.

Castellac flinched. Had he heard her again?

"You really should talk," Haleki told Anskar. "So much less painful that way."

Castellac chuckled. "Of course, Anskar, it may be that we can turn this fortuitous meeting to our mutual advantage. Considering from between whose legs you slid into the world, I'm guessing you know a thing or two about Lengar. Perhaps even how he broke into the Scriptorium all those years ago?"

Anskar clamped his lips shut.

"I see that you do," Castellac said with a sigh. "Playing hard to get, are we? Personally, I prefer to dive straight in and start thrusting. Ultimately, that's all everyone wants, really."

"Lengar could have told us how to get inside the Scriptorium," Haleki added. "But he chose to scream instead. Quite a lot, actually. Some would call it brave. Personally, I think it's the height of stupidity."

"Some people will go to all sorts of trouble to thwart the Tainted Cabal," Castellac said. "I just don't understand it. According to the Abbess, you enjoyed your first taste of our ceremonies, Anskar. You felt the presence of the lord Nysrog. Go on, admit it: you still dream about that day, don't you? The Abbess told us you were hard for her."

Anskar struggled against the bonds that held him. "Let me go," he snarled. "You're twisted. Evil."

"I thought so at first too," Castellac said somewhat sadly. "But people change. They become acclimated."

"Never!" Anskar said. "I will never change!"

Haleki scoffed.

"I'd wager you've already changed," Castellac said. "You are no longer the idealistic boy brought up by the Order of Eternal Vigilance. I imagine you've seen things among your peers and betters that gave you pause. There is a taint in every institution, Anskar, not only the Cabal."

"And at least we're honest about it," Haleki said.

Did this disgusting man know what Anskar had experienced within the walls of Branil's Burg? What he had observed at the Mother House in Sansor? About the slaves the Grand Master's ship had delivered to Atya? Did he know about the "secret few" who were encouraged to use forbidden abilities in the name of

Menselas?

He felt a rising need to tell Castellac all, a desire to trust the man. But did the desire come from within, or was it being drawn out of him by some hidden sorcery?

"If you have a plan for entering the white tower," Castellac said, "do share it with us. I am running out of options, and the only one that remains to me is not without risks. Help us out. Whatever you're after, I'm sure it's not the same thing we came here for. Work with us, Anskar. You won't regret it."

"Never."

Sparks danced along the length of Haleki's rod.

"A pity," Castellac said. "Then we shall have to settle for the consolation prize."

"And what's that?"

"You."

The invisible restraints holding Anskar fell away, replaced by Haleki's rod pressing against his chest.

"So you can walk out of here," Castellac explained. "But run, and Haleki will hurt you."

"Badly," she added. "Maybe so badly you'll never hurt again."

"And before you think of shadow-stepping," Castellac said. "Oh, yes, I know all about your dark-tide abilities—don't bother. With scarce a thought, I can dissolve the shadows, and while you might still make your escape, it will be in a thousand scattered pieces."

*Now!* Queen Talia said.

Castellac's eyes widened and he stepped back.

Anskar's dark-tide repository ruptured. His stomach flipped inside out. His heart faltered and stopped. Shards of shadow solidified out of the air, whirling around him in a vortex. His heart stuttered back to life, he gasped in a breath, and then the black shards exploded outwards, smashing the window, punching holes in the walls, and ripping Haleki to shreds as her iron rod clanged to the floor.

Not Castellac, though. At the last possible instant, the fat man poured himself into the shadows and was gone.

Anskar stood there, panting for breath, staring at the carnage. The walls, ceiling, and floor were riddled with holes, Haleki was a bloody mess at his feet, and cold night air was blowing in through the broken window.

Shouts of alarm and the peep of a whistle reached Anskar from the street. Footsteps clanged up the iron staircase outside the tower. Before they could reach the door, Anskar ran across the room and leaped through the broken window, calling upon a surge of the dusk-tide to propel him across the gap between the two towers.

The street hundreds of feet below sped past in a blur, and the Scriptorium loomed before him, its white bricks expanding to fill his vision. He threw out his hands and struck the wall of the Scriptorium hard.

Pain jolted through his arms and chest, but he didn't fall. The dark-tide was now flowing through his fingers and his booted toes, sticking him to the stone.

His guts clenched, partly from so much use of the dark-tide, partly from the sheer drop beneath him. He could see the specks of guards in the street below. No one seemed to have seen him. Sweat dripped from his hair and into his eyes, and he shivered from an icy chill in his bones.

A few feet above him was the window opposite Lengar's—he had only dropped a short way below it during his leap. Tentatively at first, in case he had misjudged the new abilities Queen Talia had taught him, he started to climb as if he were a lizard.

When he reached the sill, he clung on for a moment. His head was muggy, and the chill in his bones had given way to a burning fever. At the same time, his shivering intensified and his teeth chattered.

One of his hands came away from the windowsill, sending him swaying out over the drop. With a yelp, he recovered and pulled himself up onto the sill—just as the dark-tide that made his hands and feet stick to the stone ebbed away to nothing. His heart began to pound. Another second…

Anskar pressed up close to the window, fighting the terrifying urge to let go and fall backwards. The window was tall and narrow, with panels of stained glass in deep reds and blues between a latticework of lead. He tried to pry the window open using his fingertips, but could find no purchase. When Lengar had made the same leap, Talia had told him, the window had been open a crack to air the room within.

Anskar peered through the colored glass to gauge the shadows inside the room, but everything was dark, and he had no idea where the empty spaces were into which he might safely shadow-step. Not only that, but he had already used too much dark-tide. Any more and he felt certain he would vomit, then plunge unconscious to his death. Even now, though, he could feel the seep of the dark-tide entering through his pores, gradually replenishing; but he didn't have time to wait.

He needed metal, but didn't have room on the windowsill to draw his sword. He fumbled for his coin pouch, but couldn't unstring it from his belt without losing his balance. Then he remembered the vambrace.

He slid his arm up the glass, using his teeth to tug back his shirtsleeve. The divine alloy glowed a dull blue in the scant moonlight, for a bank of clouds now smothered the sky, admitting only the slightest glimmer from Chandra.

Once he had the vambrace in position against the window's edge, he spoke a cant. Dusk-tide tempered by the dawn flowed through the vambrace. There was a fizz, a wisp of smoke, and the faintest of cracks. The window popped open enough for him to insert his fingers.

He crabbed to one side of the sill, clinging to the window frame with one hand and using the other to open the glass outward, away from his body. As soon as there was enough of a gap, he slipped inside and dropped down lightly to the floor.

Anskar pushed the window to, but it wouldn't stay shut. The inner catch had been damaged by his entrance, so he sent another surge of dusk-dawn-tide through the vambrace to weld it closed.

Despite the dark, he could see in shades of gray. It must have been his altered eyes. There were floor-to-ceiling bookcases crammed with cloth- and leather-bound tomes, heaped-up scrolls, rolled maps, stacks of vellum and parchment. Cobwebs hung from the upper shelves and draped from the ceiling. The floor was covered in a thick layer of dust that showed no footprints other than Anskar's own. Clearly the room hadn't been used for quite some time. Years, probably.

After a quick perusal of the shelves, Anskar found what he was looking for wedged between two folios in a section reserved for rare and original copies:

The necromancer Tain's notebook.

The book's pliant leather cover was thick with mold, and the pages within were damp and musty. Anskar riffled through quickly, noting that the swirling, handwritten Skanuric script was still legible, though it had run in places and was faded throughout. He slipped the notebook beneath his shirt and turned back to the window.

Across the street, shapes passed back and forth behind the broken window of Lengar's apartment—presumably the City Watch. There was no going back the same way.

A quick examination told him his dark-tide repository was no longer empty, though the thought of using it again set his head throbbing.

He looked down at the street below, dimly lit by alchemical globes, and located a pool of shadow beneath one of the poplars that lined the road.

He turned back to the trails of footprints he'd left on the floor, drew upon his braided repository, and uttered a cant that sent a gust of wind swirling through the dust to cover his tracks.

With a swift prayer to Menselas that felt blasphemous, given the circumstances, Anskar poured himself into the shadows.

Before he had taken his first step away from the tree hundreds of feet below, he doubled over and retched.

When the nausea passed, he stood and wiped bile from his chin. Mouth sour, and sorely in need of a drink, he turned in what he hoped was the right direction and began the long walk back to the barracks.

# TWENTY-SIX

BROTHER BONAVIR WASTED NO TIME copying the parts of the necromancer Tain's notebook that described the ores and, oddly, precious stones and even wood required to produce the divine alloy. For Hrothyr's benefit, he translated the text into Nan-Rhouric from the original Skanuric.

There were still a few days before Anskar would ride north with the King, so he left Brother Bonavir to continue with his copying, and proceeded to the next step of their plan.

He tucked the list of ingredients in his shirt pocket, then took a two-wheeler trap to the city's merchant district in the old quarter. It was the middle of the day, and though he felt tired from his break-in at the Scriptorium and the walk back to the barracks the previous night, the excitement about where he was going gave him energy—although it was tinged with an equal measure of fear.

The trap clattered along broad roadways between massive

warehouses. Wagons and carts filled the roads, traveling to and from the warehouses with cargos of timber, weapons, and foodstuffs. Others were covered, so there was no telling what was inside. There were hawkers outside some of the warehouses, claiming their wares were the cheapest in the city, and harlots solicited on every corner. Wintotashum seemed filled with them. Anskar shivered, thinking how cold the scantily clothed women—and not a few young men—must be in the biting wind that had been building since the early hours.

The trap pulled up outside the Ethereal Sorceress's depot, an imposing cube-like structure that loomed above the neighboring warehouses. Anskar paid the driver and climbed out.

Doubt prickled his scalp as he approached the building. It had no windows and looked as though it had been made from one seamless block of stone. It was said that the sorceress had identical depots in every major mainland city, and even more farther off. There had been one, Anskar recalled Lanuc telling him, even in Atya.

There was something about the building that agitated his sorcerous senses as he ascended the steps to a blackwood door bound with iron. The door was set into a granite-like wall with barely visible seams. The whole edifice looked like something that had been created using sorcery or built overnight by summoned spirits. It also looked impregnable, which was why, Anskar supposed, the wealthiest nobles, jealous sorcerers, and even the Church of Menselas itself trusted their goods—worldly and otherwise—to the Ethereal Sorceress's protection.

Before he had a chance to knock, the door swung open to reveal a polished checkered floor of white and green marble, and a man in a dark gray coat and a varnished blackwood mask that covered his entire face. The mask had no features save for two eyeholes, from which dark eyes studied Anskar impassively. The man's long hair fell about the collar of his coat, twisted into ropes and bound with many braids.

Stark light from chandeliers of crafted globes illuminated the chamber. A dozen or more blackwood doors studded the wall opposite, and it was to one of these that the man led Anskar, the clip of their footsteps on the marble floor echoing off the impossibly high ceiling.

The man opened the door with a brass key to reveal an iron cage that was big enough to hold several people. He gestured to the cage, and when Anskar hesitated, the blackwood mask bobbed in reassurance.

Anskar stepped inside, and the cage swayed ever so slightly. When the functionary remained outside and shut the door, plunging him into darkness, Anskar's heart lurched. He instinctively reached for his braided repository, intending to produce a dawn-tide light, but no sorcery came. It was as if a wall had sprung up between his mind and the powers within him. His palms grew clammy, and his heart raced as the cage started to descend.

That surprised Anskar: he had assumed the cage would take him up. He suppressed a twinge of panic by persuading himself that the Ethereal Sorceress's depot probably had its most secure holdings underground, or maybe her living quarters were down there.

There was a metallic groan and a clunk from far above, and the cage stopped in line with another door. Anskar pushed it open and stepped out into a corridor carpeted with a deep green pile that looked almost like grass. The corridor was lit by crafted globes in wall sconces. At the far end, a figure was waiting in front of a closed blackwood door.

Although the figure was wearing thick dark robes with severe pleats and edges, as if the fabric had been starched and pressed, Anskar had no doubt that beneath them was a woman. An orange-tinged mask fashioned from orichalcum metal covered her face. It had a cross-shaped opening, but he couldn't see her eyes through it, only an impenetrable blackness. Long gloves of black silk covered her hands, which were clasped in front of her almost in an attitude of prayer.

The orichalcum mask inclined toward Anskar as he approached.

"Are you the Ethereal Sorceress?" he asked.

The voice that replied reminded him of birdsong.

"A name by which to trade with superstitious men, and not a few women. Are you superstitious, Anskar DeVantte?"

She knew his name? But then he worked it out. "Brother Bonavir told you I was coming."

"A wise fool," the Ethereal Sorceress replied. "Also superstitious. You have not answered my question."

Anskar thought of the many beliefs he had swallowed hook, line, and sinker from listening to Brother Tion—all the promises and threats of Menselas to those who were faithful and those who were not. Wasn't that a form of superstition? And surely only a superstitious fool would undertake a quest for a mythical suit of armor that bestowed immortality and might bring a dead queen back to life?

"I think I am superstitious," he said, feeling like a child confessing to some sort of wrongdoing.

"Then my judgment is that you are not," the Ethereal Sorceress said in her musical voice, not at all muffled by the mask. "For the superstitious rarely doubt their fantasies."

She glided closer, stopping mere inches away from him. Anskar's skin tingled at her proximity.

"And not all that is fantastical is untrue. A power churns

within you, Anskar DeVantte. Who were your parents? Your eyes—you are at least part Niyandrian, I see."

"I don't know who my father was," Anskar said, having already abandoned any ideas of deception. He had the feeling there would be no point.

"And your mother?"

He hesitated.

"It shames you, the knowledge of where you came from?"

"No!" he protested, then more quietly: "Yes."

He felt Queen Talia's seething presence within him. The Ethereal Sorceress's mask pivoted slightly, as if she had felt it.

Instinctively, Anskar went to refashion the wards he had set against his mother, but once more his sorcerous power eluded him.

"Where were you raised?" the Ethereal Sorceress asked.

"Niyas."

"Niyas is a large island…"

"I was raised at Branil's Burg."

"By the Order of Eternal Vigilance." A hard edge had crept into her voice.

"You know about Branil's Burg?"

"Your white cloak betrays what you are," she said, "but yes, I am aware that the Order of Eternal Vigilance captured the citadel during the war with the Necromancer Queen, and that they direct their subjugation of Niyas from there. What are you, Anskar, almost twenty years of age?"

"Soon I will be eighteen."

"Ah!" The Ethereal Sorceress moved even closer, until the orichalcum mask was a hair's breadth from his face. Still, he could see nothing but darkness behind the cross-shaped gap. She smelled of forge-heated iron and something else… maybe vinegar.

"The child who was lost," she continued, gliding back to a more comfortable distance. "I heard that Queen Talia had a secret daughter, but it seems my information was… incorrect." The last was said with a hint of incredulity, as if she could not conceive of being misinformed. "She has contacted you, I perceive. With your connivance, or otherwise?"

"A bit of both," Anskar said.

"A bit of both," she repeated. "What is it you want from me, Anskar? What service do you wish to purchase?"

Anskar fumbled in his pocket and produced the list of ingredients Brother Bonavir had made. The Ethereal Sorceress took it in her gloved hand.

Without even glancing at the Skanuric writing, she said, "You intend to craft Armor of Divinity. Your mother's idea?"

Anskar nodded.

"And you trust her?"

"I… no."

"But you are your own man, and you want to see how this plays out?"

Anskar frowned this time, his eyes riveted to the cross of blackness on the orichalcum mask. "Will you help me?" he asked. "Do you have all the ingredients here?"

"I do not. Blackwood is grown in the forests of Sevalio beyond the Trackless Ocean. Khorun pearls are harvested in the southern Jargalan desert by the Orgols. Sunstone forms deep beneath the soil of the isles of Ak-Settur. Astrumium is a combination of orichalcum and star-metal, which falls from the sky. It is manufactured by dangerous men in Kaile, and its supply is monopolized by the Order of Eternal Vigilance. Red-gold is rarer than yellow, and what stores remain are jealously guarded in Ruruc in the Wastes of the western continent. And the powdered horn of a nietan… you will have to obtain that for yourself. But first you must agree to my contract."

"A nietan?" Anskar asked. "Is it some kind of beast?"

"That is for you to discover. The necromancer Tain hired a team to accompany him on that part of the quest, and he was the only one to return. Whether or not he obtained the horn of a nietan we shall perhaps never know. Afterwards, he seems to have abandoned the idea of making his armor from scratch."

"So he never made the Armor of Divinity?"

"You use the definite article, Anskar, but there is more than one suit. In Niyas, the practice of encasing the mortal body in metal imbued with sorcery, in the hopes of becoming divine, is older than written history. Niyandrians have such strange dreams. Save for a nietan's horn, I will have the ingredients on this list brought to my depots around Wiraya. They will be here this time tomorrow."

"Tomorrow?" Anskar said. "But—"

"That will be more than enough time for you to travel to the ice plains beyond the Wastes to find a nietan and take its horn."

"But that's a journey of weeks by land and sea."

"Not if we have a contract."

"Surely there must be some other way," Anskar said. He drew out his coin pouch. "I have money."

"Not enough. In any case, coin is of little interest to me."

Anskar started to protest, but the Ethereal Sorceress held up a black-gloved hand. "For these items listed by the necromancer Tain, not even the wealthiest nobles of the Thousand Lakes could afford to pay. Not even the elite of Kaile. It took the fortunes of a burgeoning empire to pay for what Tain needed. It took the treasury of the then King of Niyas."

Anskar returned the coin purse to his pocket. "Then I have

wasted my time."

And again those words: "Not if we have a contract."

Anskar stared at the orichalcum mask, every sense telling him to leave now before he got entangled in something he might never extricate himself from. But he had already come so far; already committed himself by stealing the notebook from the Scriptorium. And Brother Bonavir would keep pressuring him, not to mention Braga.

"What kind of contract?" Anskar asked warily.

"A service rendered is a service owed," the sorceress replied.

"And you will obtain these ingredients for me—from all over Wiraya?"

She nodded. "I will count that as one service. A bargain, for you."

"But I must find the powdered horn of a nietan myself?"

"If your time is short, I will get you there, but that will entail a second service."

"So, I would owe you twice over? What kind of service would you want from me in return?"

"Later," the Ethereal Sorceress said. "Are we agreed?"

"What service?" Anskar asked again. This time he was met with stony silence. Eventually, he sighed, sure he would regret his words in the future. "Fine, I agree. When do I leave for these ice plains?"

"Now, if you wish."

"I have to be back within three days. I have a commitment to the King."

This business with the Soreshi raiders was becoming an annoyance he could well do without. Everything he needed to learn about himself was slowly coming into focus. The quest for the Armor of Divinity might have been his mother's plan, but his destiny was intertwined with hers. Of that he no longer had any doubt.

"If you survive, you should return with time to spare," the Ethereal Sorceress said. "You must travel to the Wastes first, where a guide will be waiting to take you to the ice plains. She will not venture with you into the nietan's lair, but will be on hand for your return trip."

"How long will it take me to get there?" Anskar asked.

"Not long." She opened the blackwood door behind her.

"Wait! Ethereal Sorceress!"

Over her shoulder she said, "Those not afflicted with superstition call me Sheelahn. Now come."

She glided along the carpeted passageway beyond the door; Anskar followed cautiously until she turned a corner and was lost to sight. He jogged to catch up and followed her into a room with a polished granite floor. Set into the stone was a circular band of orichalcum rimmed with Skanuric runes.

The Ethereal Sorceress offered Anskar a gloved hand and led him into the center of the circle, where she chanted Skanuric words. The light in the room dimmed and flickered, and Anskar plummeted into darkness.

He cried out, then felt Sheelahn's silk-clad fingers squeezing his hand, and anchored himself on her. He was blind, until bright motes and sparks raced past him to the accompaniment of peals of thunder and the smell of burned wood.

Anskar screamed as his flesh was shredded into a thousand gossamer fragments borne along on the tide of night.

And then there was light.

He pitched face-first to the granite floor. His thoughts hazed over with concussive pain, his ears rang, and his eyes wouldn't focus.

Pushing himself up onto his elbows and knees, he shook his head, blinking until he could see the Ethereal Sorceress standing beside him, seemingly untouched by whatever he had just experienced.

He looked around and realized he was in the same room, at the center of the orichalcum circle, only the lights had ceased to flicker.

"Come," Sheelahn said.

"Let me guess. We've arrived in the Wastes?"

"You have traveled in this manner before?"

"Twice. Once by sorcery, when I was kidnapped at Branil's Burg, and again when I entered a ruined city miles below ground."

The Ethereal Sorceress turned her mask toward him. "You have been to Yustanwyrd and survived?"

"Do you know of it?"

"I may have need of one such as you. Of course, the transits you experienced before were over relatively short distances. The *izindel* we have just passed along is of a different order to the crude sorcery your captors must have employed, and also to the lore of the wraithes of Yustanwyrd."

Sheelahn gestured for him to go back through the door they had entered by. She didn't accompany him.

The door opened onto the exact same corridor they had come down. Around the corner, he came to yet another blackwood door, which opened onto the cage that had brought him down into the roots of the building. He stepped inside, and the cage ascended.

When it came to a stop, he opened another door and emerged into the room with the checkered floor of white and green marble, lit by chandeliers of crafted globes.

The functionary with the blackwood mask and dark gray coat approached, his boots clipping on the polished floor.

Without a word, he guided Anskar to the door leading to the street and pulled it open.

# TWENTY-SEVEN

FOR DAYS, THE NECROMANCER TAIN'S head had directed
Carred's group north towards the Niyandrian coast. The wind
was always behind them, giving them a helpful shove, as if they
were heading the way it wanted them to go. It was hard not to
consider where the wind came from; or rather, who sent it.

Carred frequently hung back behind the others. Not just
because she felt discomfited about what lay before them but
because Noni wasn't exactly good company, and Orix and Tain
were as irritating as the thousand flea bites of Theltek. They had
done nothing but argue about words all day. Tain disparaged
virtually every Nan-Rhouric term that Orix taught him, and for
his part only fed the Traguh-raj lad curse words and perversion.

"I've no use for pious drivel from your holy scriptures," the
necromancer complained to Carred, after Orix had translated
one of the aphorisms of Menselas he'd been taught as a postulant
knight. "I need to know the kinds of things he says to the ladies."

"He grunts, by and large," Carred said.

"What did you say?" Orix asked her.

"Ask Tain—in Niyandrian."

After that, she had dropped behind, where she could be alone with her ghosts and her memories.

She couldn't say why, but she indulged in the heartache; lost herself in mourning. Not for Talia. She was the one responsible for those who'd been killed, and if Carred never saw Marith again, that was also Talia's fault. When she tried to convince herself that Talia wasn't all bad, that they had once shared a bed, all she could think about was how cold the Queen had been; and though she knew she was imagining it, her memories of their lovemaking were tainted with the stench of rot.

As they emerged from the shelter of a basin, the wind had a change of mind. After blowing at their backs night and day, it now swirled around them, then came at them from the front, making them fight for every step. A coincidence? A warning? Carred wondered if she should take the hint and turn back.

But where would she go? Back to Marith's? Persuade her to come away someplace safe, preferably far away from Niyas? But was there anywhere safe? Talia had already shown just how long her reach was from the realm of the dead, and if Carred refused to do her bidding, would the Queen simply let her go? It seemed unlikely. She would see it as a betrayal, a dereliction of duty, and Carred would be the first to agree with her.

They followed the tang of the brine, the spit of the wind, until Tain brought them to a fishing village that skirted a sandy cove. The necromancer told them what he needed, and Carred entered the village alone to buy a large net and a coil of rope.

"You took your time," Tain complained when Carred rejoined the group.

"Next time, *you* try explaining to a fisherwoman why she should sell her net."

"I wouldn't need to," Tain said. "A minute alone with me and she'd give it to me as a gift, along with anything else I desired."

"Just to get you to shut up," Carred said.

Waves crashed against the shore as they continued along the coast. The wind howled, yet the sky was clear and the sun blazed down.

After several miles, the sandy shoreline gave way to shingle as they approached a bay defined by outcroppings of blue-gray stone. Carred climbed the rocks, slipping once or twice on the still-damp seaweed that clung to the stone. Anemones nestled in depressions, and barnacles scabbed the surface. The far side of the outcrop dropped sharply into the sea.

The water, six or seven feet below, was sparkling and green, virtually still, sheltered by the natural rock wall of the bay. Not far from the shore, the shadow of a reef stood out from the ocean shelf, and poking up through the coral that had grown around it was the broken mast of a ship, more barnacle than wood, nothing left of the sails it had presumably once held.

Carred turned as Orix came up behind her, holding the necromancer's head.

"Why are we here?" Carred asked.

"The armor, remember?" Tain said.

"We're leaving Niyas? You're going to need a better ship. Preferably one that's still afloat."

"Everything we need should be right here," Tain said. "Or rather, there, beneath the waves."

"The shipwreck? And you're going to be the one to swim down there, are you?"

The head gave a smile of mock regret. "No, my succulent piece of meat. You are."

"Forget it. There are sharp-tooths in the coastal waters."

"And you fear them more than your mistress?"

"Yes."

She met Orix's eyes. He took a second to register. He looked bored, as lost in his own world as Noni was in hers. She couldn't blame him: the poor boy still couldn't understand a word of Niyandrian, save the ones that would require him to go to confession.

"Give me the head," she told him in Nan-Rhouric. "You're going down there."

"Me? I would, only…"

"You can't swim."

"Sorry."

"Well?" Tain demanded. "Or perhaps we could send the girl. She is possessed by Queen Talia, after all. Sharp-tooths are notoriously superstitious. They'll not approach the stink of necromancy."

Noni was sitting back on her haunches, stirring a rockpool with her finger, head cocked to one side as she tracked the movements of a tiny white crab.

"I never said it would be easy," Tain said. "But this is the site of the wreckage of the *Umaneia*."

"So?"

"The *Umaneia* was a merchantman from the mainland, before the invaders arrived from across the Trackless Ocean. It was crewed by the distant ancestors of the Soreshi."

"Sorcerers," Carred said. More so even than Niyandrians.

"Knowledge seekers. They must have learned about the Niyandrian attempts to manufacture an Armor of Divinity. The legends I studied claim the Soreshi came to the vicinity of the cairns and offered to trade for one of the interred suits. When the priests refused, the Soreshi used their sorcery and took it."

"And when they set sail for home, they sank?"

"Interesting, isn't it? I doubt it was a coincidence. The scrolls I studied in Wintotashum's scriptorium back in the day say nothing about what happened. All we know is that a ship came here looking for some undisclosed relic, and that it never made it home."

"So how did you find it?"

"If I had a finger, I would tap my nose," Tain said. "Suffice it to say, I am a necromancer. The dead talk to me, and even when they don't, I have learned a language of immeasurably more worth than Nan-Rhouric: the language of wood, stone, and metal.

"It is an effect of the earth-tide that the materials produced by Wiraya retain impressions, each to their own degree, and that the strongest impressions, read by the most proficient wielders of the earth-tide, are akin to memories.

"Don't look so surprised. Even the Church of Menselas is aware of the lore: they still possess memory crystals from before the demon wars—though I doubt the Church had anything to do with making them. There are many such relics at large in the world. All I had to do was find some antiques from the right period and hold them in my hand, and I had the inkling of a trail to follow."

"Then why didn't you come here and retrieve the armor?"

"Because by then I had discovered the location of the cairns, and that seemed to me a far easier undertaking."

"But not now, eh?" Carred said.

"There you go again! It was an accident."

"The creation of the shadow things, or the murder of your helpers? Well, it looks like you've wasted our time."

"What?"

"It's all well and good bringing rope and a net, but it's not much good if I can't breathe underwater. Orix," she said, switching to Nan-Rhouric, "fling the head in the sea."

"Really?"

"No!" Tain cried. "The wreck is deeper than I thought."

"So what do you suggest?" Carred asked.

"How long can you hold your breath?"

"Not long enough. Sorry, Talia," Carred said, "but this is a dead end."

Noni stood from her crouch. "You are wrong, Carred. You *can* breathe underwater."

"Oh, really? Did Talia tell you that? No, wait: you are Talia, aren't you? Noni's just—what?—an overcoat to be discarded whenever she's not useful?"

"Carred…" There was ice in Noni's voice now. A warning. "There is a way for you to breathe underwater."

"More earth-tide sorcery? No, I'm not doing it."

"Not the earth-tide," Talia said. "The dawn. If I were here, I would work the sorcery for you, but I can't use the dawn-tide from the realm of the dead. You will have to do it yourself."

"Like I said: a dead end. My repositories have atrophied from lack of use."

"I can show you what to do."

"Ask Tain," Carred said. "He's not in the realm of the dead. At least, his head's not."

"I'm afraid I must disappoint—not something I am given to with the ladies," Tain said. "There is not the slightest drop of dawn-tide essence in me. Like you, I've never had any use for it, and have focused solely on the earth-tide. I am something of a specialist."

"I'll show you," Talia said as Noni stepped nearer and reached out a hand to touch Carred's face. "It's about time. You will have to use your repositories, Carred. I will guide you."

Noni's hand came round the back of Carred's head and pulled her into a fierce kiss. Her breath was rank, and there was a metallic taste to her lips.

Lightning sheeted behind Carred's eyes, and her guts flipped into her mouth.

Gone was the taste of blood on Noni's cracked lips, replaced by the aniseed Talia used to freshen her breath.

Carred was back in the Queen's bedchamber in Naphor, only it felt different this time. There was no chill from where their skin—they were both naked—touched. Talia was as hot as a furnace. Sweat squelched between them. Fire blossomed within Carred's chest, burning hotter and hotter as it shot up her neck and filled her skull. There was a fizzing sensation in her head. Something popped, producing a pleasant pain, then an oozing warmth beneath her scalp.

"Good," Talia said. "Now, listen and learn. Quickly, though. I can't be in two places at the same time."

"What do you mean?" Carred asked. "Where else are—?"

"Actually, it's three, if you count the realm of the dead. But hush, Carred. We don't have long."

Warmth flooded Carred's belly as she moaned, straining for the Queen's embrace, but Talia held her at arm's length and repeated the same cant over and over, the words neither Niyandrian nor Skanuric but something in between.

After an agony of longing, of straining to be touched, Carred dropped to her knees, but not on Talia's bed: on hard rock.

She breathed in the sea breeze, smelled the brine. She was exhausted, turned inside out. She'd not felt so drained since

Kovin, who never knew when to quit in bed.

She opened an eye a crack.

Beside her, Noni was quivering on the ground. Orix was stony-faced, swallowing repeatedly. The head he held—Tain's head—licked its lips and tried to affect a look of nonchalance.

"I know what to do," Carred said as she stood on wobbly legs.

"What just happened?" Tain said. "I don't want to pry, but the amount of earth-tide coming off you two was staggering."

"How much did you see?" Carred asked as she kicked off her boots.

"A kiss, if you could call it that," Tain said. "Not even a touch of tongues. After that, a lot of shuddering and groaning—nothing arousing. It had more the feel of those poor unfortunates we necromancers sometimes raise from death."

"Did I die?"

"Don't… be… foolish," Noni said, her face pressed against the rock she lay upon, drool trickling from the corner of her mouth. "You've never been more… alive."

She might have been right. Something was buzzing inside Carred's head. Something that had been barely discernible moments before.

Her dawn-tide repository was twice its former size, and brimming with energy.

"How?" she asked, feeling her scalp.

"I… refashioned it," Noni said. "With the earth… tide."

Unbuckling her sword belt as she went, and cursing when she cut her foot on a barnacle, Carred made her way across the rocks toward the sea.

"Don't forget these," Orix said, hurrying after her with Tain's head under one arm, the net and the coiled rope in the other.

Carred grunted her thanks, then bundled up the net and slung it over her shoulder. She tied one end of the rope around her waist and handed the other to Orix. She turned to the sea, toes curling over the edge of the promontory as she readied herself to jump.

"Is that a dorsal fin?" Tain asked.

"Where?"

She glanced over her shoulder. Tain's chin quivered as he tried not to laugh.

"Bastard," Carred said, then added to Orix in his own tongue, "Shut him up."

"No!" Tain protested as Orix closed the face plate.

"Anything happens to me," she said, "cast the helm in the sea."

"You'll be all right," Orix said.

"I hope so. Because if I start to drown, I doubt Noni will leap in and save me. You cannot swim, and Tain…"

She turned back to the sea, scanning the clear water. Silver fish undulated beneath the surface, pursued by the shadows of seabirds that wheeled overhead. There was no sign of anything big enough to pose a threat, but now that Tain had joked about sharp-tooths, she couldn't stop thinking about them.

She focused on the reef and the wreckage enmeshed with it. She'd heard from someone that sharp-tooths avoided coral. Probably it was Jada who'd told her. Before grief could take hold of her again, she turned it to anger, and then she dove.

Cold water closed over her. Fish scattered. Sand and rocks up from the bottom rushed to meet her, but then the ocean shelf dropped away, and she was swimming towards the reef.

In her mind, she recited the words of the cant Talia had somehow communicated to her. There was an answering fizz in her dawn-tide repository. Thousands of tiny bubbles surrounded her. Her skin prickled and her veins throbbed. She expected her lungs to burn with the need for air, but the sensation never came.

Deeper and deeper she swam, her confidence in the dawn-tide sorcery growing with every stroke. Was this what it felt like to be a fish? She wanted to laugh and cry out, "I'm a fish!" Theltek's eyes, if only she'd not neglected her repositories all her life, what else might she have achieved?

Pressure built in her ears the deeper she dove, and as the thrill of breathing underwater wore off, she realized her foot stung from where she had cut it on the barnacle. She craned her neck, expecting to see the water behind pink with her blood, but there was nothing. That was a relief: Jada had also told her that sharp-tooths could detect a single drop of blood in the water from miles away.

Movement below drew her eye. A shadow emerged from the coral, causing her heart to stutter. She backed up in the water and waited, watching as something long undulated away out of sight. Definitely not a sharp-tooth, but it was big, maybe twice her length or even longer.

Gritting her teeth, Carred reoriented herself and struck out for the wreck.

Wood and iron had fused with coral where the reef had grown up around the sunken ship. She could just about make out the gaps between strakes encrusted with anemones, shells, and bone-like coral structures.

The keel was half-buried in spongelike growths. It had been breached at some point, the hole charred black around its splintered edges.

She swam around the ship's prow, past the purplish lips of huge clams, and then rose level with the gunwales, where seaweed draped like curtains.

Carred pushed out across the deck, which now formed the bed of a new reef. A skeleton clung to the ship's wheel, both green with algae.

Something brushed against her leg, and she screamed. Water flooded her lungs. She panicked, thrashed about, and started to swim for the surface until she realized she could still breathe. The water filling her lungs just seemed to evaporate. At the same time, a throb commenced within her skull, and her dawn-tide repository clenched. She could feel its essence draining away.

Fighting for calm, she looked about but couldn't see whatever had touched her. The wreck amid the reef was now a hundred feet below. Cursing herself for losing control, she dove back towards it.

Other than the splintered mast, the highest part of the ship—and therefore the closest—was the aftcastle, the elevated fighting platform at the stern. It told her that Tain—or the legends—were wrong, or had been liberal with the truth. This was a warship, not a merchantman.

Strewn across the deck of the aftcastle were dozens of skeletons in rusted armor, much of it plate, some of it mail, none of it divine. Weapons were clutched in bony hands: swords, spears, harpoons. One of the skeletons moved as she glided over it. A tentacle appeared from underneath, then a bulbous body. With a squirt of ink, the octopus sped away.

The sight of it made Carred smile. She turned to swim toward the main deck but then threw up her hands as something lunged toward her. Through the froth and the bubbles, she glimpsed a ribbon of darkness as it slid by her; then it turned back for a second pass.

Carred swam for the aftcastle's deck and snatched a metal-hafted spear from a skeletal hand. She swung round as the creature came at her again, and jabbed it with the spear. Blood clouded the water, and the thing turned away, writhing through the water at an impossible speed.

Got to hurry, she told herself. Blood in the water. The last thing she needed was to test Jada's theory about sharp-tooths.

She swam down to the main deck, past the algae-green skeleton at the wheel. Other than him, the deck was empty. The door to a squat cabin stood open, and she passed through and swam down more stairs into the underbelly of the ship.

Cargo was strewn about the hold: broken urns, upturned crates, clothing, and other flotsam floating in the murky waters. She was about to turn around and go back up top when she glimpsed something glinting in the beams of wavering sunlight that pierced the hull from the surface.

It was a great helm, not a hint of rust on it, held aloft in gauntleted hands. It looked as though the skeleton had been trying to place the helm over its head. The entire skeleton was armored save for its head: pauldrons, greaves, vambraces, a gorget to protect the neck, cuisses, sollerets—all perfectly molded from a silvery metal that seemed to ripple whenever the water moved. Only the breastplate was damaged, punched through the heart region by a rust-covered sword.

Carred's mind raced, trying to piece together what had happened here all those centuries—millennia—ago. There had been a fight; that much was clear from the dead piled around the aftcastle. But a fight with whom or what? Something had breached the hull. Had there been a reef back then, or perhaps a collision with a rock? Or maybe it had been something else, some kind of sorcery or beast.

But here, in the cargo hold: an armored woman—she could tell by the shape of the breastplate—in the process of putting on the helm. If Tain was right and this was an early suit of Armor of Divinity, had the woman been attempting to use the armor to escape? Or had she been about to translate herself to the realm of the gods, and some enemy had made it their business to stop her? It made no difference. The bodies in the burial chambers beneath the cairns were proof of that: this woman would have perished either way.

Needles stabbed at Carred's brain, and her dawn-tide repository shuddered. She might only have minutes left before her sorcery failed and she drowned and took her place in this ancient ship's story for someone else to find.

Quickly, Carred set about unbuckling the armor. The clasps unfastened at the merest touch; there was no sign of decay. Piece after piece of the armor she stowed inside her fishing net. Saving the breastplate till last, she gripped the sword hilt, but as she pulled, it came off in her hand and flakes of rust swirled through the water. She turned over the skeleton and took hold of what remained of the blade, then pulled the rest of the sword through the back of the rib cage.

Adding the breastplate to her net, she dragged the armor up the stairs to the main deck. She undid the rope from around her waist and tied it to the net.

Pressure built in her lungs, a burning need to breathe. Not daring to wait a second longer, she swam toward the shimmering light of the sun.

The moment her head broke the surface, she gasped in air.

"Carred!" Orix cried, standing at the edge of the promontory. "Did you find it?"

"I found it."

She clung to the rope as he pulled her toward the shore, and beneath her, the net with the armor started to rise.

# TWENTY-EIGHT

ANSKAR STEPPED OUT OF THE Ethereal Sorceress's depot into blinding sunlight and a scalding breeze. He found himself atop a low mesa overlooking a settlement of tents and lean-tos bustling with people. To his right, black mountains were just visible in the hazy distance, and beyond the sprawling settlement there was an expanse of glimmering ice—which made no sense in all this heat.

As he moved away from the depot, toward the broad, switchback roadway cut into the face of the mesa and began his descent, heat prickled his skin. The arid air dried his throat and burned his lungs as if he were inhaling steam. The sun's glare was so strong it pained his eyes, and he had to shield his brow with his hand.

When he reached the bottom, he passed between dust-caked tents and shelters made from the wreckage of wagons with awnings of stitched-together cloaks propped up by spears. Most of the people here were ruddy-skinned Traguh-raj, which made him think of Orix.

There was a lot of flesh on display: the locals wore little more than loincloths of linen, and the women were bare-breasted.

Anskar heard snatches of conversation in a language he didn't understand, though he thought it was traders haggling with one another. The scent of spiced meat reached his nostrils, and he turned to see a man roasting skewered lizards over burning coals. The lizards were the length of Anskar's arm, their scales red, yellow, and purple. Other traders offered cups of water kept cool in the shade of their awnings. Several wagons were open to reveal racks of weapons—spears, scimitars, daggers, bows, sheaves of goose-fletched arrows.

A gray-haired crone, seated at a table on the back of a wagon, beckoned Anskar with a curled finger. On the table in front of her were carved sticks of bone, and Anskar's sorcerous senses recoiled from the taint of the crone's repository. He couldn't tell if it was dawn- or dusk-tide or something else, only that it felt like a wound that had grown infected. She tracked his passage with slitted eyes and called out what might have been a curse.

He emerged from the clustered tents and wagons to find a woman waiting for him a mere few hundred yards away from the start of the ice plains. She was standing beside a wooden sleigh, to which was tethered a lizard the size of a pony. It was black-scaled, with bands of mauve encircling its neck and belly. Its clawed feet were encrusted with glistening granules of salt or ice or maybe crystal.

The woman's brownish-red skin marked her as Traguh-raj, and she had black hair braided close to her scalp. She wore a slender warrior's harness over her bare torso and a studded leather kilt that left her long, lithe legs exposed. As Anskar switched his gaze from her small breasts to her bare feet, he caught the glint of a scimitar hanging from her harness.

"Welcome, Anskar DeVantte," she said in broken Nan-Rhouric. "I am Uraxa of the Agalot. Ride with me."

"The Ethereal Sorceress sent you?" Anskar asked, not knowing where to look. He settled on her broad, angular face, and saw that her green eyes sparkled with either amusement or excitement.

"We hunt for nietan," she said, and gestured for him to climb aboard the sleigh.

The lizard moved at great speed, its feet barely touching the granulated crystal of the plains. It was a disconcerting sensation for Anskar, being beneath the glare of the blistering sun while at the same time traveling deeper into a land that had the appearance of ice. As the sleigh slipped and slid, at times veering wildly on the coarse surface of the ground, he clung to the wooden rail.

Uraxa of the Agalot remained standing at the front, swaying with the sleigh's movements, her hands clutching the reins. Her ruddy skin glistened with a sheen of sweat that highlighted her lean and muscular frame. She cast frequent looks back at Anskar, her face bright with elation. He could tell this was her element, her passion, and her enthusiasm was contagious.

"Keep your eyes open," she called over her shoulder.

"For what?"

"Faults, craters, a crevasse. The nietan live beneath the surface."

"You want me to go underground?"

"I do not want anything," Uraxa said with her infectious smile. "But if you require the horn of a nietan, you will have to take it for yourself."

"What if I pay you to get it for me?"

She laughed. "I don't think you have enough coin, Niyas man. And besides, I am not that foolish."

"Niyas man?"

"I am mistaken? Then forgive me. I thought, your eyes…"

"I'm only half Niyandrian."

"There's a hat beneath the bench you're sitting on," Uraxa said, noticing that the relentless sun was burning his face. "You brought water?"

"No."

"Then we will go to the water," Uraxa said, and the sleigh veered left in a long, looping arc.

Anskar fished a wide-brimmed hat from beneath the bench and settled it on his head. It was a small relief, but at least it shaded his face and eyes from the glare.

The lizard continued at the same galloping pace, the sleigh skimming along in its wake and leaving twin furrows in the crystalline carpet behind them.

Anskar began to notice long-legged birds stalking the plains, dipping their curved beaks beneath the surface. Once they passed a gigantic reptile with a shell covering its back, and as they sped by, the creature's head and legs disappeared inside the shell. Another time, Anskar spotted a scorpion the size of a man, its body seemingly made of glass.

At length Uraxa brought them to a glimmering pool where water had collected in a crater. The sleigh came to a stop, and the lizard flicked out its long, purplish tongue and drank.

"This depression was once a nietan lair," Uraxa explained. "But the creature was killed, and the tunnels it inhabited have long since filled with crystals flowing from the surface."

"They flow from beneath the surface?"

"Only at night."

"What happens then?"

"The crystals become liquid for a time. We call it the night tide. It is not good to be out here then."

"Why? What would happen?"

"For one, we would sink. Liquid crystal isn't like water; you cannot swim in it. It is more akin to quicksand. But there are things that *can* swim in the night tide, and you would not want to meet them."

Anskar gazed nervously around. "How long do we have?"

Again Uraxa laughed, this time a joyful, tinkling sound. "Do not fret, Niyas man. I will keep you safe."

They climbed out of the sleigh and drank their fill of the water, which, despite being exposed to the blazing sun, was ice cold. When Anskar looked at Uraxa for an explanation, she smiled.

"There is ancient sorcery here, left over from a long-ago cataclysm. Where these plains now lie, there used to stand a mighty city."

"Where is it now?" Anskar asked. "Surely there must be ruins?"

"All gone." She scooped up a handful of crystal powder and let it fall between her fingers.

Uraxa produced half a dozen canteens from inside the sleigh, and they filled them with water, then climbed back aboard and set off again.

As the sleigh skidded across the plains, Anskar began to despair that they would ever find the lair of a nietan. All around them was a glistening sea of crystal dust, and he could no longer see the settlement they had started from. The sun had long passed its zenith and was slowly edging into the west. He worried about what would happen when the sun finally set, the crystal plains turned to liquid, and whatever predators hid beneath the surface came out to hunt.

At last, though, Uraxa spotted what she had been looking for. She reined in the lizard near the lip of a crevasse that cut a jagged line across the plains. It was at least a hundred yards long and ten or more wide.

Uraxa unhooked a rope and grapnel from inside the sleigh, and together they climbed down into the crevasse. The compacted crystal of the walls abraded Anskar's arms whenever he came into contact with it.

They descended for perhaps thirty feet, Anskar's boots crunching against the wall, yet Uraxa, despite being barefoot, showed no signs of discomfort. At the bottom, tunnels had been bored through the lower parts of the walls on either side, and Uraxa bade Anskar enter one.

"I know nothing about nietan," he said. "How do I kill one? With this?" He half-drew *Amalantril*.

"You could try," she said unhelpfully.

"How many will there be?"

"Just the one, though there may be unhatched eggs, which you must not touch. Nietan are solitary beasts, only emerging from their lairs to mate."

Anskar nodded. "All right. Let's go."

"Just you," Uraxa said. "I shall wait for you here. Nietan are sacred to my people. But sometimes outsiders come for their horns, and we Agalot are sworn to the service of those who send them."

"The Ethereal Sorceress?" Anskar asked.

"She is but one. I am permitted to say no more than that. But I will say this: do not become embroiled in Sheelahn's designs, Anskar DeVantte. Perform this task, if you must, then go about your life freely while you still can."

"Is the Ethereal Sorceress evil?"

Uraxa laughed. "Things are never that simple." Then she looked sad. "I cannot aid you further. It pains me to betray a nietan, and I will play no part in its death."

"Must it die?"

"How else will you obtain the horn?"

Anskar nodded grimly, then set off alone down the closest tunnel.

Walls, ceiling, and floor glinted with reflected sunlight from above the crevasse, but as he rounded a corner, the light died. On instinct, he reached for the dawn-tide and held out his palm to receive its light, then cursed and shook his hand. He had been burned. This time, he proceeded with caution as he focused his awareness inside himself and felt along the interwoven threads of his dawn- and dusk-tide repository. He had used the same mental incantation to produce light as he always did, only this time the dawn's flow had been tainted by the dusk.

Carefully, he picked at a few threads of what to his sorcerous sight appeared as glowing strands of gold. As they separated from the knotted mass of his repositories, he knew they were formed from pure dawn-tide. He recited the cant again, and a pearly radiance appeared on his palm. As he fed it more dawn-tide essence, its light increased, reflecting from the crystal of the tunnel.

He walked for a while, taking tributary passages at random. He kept a lookout for any signs of which way to go, but there was no spoor of any beast. Perhaps Uraxa had gotten it wrong, and this wasn't a nietan lair. Or perhaps it had been once, but the creature that had lived here had long since died or moved away.

He began to wonder if Uraxa would still be waiting for him if he ever found his way back to the entrance. Had he been too ready to trust the Ethereal Sorceress with the knowledge of what it was he planned? Sheelahn had seemed willing enough to go along with his quest for the divine alloy. What if she secretly sought to oppose him and had sent him on a fool's errand? Or worse still, had sent him to a slow, lonely death beneath the crystal plains? Because if Uraxa hadn't been lying about the crystal turning to liquid when the sun went down, these tunnels would flood.

He came to a cavern with the narrowest of paths leading between hundreds of perfectly smooth crystal eggs heaped up on either side. Within the eggs, clusters of smaller crystals shimmered, and when Anskar stepped closer, he could see that these particles were rotating. There were three or four within each egg, connected by hairs of what looked like quicksilver.

He reached a hand toward an egg, then remembered Uraxa's warning and withdrew it. As he did, he felt the weight of a presence behind him, and he turned.

At first, he was too astounded to breathe. He merely stared, until he became aware of his mouth hanging open.

A child stood before him. A child that came up to his waist, and was crudely formed from compacted crystal. Light from Anskar's palm reflected from the millions of quartz-like granules that formed the child's skin. Its head was an egg-shaped lump with no mouth, nose, or eyes. It had no ears either, only a single horn of smooth crystal jutting from the center of its forehead. Its hands were flat spades of crystal with slender thumbs, and its feet seemed to sprout from the ground.

The creature didn't move. Though it had no eyes, Anskar felt certain it was watching him, waiting for him to do something.

He let out the breath he had been holding, and became aware of his stranglehold on the hilt of his scabbarded sword. He willed himself to relax his fingers.

*Kill it,* Queen Talia said in his mind. *Take the horn.*

Anskar half-drew *Amalantril*, and the nietan retreated. It didn't walk exactly; its rooted feet flowed backward through the crystal floor, and the rest of the creature followed—a graceful, gliding motion that seemed effortless. And then it stood still again and resumed watching him.

Again, Anskar relaxed his grip on his sword, though he could feel his mother's impatience as a painful agitation within his mind. Thoughts came unbidden and tangled with his own—of rage and death and grasping; of hope and despair and goading. A panoply of reasons why he should act now, and the dire consequences for both him and his mother if he did not.

Anskar shut the thoughts out by re-forming his wards against Queen Talia. He heard a yowl like a tortured cat, and then she was gone.

The crystal child glowed golden, then red, then violet for an instant, before returning to its former transparency.

He became aware that the nietan was standing between him and the way he had come.

He stepped toward the creature and it flowed to one side. As he took another step, it began to shake and rattle, and as its rattles became more violent, it grew. It seemed to Anskar that the crystal body was turning to a viscous liquid before his eyes— as Uraxa had told him the crystal plains above would turn into an ocean of quicksand when night fell.

His heart thudded wildly with fear that he had delayed too long and the crystal waters were even now cascading down the crevasse to drown him, bringing the sharp-toothed predators that could swim in its thick, unnatural fluid.

The floor beneath his feet remained solid. Only the creature in front of him changed, swelling into a monstrous horned beast with four tree-trunk legs and a scorpion's tail. Its head was like a lion's, only formed from compacted crystal, which shimmered in the light still burning upon Anskar's palm. Its eyes were ablaze with silver, and its cavernous maw was ringed with razor shards of glinting quartz.

As the nietan lumbered toward him, no longer flowing but thumping and thudding with its clawed crystal paws, Anskar retreated. He felt the dark-tide swell within him. With it came a stench he'd not smelled before—of sulfur, coppery blood, and rot. In his mind's eye, vines of blackness twined about his bones, insinuated their way into his veins, and sprouted like mist-formed hairs through his skin.

The creature roared—a booming, rumbling sound that shook the crystal passage and reverberated around Anskar's skull.

He retreated faster, almost tripping and falling. Dark-tide energy coalesced around his clenched fist, snuffing out the dawn-tide glow on his palm and plunging the passageway into blackness.

The crunch of crystal told him the nietan was getting closer, so close it almost touched him. He could feel its breath on his skin, hot and scalding.

Yet he was still standing, still breathing. If the nietan wanted him dead, he already would be. With that realization, Anskar let the dark-tide essence drain away, back into his repository.

Something massive brushed lightly against his face, followed by an outrush of breath. He steeled himself against its burn, but it was a biting winter wind he felt, which left him cleansed and invigorated.

"Menselas," he muttered, "show me what to do."

There was no answer. There was never any answer.

A fist of warmth ignited deep within him. He sent his

sorcerous senses inward, but it wasn't from any of the tides. Was the nietan doing something to him? No: he felt the beast's weighty presence withdraw; heard the crystal beneath its paws crunch as it backed away.

Had the god, in some small measure, replied?

Suddenly, Anskar knew he was alone in the darkness. Panicked, he reignited the dawn-tide light upon his palm.

The nietan had gone.

He had failed.

In part, he was relieved. If he couldn't get the nietan's horn, he would be unable to continue with the quest to make the Armor of Divinity. At the same time, he was flooded with anger, disappointment, and despair.

The strength of the feelings shocked him, and he dismissed them as belonging to Queen Talia—though how she could still be infecting him when he had shut her out with his wards, he had no idea. Perhaps he was deluding himself, and the feelings were indeed his own. Maybe his mother's goal had slowly become his own.

He shook his head in denial. He had no desire to become a god.

And then he remembered Uraxa's warning about the crystal plains turning to liquid, and hurried to find his way back to the foot of the crevasse. After taking one turn and then another, and another, Anskar became convinced he was lost. He called out Uraxa's name, desperate now, and to his relief, she called back.

His heart racing, panting for every breath, he followed the sound of Uraxa's voice until he reached the crevasse.

The rope they had descended by hung down from the sleigh above, and Uraxa stood waiting, her expression serene and softened by a gentle smile.

She was not alone.

Beside her, clasping her hand, was the crystal child.

The nietan looked different. The horn was gone from the center of its forehead, replaced by a circular depression. It was clutching the horn in its free hand. As Anskar approached, the nietan held it out to him.

He wavered, glancing at Uraxa for an indication of what he should do, but there was no clue in her smile.

He reached tentatively for the crystal horn, then withdrew his hand. "Why?" he asked.

A faint, musical chiming sound came from the nietan.

"You have the nietan's blessing," Uraxa said. The chimes changed in cadence. "But this thing you seek to make—the Armor of Divinity—no good will come of it. My advice is to desist while you still can."

The crystal child once more proffered the horn. Anskar took it, and cradled it in both arms with an overwhelming sense of reverence.

The nietan nodded and chimed again, then lightly touched Anskar's forearm, as if it knew, as if it could see, despite the lack of moonlight.

"As soon as you can," Uraxa translated, "remove that vambrace from your arm. If you cannot destroy it, you must cast it into the depths of the Simorga Sea."

"Why?" Anskar asked, then noticed that the crystal child was weeping tears of quicksilver. When he looked at Uraxa, she was crying too.

Overcome with guilt, Anskar offered the crystal horn back, but Uraxa shook her head and smiled through her tears.

"No, you do not understand. Our tears are not for the horn." Even as she spoke, the depression in the center of the nietan's forehead filled over, and then a new horn pushed out to replace the one Anskar had taken. "Our tears are for you."

The nietan gave a low bow, then it turned to liquid and drained away through the crystal floor.

"Come," Uraxa said, her voice thick with emotion. "We should go."

# TWENTY-NINE

ON THE SLEIGH RIDE BACK to the Ethereal Sorceress's depot in the Wastes, and then during the strange transition back to Wintotashum, Anskar fretted about the nietan's warning: that he should destroy the vambrace or cast it into the Simorga Sea.

Neither option seemed possible. He'd tried to take the vambrace off and had gotten nowhere. And that scared him. *Our tears are for you,* the nietan had said, and Anskar was beginning to see why. He was devoid of choice, swept along by the current of his mother's plan.

In her Wintotashum depot, the Ethereal Sorceress assured Anskar that the other components he needed for the Armor of Divinity had been procured and delivered to Hrothyr's smithy.

"You did not slay the nietan," the sorceress said in her musical voice.

"How do you know?"

"Because if you had, there would not be one horn, but many.

The entire crystalline structure of the nietan would form into replicas of that which you cut from its head."

"Will one be enough?" Anskar asked.

"My side of the bargain is concluded," she said. "Payment is due."

"Now?"

"Later. Until such time, I am loath to add to your debt. My orderly will see you out."

When Anskar arrived at the smithy, Hrothyr told him a cart had arrived during the night, though without a horse to pull it. It was still there, beneath the lean-to outside, the contents covered by a thick canvas.

The blacksmith had already checked what lay inside the cart: blackwood, Khorun pearls, sunstone, astrumium, and red gold. Enough for an entire suit of plate armor, Hrothyr assured him. But the single nietan horn would not be enough.

By the time Braga and Brother Bonavir arrived, Anskar had made up his mind. He wasn't going through with this.

"Get it off me!" he demanded, holding out his forearm.

Braga and Hrothyr exchanged a look that Anskar couldn't decipher.

"Peace, Anskar," Brother Bonavir said. "These things cannot be rushed. At least wait until nighttime, when the vambrace is visible."

Anskar bashed the vambrace against one of Hrothyr's workbenches over and over. When Brother Bonavir tried to restrain him, Anskar shoved the priest away.

"Don't damage it," Braga warned.

Hrothyr just shook his head as he approached Anskar with a pair of pincers. "Here," the blacksmith said, and something about his deep voice was reassuring. "Roll up your sleeve."

Anskar did, and Hrothyr felt along the surface of the invisible vambrace until he found what he was looking for—presumably one of the clasps that held it closed. He moved the pincers closer until they made contact with the vambrace and scraped along it.

"Is that—?" Anskar started.

"The pincer head is made from divine alloy," Hrothyr said. "Nothing else will cut it. I cast them from a mold, years back, when I made the vambrace. Never had a chance to use them till now."

He snipped with the pincers, and Anskar felt the pressure of the vambrace about his forearm relax a little. Hrothyr found the second clasp and cut it, then the third, and the vambrace released its grip. When Hrothyr took hold of the two sides of the vambrace and pulled, they came away like a scab, and Anskar cried out at the stinging pain.

Hrothyr carried the invisible vambrace to another bench, deposited it inside a wooden box, and closed the lid.

"You shouldn't—" Braga started, but Hrothyr waved away her objection.

"Do you want the lad to suffer? We still have the first piece of the Armor of Divinity, and it's not going anywhere. So I don't see what your problem is."

Braga glowered, and Anskar feared she might hit her ex-husband.

"Well, I suppose it can't hurt," Brother Bonavir said.

Which was when Anskar keeled over. As he hit the ground, his body began to buck and spasm.

Anskar awoke freezing. His teeth chattered, and his skin burned with cold. His eyes came blearily into focus on the inside of a tent. A woman in a white robe was kneeling beside him.

He was lying on a sheepskin on the ground, covered with blankets. The woman lightly touched his forehead, and he saw it was Gisela.

"It's freezing," Anskar said. He noticed Gisela was shivering, too.

"We're outside the city," she said, "and it's snowing again."

"Outside? I thought… I can't remember. What happened?"

"Braga brought you to me. You suffered a spell of disorientation and fell unconscious."

He followed Gisela's gaze to where Braga was seated on a wooden chest across the tent from him. The blacksmith shook her head. "You shouldn't have removed the vambrace, ass-wipe. Hrothyr shouldn't have done it."

Gisela stood. "Given what that evil thing did to him when it was removed, I'd say Anskar made the right decision. The Five only knows what it would have done to him over time."

Braga scowled.

Anskar rubbed his forearm, where the skin was raw and mottled. What if Hrothyr managed to create the rest of the Armor of Divinity and Anskar was the one to wear it? If just removing the vambrace had rendered him unconscious, he doubted he would survive the removal of the entire suit of armor.

"I'm sorry, ass-wipe," Braga added. "It was what the ghost lady wanted, not me."

"Ghost lady?" Gisela said.

Anskar sighed. "My mother."

"Is she still within you? We should gather the healers and exorcize her."

"No!" Anskar protested, far more strongly than he'd intended.

"No," he said again, more softly. "Not yet. I can't."

"But you must. Menselas demands it."

"Does he?" Anskar asked. "How do you know that?"

"Because this spirit, or whatever it is, this thing you call your mother, is an abomination."

Anskar tensed. Acid coursed through his veins. He knew Gisela was right, so why did he feel so protective of Queen Talia's presence?

He changed the topic. "Are you speaking to your father yet?"

Gisela bridled at that and moved to hold the tent flap open. "You've been healed. You can go now."

When Anskar and Braga tried to re-enter the city, the guards at the barbican refused to let them through. Eventually, at Anskar's request, Brother Bonavir was summoned.

"Thank the Five you've recovered," the priest of the Elder said as he escorted Anskar and Braga past the guards. He glanced at Braga and grimaced before he found the words he was looking for. "Something has happened. I was at the smithy when your message reached me."

"What is it?" Anskar said. "What happened?"

Hrothyr's forge was overrun with men and women of the City Watch, as well as several priests of the Healer clustered together and speaking in hushed voices. One of the healers was making notes on a sheet of parchment attached to a wooden board. As Anskar, Braga, and Brother Bonavir entered, the notetaker shook her head sadly.

Braga saw it first and rushed to the body on the floor by one of the workbenches. It was wrapped head to toe in a sheet.

Brother Bonavir put a hand on Anskar's shoulder. "I just can't explain it."

Braga shoved aside a watchman who tried to hold her back, and pulled away the sheet to reveal Hrothyr's pale face. It was stiff in a rictus mask, his eyes wide and white. Blood crusted his lips from where he must have bitten his tongue.

"How?" Braga said through clenched teeth. "Why?" Her huge shoulders bunched up around her ears, and she shuddered as she sobbed.

Brother Bonavir went to kneel at her side. Gently, he raised Hrothyr's right arm.

The sleeve of the blacksmith's shirt was rolled up, revealing the ruined flesh. The skin was depressed, as if it had been tightly bound, and it was white, with islands of blisters that wept pus. Veins of black crisscrossed the pallid flesh, and there were angry red lines at the wrist and just below the elbow.

"The vambrace?" Anskar mouthed.

Brother Bonavir nodded, his eyes flicking around the forge.

One of the healers approached and put a hand on Braga's shoulder. "Did you know him?" the man asked.

Braga shut her eyes.

"They were married," Brother Bonavir explained.

"We never divorced," Braga added, as if somehow that fact could bring Hrothyr back.

"We can find no evidence of any violence," the Watch captain said, a heavyset woman with close-cropped red hair and a lantern jaw. "The only thing untoward is that mark on his forearm, and no one seems to have any idea what caused it."

She looked expectantly at Brother Bonavir, but when the priest offered no explanation, she sighed. "Well, unless there's anything else…"

"There isn't," Bonavir said. "Thank you, Captain. You too," he told the healers. "Will you take the body?"

The healer with his hand on Braga's shoulder nodded. "We'll prepare it for crossing the veil. We can discuss the ritual, if you like," he told Braga. "You can choose how you would like to send your husband off."

"No," Braga said. "I'm not leaving him. Not till his spirit's crossed over."

"Then you should come with us. We have rooms where relatives may sleep beside their loved ones."

Brother Bonavir seemed impatient for the Watch and the healers to leave, and when they had gone, taking Hrothyr's body and Braga with them, he pulled shut the forge's barn doors and hurried back over to Anskar.

"The vambrace must still be here. We need to find it."

"Unless someone took it," Anskar said. "How do you think Hrothyr died?"

"I don't know. Presumably a ward woven into the sorcery of the vambrace by its maker."

"By Hrothyr? But that makes no sense."

"Not Hrothyr," Brother Bonavir said, as if talking to an idiot. "He was but the craftsman working on someone else's design."

"My mother's," Anskar said.

"The vambrace was intended for her," Brother Bonavir said. "Or her heir."

"Me. So this is my fault."

"Don't be so foolish," the priest said.

"I'm serious. If I hadn't insisted on having the vambrace removed, Hrothyr would still be alive."

Brother Bonavir's silence was all the confirmation Anskar needed.

"Did you know this would happen?"

"No," the priest said. "Though I should have known. As a priest of the Elder, it is my duty to explore every avenue of knowledge. There was nothing about this in the necromancer Tain's notes, but I should have looked elsewhere, asked questions of my confreres. I was in too much of a hurry to see if we could replicate the vambrace and commence work on the Armor of Divinity."

"But why?" Anskar asked. "I still don't know what you hope to gain from all this."

"The joy of discovery, of learning something long forgotten. Such things set us apart from our confreres and ease our passage through the hierarchy."

"You're after promotion?"

"I seek the Elder's favor," the priest corrected. "Nothing more."

"And Braga? Was she just acting out of fear of my mother, do you think?"

"We would have to assume that in part, but I suspect it's more complicated. It was her estranged husband, after all, who crafted the vambrace at your mother's behest."

"I'd have thought Braga would have disapproved," Anskar said.

"Maybe she did. But she's a skilled blacksmith in her own right. Perhaps she had something to prove."

"To Hrothyr?"

Bonavir shrugged. "Marriage, I am told, is a battleground."

"So, where is the vambrace now?"

Brother Bonavir walked over to the wooden box Hrothyr had stored it in. "Not here," he said, closing the lid.

"You saw Hrothyr's arm," Anskar said. "He must have worn it."

Anskar cast his gaze around the smithy, then started toward the forge. The coals were cold, so it was doubtful Hrothyr had been working on the vambrace. Nevertheless, he ran his hand over them, half-expecting to encounter the solidity of divine alloy.

"Be careful, Anskar," Brother Bonavir warned as he commenced his own search. He picked up a slender rod of steel from a bench—the kind intended to be wound into coils and snipped to make links of mail. The priest knelt on the floor and prodded beneath the bench with the rod.

Anskar selected a steel rod for himself, and together they went around the smithy, systematically searching for the vambrace.

"It would be easier at night," Anskar observed. "We could open the windows to the light of the moon."

"I agree," Bonavir said. "But do you think you could wait until then? Besides, once word of Hrothyr's death reaches the King— if it hasn't already—he may order the forge locked up until he appoints a new master blacksmith. King Aelfyr is a superstitious man. I wouldn't put it past him to have the smithy permanently closed, or even torn down and rebuilt."

Anskar was tempted to loosen the wards on his mind and ask his mother what they should do. But another part of him suspected she would only lie to him.

A clash and a clatter behind him made Anskar turn.

Brother Bonavir was standing stock-still, wide eyes staring at Anskar. "Don't move," the priest mouthed, holding a finger to his lips.

Something scraped on the stone floor, and Anskar's heart began to race.

He poked around him with his steel rod and met something solid. He glanced at Brother Bonavir and poked again, and in response heard the grate of metal on stone.

The vambrace, he realized, was moving.

"We should get out," he hissed.

Brother Bonavir shook his head, prodding the floor with his own steel rod. "If we don't find it, if we don't press on with the creation of the divine alloy, Hrothyr's death will have been for nothing."

Something scuttled about Anskar's feet. He turned in a wild circle, striking the floor with his rod.

The scuttling grew faster, and its rattling din increased.

Anskar gasped as something hard punched him in the chest. He stumbled and threw up his arm to protect himself, and something cold and hard clamped itself around his forearm.

"Did it just—?" Bonavir started.

Anskar rubbed his fingers over the invisible vambrace he once again wore. Hrothyr must have repaired the clasps he'd snipped. "It did."

"Oh," the priest said. "That's not good."

Yet something told Anskar that Bonavir was secretly pleased. And he had the impression his mother was laughing.

# THIRTY

HROTHYR'S FUNERAL WAS HELD AT the tiny church of the Warrior tucked away in the old quarter of Wintotashum. The church was peculiar among the structures of the city in that it was built from roughly mortared flint stones and had a much-patched and rotting pitched wooden roof. At one end, two crossed swords had been mounted on the gable. Brother Bonavir said that Hrothyr used to worship here most days, and Braga said that was because long ago Hrothyr had a vocation to the Warrior's priesthood. Something had happened just before his ordination and he'd left. When he and Braga were married, he'd refused to talk about what that was.

The half-dozen Warrior's priests who attended the funeral offered their commiserations to Braga. Her husband, it seemed, had retained good standing with his former confreres.

Inside the church, King Aelfyr was seated in a position of honor beside the plain stone altar. Behind him stood priests of the various aspects. The front pews were occupied by armored men and women of the King's household guard.

Anskar nodded to Lanuc, who was seated beside Nul on the second pew from the front. Of Rindon and Borik there was no sign. Either they hadn't known Hrothyr well or they were commiserating at some tavern or other.

The ceremony wasn't what Anskar had expected. The priest of the Warrior conducting the funeral spoke with barely suppressed violence about how Hrothyr's corpse would be hacked into pieces by the Warrior's servants, so his body could be reassembled in the afterlife, stronger than before, faster, indestructible.

Anskar glanced at Braga to see how she was taking it, but she appeared rapt in the ceremony, her eyes moist with unshed tears.

Brother Bonavir, seated beside Anskar, leaned in and whispered, "I have been thinking about why Hrothyr's arm was such a mess; why he died and yet you live."

Anskar had been thinking the same thing. "He lacked Niyandrian blood," he said, sharing his own conclusion.

Bonavir nodded. "And I suspect not just any old Niyandrian blood. The blood of Queen Talia's son and heir. Certain apocryphal references in my confrere's somewhat tedious and longwinded thesis, which I have been poring over all night, allude to a process whereby demon smiths attune void-steel weapons and armor to those they are intended for. Anyone else attempting to use them is rejected, often quite violently. Void-steel only being found in the abyssal realms, of course."

"So only I can wear the vambrace?" Anskar wondered aloud. He could feel the vile thing on his arm, tight against his skin.

"Or your mother, I would have to assume, were she still alive."

At the conclusion of the funeral rite, Hrothyr's casket was carried through to the sacristy—where, Anskar supposed, the

Warrior's priests would make good on their promise to hack the body to pieces.

King Aelfyr signaled to a gray-haired woman in tatty, much-patched robes—no doubt a priest of the Elder. She stepped forward to address the mourners.

"Under Thousand Lakes law," she said, "and at His Majesty's decree, Braga will inherit Hrothyr's house. Furthermore, the King would like to offer Braga her ex-husband's position as royal blacksmith."

Braga actually looked taken aback.

"Hrothyr always spoke with pride about your skill," the King said as he stood to leave, accompanied by his entourage of priests.

Braga sat for a moment, face buried in her hands, then made her way to the church's entrance, where she accepted condolences as the others filed out.

When Anskar clasped her hand and said how sorry he was for her loss, she replied, "We need to finish the armor."

Anskar glanced past her to where Lanuc was standing, waiting to speak with him.

Braga noticed and said, "While you ride north with the army, I'll start work on the alloy."

Anskar nodded, though he wasn't exactly enthusiastic about the idea. "The supplies from the Ethereal Sorceress are at the smithy. There isn't enough nietan's horn for the entire armor, but it should be enough to get started on a few smaller pieces."

"I'll give you the translation I made of the necromancer Tain's notes," Brother Bonavir told Braga. "As to the original, Anskar, when do you plan to return it?"

"Before we ride north." It wasn't a task he was looking forward to.

And then he went to speak with Lanuc.

Later that night, alone in his barracks room, Anskar prepared to confront his mother about Hrothyr's death and to demand that she tell him how to rid himself of the vambrace.

But when he felt her stir within his marrow, pulsing in time with his heartbeat, he knew he was lying to himself. Some part of him he'd never even suspected of being there feared displeasing his mother. He was terrified of losing her.

Or was that due to some sort of glamor the Necromancer Queen was using to control him?

He pushed the thought aside. Right now, he had other things to worry about, and though he hated having to do it, he once again asked for Queen Talia's help.

With a motherly warmth that had not been there before, she talked him through the method of using the dark-tide to wreathe shadows around him like a cloak.

At first his efforts left him reeling with nausea, but she showed him how he only needed a minuscule amount of dark-tide essence, and that if he bit down and weathered the storm, the nausea would pass.

After much practice, Anskar returned to the white tower of the Scriptorium and, shrouded from the sight of the guards, climbed up the outside, sticking to the stone like a spider. When he reached the window near the top, he opened it with a surge of dusk-tide modified by the dawn, returned Tain's notebook to its place on the shelf, and left the same way he had entered, fusing the window shut behind him.

Elated at how easy it had been this time, he hurried along dark and silent streets back to the royal barracks.

A little after dawn, when the two moons still ghosted between the clouds and the rising sun bathed the horizon red, the army rode through Wintotashum's barbican in a long procession of clattering hooves and clanking armor.

A small crowd had gathered to watch them go, but there was no cheering. Atop the battlements, the warriors left behind to man the defenses saluted.

King Aelfyr was in good cheer, riding with the vanguard, where he'd invited Rindon, Nul and Borik to join him. The reason he was taking such a large army—some six hundred men and women—he had explained in a brief speech before they left, was to inspect the newly built fortifications along the way, and to convey strength and confidence to the towns and villages in the north. And if the opportunity presented itself, King Aelfyr had finished, maybe his warriors would get a chance to bloody their blades on any Soreshi war bands they might run into.

In addition to the King's six hundred, Lanuc brought his entire force of almost a hundred knights plus their retainers. Zek was taken along too, as an advisor against Soreshi sorcery, and although his hands were unbound, he was closely guarded by four riders of the King's household guard.

Anskar rode behind Zek and his guards, under strict instructions from Lanuc to monitor the prisoner's repositories and to counter any attack should Zek prove dishonorable.

They made good progress along the Iron Road that led north across the kingdom. There was still snow on the hilltops and the distant mountain peaks, and several of the lakes they passed were frozen solid. The road itself was clear, save for patches of black ice, and for the most part had been well maintained, apart from a few places where its surface was cracked and weeds poked through. Occasionally they came across wagons, which pulled over to the side of the road to let the army pass.

Toward the end of the first day, they saw two plumes of black smoke twisting into the sky, too distant to know which towns were burning. The smoke came from beyond a range of hills they would have to pass through late the next day.

The army stopped a few hours before dusk, and Anskar was impressed when the King sent warriors to clear a deep, overgrown ditch around an earthworks crowned with an ancient palisade. Others uprighted any fallen trunks of the palisade, packing the holes they fit into with earth and stone, and hunters were sent into a nearby forest.

Before night had fallen, dozens of cook fires were crackling and spitting inside the protective cordon, and the air was filled with the smell of roasting meat from the boars and snow foxes the hunters had brought back. No dried rations were to be used, by order of the King, until they reached the mountains and there was no fresh meat to be found.

Anskar found Zek seated on a blanket at a fire, eating roasted boar and drinking from a canteen. The Soreshi was chatting amiably with his four guards—two men and two women, all of middle age. They acknowledged Anskar and made room for him to sit beside Zek.

"Are they treating you well?" Anskar asked, offering the guards a smile.

One of the women rolled her eyes, but the others were too intent on ripping into their fresh-cooked meat.

"Terribly," Zek said. "Want some boar?"

Anskar took the proffered meat. It was overcooked, smelled

of charcoal, and was dripping with fat, but he ate it anyway. Despite the blankets thrown on the ground where the snow had been cleared, he was chilled to the bones, and couldn't stop himself shivering beneath his cloak.

"I know a dawn-tide cant that can warm you from the inside out," Zek said.

Anskar smiled. "That seems unfair to the rest of the army."

"True, but it didn't stop me using it on myself and my four new friends here." Zek indicated the guards, all of whom grinned and seemed utterly content, not at all suffering from the cold. "I'll teach you the cant, if you like."

It was a simple Skanuric cant, the calculations and the words easy to memorize, and within less than a minute Anskar felt a gentle, steady pull on his braided repository as threads of dawn-tide essence extricated themselves from their fusion with the dusk and dispersed through his marrow. Warmth suffused his skin, and he ceased shivering.

"We still need to work on untangling your repository," Zek said, "though already it seems a little less confused. It is good that the dawn and the dusk are interwoven, but they need to be more differentiated, easier to access in isolation." The Soreshi paused. "What is it, Anskar? Why so glum?"

Anskar hadn't realized he'd been only half listening. He glanced at the four guards, who were talking among themselves and paying no heed to him and Zek. So he explained about the vambrace and what it had done to Hrothyr. And how, when he had found it in the smithy, the vambrace had fastened itself back on his forearm.

"What should I do?" he finished. "Find some way to destroy it?"

Zek looked away, thinking. "I would not do that."

"Why? It's evil," Anskar whispered. "It killed Hrothyr."

Zak shrugged. "Your vambrace is a source of new knowledge."

"Now you sound like Brother Bonavir."

"Besides," Zek said, "if you cannot remove it, how can you destroy it? I suppose you could always cut off your arm…"

The next day, the army's progress slowed as they came into hill country, where snow lay heaped on the slopes. The Iron Road, though, was a channel through the whiteness on the ground and between the hills themselves, as if at some point long ago a path had been blasted through them with potent sorcery.

Sporadically, messengers from local lords arrived with news for the King and to inform him of their readiness to send warriors to swell his army. Aelfyr sent word back that the lords were to stay put and bolster their defenses. In time, the combined might of the Thousand Lakes would be called upon to drive the Soreshi from this side of the Ymaltian Mountains, but that time was not now. The returning messengers were also instructed to summon their lords to a full war council in Wintotashum.

Farther along the Iron Road, the army passed columns of refugees coming south. When they spotted the King, the travelers doffed their hats and knelt on the snow-covered ground. Aelfyr instructed the healers to tend the refugees' wounds and the sickness many showed signs of—weeping pustules on their skin and a hacking cough speckled with red.

"The pestilence," Brother Bonavir told Anskar while the healers did their work. "Usually it disappears with the coming of the snow."

"What causes such a sickness?" Anskar asked. "Sorcery?"

Brother Bonavir shrugged. "Does it matter? Of course," he added conspiratorially, "it was the priests of the Elder who discovered the cure in the scrolls of the ancients."

Once the refugees had been treated, King Aelfyr sent fifty warriors to escort them on their journey south. They had been heading for Wintotashum, but the King ordered them instead to the city of Gutishon, promising that the walls were high and well-manned by a seasoned garrison.

During the afternoon, the army came to the burned-out ruins of a village. Wisps of smoke still coiled from the fire-blackened husks of stone buildings whose thatched roofs had been burned. Trails through the snow showed that livestock had been herded away, and ice-hardened corpses lay in the streets. Some had dark-fletched arrow shafts protruding from their frozen flesh. Others were horribly misshapen, contorted into grotesque parodies of people.

"Dusk-tide sorcery," Zek explained. "Unmitigated by the dawn. Among my people, such destructive sorcery is considered abominable."

"Then why use it?"

In truth, Anskar was as fascinated as he was horrified. Sorcery that could wreak such carnage was as intriguing to him as a library full of scrolls would have been to Brother Bonavir. More than intriguing, he realized. He felt a thrill of excitement at mastering such sorcery himself.

Of course, he would use it for good. He'd heard the priests of the Warrior say that peace and security were negotiated by the strong, not the weak—and just think what peace could be achieved with the threat of such power.

Zek was watching him, seeming to read his thoughts. "When we return to Wintotashum, I will continue to help you with your braided repository, but I will not teach you this."

*Then I'll learn it for myself,* Anskar thought, even as he nodded.

The virulence of his thoughts, the desire for more and more destructive sorcery, shocked him.

*Menselas, forgive me,* he silently prayed. *Ward me from temptation.*

But it was a half-hearted petition.

# THIRTY-ONE

AS THE ARMY RODE ON, leaving the charred village behind, Anskar saw more thick plumes of smoke twisting into the darkening sky in the northeast and northwest. At least three more towns or villages were burning, and the mood among the Thousand Lakes warriors grew grimmer and full of vengeance.

In the morning, after they broke camp, they followed a winding decline into a snow-banked valley, at the far end of which stood a town surrounded by a stout palisade.

The army's vanguard stopped where the valley widened. Anskar could see the heads and shoulders of warriors above the palisade. They had long hair braided with colorful bands, angular faces, and almond eyes. Most were armed with short hunting bows.

"Soreshi," Zek said.

The army's commanders barked orders, and riders started to dismount.

"Are we going to attack?" Anskar asked, as he saw Lanuc

signaling him to rejoin the knights of the Order.

"I guess we'll soon find out," Zek said. His guards ordered him to climb down from his saddle so they could bind his wrists together.

"You don't trust him?" Anskar asked.

One of the women scowled. "Like it matters what I think. King's orders. You want to tell him he's wrong?"

Anskar stood next to Lanuc in the long line of knights facing the town's palisade. His palm gripping the hilt of *Amalantril* was slick with sweat.

King Aelfyr had placed the Order of Eternal Vigilance in the front line of attack, so their ward spheres could draw the sting of Soreshi arrows. Of course, the Soreshi were more than just archers. They were sorcerers from birth, and Anskar suspected the knights were meant to absorb more than broad-headed steel arrows on behalf of the King's army.

The sky was packed with swollen clouds, and a bitter wind was blowing from the north, out of the Ymaltian Mountains.

"This should be fun," Rindon said farther along the line. "I've not faced Soreshi before. Save for one time in a tavern bedchamber, and she wielded an entirely different kind of sorcery against me."

The knights closest to him shook their heads and chuckled.

Beside Rindon loomed the massive Borik, his gauntleted hands resting atop the hilt of the Sword of Supremacy. The blade, for once, was exposed, and wouldn't be wrapped in its oilskin again until it had been sated with blood. It was scabbed with brown rust and nicked all along its great length. Borik's eyes scanned the Soreshi with their strung bows atop the palisade's fighting platforms.

Nul was a study in calm, as if he had seen it all before and this was just another day on the practice field.

Behind the single line of knights stood King Aelfyr's household warriors, with the King himself at their center. Next came the massed ranks of Wintotashum's garrison. To either flank, Aelfyr had stationed fifty mounted warriors in case the Soreshi tried to flee.

Farther back in the valley, the servants and priests waited with the rest of the horses and the supplies. Twenty soldiers had been left to protect them, and several of the priests, Anskar had noted, were priests of the Warrior.

"How many defenders?" he asked. Above the palisade he could make out no more than fifty archers.

Lanuc shrugged. "Veranoth isn't a large town. The King tells me the garrison was small, less than thirty warriors, and most of them old veterans."

"And the townsfolk?"

"Dead, most likely. My guess is the Soreshi haven't burned Veranoth due to its fortifications. They're using it as a stepping-stone in their progress south toward Wintotashum."

"Advance!" came the order from behind—one of the household warriors closest to the King.

A cry went up from the Wintotashum warriors, and they banged their weapons against the willow boards of their shields.

At a signal from Lanuc, the Order knights began a slow walk toward the palisade, dozens of ward spheres blazing into existence around them.

Not wanting to draw attention to himself, Anskar extricated threads of dawn-tide from his braided repository and matched the silver glare of the other knights' wards.

Arrows streaked from the top of the palisade. Most fell short, but several struck wards and bounced off. A second volley of arrows arced through the air before the knights had advanced another step. Again the slender shafts failed to breach the ward spheres, and from behind, King Aelfyr's warriors jeered at the archers.

But the third volley was different. Anskar felt the oppressive atmosphere of dusk-tide sorcery. He recognized it easily now, as a result of the melding of his repositories. It was like the pressure before a thunderstorm, and the air smelled of hot metal.

"Brace!" Lanuc cried.

Ward spheres flared as sorcerously enhanced arrows ripped into them. One knight's ward erupted in a shower of sparks and she screamed, pitching backwards with a black-fletched shaft jutting from her throat. It had penetrated the steel gorget that was supposed to protect her neck.

A glance behind showed Anskar that the Thousand Lakers were crouching behind their interlocking shields, for all the good it would do them.

"Charge!" Lanuc yelled, and the ragged line of knights surged toward the wooden gates of the palisade.

As they ran, Anskar unleashed the full potency of his braided repository. Gasps erupted around him as his silver sphere swirled with prismatic brilliance. With a shouted cant, he extended his ward into a flat barrier that covered the center of the line. Dusk-tide arrows *thwacked* into it, incinerating on impact. But on the flanks, knights continued to drop.

Borik pulled ahead, extending the Sword of Supremacy in both hands. As arrows hit the earth around him, his ward sphere coalesced around the greatsword, then rose along its length and burst from the tip in a streak of silver that punched a massive hole in the gates.

"Boar's head!" Lanuc commanded, and the knights formed with impeccable discipline into a tightly packed wedge and charged for the opening.

Still the arrows came, and still knights fell screaming. Blood misted the air. Limbs twitched. And Rindon laughed like a lunatic.

Anskar reconfigured his flattened ward, pushing out its boundaries to encompass the entire wedge. A vise squeezed his skull, and a cold sweat broke out all over his body.

And then they were through the splintered gates and separating into teams of three or four.

Dozens of Soreshi dropped their bows and bounded from the fighting platforms. They landed lithe as cats, with swords, hatchets, spears in hand, the weapons wreathed in crimson flames.

As the knights and Soreshi clashed amid the clangor of steel on steel, and sparking motes began to fly, a larger force of Soreshi flowed from the buildings flanking the main street and charged.

"With me!" Borik cried as he ran to meet the new attack.

Rindon and Nul sprinted after him, and Anskar followed in their wake. The Sword of Supremacy hacked and cleaved, opening a bloody path in the Soreshi ranks. Rindon came in hard on Borik's left, twin hatchets a blur, slinging blood in arcs. Nul, on Borik's right, fought with calm and precision, blocking and countering with masterful sword work. The Soreshi center faltered under the ferocity of the heroes' attack.

Anskar parried and thrust, and a Soreshi went down. And then he was in the thick of it, slipping on gore, sidestepping, blocking, hacking for all he was worth. Blood stank in his nostrils and spattered his face. The clamor of battle deafened him. He had no sense now of the rest of the army, couldn't even tell if the knights and the Thousand Lakes warriors were winning or losing. All he saw was the blur and haze of the melee all around him, the rise and fall of blades.

But he was pressing forward. They all were—Anskar and Rindon, Nul and Borik.

A Soreshi woman pushed to the front of the enemy, blue eyes blazing from the tanned skin of her face. Sun-bleached hair blew about her head in a blood-speckled halo. As she came at Borik with a hatchet, Anskar saw an eagle's claw fetish hanging from her neck. Borik brought up his great blade to block her blow. Steel met steel with concussive force.

And the Sword of Supremacy shattered.

Rindon roared a warning as the Soreshi reversed the swing of her axe. Nul tried to disengage from his own attacker. But they were too late.

Borik threw up an arm to protect his face, but the hatchet cleaved straight through his hasty defense and smashed into his teeth. A third blow split his head open, and the big man fell.

"No!" Anskar screamed, throwing himself at the woman.

She blocked his swing with ease, then blasted him from his feet with an eruption of white fire from her fist. The only thing that saved him was his ward sphere, though it contracted under the impact, so that it sheathed him like a scintillant skin.

She blasted him again, and strode toward him, hatchet raised.

Anskar dropped to his knees as his ward sphere winked out. The woman smirked, white fire dancing once more on her palm.

Anskar reached for the sorcery Zek had taught him to blow out the lock on the Scriptorium's window. Only this time he didn't mitigate the blast with the dawn-tide. This time, he unleashed the full virulence of his dusk-tide repository with a snarled cant.

A scorching blast of flame slammed into the Soreshi woman. Though it forced her back, it didn't burn. Instead, its fire bent around some invisible barrier protecting her, and though her face was strained with effort, the woman's blue eyes sparkled in defiance.

Then the surging dusk-tide within Anskar ignited something he'd forgotten about: the Warrior's Fire. His back arched as he rose into the air screaming—and a wall of white-hot flame roared forth, incinerating everything in its path.

He heard Rindon curse. Nul called his name. Then he fell back to earth with a skull-juddering thump, his vision a haze of white.

He felt someone cradling his head… Nul?

Anskar's blurred vision resolved into the slow fall of ashes—all that remained of the Soreshi horde.

Behind him came the pounding of hooves.

"They're routed!" Lanuc cried.

The Thousand Lakes cavalry galloped in pursuit of the fleeing Soreshi, cutting them down from behind.

Anskar felt Nul shudder as he sobbed; heard Rindon's voice thick with emotion as he spoke Borik's name.

And then he felt a tug at his core, the answering ripple of his dark-tide repository. He sat up suddenly, as if struck by lightning, and Nul released him.

"What is it?" Lanuc asked.

Anskar scanned the scorched street ahead.

There, gazing out of an upper-story window: a pale-faced man in black plate armor. Anskar pointed, and the man inclined his head, his yellow eyes narrowing to slits.

"Tainted Cabal," Lanuc hissed, already advancing on the building.

The dark-tide surged, causing Anskar to groan, and then the man was gone. Where he had been standing, a wispy plume of smoke spiraled up through the thatched roof and lost itself in the snow-swelled clouds.

# THIRTY-TWO

"I'VE ARRANGED FOR A CART to take us south in the morning," said Carred when she returned to their lodgings.

For two nights they had lain low in an abandoned single-room shack on the outskirts of Rheyll, a coastal town of fewer than a hundred residents that had completely escaped the attention of the Order of Eternal Vigilance. She'd needed the rest. They all had—especially from Tain's incessant chatter, which was why she'd left him shut in his helm since returning from the shipwreck with the Armor of Divinity.

The necromancer's head sat on the nightstand. Against her better judgment, Carred had finally opened the face plate before she went out.

She repeated her news in Nan-Rhouric.

"We're returning to the hideout?" asked Orix, seated on the edge of the room's only bed. He gave her a smile that seemed to ask if everything between them was now fixed. It wasn't.

"Naphor," Noni said from her chair in the corner. Queen Talia, who had despised Nan-Rhouric in life, seemed to have learned how to understand it in death.

"Hello!" Tain said. "Excuse me! Could we all please speak the language of the civilized. Naphor, I understood, but what did the oaf say?"

"Why Naphor?" Carred asked, but Noni closed her eyes and interlaced her fingers in her lap.

"You want us to travel to Naphor?" Tain said. "What in Theltek's name for?"

"*My* plan," Carred said, glancing at Noni, "was to return to the hideout and face Vilintia."

"Oh, please," Tain said. "Still ruminating on that Taloc fellow? I have to say, he did a better job of carrying me than Orix the savage, but at the end of the day, he was still just a grunt."

"I'll let you tell that to Vilintia."

"I will, and then I'll make it up to her... with this." The necromancer flicked his tongue out and Carred came close to kicking him across the room like a ball.

Orix stretched and lay down on the bed, then instantly rolled off it and stood, brushing himself down. "Something bit me," he complained.

Carred pinched the bridge of her nose. It was going to be another long night.

"So, why Naphor?" Tain asked. "I assume the idea is the bitch Queen's and not the crazy girl's. It's been a while, but the whores were always excellent in Naphor."

"Naphor was destroyed," Carred said. "Didn't Queen Talia tell you that?"

"She must have forgotten to mention it," Tain said. "Poor old whores. But you haven't answered my question: why there?" His eyes flicked to Noni. "Hello? Is there anybody home?"

"I'm sure she'll tell us when we need to know," Carred said.

"Oh, yes," Tain said. "Blind faith. I like it. You sound like a devotee of Menselas." Now his eyes moved to Orix. "Must be the company you keep. Well, I see no point wasting any more time. I do have a body to find, you know."

Something pinched beneath Carred's scalp as Tain's eyes flashed green, and then the room was filled with wavering light. She looked up at the oil lamp suspended by a chain from the ceiling. It had been dead when they arrived, but was now burning steadily.

Carred rubbed the top of her head. The discomfort beneath her scalp was already a memory. It seemed Talia hadn't just awakened her dawn-tide repository. For the first time since she was a child, she had felt the dusk—merely an echo in response to the sorcery Tain had just used to light the lamp.

"What are you doing?" Carred asked.

"Light to work by," the necromancer said. "I have many talents, but seeing in the dark is not one of them."

"Carred, is everything all right?" Orix said, sidling towards her with his eyes fixed on the necromancer's head.

She held up a hand: *Wait.*

"Fetch the breastplate," Tain said.

Carred frowned at the armor within the net. "Why?"

"If I had hands, I'd do it myself. The reason: it must be repaired, and then the entire suit must be modified, unless you want to suffer the same fate as the previous owner."

"Me?"

"It is a woman's suit, and I for one don't want to wait around till we find a forge hot enough to melt it down and remold it."

"But—"

"We have a deal, remember? You help me find my body, and then I will help you modify the armor for the purposes of your queen."

"How about we let Queen Talia decide?" Carred said.

"Or," Tain said, "we could do nothing." He closed his eyes and pressed his lips tightly together.

Carred looked to Noni for direction, but the young woman's eyes were also closed. She might have been resting; might have been in a trance.

"Fine," she said, starting toward the armor.

"Not you," Tain said. "The savage."

"Why him?"

"You'll see."

Carred shrugged. "Orix, bring the breastplate."

"Breastplate? Oh, from the net?"

Carred rolled her eyes, perhaps a little unfairly.

"Where do you want it?" he said as he opened the net and removed the breastplate.

"Do you need to be in contact with it?" Carred asked Tain.

"No, but he does. Tell him to come here, and to hold it out to me."

Carred indicated where Orix should stand with a wave of her hand.

This time, when the necromancer's eyes glowed green, she felt nothing within her head, only smelled something like rotten fruit.

Orix's hands holding the breastplate trembled. He craned his neck to look at Carred, eyes wide. "What's he doing to me? I can't let go."

"Tain?" Carred demanded. "Tain!"

"Be silent! You'll ruin my sorcery."

The breastplate shuddered in Orix's grasp. The metal around the puncture made by the sword grew red, then white, then started to smoke.

"Stop!" Carred said. "His hands are burning!"

"On the contrary," Tain said. "His hands, like the parts of the breastplate I do not need to heat, are icy cold. Don't say I'm not considerate."

"Orix?" Carred asked.

His teeth chattered, and when he tried to speak, only froth came out of his mouth. He looked different somehow. Thinner.

As Carred watched, the rent in the breastplate knitted together until there was no sign it had even been there. The white-hot metal cooled in an instant, and Orix dropped to his knees.

"Now the rest of the armor," Tain said. "Arrange it on the floor. Make sure there is contact between each piece."

Warily, Carred pried Orix's fingers from the breastplate and laid it on the floor.

"Are you all right?"

He nodded.

He didn't look all right. He looked as though he'd not eaten in weeks. Black rings surrounded his eyes, and his cheeks were hollow.

"What have you done to him?" Carred asked.

"Rendered him useful. I thought you'd approve."

"Useful how?"

"The earth-tide isn't just a free resource, you know," Tain said.

"You used the earth-tide to repair the breastplate?"

"What else would I use? Earth-tide's not just about raising the dead. I thought you'd have realized that after what the Necromancer Queen did to your repositories. The earth-tide is primarily for the shaping and quickening of matter—and yes, that which exists in the realm of the dead is just a subtle form of matter, hence the possibility of necromancy. But there's a cost; a give and take."

"What cost?"

"Earth-tide has no power to create, only to transform. Its currency is invisible to us, and it constitutes all that there is."

"Essence?" Carred said.

"Essence is one term for it, though I've always found it inadequate. Imagine that everything that goes to make up the world is made of tiny building blocks, invisible to our sight. Picture a grain of sand. In your mind's eye, split the grain into a thousand particles, a million, a hundred million, and still you would not be close."

"You repaired the breastplate one grain at a time? But there was a hole in its center. That means you had to create new matter."

"Or transfer it," Tain said with a smug smile.

Carred's eyes came to rest on Orix. She crouched beside him and held him close. "You bastard."

"What are you talking about?" Orix said. "What did he do to me?"

"Something I'll not permit him to do again. You hear that, Tain?" she said, switching to Niyandrian. "That's the last time you do anything like that."

"I haven't finished yet," Tain said.

"Yes, you have."

"The savage will be fine. All I need is his sword."

"His sword?"

"Tell him to draw it. I'll do the rest."

"He wants you to draw your sword," Carred told Orix. "I have no idea why."

"I can guess," Orix said. "Astrumium. When we forged our

blades for the trials to become knights inferior, we were taught to blend astrumium with the metal so the sword's keen edge would never blunt."

"You need the sword's astrumium?" Carred asked Tain.

"Unless you know a dealer in astrumium close by? Of course you don't. Do you even know what it is? Two parts orichalcum, one part star-metal. Without astrumium, the armor is useless. Worse than useless: it's a death trap."

To Orix, Carred said, "But your sword… is it not worth much to you?"

"Everything," Orix said. "But not as much as this armor is worth to you."

*Not to me,* Carred thought. *To Talia.*

Carred was no longer certain she shared the Queen's dreams, but what she wanted didn't seem to matter. Not to Talia. Probably it never had.

"Anskar helped me with the adding of the astrumium," Orix said. "Without him, I'd have failed the test."

"Do you regret not going with him when he came through the portal looking for you?"

"He's my friend," Orix said. "But…"

He looked into her eyes, and she turned away.

"Draw your sword," she said.

Orix passed the blade to Carred, and she held it out before Tain.

"Place it atop the breastplate," the necromancer said. "Then make sure every piece of armor is in contact with another piece."

"And then?" Carred said, doing as he asked.

"Stand back and watch."

Once more Carred's hand went to her head as a ripple ran through her dusk-tide repository. Orix's sword glowed red, then white, then started to melt. Rivulets of silver oozed in every direction, living lines that seemed to know where they were going. The very substance that had constituted the sword gave the impression of being alive, under the direction of Tain's sorcery. The blade, now a splash of liquid metal atop the breastplate, continued to shrink as it flowed away in veins and seeped into every connected piece of armor.

"Transmogrification," Tain said. "The sword does not cease to exist. Its substance remains, though the accidents of its appearance are altered, melded with the matter of the armor."

"The same thing you did to Orix just now? He's part of the armor."

"He has given that we may succeed."

Orix watched as all trace of his sword disappeared.

"What are you thinking?" Carred asked.

"That I don't need it." He seemed to shudder, though it may have been a sigh of relief. He looked her in the eye. "I'm with you now, not the Order."

Carred swallowed and then nodded.

"It will cool rapidly," Tain said. "Then you can put it on."

"Here?" Carred said. "Now?"

"Location is not important when traversing the realms," Tain said. "And now is as good a time as any. I've been separated from my body for far too long."

"And you don't want to miss out on the fun?"

Tain gave a wry smile. "Don't take everything I say literally, my scarred, sinewy, hatchet-faced Carred."

They shouldn't have affected her, but the words stung. "Are you sore because I rejected you?"

"Due to my perceived impotence?" Tain said. "Words are akin to sorcery for me, Carred. I say a lot of things. Some I mean.

Mostly I weave webs of misdirection. I know full well what you think of me. After all, it was my words that determined your opinion."

"He means he's not the lascivious idiot he comes across as," Noni said. "I, however, was not fooled by his antics. I do know what he is, and you must not put on the armor, Carred. Not now. It isn't ready."

"Ah, yes, the missing ingredient," Tain said. "I think I've worked out what it is. I assume you've not told Carred where she'll have to obtain it? Not that it makes any difference to me. I have no need for a return journey."

"And what about me?" Carred said. "You need me to take you wherever it is you're going. How do I get back?"

"You don't," Noni said, rising and coming towards her. "Which is why you mustn't wear the—"

Noni stopped abruptly. The room was filled with a mephitic stench. The wood of the floor flowed over and around her feet, holding her in place. Her lips knitted together, then faded away to a line, and then even that was erased. Her eyes were at once startled and indignant.

Orix groaned and slumped to the floor. Carred dropped to one knee beside him and felt for a pulse—thready and weak. He had lost even more weight, so much so that his skin was almost translucent, riddled with blue veins.

Carred drew her sword and spun toward Tain's head. "You're killing him."

Tain pursed his lips. "Put another way, your beloved Queen Talia is killing him by trying to intervene. All she has to do is stay out of it and I'll have no need to use earth-tide sorcery to restrain her, so no need for Orix to provide the necessary raw material. Of course, now that you are threatening me with a sword, I shall have to draw upon more of his 'essence,' as you call it, if only to defend myself."

The necromancer's eyes flared green.

Carred hesitated, the tip of her blade wavering. What if she struck fast, before he could complete whatever cant was needed for his sorcery? Could she risk it? Tain had stopped Noni— Queen Talia—without uttering a sound. *It's only Orix*, she tried telling herself. But still…

She lowered her sword.

"Better," Tain said. "I knew you'd see it my way eventually. Return your sword to its scabbard."

Carred did so.

"Good girl. Now, put on the armor."

Noni's eyes narrowed in warning.

"There has to be another way," Carred said.

"Quite possibly, but this is the way for you and me. I insist."

Her scalp began to throb. On the floor, Orix's skin visibly stretched, and he let out a long, agonized moan.

"Wait," Carred said. "I need time."

"Time for what? To think? Don't trouble yourself, Carred. You've proven yourself inept in that regard."

Again the necromancer's eyes flashed. Orix sat up with a start and wailed. His face writhed and twitched and then became a blur. Carred squinted at him, but her vision was distorted. When Orix's face snapped back into focus, his eyes were where his mouth should have been, his nose upside down, and his mouth just beneath his hairline. His legs were as thin as sticks, and she could see the bones through his skin.

"Shall I continue?" Tain asked. "I suppose I could clump Orix's matter together with Noni's. That would make an interesting experiment. Of course, I might need to borrow from you to power it."

Carred glanced at Noni—no help there.

"All right," she said. "I'll do it."

"I knew you would."

She reached down, caressed Orix's disfigured face, and mouthed, "I'm sorry."

"The effect will fade," Tain said, "if I will it to."

His eyes still glowed green, and his forehead glistened... with sweat? That gave Carred the inkling of an idea.

"I'll need Noni to fasten the armor for me," she said.

"Her hands are free," Tain observed. "Commence."

Carred bent down and picked up a cuisse and placed it over her thigh. Behind her, Noni bent from the waist and fastened the straps. As Carred situated the second piece, Noni discreetly rubbed the back of her hand. Did Talia know? Did she approve?

Piece after piece, Carred held the armor in place so that Noni could secure it. The metal plates vibrated slightly atop her clothes, and the joins between them grew smaller, as if some quality of the divine alloy caused the armor to shrink to fit her.

At last she passed Noni the helm.

"Wait," she said, before Noni could place it on her head. "Orix, pass me Tain."

The necromancer's eyes widened in surprise, but then he smiled. "Good thinking. I almost forgot! The moment the helm seals with the rest of the armor, the translation will be complete. You almost left without me."

Orix stumbled as he crossed the room with the head. With his eyes where his mouth should have been, it must have been hard to see.

"Careful, idiot!" Tain said. "How many times do I have to tell you? Drop me and it could be the end of me—which means the end of you, too. All of you!"

Carred glanced at Noni, who winked. That confirmed her suspicions and gave her the courage for what she needed to do.

Orix held the necromancer's head out to Carred, one trembling hand on either side of the helm.

"Well, don't just stand there," Tain said.

Carred reached for the helm, then instead grabbed Tain by the nose. The necromancer yelped.

"Don't let go of the helm!" she told Orix, and then she yanked on Tain's nose and pulled his head free of its metal casing.

"Nooooooo!" Tain cried as he crumbled into dust that sifted between Carred's fingers.

Noni gasped and took a lunging step toward Carred, her feet no longer merged with the floor, her lips restored.

As Carred had guessed, the warping of matter had been held in place by Tain's will, and Tain had only remained in existence due to his encasement in Divine Alloy.

"Keep his helm," Talia said through Noni. "In case we need a spare."

"Orix…" Carred said. She had expected him to be restored, but his face was still a jumbled mess, and he had lost so much substance.

"Tain went too far with him," Talia said. "The change is permanent. Still, it's an improvement."

"When did you become so callous?" Carred asked.

"When do you think? And I'm not callous. I'm focused on what really matters."

"Orix matters."

"He didn't before, when you grew tired of him. And that didn't take long."

"Everybody matters." Everyone who had suffered or died.

Everyone she was responsible for.

"No, Carred. Anskar matters. The *Melesh-Eloni*. That is all."

"Not even you?"

"I gave my life for Niyas, and I'm still giving in death."

*Of course you are.*

"Are you still loyal, Carred?"

Noni brushed Carred's face with her fingertips, then her neck, her breast.

Carred swallowed down bile and looked away.

"I'm loyal," she said.

"Good. Because where you must go next, I cannot come. You will be on your own."

# THIRTY-THREE

IT TOOK A FULL DAY for the servants and healers to dig a mass grave for the slaughtered inhabitants of Veranoth.

Lanuc arranged for Anskar to be taken into an abandoned house, where he lay on a flea-ridden bed, too exhausted to move. He felt empty inside, and even when a healer brought him hot broth and hard bread, he felt no better. At dusk, when the tide blowing through the open window washed over him, there was no thrill, no violent ecstasy. The sensation made him think of a pond slowly filling with rainwater during a light drizzle.

Throughout the day, the army had taken up occupation of the other town buildings, and the taverns were raucous with King Aelfyr's jubilant warriors. None of the Order knights joined them. During a visit to Anskar's sickbed, Lanuc explained why. On campaign, the knights were expected to adhere to the strict ideals of the Order of Eternal Vigilance. There was to be no slackening of discipline nor deviation from the vows of consecration.

"This is why I love war so much," Lanuc said. "It's the only time we are all that we profess to be."

In the evening, Zek came to see Anskar. His guards waited for him outside the room. The Soreshi was sullen and barely spoke. Anskar realized that Zek hadn't come to see how he was recovering; he had come for solace.

"You feel responsible for the attacks?" Anskar asked, at last able to sit up in bed.

"I feel ashamed," Zek said. "Ashamed of being a Soreshi. All these people slaughtered, many in their own homes. This is not our way."

"No, it isn't," Anskar agreed. "Your people are victims, as much as everyone else. Victims of the Tainted Cabal."

Zek shook his head. "They should have been stronger. They should have been able to resist."

In the morning, after welcoming the dawn-tide, Anskar started to feel more like his old self. He joined the assembled army in the street, where they stood in disciplined phalanxes awaiting the King.

Aelfyr made his entrance mounted on a white mare, and wearing a crimson cloak trimmed with ermine.

Already, the King told them, messengers had been sent to the outlying lords, commanding them to send warriors to Veranoth.

"We will hold this town now that we've retaken it," Aelfyr said. "Veranoth will be a bulwark against the hordes, a buffer between them and Wintotashum. This far the Soreshi can come and no further! I am leaving a garrison of one hundred warriors behind for now. And in addition to the warriors the lords will send, I have demanded as many fighting priests as the Warrior's Abbey at Cloven can spare."

Aelfyr also planned to leave two priests of the Elder with special knowledge of sorcery, claiming they had been working through the night on defenses against the kind of dusk-tide assault the army had witnessed yesterday. He glanced at Anskar. "They learned a good deal from observing what you did, young man."

Cheers erupted, and Anskar dipped his eyes. He felt pride, but it was smothered by grief and horror and a niggling sense of sin.

"Veranoth's new garrison will not be idle," Aelfyr continued. "The palisade and gates must be repaired, buildings turned into fortresses, strategies hatched, traps laid. The Soreshi must not be allowed to return. Veranoth will be *our* stepping-stone for when we march on the north."

The King himself would go with the army back to Wintotashum. He had seen now what they were up against: not just a horde of unusually aggressive Soreshi, but some dark scheme of the Tainted Cabal. After the war council, Aelfyr said, their army would strike back and hit the Cabal and their Soreshi allies hard.

Finally, the King dismounted and opened his arms to Nul and Rindon, who knelt before him. The King gave an impassioned speech about Borik's heroism, and the example the three heroes had set in their brave stand against the Soreshi.

"You too, Anskar DeVantte," Aelfyr said, beckoning him.

Anskar approached self-consciously, and took a knee beside Nul.

"Whatever it was you did," the King said, "whatever sorcery you employed, we will have need of it again. You are too valuable for us to lose. The Grand Master is lucky to have you."

The King's army dispersed to pack up in preparation for the return journey, but Lanuc commanded the Order's knights to remain in the street.

Nul and Rindon buried the shattered fragments of the Sword of Supremacy, while a priest of the Healer chanted prayers over the dust pile left by Anskar's sorcery. Somewhere in the dust was all that remained of Borik.

King Aelfyr set a relentless pace for the return journey to Wintotashum, and the army only made camp for one night, and then for just a few hours.

Anskar rode toward the rear of the column, no longer responsible for keeping an eye on Zek. Brother Bonavir rode alongside him.

"I have told the King about your encounter with a Tainted Cabalist in Wintotashum," Brother Bonavir said after a time of silence.

Anskar should have said something himself, or at least reported the encounter to Lanuc.

"The King is angry," Bonavir continued, "but you have no need to worry. He saw what you did back there at Veranoth, and he knows your value in the coming conflict."

"So, what will he do?" Anskar asked.

"Scour Wintotashum for enemy agents. But the Cabal will expect that. I imagine they are long gone."

"They were after something," Anskar said. "Something in the Scriptorium."

"The King has sent riders ahead with instructions to increase the guard on the tower, and for the priests of the Elder to set wards," Bonavir said.

"Will it be enough?"

"Of course it will be enough. We priests of the Elder are experts in our fields. Some of us have more than one talent, too. Those among my confreres who study sorcery are, shall we say, among the most adept sorcerers in Wiraya. Will it be enough!"

By the time they reached Wintotashum, everyone was beyond exhausted. Anskar was asleep the moment his head hit the pillow in his barracks room. Zek hadn't been permitted to return with him.

In the morning, Anskar collected a couple of still-warm bread rolls from the refectory, a few slices of ham and cheese, and two mugs of steaming hot tea, and took them to the dungeons.

The guards were suspicious at first, but Anskar told them he had Brother Bonavir's permission to visit Zek, and they accepted his word. He cringed at telling yet another lie. It was becoming too easy, the path of least resistance, and he no longer knew if he wanted to do anything about it.

When Anskar entered the cell, he found Zek weeping in the dark. Without a word, Anskar seated himself cross-legged on the stone floor in front of his friend and handed him a mug of tea.

Zek accepted it with a thin smile.

Anskar unwrapped the bundle of food he'd brought and encouraged Zek to eat. The Soreshi didn't need telling twice. He wolfed down the bread, ham, and cheese, then drained his mug of tea.

"Why did you come, Anskar?"

"I thought you might be hungry."

"Is that all?"

Anskar tried again. "I thought you might want to talk."

"I do, but that is not why you came."

Anskar sighed. "I need your help."

"Sorcery?"

"What else?"

Anskar explained how, in Veranoth, he'd modified the technique Zek had shown him for opening the lock on the Scriptorium window, and what had happened when the Warrior's Fire he'd stolen from Gann was added to the mix.

"You probably shouldn't have done that," Zek said when Anskar had finished. "You do not have a natural affinity with the dusk-tide. Limited use is fine, so long as it's contained by the interwoven threads of the dawn-tide, but an unmitigated blast of the dusk… It's a wonder you are still alive."

"It drained me entirely," Anskar said. "I've still not fully recovered."

"The dusk-tide is like the black powder they've developed in the far south," Zek said. "Touch fire to it and it explodes. Anything combustible in the vicinity burns too. First it would have incinerated all the dusk-tide in your repository, plus the residual amount in your body, and then it would have consumed any lingering in the air from the tide's passage the evening before. After that, it would have leaped to burn up the dusk-tide stored within the Soreshi who opposed you. Just thank your god of five aspects that the knights fighting alongside you had no dusk-tide repositories of their own."

"Else they would be dead?"

Zek nodded.

"Then what should I do?"

"Do you plan to use the dusk-tide in the future?"

"I must, if I'm to ride with the King against the Tainted Cabal and their Soreshi allies."

Zek chewed his lip for a long while before he spoke again.

"The dawn and the dusk are the same light, refracted differently," he explained. "The dawn builds up; the dusk breaks down. Modify the dawn with the dusk, and you have a potent healing energy that is able to scourge disease from the body, a brighter illumination, and a swifter recovery from exertion. You already know these things. Without the dawn to contain it, or at least mitigate its flow, the dusk-tide is pure destructive force. It burns up in an instant—a catastrophic flash of released energy—and then it's gone, and you are spent… if you are not consumed by the blast." He gestured toward Anskar: "Your braided repository is a mess—the result of an accident, not careful crafting and nurture. View my own, for example."

Anskar felt the lessening of a barrier between them that he'd not previously been aware of. Under Zek's approving gaze, he reached out with his sorcerous senses and *saw*.

Zek's repository was a latticework of gossamer strands of the dawn-tide interwoven in perfect balance with the dusk, each thrumming with a measured flow.

"Do your people practice the craft of knitting?" Zek asked.

"The priests of the Mother do."

"Well, the tides must be knitted together following a pattern. Mine is basic, but serves its purpose. When one tide is used, the other shifts to check it, to keep the flow in balance. It means I cannot easily discharge the kind of power that you did during the battle, but I have more control, more endurance. You saw how my people augmented their weapons. That is one effect of many. Once you feel the play of the patterns, you'll be able to create fire at will, as well as dowse it. You might deliver focused blasts of lightning or a corrosive mist or choking fumes."

"And if I need something more?"

Zek studied him with narrowed eyes. "Then you will need

your mother's advice, not mine. Come, let me show you where to start."

Anskar recoiled as he felt the probe of Zek's senses inside his skull, but then he relaxed and let the Soreshi go deeper.

"Try to follow what I'm doing with your senses," Zek said.

With great care, the Soreshi unpicked a single thread of the dawn-tide from the knotted mass of Anskar's braided repositories. Next, he teased out a dusk-tide strand, then lay a second thread of dawn-tide across them.

"Now you," the Soreshi said.

Anskar fumbled a dusk-tide thread free. When he hesitated about where to place it, Zek said, "You decide. It is your pattern. The only requirement is balance. I'll leave you to it. This is your task alone."

Anskar worked through the remainder of the morning and most of the afternoon, and eventually fell into a deep and dreamless sleep on the cold stone floor. He was awakened by the sound of the cell door opening.

"Do you have any idea how long it's taken me to find you?" Brother Bonavir said. "I must be demented. According to the guards, I granted you permission to come here!"

Anskar started to apologize, but Bonavir waved him quiet.

"Are you hungry?"

"Starving," Anskar and Zek said at the same time.

"I'll tell the guards to hurry up with your food," Bonavir told Zek. "You, Anskar, can eat on the way."

"Where are we going?"

"Hrothyr's forge. Braga, it seems, has made some progress."

Despite the late hour, the orange glow of the forge was visible through the smithy's windows.

Bonavir climbed down from the carriage that had brought them from the dungeons, and Anskar followed him.

It was quiet inside the smithy when they entered. Braga was seated on a bench, hunched over and reading from a sheaf of parchment.

"My translation of the necromancer Tain's notebook," Brother Bonavir observed as they approached her. "I trust it is accurate."

Braga snorted and set down the parchment. "Judge for yourself."

She led them to the forge, beside which sat three ingots. At first Anskar thought they were of iron, but as he drew nearer, he saw they had a swirling, shifting sheen that gave them the appearance of mother-of-pearl.

"Divine alloy!" Bonavir said.

"And we can see it," Anskar observed.

"Obviously," Braga said.

Bonavir explained: "Tain's notes say nothing about imbuing invisibility. I assume that was your mother's contribution to the vambrace. The other sorcery it contains *is* described in Tain's notes, though I must admit I barely understand it. There are some among my confreres who might know more—but that is far from certain. It would require a sorcerer of rare talent to complete the Armor of Divinity."

"But this is the first step?" Anskar said, reaching out to touch one of the ingots. It was perfectly smooth and icy cold, and he felt a slight vibration emanating from the alloy. The vambrace on his forearm responded with a thrum of its own.

Bonavir nodded excitedly. "Do we have any of the nietan's horn left?" he asked Braga.

"I only used a pinch for these ingots. I'd say we have enough for a few of the smaller pieces."

"Smaller pieces of what?" a voice said from the open doorway to the street.

Anskar turned, and a shiver ran along his spine.

It was Castellac, the Tainted Cabalist who had murdered Lengar. He was wearing a black robe, the cowl obscuring his piggy face.

"Whatever you're up to at this time of night," Castellac said, stepping into the smithy, "it can't be good."

"Clear off, you shit-eating goat," Braga said, snatching up a hammer.

Anskar felt the swell of dawn-tide essence beside him, and a wavering ward of bluish light appeared around Brother Bonavir.

"Where did you learn that, priest?" Castellac said. "Let me guess: the scrolls of Evoker Magrius?"

"You know of them?" Brother Bonavir said.

"Knowledge is power," Castellac said. "Isn't that what you priests of the Elder say? And power is essential to us Cabalists. Without it, we don't tend to last long. I will admit to studying Magrius rather more assiduously than any of my confreres. The blue ward sphere is a neat innovation, don't you think? Turns away the dusk-tide as well as the dawn; but not, I think, the dark."

Too late, Anskar felt the surge of shadow from within the Cabalist. Tendrils of inky blackness snaked across the space between Castellac and Brother Bonavir. The blue ward dissolved into a shower of sparkles, and the priest of the Elder screamed. His robes fell to the floor in a crumpled heap, but of Bonavir himself there was no sign. He had simply vanished.

"Oops," Castellac said. "Never mind. It is you I have come for, Anskar."

"I thought I told you to clear off," Braga growled, slinging her hammer at the Cabalist.

Her aim was true, but the hammer struck only air, then crashed into a workbench and clanged to the floor.

Castellac was suddenly beside Anskar, whispering in his ear. "Come with me, and no one else needs to die."

Braga grabbed at the Cabalist, but Castellac was suddenly back in the doorway. Braga snarled and ran at him.

"Braga, no!" Anskar cried.

He threw out his multicolored ward to cover her as dark flames burst from Castellac's hand. Braga recoiled. Darkness licked over the ward, breaking like waves around a rock, then dissipated.

"I'm impressed," Castellac said. "This is why we want you, Anskar. The Abbess could use such a powerful sorcerer. But of course you already know that, don't you? You and the Abbess are intimately acquainted."

Still protected by Anskar's ward, Braga stalked toward the Cabalist. He backed outside the smithy and closed the door. Braga glanced back at Anskar, who raised his hands to caution her as she went to open the door.

"It's stuck," she said, pulling on the handle. The door shook and shuddered but wouldn't open.

"Fused with sorcery," Anskar said.

He dropped the ward he'd placed around Braga and sent his sorcerous senses into the door to gauge exactly what Castellac had done. Before he could find a way to counter the sorcery, Braga gasped.

Anskar turned as a figure materialized out of thin air. It was thin and spindly, with yellowish eyes. A demon, like the ones that had attacked him when he fled the abbey. Only not quite the same.

Its livid skin was covered in thorny spines from head to foot. Heaviness radiated from the demon, despite its slight build, and the atmosphere inside the smithy grew dense with some invisible charge. A confusion of scents filled the air: sulfur, rot, and a stench of piss and leather that reminded Anskar of a tannery.

As the demon stalked toward Braga, she backed away to a workbench, where she had left her sword. She fumbled behind until her fingers grasped the hilt, then she brought the blade around so it wavered before her.

Anskar tried to ward Braga, but his sorcery fizzled out, and the demon let out a gurgling laugh.

"Mother…" Anskar hissed, loosening the wards that kept her in check.

*You need me now, do you? Why not run back to your Soreshi friend and ask him to help?*

Braga moved along the edge of the workbench, and the creature kept pace with her. A gash-like grin split its spine-covered face, revealing row upon row of needle-sharp teeth.

"Do you want Braga to die?" Anskar demanded. "Who will make your precious Armor of Divinity then?"

*Braga is already dead. The demon has been summoned to feast on her soul.*

"What can I do to stop it?"

Braga had run out of space. She stood with her back pressed up against the wall.

*You can't stop it. Shadow-step to safety,* Queen Talia urged, *lest it break the terms of its summons and come after you next.*

Anskar met Braga's gaze and saw the fear in her eyes. "I can't," he said, reaching into his dark-tide repository.

*Don't be a fool,* Queen Talia warned.

But it was too late.

Anskar formed calculations in his mind and spoke a cant, sending spears of shadow streaking across the smithy toward the demon. They faded away to nothing before they struck.

The demon turned to face him, yellow eyes narrowed to slits.

With a roar of terror and rage, Braga slammed her sword into the back of its head. She cried out in pain as the sword rebounded and went flying into the wall.

White-hot barbs pierced Anskar's scalp, and instead of the scene before him, he was suddenly splayed out upon a scalding rock in the midst of a burning lake, while an evil-looking crow pecked at his liver. Screams rent the air, none of them louder than his own.

*Resist!* Queen Talia commanded. *Wreathe your thoughts in shadow.*

Anskar drew a pall of dark-tide over the images in his mind, and then he was back in the smithy, watching as the demon leaped for Braga.

At the same instant, Anskar flung himself into the shadows at the base of the wall. He grabbed Braga and dragged her with him as he focused on a pool of darkness out in the street. But as the shadows swallowed them and the usual nausea washed over him, Anskar felt something else traveling beside them. Braga screamed, and Anskar panicked as he felt her sudden absence. He stumbled as he emerged from the shadows on the opposite side of the street. Alone.

"Braga!" he cried, turning frantically.

*It has taken her,* Queen Talia said. *Ripped her from the shadow-step and scattered her essence to the dark.*

"No!" Anskar screamed.

*She is gone. Not even I could bring her back.*

Anskar heard whistles and the pounding of boots approaching

along the street. The Watch were coming, and though he had done nothing wrong, he felt a desperate need to get away.

He turned into an alley, but Castellac was there, waiting for him, hands tucked into the sleeves of his black robe.

"You could make things much easier on yourself," the Cabalist told Anskar. "I will not return to the Abbess empty-handed; you must know that. It would be suicide."

The footfalls of the Watch grew louder. Someone entered the alley and called, "Who's there?"

"This is not over," Castellac said as he shadow-stepped away.

Anskar shadow-stepped again too, his guts clenching from using too much dark-tide in so short a time. He re-emerged from the shadows inside the smithy.

The Watch were hammering at the door, demanding to be let in. How had they been alerted to what had happened inside? Probably someone in the neighboring buildings had heard the commotion and reported it.

Quickly, he snatched up Brother Bonavir's translation of the necromancer Tain's notes, then grabbed the three ingots of divine alloy and placed them in a sack. He stuffed the pouch that contained the remainder of the powdered nietan horn on top of the ingots and, as the door burst open, shadow-stepped to safety.

# THIRTY-FOUR

"BROTHER BONAVIR IS DEAD?" KING Aelfyr said.

"The Cabalist Castellac killed him, sire," Anskar replied.

Anskar hadn't known what else to do, so he'd gone to Lanuc and confessed what had happened at the smithy—not only Castellac's attack and his summoning of the demon, but the whole story concerning the Armor of Divinity. Well, most of it.

All the while, Queen Talia had hissed and warned and threatened in his mind, but Anskar ignored her. Too many people had died.

Lanuc had immediately sent word to the King.

They were summoned to the great hall within the hour, but Aelfyr was a subtle man and insisted on speaking with Anskar alone, except for the presence of a priest of the Elder called Brother Iantos.

"And it was the same Cabalist you encountered before?" the King said. "But I don't understand. Why was Bonavir even there? What was his involvement in all this?"

"Knowledge, Majesty," Brother Iantos said. "It is all that motivates us priests of the Elder." He peered over the top of his eyeglasses at Anskar.

"But we already have knowledge of the Armor of Divinity," the King said. "The necromancer Tain's notes have been in the Scriptorium for centuries."

"Ah, but not the practical know-how. Such knowledge is pleasing to the Elder and would have brought Brother Bonavir great esteem."

"And Bonavir pressured you into this… this quest?" King Aelfyr asked Anskar.

"Him and Braga."

"Hrothyr's wife." The King grimaced. "A difficult woman by any standards. And she is dead too, you say."

Anskar nodded. "Killed by the demon Castellac summoned."

"If I may, Majesty?" Brother Iantos said. "What progress did you make with the divine alloy, young man?"

"None," Anskar said. With each lie he told, it grew easier. "Brother Bonavir had only just made a translation of Tain's notes."

"After you broke into the Scriptorium," the King added, "and stole the original."

Anskar dipped his head. "I returned the notebook as soon as we had the copy, Majesty."

"How very decent of you."

"And the Tainted Cabal," Brother Iantos said. "Do they also plan to make Armor of Divinity?"

"I don't know. But I don't think so. Whatever they seek, though, is also in the Scriptorium. Castellac tried to make me break in and retrieve it for them."

"Your reputation precedes you," the King said.

"And how were you to find it, if you didn't know what it was?" Brother Iantos asked.

"If I'd agreed to break in, I'm sure Castellac would have told me."

"I'm sure he would." Brother Iantos removed his eyeglasses and turned to the King. "It can only be the memory crystal of Morudjin, sire."

Aelfyr pinched the bridge of his nose. "Well, this certainly explains a great deal. You should have come forward with this information earlier, Anskar. It is a black mark against you that you did not."

"I'm sorry, Majesty."

"Not nearly sorry enough," Brother Iantos said. "Do you have any idea what the Tainted Cabal will do with the memory crystal of Morudjin?"

"I don't even know what that is."

"Morudjin, a priest of the Elder, was responsible for the first summoning of Nysrog into the world," the King explained. "That was the start of the cataclysms that have afflicted Wiraya ever since."

"Morudjin died for his sins," Brother Iantos said. He might have shuddered.

"You do not share in Morudjin's guilt, Brother," the King said. "That was all a long time ago. Centuries."

"But he was still a priest of the Elder."

"Yes," the King said, "and we should see his life as a lesson about what can happen when the pursuit of knowledge becomes an unchecked obsession. A lesson that fell on deaf ears, it seems, when it came to Brother Bonavir."

"It was Castellac who killed Brother Bonavir," Anskar said.

"Not the Armor of Divinity."

"Nevertheless," Brother Iantos said, "if Bonavir had not been trying to make a name for himself through his involvement in this Armor business, it is doubtful he would have been at the smithy when the Cabalist struck."

"Castellac was after me," Anskar persisted. "It was never about the smithy or the Armor of Divinity."

"And now?" the King said. "What do you think we should do, Anskar?"

"Could you destroy the memory crystal before the Tainted Cabal find a way to steal it?"

"For centuries, the rulers of Wintotashum have tried exactly that," the King replied. "Whatever sorcery was used in its creation protects the crystal, and it cannot be shattered. And so we are left with one option, the same we were already pursuing: war. As for you, Anskar—" the King speared him with a hard look "—what should we do with you?"

This was it: the moment Anskar had been afraid of since being summoned. He had heard that any transgressor of the royal law endured a long and painful death at the hands of the King's torturers. At best he could expect to join Zek in the dungeons; only in his case, he might never be allowed out again.

"You have worth," the King continued. "You will be useful in the upcoming battle against the Soreshi and the Tainted Cabal. So I will pardon your break-in to the Scriptorium and your failure to report the activity of the Tainted Cabal within my walls. In return, I will exact from you an oath."

"Majesty?"

"You will never enter the Scriptorium again. Swear it in the name of all five aspects of Menselas."

Anskar swallowed.

"I won't ask again," the King said.

And so Anskar swore, on all that he held sacred. Despite his ailing faith, he didn't feel he could ever break such an oath.

But in case he did, King Aelfyr added, "Menselas has a forgiving aspect, but I do not. If you break your oath to me, I will have no choice but to make an example of you." He glanced at Brother Iantos, whose expression implied that the priest of the Elder would enjoy that very much. "Remind me of your special field of interest, Brother."

"Pain," the priest said. "And the ability to keep a person in agony, on the threshold between life and death, for a very long time."

The streets of Wintotashum were swarming with the City Watch and armored warriors. Priests of the Elder went from door to door, asking questions. King Aelfyr was leaving no stone unturned in his attempt to root out the enemy within, but Anskar suspected that Castellac was long gone.

Anskar found himself at a tavern in one of the poorer regions of the city. The building was run-down, but it had a wide hearth heaped with steadily burning logs. And when he ordered a meal, the bread was fresh baked, the ham tender and lightly salted. He washed it down with a dark hop beer, then sat brooding by the fire as the lunch crowd slowly emptied out.

*Happy birthday,* Queen Talia said in his mind.

"I'm surprised you remembered."

Anskar had tried his best to forget. He was in no mood for celebrating, and even if he were, who would he celebrate with?

*Oh, I remember your birth,* his mother said. *On its true date,* not the arbitrary one the Order of Eternal Vigilance gave you when they took you in.

"You mean I'm not yet eighteen?" Anskar asked, then remembered to keep his voice down when the tavern keeper glanced at him.

*You were eighteen several weeks ago, on the feast of Culinor.*

"Culinor?"

*One of the old Niyandrian gods, though once he was mortal, like you and I.*

"Are you still mortal?"

She didn't answer, telling him instead how grief-stricken she had been to send him into hiding when he was a baby.

*The mainlanders were closing in on Naphor, and the end was inevitable. But I laid plans, Anskar. Plans for you, plans for me. I know how much you have suffered, and I have suffered too, but in the end we will win through, and then it will all have been worth it.*

"Will it?"

*You will see, my child. And so will our oppressors. One day, not so long from now, it will be their turn to suffer.*

"You sound like Carred Selenas," Anskar muttered under his breath, signaling to the tavern keeper that he wanted another beer.

Talia sighed. *Poor, sweet Carred. So loyal, so naive.*

"She didn't seem naive to me," Anskar said.

The woman he had met was a veteran of many fights, a planner and a schemer.

*The years change us,* Talia said, and there seemed to be genuine sadness in her voice. *Innocence is corrupted, love turns cold, but loyalty... Carred's loyalty was never in question.*

"She's obsessed with you," Anskar said, then fell silent as the tavern keeper brought him a fresh mug of beer and set it down on the table without a word. Flames spat in the hearth from where a boy added more wood and raked the embers with a poker.

*Less than she once was,* Talia said. Her voice in Anskar's head almost sounded sad. *You did well to take Tain's notes, the ingots of divine alloy, and the powdered horn of the nietan, but where will you find another blacksmith accomplished enough to produce more divine alloy and craft it into the Armor?*

"I won't," Anskar said, taking a sip of his beer, hardly noticing the bitter taste. "I took those things from the smithy so no one else would find them, but I want no more part of it. This vambrace"—he rubbed the invisible metal that covered his forearm—"is evil. It killed Hrothyr."

*Foolish boy. Hrothyr should never have removed it from you, and he most certainly shouldn't have tried it on. The vambrace is for you alone, Anskar. It was always intended for you. I imbued it with sorcery and sealed it with my own blood.*

"I thought you wanted the Armor of Divinity for yourself," Anskar said.

*Perhaps once,* Talia said, *but I ran out of time. Hrothyr had completed only the vambrace when the mainland armies came against us, and so I prepared it for you and hid it away in the tomb constructed for me atop Hallow Hill.*

"With a wraithe to guard it?"

*Without the wraithes, there would never have been any Armor of Divinity. It was their lore, augmented by the necromancy of Niyas, that made the Armor possible.*

"So the wraithes wanted our people to become gods?"

*I doubt that. They don't approve of our alterations to their original design. The necromancer Tain was once almost killed by wraithes, which is why he hid away in Mount Phyrith. But I learned—do not ask me how—that wraithes can be compelled like demons if you discover their names. I bound a wraithe to fulfill a task for me before it was released.*

That made Anskar think of the Ethereal Sorceress and the two favors he owed her. It wasn't a comforting thought.

"What about Tain, then? Is he a god? Did the Armor of Divinity work for him?"

*It was not altogether successful.*

"So, what happened to him? Where is he now?"

Queen Talia chuckled. *He is around. Here and there. He may still be of some use to us. And if not, you at least have his notes.*

"But even if I wanted to go on with this—which I don't—we don't have enough nietan horn for a full suit of armor."

*Then fetch more.*

And be further indebted to the Ethereal Sorceress? "I can't."

*Or won't? Then it's fortunate that loyalty abides, even when obsession dies.*

"Oh?"

*You think I have only one plan? You will have the armor, Anskar, whether you make it anew or modify an old suit. But either way, you must find a new blacksmith with the ability to work divine alloy.*

"The way Braga and Hrothyr spoke, I don't think there is anyone. And even if there were, Wintotashum's forges are the only ones hot enough."

*Then you must bring him back.*

"Who?"

*Hrothyr. There is no bringing back Braga. The demon plucked her from the shadow-step and scattered her essence across the abyssal realms. Nothing of her remains in this world.*

"You want me to raise Hrothyr from the dead? How?"

*I will show you.*

Anskar's beer spilled as he gripped the mug so tightly it shook.

Was there nothing his mother wouldn't do?

"If you know how to raise Hrothyr, why didn't you raise yourself?" he asked.

*Because there was nothing left of me, unfortunately. To bring someone back, there must be an intact body to work with. I was at the very center of the blast that destroyed Naphor.*

"Well, I won't do it."

*You must!*

"I will not."

*Then all our work has been for nothing!*

"Your work, not mine."

*You don't care? You don't care about me? About the fate of the Niyandrian people?*

"All I'm saying is that I want no more to do with your scheming. Now leave me alone."

Anskar raised his wards again, shutting her out.

He finished his drink and stalked from the tavern. He hesitated in the street, not sure of where to go.

Then he knew.

"No, Anskar," Gisela said, not even granting him admission to her tent. "We had an agreement, remember? You must find another priest to hear your confession."

"But I don't trust anyone else," he said. "And no one else can know my secrets."

"Why?" Gisela countered. "Because they might think less of you if they knew? That's the point of confession, Anskar: to share your failings with the Healer's representatives on Wiraya."

"But I'm ashamed."

"Shame is humbling," said Gisela, and shut the tent flap in his face.

Anskar stood there for a long moment, smoldering with barely suppressed rage.

"Are you all right?" a man asked.

Anskar turned to see a white-robed healer watching him.

"No, I'm not all right."

"Would you allow me to hear your confession?"

"To the abyss with confession," Anskar growled. "To the abyss with forgiveness, with the Order, and even Menselas himself!"

He stormed past the gawping priest and headed back through the barbican. He was done being pulled between his mother and Menselas. It had to be all or nothing, as far as he was concerned.

He'd tried to give himself entirely to the Order—until he'd noticed that few others did the same, least of all his superiors. As for Queen Talia, he didn't trust her in the slightest. Yes, she'd come to his assistance once or twice, but not out of motherly love, that was for sure. She was using him.

What he needed right now was clarity—the sort of clarity that came with a righteous cause, with a sword in hand on a battlefield.

King Aelfyr was holding a full war council tomorrow; he was determined to drive the Tainted Cabal and their Soreshi allies from his land and avert a second coming of the demon lord Nysrog. What better cause could there be than that? Anskar would pledge his allegiance to the King and have nothing further to do with the Order of Eternal Vigilance or the long-dead Queen of Niyas.

# THIRTY-FIVE

FOR THE JOURNEY SOUTH, CARRED sat up front with the driver while Orix slept fitfully in the back, Noni seated beside him, watching the hills and the trees go by with childlike awe. Talia hadn't said a word since the night before. The driver was an older Niyandrian man who responded to Carred's attempts at small talk with grunts. Every now and again he would glance behind at Orix and shake his head disapprovingly while making a circle of his thumb and forefinger—the Niyandrian ward against demons.

Poor Orix. When Carred had bought food as they waited for the cart to pick them up, Orix hadn't been able to feed himself, with his eyes and mouth in the wrong place. Carred had helped, but chewing had been messy, and Orix had gone hungry. He'd tried to speak, but his lips and tongue were uncoordinated, as if his brain had trouble communicating with them now they had been relocated to his forehead. Perhaps when this was all over, Talia would deign to restore Orix to normal, assuming her ability with the earth-tide was comparable to Tain's. And if not her, perhaps Anskar would. He and Orix had been friends, at least until Carred had come along.

Little by little, the surrounding countryside grew familiar, until at last the cart drew up at the brink of a hill, where the road descended toward a vast building site a mile or so distant: Naphor, the place of Queen Talia's defeat and, later, of Carred's at the hands of Eldrid DeVantte.

"Here and no further," Noni said, standing and climbing down from the cart. "We must not be spotted by a patrol."

The sun was low on the western horizon, and there was no activity upon the scaffolding surrounding the massive keep that was nearing completion. A few dark specks were moving about the mud-churned streets, amid stone buildings that had been repaired with thatch and wood. The mainlanders lacked the skills of Niyandrian stonemasons, but even so… It was one step up from hovels built with dung.

Carred hopped down and reached into the bed of the cart to shake Orix awake. She felt guilty rousing him to the realization of what he had become. He groaned, the eyes on his chin blinking blearily and his misplaced lips curling into a snarl. She guided him to the ground.

She dragged the net that contained the armor from the back of the cart.

Carred paid the driver, who snapped the reins and headed back north without a word.

"Follow me," Noni said as she walked towards the woods.

Carred hefted the armor to her back, looped her arm in Orix's and followed.

"I have not been idle during my time in the realm of the dead,"

Noni-Talia said. "It took some persuasion, but there are spirits here with me who are impossibly ancient, and who know a thing or two. Tain only discovered one of the missing ingredients, which is why he could not have returned even if he'd wanted to. Have you guessed what the other one is yet?"

Noni stopped and slipped her hand inside Carred's shirt. She brought out the ring on its slender chain that Talia had left for Carred.

"Void-steel?"

"So, you worked out what the ring is made of." She released the ring and walked on through the trees.

"I had help." Marith had been the one to identify the ring.

"And do you know what it is for?"

"It saved me from the sorcery of Luzius Landav, when he took me some place to meet with some secretive rich types from the mainland in the hope that I would betray the rebellion."

"Fortuitous," Noni said, "but not the ring's intended purpose."

"Which was?"

"You will see soon enough."

"Void-steel is demonic," Carred said.

A pained look crossed Noni's face.

"I used a little in an experiment with the vambrace Anskar now wears. It had unfortunate side effects, and the vambrace developed a sort of animal sentience, which I was able to train to some extent. The vambrace clings to Anskar like a loyal dog, and it does harm to others who may try to use it. I now need more void-steel to add to the armor you retrieved from the seabed."

"Hence the ring?" Carred said.

"More than that. Ten times that amount, at the very least."

They came to a clearing overgrown with brambles. The ruins of a mansion stood smothered by creepers, a huge oak growing up through the remains of the roof.

"Go inside," Noni said. "There is a closet in the entrance hall. Within, there is a pouch containing star metal. Take this and leave the armor inside. It will be safe here. Few know of this place, and fewer would dare to come here."

"Wait here," Carred told Orix, then fought her way through the undergrowth until she reached the partially collapsed portico.

Inside, the vegetation had not only invaded but taken over. Crumbling walls had plants growing in the cracks, and the ceiling was bowed and split down the center. Black mold speckled every surface, and the air smelled of pepper and loam.

Farther in, Carred came to a hallway where the floor at the far end had rotted away, revealing the flooded basement below.

She opened the door to her left onto a large closet. As Talia had said, there was a drawstring pouch inside, partially hidden behind a bucket and a mop. She took the pouch and tied it to her belt, then removed the mop and bucket to make room for the armor.

She couldn't leave the ruined mansion fast enough. Noni then guided them around the edge of the estate to a narrow stone path carpeted with moss. They followed it through dense forest for perhaps half a mile until they reached some kind of folly in a circle of yew trees. The structure at the center was the height of a tall man and perhaps three feet across. It had eight paneled sides of some dull metal, green with patina.

"What is this place?" Carred asked.

"Something my father built long before I was born."

Carred looked Noni in the eye. Talia had seldom spoken about her father, and then only in hints and shudders.

"Tell me again," Noni said. "Are you loyal? Can I trust you?"

Carred nodded.

"Hand me the ring."

Carred pulled the chain over her neck.

Noni took it and ran her fingers over the surface of one of the panels until she located what she was looking for: barely discernible, a circular indentation largely obscured by an accumulation of patina and moss.

Noni placed the ring in the indentation, and that section of the outer wall swung open.

"Step inside," Noni said.

Carred released Orix's arm. "What about him?"

"Noni will look after him, don't you worry."

"Noni? Or you, Talia?"

"We will not speak this way again, my love. Anskar needs me, and your task is almost done."

Warily, Carred crossed the threshold into the narrow chamber. The walls were eight panels of reddish stone, darker than ruby and veined with black. Her scalp tingled and she felt queasy. The air was filled with a low thrum that caused her innards to vibrate.

"This is a portal chamber," Noni-Talia said from outside. "A crude version of the portal stones that were instrumental in bringing about the demon wars. It took my father a long time to construct. A very long time."

"What now?" Carred asked. Every instinct told her to get out now, while she still could. Assuming Talia would permit that.

"You must go to Vulthrax. Trade with the ruling lord."

"Where in the world is Vulthrax?"

"It's not in this world. Tell him I sent you. That will intrigue him, if nothing else."

"Trade?"

"Star-metal is inimical to demons, which is what makes it so valuable to them—for killing one another, but also for study, so that one day they might find a remedy for its effect on them. It is found nowhere in the abyssal realms, but void-steel they have, though it is rare."

"You want me to go to—"

But Noni slammed the door shut.

The thrum built in Carred's ears till it sounded like a cascading waterfall. The red stone of the walls started to glow, the black veins that webbed it throbbing…

# THIRTY-SIX

ON HIS WAY TO THE great hall the next morning, Anskar had never seen the streets so bustling with activity. Clearly the King trusted the Thousand Lakes lords more than he did the Order of Eternal Vigilance, because it seemed that Wintotashum's population had nearly doubled in size overnight.

The City Watch were visible on every corner. The taverns were overflowing with customers. Some had broken windows, and the streets outside their doors were painted with blood and vomit.

Beyond the city walls, the Order's encampment was now an island within the sprawl of new tents, pavilions, and supply wagons. Hundreds of horses were pastured over several fields, with young boys and girls in attendance. Latrine pits had been dug, and already stank like the abyssal realms all across the city.

The stench inside the great hall was of a different kind: stale sweat, the moldering smell of fur cloaks sodden with rain, the charcoal from the braziers, and the smoking rushlights that cast their flickering glow across the gloomy interior.

The hall was so packed that many of the priests, servants, and commanders who had arrived with their lords were forced to stand around the walls, and more still were crowded in the entrance or huddled beneath their cloaks in the cold outside.

The rows of seats nearest the dais that held the King's throne were occupied by men and women in heavy cloaks and ostentatious chains of office. Many wore circlets of silver or bronze around their heads. A few wore gold. Each of these nobles was flanked by officials—priests, lawyers, and scribes. There was a constant hubbub of conversation as everyone awaited the King.

Lanuc, Anskar, Nul, and Rindon had been relegated to standing at the back of the hall. Rindon maintained a constant banter with Nul, most of it bragging about past accomplishments or women he had known, though Anskar thought there was a sadness in Rindon's eyes that hadn't been there previously. Nul was even more reserved than he had been before, and his usually calm demeanor had given way to a tension bordering on violence.

Lanuc, too, seemed far from himself. Once or twice he tried to engage Anskar in conversation, but Anskar couldn't face him. He didn't know how to tell Lanuc he no longer wanted any part of the Order.

The hubbub inside the hall died, replaced by the occasional cough as the stocky priest of the Warrior, Brother Kenaith, appeared from a door behind the throne, ascended the couple of steps onto the dais, and stood glaring at the assembly.

King Aelfyr followed him and acknowledged the lords with a bob of his head.

"Lords of the Thousand Lakes," the King said. "Wintotashum welcomes you as we gather together in service to the lands we rule under Menselas, the Five."

Anskar noticed several lords exchange looks at that. Perhaps not all the nobility of the Thousand Lakes shared the King's piety.

"Our subjects in the north have been ravaged by the Soreshi," the King continued. There were angry murmurs in response. "Our towns and villages have been burned, our people dispossessed. We have offered refugees succor on the Iron Road and arranged safe escort to Gutishon."

More murmurs and exchanged looks, most of them directed at a fierce-looking woman in the front row. Her gray hair was wound into buns that covered her ears, and she wore a heavy cloak of wolfskin.

King Aelfyr nodded to her. "My thanks, Baroness Helva, for welcoming the refugees with open arms."

Anskar couldn't see the baroness's face from the back of the hall, but he thought, from the bunching of her shoulders, that she might be scowling.

"Today," the King went on, "the combined might of the Thousand Lakes says 'Enough!' Today, we do our service as the shepherds of the people we govern, and we protect them from the wolves that have invaded our lands."

"About bloody time," a man near the front growled.

"Our response would have come sooner," Aelfyr said, "if our allies from Kaile had heeded our call without delay. The enemy has struck like lightning, burning isolated towns in the north and then disappearing back into the mountains. Some settlements have been taken, it is true"—he raised a hand to forestall an interruption from a lord wearing a voluminous crimson robe— "all of them along the Iron Road. It has been clear for some time that the Soreshi are cutting a path to Wintotashum, but it has taken us until now to work out why."

The hall hushed as the King's eyes scanned the lords. "The

Tainted Cabal." Aelfyr let the words sink in. "That is who is behind this Soreshi aggression. They have insinuated themselves into the Ymaltian Mountains, taking over a long-abandoned Soreshi citadel. And they have used beguilement to turn the Soreshi against us."

"But why?" the lord in the crimson robe asked. "What would draw the Tainted Cabal to the Thousand Lakes?"

"The Scriptorium here at Wintotashum," the King said.

"They want our scrolls and books?" the lord said, his voice dripping with scorn.

"Lord Dismar, Wintotashum is an ancient city, and it holds secrets that would stop you from ever sleeping soundly again, were you to be made aware of them. But, as King, it is my responsibility to know of them, and to protect them from falling into the wrong hands." He glared around the hall, then gave a wry grin. "And at times, I might even get to sleep."

The lords dutifully chuckled, but the King pressed on, once more deadly serious.

"We have all heard the whispers about the Tainted Cabal, about what their aims are. Many of us have mocked them, have accused them of living in a fantasy world where they confuse myth with reality. But let me assure you, and if you do not believe your King, then consult with your priests of the Elder, or if you still have them,"—and this time he looked directly at Lanuc—"your priests of the Hooded One."

So King Aelfyr knew about the Grand Master commandeering the Hooded One's chapel in Branil's Burg.

"Ask them about the truth of the old stories, of the times when the demon lord Nysrog walked the surface of Wiraya. Ask them about the fire, the blood, the shadow that spread across every land. 'What concern is that of ours?' you may say. 'Nysrog was defeated and sent screaming back to the abyssal realms.' But at what cost? How many thousands died? How many millions?

"'But that was in the distant past,' you might object. Not so. The Tainted Cabal want to usher in a new age of Nysrog, and they have plotted for centuries to make the demon lord's return a reality. They believe they know how, but have always lacked one thing: the memory crystal of Morudjin, the priest of the Elder who learned the mysteries of the abyssal realms and first brought Nysrog's terror upon Wiraya.

"That crystal is heavily warded here in Wintotashum, behind our impregnable walls in the heart of a kingdom of garrisoned towns and cities. But somehow, the Tainted Cabal have learned of its whereabouts. Even while they use the Soreshi to harry the north and cut a path to Wintotashum, the Cabalists have infiltrated our great city in an attempt to steal the crystal.

"That, my lords of the Thousand Lakes, is why you are here. That is why the knights of the Order of Eternal Vigilance have journeyed all the way from Sansor in Kaile to fight at our side— though I would have preferred greater numbers and more haste. But our enemy has struck a mortal blow that may render all our efforts futile. During the night, the Scriptorium was entered— not broken into—and all the guards within were slaughtered, mutilated, defiled."

Cries of outrage and questions broke out among the lords.

Lanuc turned a look of shock on Anskar, who swallowed, his mind racing as to what might have happened.

"It is gone," the King said. "The memory crystal of Morudjin has been taken." Overcome with weariness, he folded himself into his throne.

"Why is this the first we are hearing about this crystal?" one of the lords demanded.

"Morudjin is a myth," someone else added. "What's really going on?"

The King's household warriors lining the hall grew more alert, and their hands went to their sword hilts.

"If the Tainted Cabal already have the crystal," the woman in the wolfskin cloak asked, "does that mean we're doomed?"

The hall erupted into shouted questions and demands to know more. Lords argued with other lords—some of them incensed at the disrespect shown to the King.

All the while, Aelfyr sat slumped on his throne, one hand covering his eyes. Anskar assumed the King was as despairing as half the lords seemed to be, that he had given up hope now that the Tainted Cabal had taken what they wanted. But it made no sense. Aelfyr had seemed confident and in control only moments ago, and he must have known about the crystal's theft before the council had even started.

Brother Kenaith gave instructions to one of the warriors, and the woman hurried through the door behind the throne. Moments later, she re-emerged, a priest of the Healer following behind.

While the lords continued to yell at each other, the healer approached the King and placed her hands on either side of his head. Anskar expected to sense a discharge of dawn-tide essence, but there was nothing. The healer's lips moved, but it seemed more like a prayer than a cant. The King shuddered and gasped, then shook himself like a man who had just fallen asleep and been loudly awakened. The healer placed a hand over the King's belly, and pain and tension slowly melted from Aelfyr's face.

As the healer left the hall, King Aelfyr raised a tremulous hand for silence, but either nobody noticed or they chose not to obey.

The King nodded to Brother Kenaith, who stepped to the front of the dais. Anskar sensed the dusk-tide essence rolling off the Warrior's priest, and when Kenaith spoke, it was with a voice like thunder that shook the hall and silenced the squabbling lords.

"Shame!" Brother Kenaith declaimed. "Shame on you all! Do you forget where you are? Who you are seated before? Get off your chairs, you craven so-called lords of the Thousand Lakes. Get off and kneel to your sovereign."

To Anskar's amazement, the hundred or more lords and their retainers pushed back their chairs and knelt on the hard-packed earth of the floor. Some had to be helped down by their servants. Knees creaked, shoulders stooped, heads bowed. Looks were exchanged, some of them venomous, but still all the lords bowed.

Only Lanuc's group didn't kneel, and though Brother Kenaith swept his gaze toward them, he didn't insist that they comply.

Rindon, Nul, and Lanuc hadn't said a word during the chaos, only shared concerned looks. Their conduct throughout had been impeccable, and Anskar realized that he felt proud to be standing with them.

That surprised him.

The King stood, narrowing his eyes as he scanned the kneeling lords. When he switched his gaze to the warriors lining the walls and nodded, dozens of swords hissed from their scabbards, and a collective gasp went up from the lords. A second nod from the King and the swords were resheathed. A look passed between King Aelfyr and Brother Kenaith, and then the King resumed his throne.

"You may return to your seats," Brother Kenaith said, this time without the dusk-tide enhancing his voice. He waited until the lords had settled themselves back on their chairs before he continued.

"The memory crystal of Morudjin was in the most secure part

of the Scriptorium, a basement vault lined with orichalcum and accessed through a steel door a foot thick and locked with a Sandoval mechanism. Sorcerous wards of the highest order protected the door, the floor of the vault, and the crystal itself. There was no sign of entry, either to the white tower or the vault. The wards had all been triggered, but none of them had their designed effect. In fact, Brother Yonas, our priest of the Elder who specializes in such things"—he indicated a decrepit-looking old man wearing a charcoal robe, with just a few wisps of white hair clinging to his liver-spotted scalp—"reported that the wards' destructive effects had been contained somehow, and simply allowed to peter out."

Brother Yonas nodded his agreement but said nothing. Anskar wondered if the old man was even capable of speech.

Brother Kenaith glanced at Anskar as he went on. "The number of guards inside the Scriptorium had been doubled since a recent break-in, but all were found dead, their bodies mutilated or defiled. Some were spread-eagled on the ceiling, with nothing tangible holding them there. Others were impaled against walls or ripped to shreds."

A hushed tension fell over the great hall.

"You all know what this means," Brother Kenaith said. "The Tainted Cabal are known to consort with demons. But this slaughter wasn't the work of lesser demons. Only higher-order demons have such power, perhaps even a demon lord. No human could possibly bind a higher-order demon for more than a few minutes, which tells us that whoever summoned the demon or demons for this task must have been inside our city. If Brother Yonas is right about that, the cost to the Tainted Cabal would be huge. Even they cannot command higher-order demons without significant sacrifice. Menselas only knows how much of their blackened souls the Cabalists lost in the process, but it shows how important Morudjin's crystal is to them. They are convinced that it will bring them what they most desire: the return of Nysrog."

It had to have been Castellac who had summoned the demons, Anskar thought. What sacrifices would the Cabalist have made to achieve that? Was Brother Bonavir's death connected to the summoning? His corpse had disappeared. Or Braga's? Or had Castellac given something of his own?

"We were already aware that the Tainted Cabal's agents have been at work amongst us," Brother Kenaith said. "King Aelfyr has sent word to the City States, the Pristart Combine, and the Patriarch of the Church of Menselas in Kaile about the dire peril Wiraya is once more facing." A murmur of questions and protests erupted, and the Warrior's priest held up his hand for silence. "Word was sent by special means to swiftly reach each destination."

Anskar's mind instantly flashed to the Ethereal Sorceress and her mysterious mode of travel. He wondered what Sheelahn had demanded from the King in return.

"Thank you, Brother Kenaith," Aelfyr said, rising from his throne. His eyes were piercing and blue, and he looked invigorated by whatever the healer had done to him. "Despite the rapid delivery of our messages, it will be weeks before aid arrives, so I have advised the Patriarch of Kaile and the rulers of the Pristart Combine and the City States, to scour their own lands and purge the Tainted Cabal from among us. No stone, I am certain, will be left unturned. The stakes are too high for that.

"In the meantime, my lords of the Thousand Lakes, we must act, and act quickly. Our combined forces will converge on the newly garrisoned town of Veranoth, and from there we will march north, to the ancient Soreshi citadel in the Ymaltian Mountains. On the way, we will give no quarter to our enemies. The Tainted Cabal, and the Soreshi who currently serve them, will all be killed. The mountain passes will run with Soreshi blood, and if any escape, we will pursue them to the shores of the Trackless Ocean. And we will start the cleansing here at home, with the Soreshi piece of filth languishing in our dungeons."

Any thought Anskar had of swearing allegiance to the King and abandoning the Order of Eternal Vigilance vanished at these words. But before he could open his mouth to protest, a priest of the Healer burst into the great hall with two warriors in tow.

It was the man from outside the city walls who had offered to hear Anskar's confession. He was pale-faced and shaking, and dropped to his knees in the gangway between the seats of the lords. When he spoke, he had to pause between words to catch his breath.

"Majesty, forgive my interruption." He fumbled a folded piece of parchment from his robe pocket and held it up. "One of our healers has been taken. By a man in black. He escaped with her in a carriage that sped north along the Iron Road."

"And no one stopped him?" Brother Kenaith said. "There must be thousands of warriors outside the city."

"The carriage was clouded in a dark mist," the healer explained. "Those who approached dropped like flies. Seven warriors are dead."

"A healer, you say?" Lanuc asked. "A woman?"

The priest turned to face him. "Your daughter, Gisela, Commander."

Lanuc staggered back a step, his face draining of blood, then turned to leave the great hall.

"No, Lanuc of Gessa," the King said. "There will be no solo

action. We ride north together to crush the enemy."

Lanuc stiffened and turned back to face the King. "But my daughter—"

The King cut him off. "I'm sorry, but we are at war." He returned his attention to the healer. "What is this parchment you hold aloft?"

"It is a letter, sire, for Anskar DeVantte."

Aelfyr nodded for Anskar to take the parchment.

Anskar unfolded it and started to read. "It's from Castellac, the Tainted Cabalist," he said, glancing at Lanuc. "He observed me when I went to see Gisela yesterday. She refused to hear my confession."

Lanuc frowned, but Anskar pressed on.

"He's taken her north to…" He squinted at the strange words. "Nax-ur-Vadim?"

"The language is Nazgrese," Brother Yonas said, surprising everyone. His voice was frail and reedy, yet it carried across the hall as if he were whispering in Anskar's ear. "The language of the abyssal realms. It means 'Fortress of Shadow.'"

"The abandoned Soreshi citadel," Brother Kenaith said.

Anskar returned the letter to the healer. "Castellac doesn't really want Gisela," he told Lanuc. "He's using her as bait to get me to this citadel. If I give myself up to the Tainted Cabal, he promises to release her."

"Unharmed?" Lanuc asked.

"He doesn't say."

"Out of the question," King Aelfyr said. "Your sorcerous powers will be needed for the coming battle."

Anskar scrunched the parchment into a ball, dropped it on the floor, and turned to leave.

"Anskar—" Lanuc started, but Nul caught Anskar's eye and

gave the slightest of nods.

"I said no!" the King shouted from the dais, and warriors moved to intercept Anskar, swords drawn.

Anskar whispered a cant, and his multicolored ward sprang into existence around him. The closest warriors backed away, covering their eyes against the glare.

A surge of dusk-tide essence behind him made Anskar turn. Brother Kenaith, ablaze with the Warrior's Fire, streaked toward him, power radiating from every limb.

And then the Warrior's priest tripped and sprawled face first on the floor.

"Oops," Rindon said, pulling back his foot.

Anskar shadow-stepped away, emerging in the shadows beneath the wooden Church of Menselas. He slipped inside the open door.

The nave was wreathed in gloom because the window shutters were closed. Reaching into his dark-tide repository, he wove himself a cloak of shadows.

From outside he heard the shouts of warriors: commands to secure the city gates, to watch the walls, to check the barracks. But they had misjudged his intent if they expected him to rush blindly north to exchange himself for Gisela.

For one thing, he didn't believe Castellac would honor the terms of his letter. Anskar had seen enough of the Tainted Cabal to know that they were ruthless, dismissive of human life. If she wasn't dead already, Gisela would be disposed of once Castellac had what he wanted.

But Anskar couldn't bring himself to abandon Gisela either. She was Lanuc's daughter, a sister in the Church of Menselas. The moment he heard about her abduction, he felt as though it were an attack on his family. It was an odd realization, given he'd been on the brink of turning his back on the Five and pursuing a different path.

Castellac was going to pay for this.

But first Anskar had another matter to attend to.

# THIRTY-SEVEN

A WARRIOR ENTERED THROUGH THE open church door—a young woman with a round shield, her sword held out before her.

"Anything?" a man called from outside.

"Nothing," she answered.

"Even so," the man said, joining her inside, "best to make sure."

The two made a cursory check of the interior, then passed through the door behind the five-faced bust of Menselas and into the sacristy.

Anskar's heart thudded in his chest as he watched, a silent shadow. When they emerged from the sacristy and headed back toward the main door, the woman frowned in Anskar's direction, and he thought she had seen him. But then she followed the man outside.

Anskar waited as long as he dared, which wasn't long.

Zek was in danger.

Once the noise from outside had died down, Anskar went into the sacristy and found a side door used by the priests. It was locked, but a measured surge of dusk-tide sorcery, contained by a sheath of the dawn, took care of that. He peered out into the street, looking both ways, then set off at a run for the dungeons.

There were three guards on the doors when he got there, and a group of six warriors led by Brother Kenaith were tramping toward the building from the direction of the great hall. The King hadn't wasted any time.

Anskar hesitated at the corner of the adjoining street, racking his brain for what he should do.

Brother Kenaith and his warriors were within twenty yards of the entrance to the dungeons, and the guards on the door were now standing stiffly to attention.

Dusk-tide. The intuition hit Anskar like a thunderclap. He'd seen how devastating dusk-tide sorcery could be, and under Zek's tutelage he had begun to develop precision and control.

He made some calculations and mentally prepared a cant, then reached inside the balanced mesh of his joined repositories and eked out more dusk than dawn.

Just as Brother Kenaith and his warriors came level with the alley, Anskar unleashed the cant along with a surge of tidal force. There was a blinding flash and a thunderous boom, and Brother Kenaith and his warriors ducked, then scattered. Black smoke roiled from the mouth of the alley, and the thatched roofs of several houses caught fire.

Amid cries of alarm and screams, Brother Kenaith barked commands above the din. Two of his warriors inched down the street, covering their mouths and noses against the fumes. The three guards on the dungeon door rushed over to join them, and as they did, Anskar ducked back into his street, took a right turn, and emerged by the side of the dungeons.

The windows were barred, but that didn't matter to Anskar as he poured himself into the shadows inside.

The transition through the dark was harder this time. He felt as though the shadows were tugging at him, wanting to rip him apart, as they had Braga. He was too distracted, he realized, by the consequences of storming out of the great hall, by Gisela's abduction, by the danger to Zek. He dropped to one knee and dry-heaved as the shadows inside the building released him.

He could still hear yells and screams from outside, and the stench of burning thatch came through the windows and under the front door. It wouldn't be long till the fires were brought under control, and then Brother Kenaith would come and Zek would be dead.

Lighting his way with a globe of dawn-tide radiance, Anskar proceeded down the winding stone stairs until he reached Zek's cell. He blew out the lock with another measured burst of sorcery.

Zek gasped and sat up.

"Come with me," Anskar said, already starting back toward the stairs.

As Zek followed, he asked, "What's happening?"

"The Tainted Cabal have taken Gisela, and we're going after her."

"We are?"

"Unless you'd prefer to wait until the King's men come to your cell and kill you?"

"Why would they do that?"

"I'll explain later," Anskar said. "For now, you'll just have to trust me."

They reached the ground floor, and Anskar doused his sorcerous light. He heard voices from outside, then the grate of a key in the lock. As the door started to open, he grabbed Zek by the arm and shadow-stepped both of them beyond the barred window and into the alley. This time, when the shadows relinquished their hold, Anskar collapsed into a pile of stinking refuse.

Zek crouched beside him, and Anskar felt the warm thrill of dawn-tide essence seeping beneath his skin, washing away his exhaustion. It could do nothing for the twisting of his guts, though, the hollowed-out feeling of using so much dark-tide.

"Thanks," he muttered.

"No, thank you," Zek said, glancing over his shoulder at the warriors entering the dungeons. "Why would the King do this?"

"Because the stakes are so high."

Anskar explained that the Tainted Cabal had stolen the memory crystal of Morudjin, which they hoped to use to accelerate the return of Nysrog to Wiraya.

"How much time do we have until the world is plunged into shadow?" Zek asked.

Anskar shrugged. "I imagine Castellac, or whoever took the crystal, has to take it north first, to wherever his superiors are lurking."

"Molas Drythe," Zek said. "My people's name for the ancient citadel in the Ymaltian Mountains."

"You know the way?"

"Just follow the Iron Road. But we'll need horses if we are to catch up with this Castellac. What I do not understand is what he hopes to achieve by kidnapping a healer."

"He's after me," Anskar said. "I am to be Gisela's ransom."

"Then don't go."

Anskar shook his head. If only it were that simple.

"What about the memory crystal?" Zek added.

"That's a problem for the King and his allies. He plans to lead an army north and scourge the Soreshi and the Tainted Cabal from his lands, and in so doing recapture the crystal."

"All the Soreshi?"

"All."

They lay low amid the rubbish until the yells from the street died down and the flames came under control. Then they made their way to the far end of the alley, past scurrying rats and a hissing cat.

"How will we get out of the city?" Zek asked.

"We'll think of something."

As he spoke, two men stepped across their path. Instinctively, Anskar brought his prismatic ward into existence around him. Beside him, he felt dusk-tide mingled with the dawn seething within Zek. The Soreshi's fist sparked as he held it up.

Then Anskar recognized the two men.

"Rindon! Nul! Why are you here?"

"Charming," Rindon said.

Nul merely shook his head.

"I've been meaning to tell you how much I like that ward of yours," Rindon added. "All the colors of the rainbow."

"You're not here to stop us?" Anskar asked.

Nul cocked his head to one side. "Stop you from what?"

"Getting out of the city."

Rindon shoved his fists into his hips and widened his eyes in mock surprise. "You plan to go after Gisela?"

"It's me the Tainted Cabal really want," Anskar explained, "not her."

"So you're going to exchange yourself for Lanuc's daughter?" Nul asked.

"If I have to."

"And if you don't?"

"Then I'll kill the bastards who took her. Kill them all."

Rindon grinned. "Spoken like a true servant of Menselas."

"What I mean is—"

"I know what you meant," Rindon said. "And I approve. We suspected as much but just wanted to be sure. And you," he said to Zek, "are the guide?"

"I am more than that," Zek said. "The Tainted Cabal have corrupted some among my people. They will pay for that."

"Better and better," Rindon said. Then to Nul, "Still think we should help them?"

"Come," Nul said, turning and leading the way back up the alley.

"How did you find us?" Anskar asked, lowering his ward as they followed.

"We're not completely blind to the emanations of dark-tide sorcery," Nul said.

"All the battles we've fought in," Rindon said, "all the quests we've been sent on by the Church of Menselas, we've picked up a thing or two."

"We've also spent considerable time in Wintotashum before," Nul said. "Back when the Order had a compound here."

"What happened to it?" Anskar asked.

"King Aelfyr didn't trust us. Or rather, he began to suspect the Order of Eternal Vigilance had designs on his lands."

"And did it?"

"It's a moot point now," Nul said. "Anyway, Rindon here once had to leave the city without being seen, and he came up with a rather ingenious plan."

"Though smelly," Rindon added.

"What do you mean?" Zek cast a nervous look at Anskar.
"You'll see."

Rindon and Nul led them away from the center of the commotion and into the less salubrious areas in the east of the city. Whenever they came to an intersection, one or the other of the heroes would check the way was clear. Once or twice they came across patrols, and while Anskar and Zek hid, Rindon chatted amiably with the warriors, pretending that he and Nul were part of the pursuit.

"They're being very thorough," Nul said. "The King must really want you for the coming battle. Either that, or he's worried what might happen if you fall into the Tainted Cabal's hands."

"He'll have my sorcery once Gisela is safe," Anskar said.

"I'll be sure to tell him that," Rindon said. "And Lanuc."

"Lanuc disapproves of my actions?" Anskar asked.

"On the contrary," Rindon said. "It was Lanuc who sent us to help you."

At length they came to a hub of hard-packed earth at the intersection of four roads. The hub was roughly circular and big enough to accommodate half dozen carts that were parked there. The stench of human waste was overpowering.

"Wintotashum's a very old city," Nul explained. "Built way back when they hadn't heard of sewers. Every night these carts collect the waste from the houses of the rich and from the streets in the poorer regions. Without them, the city would have disappeared beneath a mountain of dung centuries ago."

"Where do they take it all?" Zek asked.

"Huge pits away from the city. When the pits are full, they cover them with mounds of earth and dig more. Hence the range of hills northwest of the city."

"I used to think they were a natural feature," Rindon said.

"Until I offered to take a young lady into the hills for a picnic and she slapped me round the face."

One of the carts was hooked up to a pair of massive draft horses covered with flies. A man was checking their harnesses, while another was in the back of the cart, leveling the dung with a rake. Both men wore knee-length boots, muck-spattered aprons, and long leather gloves. Their mouths and noses were hidden beneath masks, and each had a filthy cap covering his hair.

While Rindon approached the two men, one hand over his mouth and nose, the other jangling a coin purse, Nul asked, "Do you know how to drive a cart?"

"I do," Zek said.

After a few words, the men stepped away from the cart and took off their aprons, hats, gloves and boots, beneath which they wore simple shirts and pants. They retrieved their regular boots from beneath the driver's bench before they headed toward a tavern, sharing out the coins from Rindon's purse.

"Lanuc is preparing to ride north within a matter of hours," Nul said. "And the King has agreed to mobilize the army and follow as soon as possible. The lords' warriors have been instructed to gather outside Veranoth, and will join them on the way."

"The King agreed to this?"

"He's not happy," Rindon said, "but without our knights, he knows the Thousand Lakes warriors don't have much of a chance against Soreshi sorcery. Without you, though, I doubt any of us will last long against the Tainted Cabal."

"I'll be there," Anskar said.

"But will it be enough?" Zek asked. "You are still discovering your abilities, Anskar. The Tainted Cabal have experience on their side."

"I can draw upon experience, if I have to," Anskar said, sounding far more confident than he felt. Even if he asked for Queen Talia's help, would she still give it?

Anskar and Zek put on the stinking clothes the two men had discarded. Rindon claimed they were unrecognizable with their hair tucked beneath the caps. And besides, he said, no one would brave the stench to get close enough to check.

Anskar climbed onto the driver's bench beside Zek, and the Soreshi took up the reins. Rindon and Nul waved as the wagon set off at a clatter through the streets.

The people they passed—even the patrols—gave them a wide berth. And when they reached the barred city gates, the guards lifted the locking beam and stepped aside, holding their noses, no questions asked.

# THIRTY-EIGHT

ZEK BROUGHT THE DUNG CART to a stop just inside the cover of trees bordering the fields where the army's destriers, light riding horses, and pack animals were pastured.

When a boy watching over the horses approached, Zek put him to sleep with a subtle application of dawn-dusk-tide, and Anskar dragged the boy behind a tree. He made sure the boy was still breathing and turned him on his side, then returned to the cart, where he and Zek stripped off the stinking clothes they had borrowed.

Nearby was a barn, where the warriors who'd entered the city had stowed their tack. Within minutes, Anskar and Zek had saddled two young coursers that looked well rested and fast, and hung four good-sized canteens from the saddles. At Anskar's suggestion, Zek borrowed his white cloak and wore it with the hood up.

They took a wide, looping course through the forest until they met up with the Iron Road, and then sped north to find Gisela.

When they passed a group of men-at-arms making their slow way to Wintotashum, no one challenged them. They were just two knights of the Order on their way north, probably to Veranoth, where the main army was assembling.

"We will greet the dusk-tide together in a few hours," Zek said. "And during the night…" He looked expectantly at Anskar.

"During the night, the dark-tide will seep beneath my skin while I sleep," Anskar acknowledged.

"Perhaps there is a way to fully welcome it?" Zek suggested. "You could ask your mother about that."

"I'm not speaking to her."

"What has she done this time?"

"Never you mind."

She wanted him to raise Hrothyr from the dead, that was what. Not something he wanted to share with Zek.

As evening approached, they walked the exhausted horses to a lake just shy of the road, where the animals could drink and Zek and Anskar could refill their canteens.

When the dusk-tide came, it was a distant gusting howl that gathered in strength as it neared them, then crashed over them like a tidal wave.

Zek threw his head back and screamed in ecstasy, reveling in the invisible storm's virulence. Anskar had always held back at the coming of the dusk, some part of him guilty at partaking in what the Church of Menselas forbade—at least officially. But Zek's wild abandonment was infectious, so Anskar let his guard down too. He screamed into the gray skies, shuddering at the forces blasting through him.

When the tide passed, he collapsed to his knees, overcome with laughter.

"What's so funny?" Zek said.

Anskar stopped abruptly as he sensed a shift in his braided repository. He sent his senses within. "The dawn-tide has replenished, not just the dusk," he said.

Zek gave him a knowing grin. "One of the benefits of a properly meshed repository."

"But it's not the same," Anskar said. "The dusk isn't as corrosive as when it had its own repository, and the dawn is less tranquil."

"They mitigate one another," Zek said. "But as you grow used to the braiding of your repository, even that will alter. The tides were never meant to be separated. They have a unified source, though its expression is altered by the position of the sun in the sky."

"What source?" Anskar asked. "Where do the tides come from?"

Zek glanced up at the sky and shrugged. "I have heard several theories."

"So, you don't know?"

"If I did, my power would be supreme. Perhaps I would rule the world."

"You're joking," Anskar said.

Zek clapped him on the shoulder.

"We should each have but one repository, attenuated to both the dawn and the dusk. The repositories your people have cultivated over the centuries—and augmented with crystal catalysts—are unnatural."

"But yours isn't?"

"We Soreshi never abandoned our sorcerous heritage. The other races of Wiraya did so at various times, and now, for the most part, their abilities lie latent."

"And the dark-tide?"

"As I told you before, it is not a talent we Soreshi are born to, and those who have cultivated it have not fared well. But the dark-tide is natural to the people of Niyas, yes?"

"I don't think so," Anskar said. "None of the Niyandrians I knew had the power."

"Except for your mother?"

Anskar nodded.

"And now you," Zek said. "I suppose that explains why the Tainted Cabal are so interested in you."

"But why? They have dark-tide abilities of their own, and demons to draw upon. What could I possibly add to that?"

Zek looked him in the eye. "I have little experience of matters pertaining to the dark-tide, Anskar, but let me tell you this. There is a yawning, churning void beneath your braided repository. A hunger that seems barely contained."

"You can see all this?"

"Dimly, as if it were a reflection in a broken mirror."

"And it disturbs you?"

"I am worried for you, my friend. Worried about what you may become."

They slept fitfully beneath the bloody crescent of Jagonath and the milky disk of Chandra. Anskar could feel the itch and ooze of the dark-tide on his skin, seeping through his pores, and his mind filled with images of the gaping pit of darkness at his core. He kept waking with a start as he felt himself falling into the black hole. Once he woke thrashing and screaming, convinced he was drowning in a sea of tar.

"The horses are rested enough," Zek said with a yawn. "We should get underway and see if we can catch this carriage before it reaches Molas Drythe."

"Agreed," Anskar said, "but first I need to eat. I'm starving."

"You brought supplies?" Zek asked.

Anskar had the feeling he was being mocked. "No."

"Then come with me, and I'll show you how we Soreshi like to fish and cook."

Zek crouched at the edge of a nearby lake and peered into the crystal-clear water. Anskar joined him, and Zek pointed to a large fish basking on the lake bed, partially hidden behind a shock of green reeds.

"It's a gar," Zek said. "Teeth like needles, and more venom than even the deadliest snake. But they are extremely tasty, and there is enough meat on that one for both of us."

"So, what do we do?" Anskar asked. "Wade out and grab it? Because if that's your plan, I'll stay here."

"Be attentive and learn," Zek said.

Anskar's senses prickled at a thrum of energy from the Soreshi's repository.

Zek jabbed his finger into the water, breaking the surface, and the thrum became a searing burst of intertwined dawn- and dusk-tide. There was a flash, the bubble and splash of water, and Anskar had to turn away to protect his eyes. When he looked again, the gar was floating on the surface.

Zek waded out to retrieve it, then held the gar before him in both hands and unleashed a measured wave of braided power. A rich, succulent smell immediately pervaded the air. The gar's skin grew crisp and brown, and steam plumed from its scales. Anskar's stomach growled in response.

"Ouch!" Zek said, dropping the fish onto the ground. "It has been a while since I did this."

Once the fish had cooled a little, Zek broke off pieces of flesh and passed some to Anskar. It was naturally salty with a slight buttery taste.

"Good," Anskar said, reaching for another piece.

"You should see me zap squirrels out of the treetops and roast them in their skins," Zek said. "And before you go getting any ideas, yes, you could do the same thing to a warrior in armor, but it takes a while."

"Because of the mitigating effect of the dawn on the dusk?" Anskar guessed.

Zek nodded. "You sacrifice destructive power for balance and control. Of course, not all of my people agree with the measured approach. There are many who deliberately separate the tides. They are the ones who band together outside our cities, testing their powers and breaking our taboos."

"You're talking about the Soreshi who are allied with the Tainted Cabal?"

"That is my theory," Zek said.

"Then, by helping me to braid my repositories, haven't you handicapped me against them?"

"Perhaps. But I rather think I've given you the control to stay the course. In an out-and-out sorcerous battle with the Soreshi, you would have been goaded into overreaching and using all your dusk-tide power in one catastrophic eruption, which probably would have harmed you and your allies as much as it did them. And they are used to such virulence. Unless you take them by surprise, as you did at Veranoth, they will have wards against such a storm. But now that your repositories are braided, although your single attacks will not be as devastating, you'll have more control over them, and greater endurance. Besides, you may have other weapons."

"The dark-tide."

"And what else?" Zek prompted.

"The Warrior's Fire?"

"That was not the answer I was looking for. I was thinking of other abilities that may have passed to you from your mother. The way I understand the history, Queen Talia surpassed all other Niyandrians in her sorcery."

"No doubt why they called her the Necromancer Queen," Anskar said.

"And what power do necromancers draw upon?"

Anskar shrugged. He was thinking about the warrior's spirit his mother had helped him to summon from the realm of the dead. He was thinking about Naul's corpse warning him when agents of Carred Selenas went after Sareya at Branil's Burg.

"There is something other than the three tides known to us," Zek said. "Something that comes from the world's core, I imagine, rather than up there beyond the skies."

"Are you theorizing again?" Anskar asked.

"Always."

They hit the road a few hours before dawn, only stopping to welcome the tide. Once more, all the interwoven strands of Anskar's repository throbbed as he took in the essence, until finally he was brimming with both the dawn- and the dusk-tide.

Just after midmorning, they saw the carriage a quarter of a mile ahead of them on the Iron Road. It was lacquered black, with red trim around the shuttered windows, and wheels that glinted silver. The carriage seemed to glide over the surface of the road, pulled by a team of six black horses.

"The way it moves, it's unnatural," Zek said as they kicked their steeds into a gallop.

"I just hope Gisela's inside," Anskar said, "and they've not done—"

Before he could finish, the carriage blurred in his vision, then was no more than a misty haze ahead of them.

"Dark-tide sorcery," he said.

Zek glanced at him. "They must have seen us."

Anskar urged his horse to greater speed, but no matter how fast he and Zek rode, the smudge of the carriage remained the same distance in front of them.

"More dark-tide sorcery?" Zek said. "Perhaps you could do the same for us?"

"I wish." Anskar was half-tempted to ask his mother for help—but only half.

His horse was tiring, and he let it slow to a canter.

Zek cursed and slowed his courser too. "So, what do we do?" he asked. "At this pace, they'll easily reach Molas Drythe ahead of us."

Anskar shrugged. "We keep following."

They kept up a good pace for several hours, only stopping once to rest and water the horses at a partially frozen lake. A light snow started to fall, though most of the flakes failed to settle on the road. When they resumed their pursuit, the hazy outline of the carriage was still there ahead of them, exactly the same distance away.

"It's as if they're goading us," Zek said.

An hour before dusk, they came upon a camp of warriors on their way north to Veranoth. Anskar advised Zek to keep silent as he spoke with the group. The Soreshi remained hidden beneath the hood of Anskar's white cloak, and though the warriors gave him stern looks, Anskar assumed it was on account of the usual tension between the Thousand Lakers and the Order of Eternal Vigilance.

The warriors were from the lands of a Lord Fulk, a day's march to the south. They treated Anskar warily on account of the reddish tinge to his skin and his tawny Niyandrian eyes, but no one seemed to doubt the story he told: that he and Zek had been sent north with messages for the garrison King Aelfyr had left at Veranoth. None of the warriors had seen the black carriage as it passed, not even the blur it had become.

"It must be fully invisible to those who lack sorcerous senses," Zek suggested as he and Anskar rode on.

The dusk-tide slammed into them not long after they had left the camp, its gusts scouring and invigorating. Zek hooted with joy and kicked his horse back into a gallop, only slowing once the tide had passed.

They discussed riding through the night, but the horses were exhausted. Instead they dismounted and made camp in the lee of a cluster of hills surrounding a lake. The firewood they gathered was damp from the snow, and Zek demonstrated how to dry the wood, then start a steady blaze using the conjoined essence of his repository.

They ate fish again, and soon after, Zek was snoring softly beneath the cloak Anskar had lent him, curled up beside the fire.

Anskar couldn't sleep. Whispers invaded his skull in a language he didn't know.

Little by little, he came to realize that the hills that sheltered them were in truth burial mounds, and the whispered voices he heard were those of the dead. It was a reminder that, thousands of years ago, before savage raiders had come from beyond the

Trackless Ocean to claim the Thousand Lakes as their own, a different race had lived here, a people lost to history.

When they set off once more the next morning, the black carriage was still there ahead of them, no longer hazy now.

Anskar couldn't understand why Castellac wasn't racing to get to Molas Drythe before he and Zek caught up with him.

It was Zek who provided the answer. "He's making sure he doesn't lose or discourage us. He wants to be certain you'll follow him all the way to the citadel."

Anskar's stomach knotted. He'd known all along that Castellac wanted an exchange—him for Gisela—but secretly he'd hoped to catch up with the carriage on the road, force a fight, and somehow win.

As they followed, he ran over and over his options. None of them were good. Certainly he couldn't countenance abandoning his attempt to rescue Gisela: he'd never again be able to look Lanuc in the eye. And, if he were ever permitted to return to Branil's Burg, what would Vihtor think?

Toward the day's end, as they came in sight of the town of Veranoth, the carriage once more blurred into a hazy smudge, and none of the warriors atop the palisade paid any heed to it. They must have recognized Anskar, though, for when he signaled to them, the gates were opened.

New tree trunks, freshly stripped of branches and bark, had already been added to the palisade, and hastily built fortifications had been erected inside the gates—barricades of wood or piled stone that funneled attackers into a killing ground before the first of the buildings.

A glance up showed Anskar that the fighting platforms around the top of the palisade had been reinforced and even widened in places. All were heavily manned.

Hundreds of warriors had already arrived, and the houses, taverns, and barracks were overfull. Tents had been pitched in the shade of the palisade all around the town. Veranoth had been brought back to life after the slaughter and turned into a fortress town.

After relaying to the garrison's commander news of what had happened in Wintotashum, Anskar and Zek spent the night in a stinking goat shelter—the only accommodation left. They had to drive the big billy away with shouts and a sharp crack to its horns with the flat of Anskar's sheathed sword.

In the morning, they greeted the dawn-tide together, bought some bread and cheese from a stall in the main street, and then were back on the Iron Road, riding north.

Hours later, they no longer saw the carriage ahead of them. They were in enemy territory now, and several times passed the fire-blackened husks of towns that had fallen to the Soreshi rebels and the Tainted Cabal.

Occasionally, Zek would point out Soreshi warriors watching them from high up on the hills that flanked the Iron Road, but none challenged them. It would have been a different matter, Anskar suspected, if he and Zek had tried to ride back south.

They rested beside Zek's sorcerous fire that night, and at the close of the following day, with the looming barrier of the Ymaltian Mountains red-lit and hazy in the glow of the sinking sun, they could see their destination a couple of hours' ride ahead of them.

Zek pointed it out, but to Anskar it looked like nothing more than a natural outcrop of rock. As they drew closer, though, he could make out the orderly slits of embrasures, saw-toothed crenellations, and monstrous buttresses, between which gaped an arch of blackness.

Molas Drythe.

As they rode closer still, Anskar saw that the citadel's stone gate was raised, and there were three figures waiting in the entrance to the gatehouse: Castellac, the pale-skinned man in black plate armor from Veranoth, and a woman Anskar had hoped never to see again.

# THIRTY-NINE

"YOU CAME," THE ABBESS SAID.

She looked older than when Anskar had met her at the Abbey of the Hooded One. Her skin was paper thin and pulled taut over her skull, her hands ridged with blue veins.

"I told you he would," Castellac said. He stood with stooped shoulders, on one side of a pale-skinned man in lacquered black plate armor—the man Anskar had spotted during the battle at Veranoth. Castellac was almost unrecognizable: a hunched, twisted thing that barely resembled a man, his hands curled into claws. The skin of his face was like melted wax, and his eyes were bloodshot and bulging from their sockets. His lips were crusted lines that did nothing to hide rotting gums and yellow teeth.

The pale man looked unimpressed. "You really think we need him?"

"Of course we need him, Uspeth," the Abbess said. "Unless you want to lead the summoning yourself, and make the exact same mistakes as that fool Morudjin."

Anskar dismounted and passed his horse's reins to Zek, who remained in the saddle.

"Your companion can leave," the pale man—Uspeth—said, which earned him a glare of contempt from the Abbess.

"Where is the healer?" Anskar hated the quaver in his voice. He addressed Castellac: "In your letter, you promised to exchange her for me."

"A lie," Castellac said. "A lie, a lie, a lie."

"What happened to him?" Anskar asked the Abbess. But he found he couldn't meet her gaze without remembering the things he had done with her.

"He overreached," Uspeth said.

"Trying to impress us, no doubt," the Abbess put in.

"I succeeded!" Castellac gibbered. "I summoned a demon lord."

"A minor one," the Abbess said. "If it's who I think it was, not really a lord at all, just an inflated egoist of the Thirty-Seventh Order."

"But I still did it! She did my bidding and took the crystal from the Scriptorium. There was blood! Lots of blood! You should have been there!" he told Anskar. "If you had only seen it!"

"I would have fled from it," Anskar said coldly. "Like I did from the other demon you summoned. The demon that killed my friend." He turned to Zek and accepted his horse's reins back. "If you won't release Gisela, my journey here has been wasted."

As Anskar spoke, he felt a surge of dark-tide energy from Castellac. It was met by the boil of dusk-tide from Zek.

The Abbess and Uspeth exchanged looks.

"You will honor your word, Castellac," Uspeth said.

"But—"

"Uspeth is your commander!" the Abbess snapped. "You will obey him."

Castellac cringed and whimpered.

"Forgive Castellac's unseemly behavior," Uspeth said to Anskar. "Contact with this phony demon lord has corroded his senses. He sought to return here in triumph, but he's lucky the demon allowed him to leave Wintotashum alive."

"Idiot," the Abbess said. She hawked up phlegm and spat it at Anskar's feet.

"Castellac did, however, retrieve that from Wintotashum which we have long labored to find."

"I did!"

"The memory crystal of Morudjin," Anskar said.

"And now Castellac has played his part," the Abbess said. "The Tainted Cabal has no further need of him."

"What?" Castellac said. "But that's not fair!"

Anskar stiffened at the surge of dark-tide from the Abbess. Castellac started to shadow-step, but the shadows he had turned to grew suddenly glistening and hard, like black ice.

Castellac whimpered. Dark tendrils sprouted from the rock at his feet and writhed up his legs. Anskar closed his eyes, but Castellac's screams echoed around his skull, until they suddenly stopped. When Anskar opened his eyes, all that remained of Castellac was a dark stain on the floor.

"He wanted to usurp my command," Uspeth said softly.

"They all do, my son," the Abbess said. "But now you have me by your side."

Son? Uspeth was her son?

"If you have the crystal, why do you need me?" Anskar asked.

"You are one of us," the Abbess said. "Why would we not

desire your presence at this most auspicious moment?"

"I'm not one of you." Anskar prepared to mount his horse.

"I say you are," the Abbess said. "We became one flesh, or have you forgotten?"

Uspeth visibly winced at that.

"What you took from me was not given willingly," Anskar said, and climbed into the saddle.

"Morudjin made mistakes with his summoning of Nysrog," Uspeth said quickly. "That much my mother has determined. Morudjin's memories in the crystal show how the power of the summoning shattered the demon lord's mind. Nysrog became a raving monster and turned on Morudjin and all who assisted him. At the instant of his death at Nysrog's hands, Morudjin realized that the dark-tide alone could not bind a demon of such power, wisdom, and intellect.

"For centuries, the Tainted Cabal have labored under the impression that we needed more and more dark-tide power, but now we understand that it was never a matter of strength in numbers. A different kind of sorcery is needed to bind a demon lord like Nysrog, but Morudjin's soul was incinerated before he could work out what. My mother believes you are the answer, Anskar.

"When we coupled, I felt something unfamiliar squirming within your marrow," the Abbess said.

Anskar felt blood rush to his face, and his stomach twisted. Zek gave him a sidelong look of revulsion.

"At first I didn't know what it was," the Abbess said. "But my agents among the Order of Eternal Vigilance have dug up clues for me.

"Your mother, Queen Talia of Niyas, was an exceptional sorceress. Unsurpassed. She was in advance of virtually every sorcerer who ever walked the surface of Wiraya, and do you know why? Because she studied the works of Giyas, Mabblethwyck, Honariuc, and Tain—the four most revered necromancers of the Niyandrians, ancient warlocks whose names are cursed by every other culture. More than studied: she learned from their own writings how to summon their shades. Not Tain's, I understand, for his spirit was not in the realm of the dead, and his body had long-since vanished from the world.

"But the other three answered her summons willingly. She raised their corpses from their tombs and made them teach her everything they had known in life and all they had learned after death. Thousands of years of sorcerous lore, all crammed into her clever little head. Can you imagine? Such a powerful woman, Anskar. I felt her presence within you back at the abbey. She speaks with you, doesn't she?"

"Let's just go," Zek said, but Anskar doubted they would be given the choice.

As if on cue, he saw Soreshi warriors creeping toward them out of the hills.

"Or maybe not," Zek said.

"What makes you think Queen Talia would aid in your summons of Nysrog?" Anskar asked.

"Because she seeks a return to power," the Abbess said. "It isn't for nothing that she was called the Necromancer Queen, and on Niyas there are still cultists who work for her return."

"They are fanatics and fools," Anskar said.

"Probably, but you are no fool, Anskar DeVantte. I sensed the power latent within you—more power than you can imagine. You are your mother's tool. Does she visit you from time to time to nudge you in the right direction? Or does she come for more... pleasurable reasons?"

Again Uspeth winced.

Anskar said nothing.

"I thought as much," the Abbess said, and turned to her son. "Didn't I say that's what she would do?"

"You did, Mother."

"Castellac promised to exchange Gisela for me," Anskar said. "Either you honor that promise, or lose this great power you say I have when I turn around and ride away."

"You mean to fight your way past thirty blood-born sorcerers?" the Abbess said, indicating the Soreshi now fanning out behind Anskar and Zek. "That will make an interesting spectacle."

"Not just him," Zek said. "Even among the Soreshi, my abilities are considered exceptional."

"Let's hope you are right," the Abbess said. "Else you shall both die."

"No, Mother," Uspeth said. "They will not. This is too important. The Tainted Cabal have worked far too long and sacrificed too much in order to bring about a new age of Nysrog; but now, in your wisdom, Mother, you have discovered another way. With Anskar's help—with Queen Talia's—we can bring Nysrog through the veil intact, restore his sanity, and bind him. This time, there will be no crazed destruction. This time, we'll impose our law across the whole world, and the Tainted Cabal will be at the heart of it. And who do you think will rule the Cabal, Mother?" He finished on a note of triumph.

She smiled, and he dipped his head in a slight bow.

"You're mad," Anskar said, wheeling his horse away. "Totally insane."

"Bring the healer!" Uspeth shouted to someone within the citadel.

Anskar turned his horse back to face the gatehouse.

"We will do as you ask," Uspeth continued. "But know this: my mother and I did nothing to the woman. Any harm committed was Castellac's."

"All that way in the carriage, just the two of them, alone," the Abbess said. "Well, save for the lesser demons Castellac summoned so he could watch them sate their appetites."

Two black-armored Cabalists emerged from the rear of the gatehouse with Gisela between them. Her once-white healer's robe was a torn, stained, stinking mess that barely covered her lithe frame. Her fair hair was unbound and crusted with filth. Bleeding cuts crisscrossed her face, one or two very close to her eyes, which were wide with shock and horror.

As she limped toward the group, Anskar heard her murmuring. No, he realized, she was singing under her breath, the sort of melody a mother might sing a child to sleep with.

When her eyes alighted on Anskar, Gisela gasped, and her song died on her lips. She made an effort to stand up straight and pull her shoulders back in what seemed to Anskar like a parody of her usual dignity. One hand tried to smooth the creases in her robe; the other ran through the tousled mess of her hair.

"I'm sorry, Anskar, I will hear your confession now," she said as tears squeezed from her eyes and ran down her cheeks. "Tell me everything, and the Five will forgive you." A crazed look came over her eyes. "Confess," she said, and now she was sobbing. "Confess."

Anger surged within Anskar. He dismounted, handed the reins to Zek, and took a faltering step toward Lanuc's ruined daughter.

She held up a shaking hand.

"Menselas loves you, Anskar. Unburden your soul. I promise I'll listen without judging. Then I will bestow the god's forgiveness on you. And he will forgive me."

The desperate hope in her voice was a knife through Anskar's heart. He glared at Uspeth, then the Abbess.

"This was not our doing," Uspeth repeated. "Castellac was unhinged by his summoning of a higher order demon. You cannot blame—"

He stopped as Gisela jerked violently and collapsed to her knees. The two guards pulled her to her feet again.

"Will you release her?" Anskar asked, glancing over his shoulder at Zek still mounted on his horse, sorcery boiling within him, begging to be discharged.

The Abbess was watching Zek too, as if she felt the threat he posed and was working out whether or not to risk facing it.

Behind Anskar and Zek, the thirty Soreshi blocked the road south, and every one of them was bristling with sorcerous power. They also held short yew bows, arrows already strung. One nod from Uspeth or the Abbess, Anskar suspected, and it would all be over.

He felt the urge to call upon his mother's help, but no sooner had he realized the thought than the Abbess grinned and wagged a finger at him. Tongues of black flame danced on her fingertip—a tiny manifestation of the dark-tide that thrashed and heaved within the old woman. Anskar knew he had no answer for such power. Not yet. Perhaps he never would.

"Will you release her?" he asked Uspeth.

"Go," Uspeth said, pointing Gisela toward Zek and the horses. "It is you we want, Anskar. Isn't that so, Mother? Just Anskar."

The Abbess's eyes narrowed at Gisela. "She is a priest of the Five," the old woman said, as if it were the bitterest curse she could imagine.

"And she will face the same fate as all other priests of Menselas,"

Uspeth said, "once Nysrog is among us."

The Abbess nodded, but continued to stare like a hungry wolf at Gisela.

Anskar took Gisela's hand. She flinched but didn't pull away as he led her to his horse and assisted her into the saddle.

"Go. Ride back to your father," he told her.

Tears streaked her cheeks. "I don't hate him," she said. "You know that, don't you?"

"Of course I know that. And Lanuc knows that too. You're his daughter. Nothing will ever change that."

"Nothing?" Gisela asked, touching her fingertips to her ruined robe. "Are you sure?"

Anskar swallowed. He glanced at Zek. The Soreshi took hold of the bridle of Gisela's horse and turned it to face the Iron Road.

At a gesture from Uspeth, the thirty Soreshi released the tension on their bowstrings and stepped aside.

Anskar watched Zek and Gisela ride away, overcome with a mounting despair. He had done the right thing, he told himself, though a niggling voice at the back of his mind said he was a fool.

For all the good it would do, he uttered a silent prayer to Menselas.

He started at a touch on his shoulder and looked in disgust at the Abbess's wrinkled hand that rested there.

"I knew you would come back to us," she said. "I know you, Anskar DeVantte, inside and out. Probably better than you know yourself."

Anskar wanted to push her away, wanted to curse her with every profanity he could muster. But all defiance had seeped from him with Gisela's and Zek's departure.

# FORTY

USPETH GAVE THE ORDER, AND the massive stone gate closed behind them with an echoing thud that seemed to resonate forever.

Anskar began to unbuckle his sword belt.

"What are you doing?" Uspeth said. "Keep it. You're not our prisoner. You're one of us now."

"You have always been one of us, Anskar," the Abbess said, running a curling fingernail down his cheek. She was so close he could smell her sour breath. "At least since you came to stay at the Hooded One's abbey, but I suspect long before."

Uspeth gave his mother a curious look, but either she didn't see, or pretended not to.

The two black-armored guards moved to Anskar's rear, but Uspeth waved them away. "You won't be needed," he told them. "I'm sure Anskar is a man of his word."

Anskar tried to keep his expression neutral. He'd lost count of the number of times he'd lied or broken promises. Too many. But he didn't want Uspeth to know that. Something told him it would be a tactical mistake.

"You accept, don't you, Anskar, the fairness of the exchange?" the Abbess said.

"There's nothing fair about kidnapping Gisela, nor the things that were done to her."

"We could have killed her…"

"And I could have remained in Wintotashum."

"But you chose to come," Uspeth said. "Why?"

"He missed me," the Abbess said. "Why else do you think? Now, Uspeth, my legs are too old for lengthy walks. Bring him to my chamber. Answer any questions he might have on the way. There are to be no secrets between us. No one leaves the Tainted Cabal, Anskar. The only course for you now is up… or down."

With that, she melted into the shadows.

"How did she do that?" Anskar asked. "She should have reemerged from another visible shadow."

"Mother does not need to see the shadows at the end of her journey," Uspeth said. "Her 'other' senses scout ahead and find them… within a limited range, of course."

"And you can do that as well?"

"Even if I can, where's the fun taking the highway of shadows? Then we'd have no time alone to talk."

"I'm all right with not talking," Anskar said.

Uspeth smiled. "It is through conversation with one another that we learn, Anskar. Strengths, weaknesses, allegiances. I'll let you into a secret: the Tainted Cabal is not at all like the Order of Eternal Vigilance. We are not all of one mind, doing the bidding of one god—even a five-faced god like yours."

"Perhaps you don't know the Order as well as you think you

do," Anskar said. "But you Cabalists: I thought you all wanted the same thing."

"We do, but it isn't necessarily what you think."

"The return of Nysrog."

"Power."

"Over what?"

"Anything. Everything. Only the strong survive."

"So you're frightened of dying?"

Uspeth's smile grew wider. It was hard to tell if he was masking what he really felt. "Did I say that? The Cabal is obsessed with order, Anskar. Everything in its place."

"And Nysrog?"

"Will impose that order."

"What then?"

"Then he will have served his purpose. But let us back up a little. Why did you come? I assume my mother was not being entirely serious. You didn't come to get your dick wet."

Anskar couldn't disguise his revulsion at the thought. To his surprise, Uspeth placed a hand on his shoulder.

"I understand how you feel. Mother told me what happened at the abbey. I… She… It doesn't matter. Come."

Uspeth started off along the corridor, and Anskar followed.

"You asked why I came here. Because of Castellac's letter. He said he would exchange Gisela for me."

"How noble of you. Menselas will be pleased."

Uspeth led him along broad corridors made from layers of different shades of rock stacked on top of each other with no sign of any join. The lighter layers closest to the ceiling sparkled with mineral deposits, whereas the darker ones closest to the floor glinted with gold and silver. There were no bricks or plaster, just these apparently natural rock formations that had somehow been rendered smooth and uniform. They created the impression that the citadel had grown out of the mountain.

They passed many doors, all of them stone, some embossed with knot-work images of thorns and vines, eagles, wolves, and bears. A solitary guard was stationed outside each door, cloaked and hooded in black, a broadsword scabbarded at the hip—every one a sorcerer. Their repositories were a murky mix of at least the dawn- and dusk-tides, often the dark too, and they were tangled like an overgrowth of briars, not neat like Anskar's now was. He felt something similar within Uspeth, too. So, the Cabal's obsession with order didn't extend to their sorcery. Perhaps they weren't as gifted as they thought.

"The citadel was once called Molas Drythe," Uspeth said. "Though the first thing we did upon arrival was change the name. We call it Nax-ur-Vadim, roughly translated as—"

"Fortress of Shadows," Anskar finished for him. "I know."

"You speak Nazgrese? Mother didn't do you justice."

Anskar had heard the translation from Brother Yonas in the great hall at Wintotashum, but he saw no reason to reveal that.

"There's a legend of a battle on this site," Uspeth continued. "The Soreshi were massacred, but eventually won the war with a cataclysmic use of sorcery. Allegedly it was a sorcery they had previously considered forbidden and would come to outlaw again. Indeed, it is my belief they have forgotten it.

"After their victory, the Soreshi built, grew, fashioned, summoned—I have no idea which—Molas Drythe as both a monument and a ward against any future attacks on their lands."

"Did it work?" Anskar asked.

"There was a second battle, and this time the invaders were cut down in the thousands as they tried in vain to storm the citadel's walls. Their mass graves lie above those of the Soreshi slaughtered in the first battle. The invaders never returned, and so, after many centuries, the Soreshi ceased garrisoning the citadel. Little by little, it was abandoned, forgotten, only of lingering interest to historians and poets."

"Why didn't the invaders return?" Anskar asked. "Couldn't they have besieged the citadel?"

"Perhaps," Uspeth said, "but I rather think they had better things to do. After the battle, they headed south to lick their wounds, and ended up founding towns and villages and even occupying the ruined cities of the old folk who once inhabited the mainland. They became the people of the Thousand Lakes."

"Who you now make war on," Anskar said.

"They had something we wanted, but now that we have it, there's no more need for war."

"King Aelfyr doesn't see it that way."

"No, I don't suppose he does. So, tell me, Anskar, does Aelfyr have siege engines capable of storming a citadel built into a mountain?"

Anskar said nothing.

Uspeth spread his hands, a smug smile on his pallid face. "In any case, I doubt he can match the sorcery of our allies… or our own acolytes."

"The Order of Eternal Vigilance can," Anskar said.

"I'm not convinced, and I don't believe you are. It will take more than silver ward spheres to turn the tide of any sorcerous battle that might ensue."

"Which is why…" Anskar started, then petered out.

"Why they have you?" Uspeth said. "I know. And now they don't."

"I won't fight my own Order."

"Nor will you need to. But tell me this, Anskar: What was it like growing up among the hounds of Menselas, knowing you were the heir of the Necromancer Queen?"

"I didn't know who my mother was."

"Really? When did you find out? Did they break it to you gently?"

"I worked it out for myself, over time. How about you?"

"Me?"

"What's it like being the child of the Abbess?"

Uspeth stopped walking. He gnawed the knuckle of his thumb as he considered his reply. "Would you be convinced if I said it was an honor?"

Anskar held his gaze until at last Uspeth said, "It is not easy."

"And your father?"

"Ah, in this we are alike. What kind of man, I wonder, would fuck the Necromancer Queen? And yes, I know you might ask the same thing about my mother, but I guess you already know the answer to that question."

"As, I suspect, do you."

Uspeth's cheek twitched, and his fingers clenched into a fist. His chest expanded as he drew in a deep breath. He smiled as he let it out.

"I can see you're going to fit in well here. I shall have to watch my back."

"You don't know your father?" Anskar asked.

"To be honest, I'm not sure I want to."

As they walked, Anskar couldn't help thinking about Uspeth's yellow eyes and the unnatural paleness of his skin. At first he'd taken both as indications of sickness, but now he wasn't so sure.

Uspeth led him deeper into the citadel, along corridors without end, past doorways that opened onto halls and chambers. There were no windows save for the embrasures Anskar had seen from the outside, yet there was always enough light to see by—a pearly radiance that seemed to come from the mineral deposits in the walls, supplemented here and there by glowing globes suspended from chains set into the concave ceilings.

They passed Soreshi warriors in the corridors and still more barracked in some of the halls, where animal pelts had been thrown on the floor as beds. It was impossible to gauge how many Soreshi there were within Nax-ur-Vadim, but Anskar guessed he had thus far seen close to three hundred. Menselas only knew how many more there were in the mountains and in the occupied northern towns of the Thousand Lakes.

He saw far fewer Tainted Cabalists. Some guarded the doors of chambers not occupied by the Soreshi, and others were gathered in halls of their own, eating together, drinking, and in a few instances openly copulating—man on man, woman on woman, woman on man. The unabashed lust reminded Anskar of the Abbey of the Hooded One, and made him so nauseous he had to breathe deeply and swallow sour spit.

Uspeth brought them to a vast hall, perfectly square, with arched entrances on each of its four sides. Its high ceiling was reinforced with struts of cut stone that resembled ribs.

Dark-robed Cabalists were painting symbols on the floor with something brown and foul-smelling. Others were replacing rushlights in their iron holders or rehearsing chants in groups of three or four or stoking the coals of eight braziers set up around the perimeter of a circle formed from fists of quartz. Two robed men and a woman were polishing broad strips of brass riveted to the floor within the circle of quartz. The strips were arranged in a massive triangle.

There were upwards of sixty Cabalists in the hall and none of them novices, judging by the murky essence coming off their repositories.

"Come," Uspeth said, leading the way through a door that had been concealed as part of the wall.

The Abbess awaited them inside, beside a circular stone table. There was a casket of blackwood atop the table, intricately carved with swirling designs, which upon closer inspection proved to be a cursive form of Skanuric that Anskar had never before seen.

The Abbess waved her hand, and the surface of the table rippled with purplish flames for an instant.

"A ward?" Anskar asked.

"You can never be too careful," the Abbess replied.

She opened the lid of the blackwood casket and removed a box formed from riveted plates of orichalcum, each inscribed with passages of Skanuric script. The lid was held shut by half a dozen intricately wrought clasps of the same orange-tinged metal, and the Abbess released them one at a time. When she had finished, a hiss sounded from within the box, and inky vapors trickled from beneath the lid.

The Abbess prised the lid off with a dirty fingernail to reveal a second lid, this one comprised of orichalcum petals around a pinprick center. The Abbess whispered a cant, and Anskar detected the merest discharge of pure dawn-tide essence, though he still couldn't sense the Abbess's repositories.

The petals of the second lid snapped open, and the Abbess reached inside the box and took out a faceted crystal that sat snugly in the palm of her hand. Filaments of light flashed within the crystal, and as she raised it to show Anskar, he saw wisps of shadow intertwining at its core.

"Take it," the Abbess said, dropping the crystal into Anskar's hand. "Hold it tight, shut your eyes, and let Morudjin's memories speak to you."

Anskar glanced at Uspeth, who nodded.

Heat suffused the skin of Anskar's palm as the crystal began to glow, brightening to a blinding radiance.

Anskar closed his eyes. At first he felt nothing save the burgeoning heat, but then the light penetrated his eyelids and flooded his inner vision with its brilliance.

He lost track of his physical senses and soared free, his spirit rising and expanding until it filled the whole cosmos.

And then, just as quickly, it plummeted.

Anskar gasped as the ground came up to meet him. In his mind's eye, he threw out his hands in an attempt to protect himself, then jolted upright with the disorientation of having been suddenly awakened from a deep sleep.

He was in a dark space—somewhere below ground? The air was dank, and through the gloom he heard the steady drip of water. His heart thudded with anticipation—of what, he didn't know.

He soared again, this time upward, until he found himself watching from an impossibly high vantage point as bat-winged horrors swarmed through purplish skies. On the ground far below there was slaughter and defilement as Nysrog raged and roared through a valley flowing with blood. Corpses littered the ground for miles in every direction, and spiny-backed demons ran among the grotesquely twisted bodies.

Anskar felt responsible, as if he had unleashed this horror upon Wiraya. He had fought fire with fire, and fire had defeated him. A lifelong pursuit of the dark-tide hadn't been enough. Rather, it had been the bait that had snared him. And with that recognition, Anskar knew that he was living the memories of Morudjin Hailoth, priest of the Elder.

Morudjin the idiot, he chastised himself. Morudjin the

hoodwinked, the blind. For the demon lord had played him.

Yet… there was a different cadence to Nysrog's roars now. They had turned into something garbled and shrill.

The scream of the insane.

Anskar's eyes snapped open and the scream was his own, a piercing howl that tore around the chamber he once more stood within.

Shaking, he looked at the crystal in his palm. It was no longer burning; its interior had grown dull and inert. He handed it back to the Abbess.

"So," she said as she returned the crystal to its orichalcum box, then placed it within the blackwood casket, "you have witnessed firsthand the error Morudjin made."

"He tried to coerce the demon lord with the dark-tide," Anskar said.

Uspeth breathed a sigh of relief. "His mind has not been shattered by what he witnessed."

"That doesn't surprise me," the Abbess said. "I told you he was strong. Morudjin assumed that, with the right amount of dark-tide essence, he could bind and command Nysrog. But the truth was, he only strengthened the demon."

"And it was too much," Anskar said. "The influx of dark-tide, the summoning and binding—Morudjin was defeated. But Nysrog…"

"The demon lord's mind was shattered into a thousand fragments," the Abbess said. "He is more brute beast now than supreme intellect, but he remains, for us, the embodiment of law."

"And we are sworn to bring Nysrog back," Uspeth added. "No

matter what.”

“Even if it means the harrowing of Wiraya?” Anskar asked. “Even if it means your own deaths?”

“Even if,” Uspeth confirmed.

“But then the Five sent you to us,” the Abbess said.

“The Five! Now you’re mocking me.”

Her face softened. She almost looked sincere. “Menselas is a god of law and order, Anskar, but there are those in positions of power within his Church, and within the Order of Eternal Vigilance, who break his laws and, by their actions, plunge the world back into chaos. You know this is true.”

“Within the Order, there is…” Anskar paused to find the right words. “Imperfection. Corruption.”

“And you would root it out?” Uspeth said.

“I would, but…”

“It is not by accident that I was placed within the Abbey of the Hooded One,” the Abbess said. “My vocation was to seek dark knowledge.”

“And it led to your fall,” Anskar said. “To the abominations you committed. To the Tainted Cabal.”

“Oh, Anskar.” The Abbess gave a weary shake of her head. “You were raised by the Order of Eternal Vigilance. Their truths became your truths, but so did their mistruths. How do you know who is wrong and who is right? No doubt you’ve been told that the taint of evil afflicts our cabal. But is it not equally possibly that the taint could be good? That it might be the first step toward the restoration of order to Wiraya, a new and golden dawn?”

“But I saw what you got up to at the abbey,” Anskar protested.

“A parody of what your own Grand Master gets up to behind closed doors,” the Abbess said. “And besides, what you’ve been taught about basic lusts and drives isn’t altogether truthful, is it?

You yourself have felt the conflict between desire and duty. You know how pleasurable it feels to indulge our natural instincts. I know you do." She smiled, and Anskar looked away. "Such desires are not wrong, Anskar. Only the way you've been taught to think about them makes them wrong. Why would Menselas give us these drives and desires if he wanted us to suppress them? Wouldn't that make him a callous god? Sadistic?"

"You are brave to strive for such a lofty ideal, Anskar," Uspeth said. "But how do you know it's the right ideal? I too once believed in purity, in honor and righteousness. And I was not wrong to believe. I was only wrong about what each of those things means. You know this too, in your heart of hearts."

Old conflicts and new clashed within Anskar's mind, and though he kept telling himself he was being beguiled by evil, he couldn't deny the truth, at least in part, of what he was hearing. He had never felt right within the Order, never felt truly at peace, and perhaps this was the reason why.

He raised his eyes to Uspeth. "What do you want me to do?"

It was the Abbess who answered. "Commune with your mother, Anskar. Contact Queen Talia. Bring her over to our side so that together we can summon Nysrog and make him whole again. With the Necromancer Queen's help, we will force him to serve us."

Anskar's hand went to the vambrace on his forearm. "I can't."

Uspeth glanced at his mother.

"Can't?" the Abbess said.

"I won't."

The Abbess scowled. "Then we shall have to compel you!"

Anskar felt a massive surge in all three tides from the Abbess and Uspeth, moments before twin walls of invisible force slammed into him and then wrapped around him. He struggled to move, but he was powerless. He reached inside for his braided repository, but a dense barrier of blackness surrounded it, and when he tried to break through, white-hot needles lanced through his head.

He dove down toward the dark-tide but was flung violently back from its churning essence. All the while, unseen forces clamped down on his body, constricting, compressing, crushing.

*Mother!* he cried out in his mind. *Mother, help me!*

Instantly, her spirit was within him, sluicing through his marrow, his veins. *Foolish boy!* she said. *This is what they wanted all along!*

The Abbess cried out in triumph, and Anskar felt his mother's essence coalesce into something like a snake that writhed in his guts. He *saw* a mesh of briars surrounding the serpent, and the more it thrashed, the more it was constricted.

"I compel you, necromancer!" the Abbess said.

Uspeth added his voice. "We compel you!"

A colossal surge of dark-tide mingled with something else welled inside Anskar. The serpent grew, and the thorny mesh around it began to stretch and fray.

"No!" the Abbess cried. "It's not possible!"

But then the serpent wilted, all its resistance gone.

Anskar couldn't move a muscle, even to speak. He assailed the barriers around his repositories, but to no avail. Tears of frustration spilled from his eyes.

"You are bound, Queen Talia of Niyas," the Abbess said, a triumphant note of glee in her voice. "You are compelled."

*No,* Talia protested weakly within Anskar. *No.*

"Do you accept your enslavement, necromancer?" the Abbess asked. "Speak through your son's lips."

With a shudder, the serpent shrank in size until all that

remained of Queen Talia's presence was a feeble thread squirming in Anskar's guts.

"I am bound," she said, using Anskar's voice. The words were Nan-Rhouric, a language she could barely speak when she first came to Anskar. Had she learned from him, the same as he had learned from her?

Anskar was sickened by the feeling of someone else controlling him. It was a defilement, a violation. Was this what demons felt when they were enslaved?

"Tell us your thoughts on Morudjin," the Abbess commanded.

And again, Anskar's lips moved, though the words were his mother's.

"Morudjin was an idiot to think he could compel a demon lord using only the dark-tide," Talia said, her Nan-Rhouric perfect.

"This much I have figured out for myself," the Abbess said. "Even Morudjin worked it out at the last—I saw it in his memories in the crystal. What I want to know is what you think we should do."

"To ensure you don't end up like Morudjin, kicking and screaming in the abyssal realms for all eternity? Abandon this madness."

"That isn't an option," Uspeth said. "We are sworn to the return of Nysrog. He will set his yoke upon Wiraya, and we will be his favored ones, until we come to surpass him."

"You will be slaughtered along with everyone else," Queen Talia said. "If you insist on going ahead with your plan, I am powerless to stop you. Know that you have only one chance, and you must take it right now, for I cannot remain here much longer. The realm of the dead calls me back."

"What chance?" the Abbess asked.

"You must perform your ritual with Anskar standing at the apex of the triangle of manifestation."

"And what then?"

Talia was silent.

"And what then?" the Abbess yelled.

Anskar felt a violent tremor within, and then his lips spoke his mother's reluctant words.

"You must use a power unknown to the demon lords. You must bring to bear upon Nysrog the full brunt of the earth-tide."

"Necromancy?" the Abbess said.

"All you have to do is compel me."

The Abbess's face resolved into a determined grimace. "Come!" she told Uspeth. "And you," she said to Anskar.

The invisible bindings fell away from Anskar's legs, and, against his will, he followed the Abbess and her son back into the hall, where the preparations for the summoning were all but complete.

# FORTY-ONE

THE HALL WAS THICK WITH smoke from eight braziers that stood around the perimeter of the circle of quartz. There was a heady aroma to the smoke, at once sweet and pungent, which filled Anskar's nostrils and almost made him gag. The rushlights had all been lit: hundreds of flickering flames that cast wavering shadows and reflected eerily from the crystals on the floor.

The symbols the Cabalists had painted both within and without the circle glistened, still wet. Some were variations of Skanuric letters twisted together, but the others… Anskar had to assume they were Nazgrese, the language of demons.

The sixty Cabalists present stood behind quartz crystals set around the outer edge of the circle. Anskar wanted to ask what the crystals were for, but he was still the Abbess's puppet, save for his inner thoughts and his relentless desire to break free.

*They amplify the will of the summoners,* Queen Talia said within his mind. *Not dissimilar to the catalyst you have embedded beneath the skin of your chest, only more cumbersome and much cruder.*

*You're not bound?* Anskar asked.

*Like you, my thoughts remain my own.*

Rushlights glinted off the triangle of brass at the center of the circle, where the demon lord Nysrog was supposed to manifest.

*Will it work?* Anskar asked.

*Oh, it will work.*

*And there's nothing we can do to stop it?*

Queen Talia didn't answer.

Uspeth guided Anskar toward the apex of the triangle. "You stand here."

Again Anskar tried to resist, but his legs were no longer his to command, and they carried him to the allocated spot. The air within the triangle felt charged, and he had the impression of teetering on the edge of a cliff with the mounting compulsion to jump.

The Abbess stood on one side of the triangle's base, Uspeth on the other.

"Now what?" the Abbess said.

Anskar realized she was talking to his mother.

Queen Talia replied, using his lips. "Whatever you originally planned to do."

"Do not be insolent, necromancer!" the Abbess said.

"You must compel me, remember?"

"You are already compelled!"

"Then be more specific. Give me the order at the right time."

The Abbess scowled, but then she seemed to understand and nodded to Uspeth.

"Commence," Uspeth said, and the sixty Cabalists began a sonorous chant, incomprehensible to Anskar save for the oft-repeated "Nysrog."

The crystals around the circle's perimeter flickered, casting wavering shadows. Smoke from the braziers swirled beneath the ceiling, becoming a vortex that churned ever faster. The Abbess added her voice to the chant, and then Uspeth did the same.

Anskar's eyes snapped into focus on the triangle of manifestation, where a shadow had begun to form.

The Abbess glanced at him. "You, now, Anskar. Add your power."

Anskar felt a swelling within his dark-tide repository, and then his body lurched as the dark-tide erupted from him in thousands of thrashing strands that extended to touch every Cabalist in the chamber and every glowing fist of quartz.

The chanting rose to new and impossible heights. The smog beneath the ceiling churned ever faster. The rushlights guttered and went out, pluming threads of dirty smoke. And the shadow within the triangle took shape.

A lumpy misshapen head emerged first, then a bullish neck and thickly muscled torso, blurry and indistinct. It had apish arms, clawed hands, and legs the size of tree trunks.

As Anskar stared, entranced, the demon lord's body grew more solid. The face, though, remained a shifting mask of hatred, rage, and insanity—yellow eyes, glistening fangs, and twin horns that curled away from its temples.

"I command you, Queen Talia of Niyas," the Abbess roared. "Unleash the full brunt of your earth-tide power! Transform Nysrog. Reshape his matter. Bring him through!"

A second eruption of power from within Anskar dropped him to his knees. This was something new, yet somehow vaguely familiar: a putrid stream of wrongness that gushed up from the depths. He gagged as it swilled through his marrow, his veins, and strained beneath his skin. Then he threw back his head and vomited a cloud of noxious fumes that encompassed the still-forming demon lord.

Nysrog shuddered and let out a roar that rocked the chamber. He was huge now: his ram's horns scraped against the ceiling, and his chill shadow fell over everyone around the circle.

"It's working!" the Abbess cried. "Look at his eyes!"

Anskar looked up at the demon's face some fifty feet above him, and saw that the Abbess was right. Before, the eyes had been yellow and blazing with bestial rage. Now they were white with slitted pupils of violet, and they took in everything in the chamber with slow deliberation. Eyes that held a fierce intelligence. The eyes of a malign god.

Nysrog turned his gaze on Anskar. Foulness rolled off the demon lord in waves. Shadows continually flicked across his face, warping it into a thousand unrelated aspects. Anskar had to look away before the sight drove him insane.

All around the chamber, Cabalists dropped to the floor, lying prone with their heads covered by their black cowls. Uspeth was on his knees at the foot of the triangle of manifestation, gazing in adoration at the demon lord. Only the Abbess still stood, a look of triumph on her face.

"Nysrog!" she shrieked. "Lord of the abyssal realms!"

The demon lord inclined his massive head to look down at her. His rage seemed to melt away in an instant, replaced by a calmness that was somehow even more terrifying.

"I have summoned you," the Abbess cried. "And now I bind you!"

A tremor passed through Nysrog's monstrous body. Anskar thought it might be laughter.

"Do you hear me?" the Abbess yelled, her voice hoarse and cracking. "You are bound."

For an instant, Anskar saw doubt enter the demon lord's eyes. Nysrog blinked and staggered back within the triangle.

"You are bound!" the Abbess cried again, stepping toward him.

The demon lord shrieked, sending a shock wave throughout the chamber. Fissures split the floor. The Cabalists covered their ears. Anskar would have done the same if he'd been able to move.

The demon's skin blistered and bubbled, then sloughed away. The stench of rot and decay filled Anskar's nostrils as Nysrog's flesh slopped in steaming puddles to the floor. Exposed muscle clung to bones of woven shadow; ligaments frayed; tendons crumbled. It was as if the demon lord, still screaming, were decomposing before their very eyes.

Inside Anskar's skull, Queen Talia said, *I did as they asked. What did they think would happen?*

The Abbess turned angry eyes on Anskar, as if she too could hear the Queen's voice. "You!" she shrieked, striding toward him, fingers splayed and ablaze with flames of shadow.

All Anskar's senses screamed at him to run, but the Abbess's compulsion held him frozen. She howled in rage and jabbed her finger toward his face, but a massive hand, more bone than flesh, grabbed her and lifted her screaming into the air.

Crimson lightning burst from the demon lord's decomposing flesh, and the corruption halted. Patches of shadow wove together to create new muscle, tendons, and skin; and all the while red lightning sparked and flickered around him.

Nysrog stood once more whole and intact, with the Abbess thrashing and screeching in his grip. He cast his implacable gaze over the chamber, taking in the Cabalists lying around the perimeter of the circle, and with an almost dismissive wave of his free hand, he sent an eruption of black fire to consume them.

Of its own accord, Anskar's scintillant ward of many colors sprang into life around him. The dark flames licked over its surface without penetrating. But the sixty prone Cabalists were reduced to ash. In that same moment, Anskar saw Uspeth shadow-step to safety.

The black flames dissipated. Nysrog laughed, a deafening rumble that threatened to burst Anskar's eardrums. Then, with the Abbess screaming in his grasp, blood oozing from her mouth, the demon lord resolved into shadow and sank down through the floor in the middle of the triangle.

Anskar could move again. He tried to stand, but instead pitched onto his face.

Queen Talia chuckled within him.

"Why are you laughing?" Anskar managed to ask, though it was an effort to speak.

*For all her supposed knowledge of me, that hag was ignorant of one crucial thing: I lie. A lot.*

"You weren't bound by her?"

*As bound as you were. But my mind was free, and it was a simple matter of telling the Abbess what she wanted to hear. I trusted that her greed for power would override her good sense and the specifics of her orders.*

Anskar still didn't fully understand. "Your earth-tide power completed the summoning? How?"

*I drew upon the corrupted tides at the core of Wiraya to lend form to Nysrog.*

"Corrupted tides?"

*The residue of the dawn- and the dusk-tides after they have filtered through the filth that comprises Wiraya: dirt and rotting vegetation; the carcasses of animals and insects; the putrefying bodies of the dead. The soil of this world is steeped in disease and death. The tides are quite different when they seep below to pool at Wiraya's core.*

"So the form you gave him was one of rot and decay?"

*It was an interesting experiment. I didn't know how much impact it would have on such a powerful demon lord. The result was only temporary, as you saw, easily reversed once Nysrog recovered from the shock.*

Anskar heard the pound of booted feet outside in the corridor. There were shouts too. He thought he recognized Uspeth's voice, urging caution.

*Move, Anskar!* his mother commanded.

But Anskar couldn't. The deluge of dark-tide that had burst from him during the summoning had exhausted him, and the other vile current that had come up through the ground and flooded him with rankness and corruption had exacerbated that exhaustion beyond belief.

*Are you so weak?* Talia said. *Gods of Niyas, I am disappointed in you!*

Anskar tried again to move, and again remained slumped on the floor.

Queen Talia sighed, but when she spoke again, all criticism had gone from her voice. *Permit me to work through you once more.* The previous time, Anskar had had no choice: the Abbess had compelled his compliance. *I will draw energy from the lingering shades of the dead Cabalists to help you. It won't be a lot, but it should suffice.*

Anskar was beyond arguing. He assented to his mother's control, and observed passively as she wove a net from the same putrid essence she had used on Nysrog and cast it out into the chamber.

As the earth-tide net fell over the piles of ash that had once been the Cabalists, Anskar felt a ripple beneath his skin. It grew to a shudder, and then violent convulsions of energy flowed into him—not dark-tide, nor dusk, nor dawn, but vitality, new life.

And then he saw the gray-misted outlines of the fallen Cabalists hovering above their crumpled robes. He felt certain they weren't visible to the naked eye, but he could *see* them, the same way he could sometimes hear the voices of the dead.

The shades shivered where Queen Talia's web touched them, and whatever life force lingered in them pulsed along the threads of the web to Anskar. As he absorbed their essence, the shades wilted and faded, then dissolved from existence.

Anskar climbed to his feet, filled with renewed strength, and wondered how far he had fallen, that he was willing to take for himself the very substance of these dying souls.

At that instant, the door swung open and Soreshi archers burst into the chamber. Behind them came a mass of black-robed Cabalists, Uspeth among them, yellow eyes blazing as the words of a cant left his lips.

Anskar shadow-stepped into the gloom at the far end of the corridor.

# FORTY-TWO

ANSKAR EMERGED FROM THE SHADOWS at a run, stumbling as a wave of nausea flowed through him. He recovered and raced along corridor after corridor, not stopping even as doors opened and Soreshi hesitated in the entranceways. Behind him came the sounds of pursuit, and very soon an alarm bell tolled throughout the citadel.

He veered down a right-hand passage as Cabalists blocked the way before him, then sprinted for a flight of narrow, winding steps.

When he reached the next level, he was shaking with fatigue. There were more steps going up, but he knew he couldn't manage them.

A Cabalist reached the top of the steps behind him and barked a cant, but before it could take effect, Anskar shadow-stepped through one of the narrow embrasures in the wall, out into the darkness of night.

When the shadows gave him up, he was floundering on his back in the snow beneath an outcrop of rock at the side of the Iron Road. His teeth chattered as he struggled to rise. On his forearm, the vambrace glowed blue in the moonlight, its radiance bleeding through the sleeve of his shirt.

*Again!* Queen Talia cried.

With a grunt of effort, Anskar lifted his head and focused on a line of fir trees cresting a hilltop. He reached for the dregs of his dark-tide repository, but all he got for his efforts was a squeezing pain in his head.

The night sky was suddenly illuminated by streaks of crimson—glowing arrows arcing from the citadel's embrasures. They grew brighter as they sped toward Anskar, drawn like iron to a lodestone. At the last instant, Anskar managed a cant, and his multicolored ward sprang up around him.

The first arrows to hit disintegrated, but several stuck within the sphere, smoldering as they slowly turned to ash. One penetrated a few inches, its barbed tip a hair's breadth from Anskar's face. The ward was weakening.

*Get up!* Queen Talia urged, as more arrows looped down from the citadel. *You must get away from here!*

But Anskar couldn't move.

A volley of arrows converged on his ward, and this time one passed right through to graze his shoulder. Bright blood splashed on the snow.

*Give yourself over to me once more,* Queen Talia demanded, and Anskar, close to unconsciousness, grunted his assent.

Foul vapors seeped into his body from the ground. He could sense their origins impossibly far below. His nostrils filled with the rank odor of decay. Pus and disease congealed in his blood. His body stiffened with rigor. The sensation passed through him, spreading out across the surface of the ground beneath the looming rockface of the citadel.

*There was once great slaughter here,* his mother said. *Two vast massacres.*

The ground shook and trembled, and fissures split the earth. More streaks of crimson arrows slammed into Anskar's ward. It collapsed, and he screamed as an arrow went through his thigh. He could see the head protruding from the back of his leg, the goose-fletched flight sticking out at the front. Another arrow gashed his cheek. A third struck his armor and snapped.

He heard the grating of the citadel's stone gate as it was raised, the crunch of booted feet on the snow, yelled orders, the clink and clatter of armor.

But then the bow fire stopped as a sound like an earthquake rolled across the Iron Road.

With his hands clasped about the arrow in his thigh, Anskar craned his neck to see what was happening.

The ground ruptured in hundreds of places, and fleshless, bony hands groped above the surface. As snow and soil and rock fell away, thousands of skulls burst into view, the rest of their skeletal bodies following.

The Cabalists and their Soreshi allies pouring from the citadel drew up sharply, creating a bottleneck in the gateway. Before them, standing on the pocked surface of the Iron Road, was an army of the dead: rank upon rank of age-yellowed skeletons, bones held together by rotting ligaments, eye sockets blazing with a fierce emerald light.

Four skeletons broke away from the back row and clattered toward Anskar. Their bony hands lifted him and bore him away south at an alarming pace.

From behind came an unearthly howl as the army of the dead

charged, and the Cabalists and Soreshi responded with brilliant bursts of sorcery.

Anskar drifted in and out of consciousness as the four skeletons carried him through the night. Finally, they set him down on the road and stood back, hiding themselves in the thick mist that heralded the dawn.

Anskar felt hollowed out, scraped clean of all power. And then the dawn-tide raced toward him out of the east and slammed into him, filling him with its purity and light. The interwoven threads of his repository throbbed with new essence—the dusk-tide as well as the dawn.

As vitality returned to him, his hands went to the arrow lodged in his thigh. But he was no healer, and even if he were, Menselas only granted the power to heal others, not oneself. He decided to leave it.

With agonizing effort, he lurched to his feet, taking all his weight on his good leg. He looked for the skeletons, but they had crumbled into dust with the coming of the dawn-tide.

He glanced north along the Iron Road and wondered how far they had carried him; how long the army of the dead had held off the Soreshi and the Tainted Cabal.

Not long, he realized. Hoots and cries echoed down from the flanking hilltops, and he saw crimson arrows streaking toward him, carried over the distance by sorcery.

His ward came up, brighter and stronger now that his repository had been filled, and though the arrows should have fallen short, hundreds of them struck, although none penetrated.

Then, from the north, out of the morning mist that obscured

the road, came a hundred or more Cabalists, all armored in black, all carrying shields and swords. At their head was Uspeth.

"You killed my mother!" Uspeth cried, as he stopped fifty or so yards from Anskar. His Cabalists fanned out behind him.

"I thought you'd thank me for it," Anskar said.

"And you thwarted the return of Nysrog with your stinking sorcery."

"Poor Nysrog," Anskar said. "I thought he was a demon lord, not a baby."

Soreshi archers lined the hilltops on either side of the road.

"You know nothing!" Uspeth said, drawing his sword as he advanced. "Nothing about Nysrog, and nothing about the Tainted Cabal!"

"I know enough," Anskar said, limping backward and drawing *Amalantril*. Blood gushed from his thigh wound, and he winced at the pain.

Uspeth's lips curled into a cruel smile as he noticed. He moved forward again. "I was going to be the one to bring back Nysrog. I expected to succeed. Failure is a weakness within the Tainted Cabal."

"And there was me thinking it was your mother who was running things," Anskar said.

Uspeth's face twisted into a scowl. "She interfered. She would never have come here if not for you and what happened at the Abbey of the Hooded One."

"Come on," Anskar said. "You seriously think you could have summoned Nysrog without her? Without me?"

"I know I could have done it, given time," Uspeth snarled. "And the Tainted Cabal was ready to make that sacrifice to Nysrog. We were all ready."

"Except for your mother."

"She sought another way," Uspeth said.

"And you went along with it. So maybe you *are* weak, Uspeth." Anskar raised his voice so the other Cabalists would hear. "Maybe now the vultures you lord it over will make their move."

Uspeth glanced behind him at the Cabalists.

"Then I shall demonstrate my strength once more by killing you," he said, turning back to Anskar.

"By killing an injured man who can barely stand, let alone walk? That should impress them."

"Oh, it will," Uspeth said. "The manner of your death will sow fear in their blackened hearts."

Dark flames licked along the length of his sword, and his yellow eyes seethed. Anskar felt the buildup of dark-tide sorcery, and then, faster than an arrow shot from a bow, Uspeth charged.

Anskar fell rather than moved back. He threw up his sword in a desperate parry.

But Uspeth's blade never met his own. It struck Anskar's ward amid a spray of sparkling motes. Anskar panted in relief. He'd forgotten his braided sorcery still surrounded him.

Uspeth came on with vicious, hacking blows, each one impacting the ward with concussive force and leaving dents and gashes in the mesh of light. Anskar crawled back, but the arrow fletching protruding from his leg snapped against the road, and he shrieked in agony.

His pain spurred Uspeth to greater ferocity. The Cabalist was relentless as he hacked and bashed at the ward. Then, with a triumphant yell, he was through, and the ward dispersed.

Uspeth opened his mouth to gloat, but Anskar felt his mother's presence dredging the darkness from his repository. Without knowing what he was doing, he flung his free hand out toward Uspeth, and a lance of pure shadow burst from his palm. Uspeth's yellow eyes widened in alarm.

A glistening black ward materialized around the Cabalist, but still he was flung back onto the road as the lance struck.

A couple of the Cabalists behind Uspeth exchanged smirks, but then he was back on his feet, yelling for them to attack. The Cabalists surged forward.

Anskar struggled to rise but fell back, and in the same moment the Soreshi either side of the road unleashed a swarm of arrows, all of which were drawn to him like bees to honey. In vain, Anskar raised his hand to protect his face. Within him, his mother wailed.

But a new ward erupted around him, emerald and bright, and the Soreshi arrows shattered against its almost solid shell.

The Cabalists checked their charge, unnerved by this new manifestation of sorcery. Uspeth pushed to their fore and glared—not at Anskar, but at something behind him.

Anskar heard the sound of hooves then, dull against the snow-packed road. He pushed himself up on one elbow to see, and his mouth fell open.

Zek was galloping toward him, one palm raised, a beam of emerald light streaming from it to create the ward that protected Anskar. A similar ward encompassed the Soreshi and his horse.

Zek drew rein and leaped from the saddle to crouch beside Anskar. The two emerald shields merged and doubled in thickness.

"Attack!" Uspeth cried, and more sorcerously charged arrows slammed into the ward, throwing off sparks and motes and fracturing the outer shell.

Zek's brow creased with concentration, and a flash of worry crossed his face as the Cabalists advanced, their swords wreathed in dark flames.

"They're certainly taking their time," Zek said, glancing behind.

"Who?"

The Cabalists slammed into the emerald ward, beating at it with their black-flaming swords, and Zek groaned and swooned under the onslaught. Arrow after arrow struck, and the ward began to flicker. Uspeth was suddenly there in front of Anskar, hacking and screaming and almost breaking through.

And then Anskar heard the pounding of hooves, and a wave of horses slammed into Uspeth and the front line of the Cabalists.

White cloaks whipped and snapped all around him. He glimpsed Rindon and Nul at the head of the charge, with Lanuc close behind. Anskar and Zek became an island wreathed in emerald as the mounted riders passed around them.

The arrows had stopped. Anskar looked up at the hills and heard a battle cry go up as the Thousand Lakes warriors charged into the Soreshi archers from the rear on both sides.

Ahead on the road, shadows and light warred in the sky, as dark streaks of sorcery impacted the knights' shining wards. The air filled with the clangor of steel on steel, the screams of men and women. A horse went down, skewered by a Cabalist's blade. The rider shrieked, trapped beneath his thrashing mount.

Atop the hills, lightning ripped into the Thousand Lakes warriors and scorched the earth black. It was met by sheets of flame that roared over the Soreshi from the priests of the Elder among King Aelfyr's army.

"Look out!" a woman cried from behind Anskar—Gisela. She had dismounted and was approaching with a handful of healers. At the same time, something hit Zek's emerald ward, and it fizzled out.

Zek screamed. Blood gushed from his open mouth. A black-wreathed blade jutted from his spine.

Uspeth emerged from the fury of battle, one leg twisted awkwardly under him, his face a mangled ruin after being trampled under hoof. A sphere of black light surrounded him, expanding to include Anskar.

Outside the ward, Anskar could hear Gisela calling his name and the clash of armies, but he could see nothing. Nothing except for Uspeth, his face contorted into a snarl of hatred.

"Now we will not be interrupted," the Cabalist said, ripping his sword free of Zek's body, then kicking the Soreshi aside.

Blood gushed from Zek's wound to pool on the frosted ground. Overcome with rage, Anskar did the only thing he could think of. He used the cant Zek had taught him for blowing out the lock on the Scriptorium's window.

Uspeth cried out as sparks erupted around his hand, and he dropped his sword. Before he could recover, Anskar repeated the cant, this time flinging explosive force in his face. But Uspeth had anticipated the move, and Anskar's sorcery petered out with no effect.

Now Anskar reached for the dark-tide. A dozen shards of shadow streaked toward the Cabalist, but with a sweep of his hand, Uspeth reversed their course. On instinct, Anskar cut the flow from his repository—only just in time. The jagged shards of darkness dissolved a hair's breadth from his face.

Desperate, Anskar called to his mother for help, but it was as if a wall had been erected inside him, shutting her out.

Uspeth smirked. "So predictable. You are but a novice, whereas I was raised to sorcery. Here, within this sphere, you are forced to face me man to man. No surprise attacks, no trickery. And I have to tell you, Anskar, you are outmatched."

As Uspeth crouched to retrieve his sword, Anskar tried to drag himself away, but the black sphere was solid and ungiving. Through its dark shell, he could see the blurry outline of Gisela hammering against the sphere with her fists, while three other healers tried to pull her back.

The sounds of battle were a muffled echo.

Again he tried to call his mother, and again he was met with silence.

"Look at me!" Uspeth commanded. "I want to see your expression when you die."

The Cabalist raised his sword, dark fire enveloping the blade, and Anskar plunged his senses into the ground, imitating what his mother had done when she had raised an army of the dead.

He felt the earth-tide. Grasped at it. Filth and putrescence sluiced through his marrow, and then belched from his mouth as he shrieked.

Uspeth recoiled, his eyes wide with horror as pustules erupted all over his face and brown drool oozed from his lips. He gasped, then lurched forward, swinging his sword, but his arm withered, the flesh sloughing to the ground and the sword tumbling after. Uspeth screamed. His black ward winked out. He teetered as his wounded leg slopped off, then his other arm. He hopped on one leg for a moment, whimpering, and then even that leg rotted away. All that remained now were his torso and head lying in a pool of pus on the ground. As he started to gibber, stinking fluids spewed from his mouth. And then, as Anskar watched in horror, all that remained of the Cabalist liquefied and drained away into the snow.

*Good show,* Queen Talia said, and Anskar felt her presence within him once more. *I couldn't have done better myself.*

# FORTY-THREE

ANSKAR MUST HAVE PASSED OUT for a moment. When he came to, Gisela was crouching over him, sobbing. His thigh was a stinging agony, and he saw that Gisela had broken off the arrowhead and pulled the shaft out. Blood gushed from the wound, reddening the road.

"I can't heal you!" she cried, her eyes glistening with tears and madness. "The power has left me!"

Two other healers pulled her gently away. A third knelt beside Anskar and covered his leg wound with her hands. Warmth seeped into his skin, and he winced at the sensation of bone and flesh knitting together. Within moments, the bleeding had stopped. He lay back on the road, exhausted, and closed his eyes.

He could still hear the clash of steel and the moans and cries of the wounded, but the sorcerous discharges were fewer, and gradually the sounds of battle died down. From somewhere behind him, Gisela continued to sob, her words, spoken in short gasps, full of despair.

Anskar lay there, cold and shivering, for perhaps an hour, until the Thousand Lakes warriors came down from the hills, wounded and bloody but in good cheer. Strong hands helped him to his feet. Already his injured leg was able to bear his weight.

"It's over," Nul told him.

"Well done, Anskar," Rindon added. "You did us all proud."

Lanuc approached on foot, his mail speckled with blood, his sword dripping with it. "We lost thirty knights," he told the two heroes, and both nodded gravely.

Lanuc turned toward his sobbing daughter and frowned. "Thank you," he said to Anskar, but Anskar looked away. Whatever he had done, it hadn't been enough. Not for Gisela. And not for Zek.

The road was soon packed with Thousand Lakes warriors and the remaining knights of the Order of Eternal Vigilance. More warriors arrived from the south, King Aelfyr riding at their head. He looked tired and was spattered with blood, but a grin was plastered over his face.

"Not the way I planned it," the King said, nodding to Lanuc and then to Anskar. "But by Menselas, we showed them!"

The King ordered warriors back into the hills to hunt down the fleeing Soreshi. Others he sent to the outlying towns and villages to report on their status. Finally, he led a force, including Rindon, Nul, and Lanuc, north, where he planned to claim the ancient citadel and retrieve the memory crystal of Morudjin.

Three days later, King Aelfyr returned to Wintotashum in triumph with three hundred warriors and almost seventy knights of the Order of Eternal Vigilance. Crowds lined the streets, cheering.

The King and his escort rode at once for the Scriptorium, where the memory crystal of Morudjin was to be returned, though with double the guards and new wards that the priests of the Elder had been charged with developing.

Rindon insisted that Anskar join him and Nul for a beer before they returned to the barracks, and though he was exhausted, Anskar couldn't bring himself to disappoint them. Lanuc and a few other knights came too, and to Anskar's surprise, so did Gisela. She was dressed in a new white robe, and her hair was neatly combed. Her eyes were still frenzied, though, and her skin was blemished with angry scars.

"Can we talk?" she asked him as he waited to be served a drink.

Lanuc caught Anskar's eye and gave a pained nod.

Rindon winked and told Anskar he would fetch the beers, so Anskar went with Gisela out onto the tavern's porch.

"I'm sorry," she said, when they were alone.

"For what?"

"For refusing to hear your confession."

"It's what we agreed," Anskar said. "It's me who should be sorry, for asking."

Her chin quivered and tears glistened in her eyes. "Can you forgive me? I was a pious fool. I saw the way you looked at me, Anskar, and believed it an affront to my purity. But now... after what happened on the way to the citadel…"

"There's nothing to forgive."

Gisela forced a weak smile and wiped her eyes. "You saw what happened at the battle site, how I was unable to heal you." Her voice rose to a cry. "Menselas has forsaken me… because of what the demons did."

"No, he hasn't," Anskar said, but Gisela had already turned away from him to run off down the street.

"Trouble?" Rindon said, stepping out onto the porch and handing Anskar a beer.

Anskar shook his head and sighed, then followed Rindon back inside.

"I don't blame you," Lanuc told him, but Anskar couldn't help feeling that he was responsible. Castellac and the Tainted Cabal had used Gisela to get to him.

The thought still haunted him as he returned to the barracks by himself.

As soon as Anskar opened the door to his room, he sensed the atmosphere inside was charged to bursting with sorcery. Automatically, his ward sphere sprang up to surround him.

Through its multicolored radiance he saw the outline of a figure seated on the chair beside the bed. At first he thought it was Gisela, but as his senses reached out, he detected twin repositories of enormous volume, one brimming with the dawn-tide, the other with the dusk. Both felt familiar.

The woman stood and held out her hand. A ball of pearly radiance blossomed upon her palm. "You must return to Branil's Burg," she said.

"Sareya!" Anskar let his ward fade away to nothing. "What are you doing here?"

He expected a glib response—Sareya had enjoyed teasing him during their training together at the Burg. Or perhaps flirtatiousness—they had, after all, briefly been lovers.

Instead, her expression was grim, her voice measured and clipped. "Vihtor is dying."

The words hit Anskar like a punch to the stomach, and he stared at her blankly.

Vihtor Ulnar had been Seneschal of Branil's Burg for all Anskar's life. It was Vihtor who had brought him into the citadel as an orphaned baby and had him raised to be a knight.

"He was wounded by a rebel arrow as he toured the new strongholds," Sareya explained.

"Carred Selenas!" Anskar said.

Sareya nodded. "Her people, at any rate. It was just a shoulder wound, and the healers tended it at once to prevent infection, but there was something else."

"Poison?"

Sareya shook her head. "The healers could have stopped that. The arrow was left over from the time when Queen Talia ruled the isle. The priests of the Elder think it was cursed. Vihtor sent me to find you. He knew I'd be able to persuade you to come."

Anskar shook his head. "I need no persuading. How long does he have?"

Cursed? What did that even mean? Had the arrow been tainted with the earth-tide… by his mother?

"They don't know. I came as fast as I could," Sareya said. "But the return journey by sea… you may be too late."

Anskar's heart raced as he tried to make sense of his feelings. Vihtor wanted to see him, of all people, before he died? Why? A clenching of his guts told him that could mean only one thing…

Anskar grabbed the sack holding the three ingots of divine alloy and the powdered nietan's horn from under the bed, and headed for the door.

"Return to your ship," he told her. "I'll travel another way."

"But—"

He cut her off. "Believe me, it will be faster."

It would also incur a third debt to the Ethereal Sorceress.

He only hoped that, when it came due, he would be able to pay.

END OF BOOK THREE

# TO MY READERS

As always, if you enjoyed the read, leaving a review supports the books and helps keep me writing! You can return to where you purchased the novel to review it or simply visit my website and follow the links: WWW.MITCHELLHOGAN.COM

There are also websites such as Goodreads where members discuss the books they've read or want to read or suggest books others might read: WWW.GOODREADS.COM/AUTHOR/SHOW/7189594.MITCHELL_HOGAN

If you never want to miss the latest book sign up here for my newsletter. I send one every few months, so I won't clutter your inbox. MITCHELLHOGAN.COM/NEW-RELEASE-ALERTS/

Having readers eager for the next installment of a series, or anticipating a new series, is the best motivation for a writer to create new stories. Thank you for your support and be sure to check out my other novels!

# ABOUT THE AUTHOR

*Photo copyright © 2018*

When he was eleven, Mitchell Hogan received *The Hobbit* and the Lord of the Rings trilogy, and a love of fantasy novels was born. He spent the next ten years reading, rolling dice, and playing computer games, with some school and university thrown in. Along the way, he accumulated numerous bookcases' worth of fantasy and sci-fi novels and doesn't look to stop any time soon. For ten years he put off his dream of writing; then he quit his job and wrote *A Crucible of Souls*. He now writes full-time and is eternally grateful to the readers who took a chance on an unknown self-published author. He lives in Sydney, Australia, with his wife, Angela, and his daughters, Isabelle and Charlotte.

Printed in Great Britain
by Amazon